CONTENTS

LIVERPOOL DAISY
7

THREE WOMEN OF LIVERPOOL
209

LIVERPOOL DAISY

ONE

The morning of the death of Daisy Gallagher's mother, Mrs. Mary Ellen O'Brien, began like any other morning.

"And yet, you know, Mog," Daisy once remarked to her aged tomcat, "it was the beginning — the cause — of me slide. I didn't fall into trouble — I slid. And at times, Mog, it was pure mairder."

Moggie stared back at her with sad, unblinking eyes, as if to indicate that, if a woman imagined that life could be anything better than pure murder, she needed her head examining.

As if to mourn the passing of Mrs. O'Brien, the clouds lay low along the Mersey; and occasionally thin rain spread up the river, like a bolt of grey georgette being hastily unrolled, a wavering wetness hardly dappling the heaving waters. Through its dimming folds, freighters and ferry boats passed like silent spectres, their lights unearthly in the poor visibility of the morning. Through the dockside streets, men clattered in worn out boots, cloth caps set low over their eyes, stained cloth coats already wet, as they went to sign on for work which did not always materialize in those hard days of 1931.

A spatter of rain swept over Dingle Point and across the Herculaneum Dock. It pattered softly on the slate roofs of the tightly packed houses, which faced each other across each street like courting cats about to spring. The house which Daisy Gallagher and her sailor husband shared with her mother was much older than the rest and did not return the stare of another house. It faced directly towards the river, and the rain struck its window-panes squarely with a sharp pit-pat, as if it were trying to rouse the dead woman within. For a hundred years the rain and wind had been buffeting its grey stone walls and solid oak door, making the windows rattle in warning of bad weather coming up the river.

"Och, who cares about the weather," Daisy would sometimes say to her dearest friend and sister-in-law, Nellie O'Brien; and Nellie, who looked so frail that a puff of wind would blow her away, would nod her greying head gently in agreement, knowing that nothing as minor as bad weather would upset buxom, cheerful Daisy.

Daisy would push an old stocking filled with sand across the bottom of the front door to keep the draught out, and would say, without fail, "Me grandmother was born in this house — just after me great-grandma come from Ireland in eighteen thirty-six. If she could stand it, I can."

As yet unaware that her mother would never again complain of the draughts, Daisy looked out of the living-room window and clucked irritably to herself when she saw the overcast day. It looked as if winter was going to set in early.

She picked up a steaming mug of tea from the crowded table and tramped slowly up the worn wooden stairs to the front bedroom.

"Here's your tea, Mam," she announced, as she marched into the low-ceilinged, chilly room.

There was no reply. Cold, unmoving eyes returned Daisy's glance. Mrs. O'Brien would never need tea again.

Pure terror paralyzed Daisy for a moment. Then she quavered, "Mam," as if she hoped to waken her. " 'ere, Mam."

Fearfully, Daisy approached the bed and tentatively touched the already cold hand on the dirty blanket. "Oh, Mam!"

"Oh, Jaysus Mary!"

She felt, as she gasped out this plea for Divine help, that part of her own body had been torn from her, the pain of separation was so intense.

She stifled a desire to scream for help; it was no use screaming if there was nobody to hear. With a trembling hand she put down the mug on the mantelpiece. Then she leaned over cautiously to cover Mrs. O'Brien's waxen face with the end of the blanket. Her lips quivered as she sought to keep herself calm.

She ran down the stairs and out of the house as if the devil was after her. The street was deserted, the pavement heavy with drops of mist. The damp pierced her tight-fitting cotton blouse; and her heavy black skirt whipped uncomfortably around her legs, as she sped round the corner and up the sloping side street to the house where Great Aunt Mary Devlin rented a room. She hammered on the door.

Great Aunt Devlin answered the knock herself, so quickly that it seemed as if she must have been waiting on the other side of the door for weeks for just such a call.

Half panting, half sobbing, Daisy announced her news.

"Me Mam! She's gone!"

She leaned against the door jamb to steady herself, while her normally rosy face drained of colour and her eyelids drooped over her deep-set blue eyes.

"I'll come, luv," Mary Devlin wheezed in reply, her wizened face puckered up in sympathy. "You should have put your shawl on, luv. You'll catch your own death."

With fingers mis-shapen by arthritis, she lifted her own black shawl over her nearly bald head; then she stepped out and closed the door softly behind her. Great Aunt Devlin spent most of her time with the dead, and her quietness could be unnerving.

After viewing the body with experienced, rheumy eyes, Great Aunt Devlin drew fourpence from her apron pocket and pressed it into Daisy's shaking hand.

"Ask t' chemist, if he's open, if you can use t' telephone. You got to tell the club man and ask him to bring the burial money. Then phone Doctor Macpherson to coom and certify her."

Obedient and still tearless, though inwardly shattered, Daisy delivered these two messages as fast as her fat legs and empty stomach would permit her.

On her way home, she knocked at the door of the house of her sister, Meg Fogarty. The house was one of a row of dilapidated brick houses opening directly on to the pavement. The door had long since lost its handles, but it did not yield when Daisy tried to push it open.

She heard the bolt squeak as Meg Fogarty wriggled it out of its socket.

" 'allo, what you doin' here so early?" Meg inquired, her black-rimmed eyes staring apprehensively out of a gaunt, tired face, as she wiped her hands on a grey apron. "What's to do?" Her chil-

11

dren crowded behind her, eager to greet their dear Anty Daise.

Meg drew in a quick breath, and her round, grey eyes with their black circles seemed suddenly much rounder. Her hand went to her mouth in a gesture of shock.

"God have mercy on us! Is it Mam?"

"Yes. I been for the doctor just now. Great Aunt Devlin's with her." Daisy lifted a corner of her apron and agitatedly mopped the sweat from her smooth, broad forehead.

Meg's toothless mouth quivered. "She's gone, is it?"

Daisy nodded, and the children gaped at her with open-mouthed, jam-smeared faces.

Meg's whole body sagged and she clutched her eldest daughter's shoulder to support herself.

"Now, Meg," said Daisy sharply. "Don't take on. Pull yourself together. I need help. Get your little Mary to go and tell Agnes and George and Maureen Mary — and Father Patrick — and all the others."

Little Mary on whom Meg was leaning ran the comb she was holding quickly through her lanky, shoulder-length hair. She said eagerly, "I'd love to go, Anty."

Her mother was dabbing her eyes with the back of her hand. Now she sniffed, and ordered, "Not now, you don't. You can go after school." She said firmly to Daisy, "I'm in a pile of trouble for keeping her home to help me last week." She shut her eyes tightly, and added passionately, "Poor Mam!"

Daisy sighed. "Well, send her after school, then."

The whole mystery and the fearsome finality of death struck her forcibly as she shivered on Meg's doorstep. She wanted to scream out loud, "Holy Angels at the Throne of God, it was unfair to take her from me. Mike's been at sea for eighteen months now, and there was only her and me in the house. You know me daughter, Maureen Mary, and her husband is too stuck up to live with me — and the rest of me children is lost to me. Dear Holy Angels, it's unfair, it is! It's unfair! I'll be alone, I will!"

But Meg's children were there, so she must be silent; and Meg was saying that she would have gone herself to announce the sad news to the rest of the family, but she dare not leave her invalid father-in-law, old Fogarty, for fear he fell out of his chair or suffered some other catastrophe.

12

"I'll come over tonight, I will," she promised. "As soon as our John gets home."

Daisy clasped her hands over her aching, empty stomach, to comfort herself, and sniffed. Surely mothers came before fathers-in-law, she thought angrily. Meg could have asked her sister-in-law, Emily, to watch old Fogarty. But she did not feel strong enough to fight Meg this morning — and Emily was a fool of the first water, she had to admit that.

She sighed, and turned away without another word, and walked hastily homeward. From time to time, she would clap her hand over her mouth, as if to keep inside her the scream she longed to give vent to.

After her unusually subdued children had gone to school, Meg sat down suddenly on a kitchen chair and allowed the tears she had withheld while the children were present to burst out of her. She swayed her skinny body back and forth and beat her breast, as she wailed aloud, "Me poor Mam! Poor Mam!"

"What you making such a racket for? What's to do?" shouted Mr. Fogarty, her irascible, crippled father-in-law. "Shut up that row and bring the pot. I want to pee."

Meg ceased her sobbing. For a moment she sat quite still as anger overwhelmed her grief. "Why couldn't it have been you, you old bugger?" she muttered furiously, as she seized a jam jar from under the kitchen sink and scurried to him.

Great Aunt Devlin laid out her niece and sat for two nights in the cold bedroom with the corpse. Two shawls were draped around her shoulders, and in one apron pocket she carried a bottle of gin; in the other one lay her rosary which she told from time to time. It was she who was paid first for her services from the money promptly brought by the agent of the insurance company.

It seemed to Daisy that in death her mother was more important and received more respect than she had ever enjoyed in life.

Father Patrick came to see Daisy and offer consolation. And the undertaker arrived on the dog-fouled doorstep before either Daisy or Meg had communicated with him.

"As if he could smell a passing on the wind," snorted Daisy.

The tiny house seemed to be full of clumsy, gossipy relations, who thankfully left all the arrangements for the funeral to Daisy, since she was now the eldest woman in the family; in this matter

13

of hierarchy Aunt Devlin did not count because she was a spinster.

Daisy's lifelong friend and sister-in-law, Nellie O'Brien, though obviously tired and ill, sat for hours on one of the kitchen chairs and listened kindly to Daisy's impatient fulminations about the laziness of the rest of the family. She had brought her only son, iddy Joey, to say good-bye to his Nan, lying cold and white beside Great Aunt Devlin, who, he was certain, was a witch. And, of course, there were neighbours who loved to come to inspect a corpse.

"I been fair run off me feet," Daisy complained to Mrs. Hanlon of the Ragged Bear, when she went to buy two bottles of rum and four of cheap port wine for the wake.

Mrs. Hanlon commiserated and tendered her condolences, as she thrust the bottles through the narrow hatch of the Off-Licence Department.

Mrs. Donnelly, the grocer, whose heart it was affirmed locally was solid flint regarding extensions of credit, also politely tendered her sympathy while she weighed and wrapped up three pounds of her cheapest currant cake.

"That'll be a shilling," she announced, putting one hand firmly over the parcel until the coin should be produced.

"You'll have to put it on me bill," Daisy replied, folding her great arms over her bosom. "I haven't got the insurance yet," she lied. Mrs. Donnelly and she had been crossing swords for nearly forty years and she saw no reason to part with good money for Mrs. Donnelly's benefit. Let the old devil wait.

Mrs. Donnelly's eyes narrowed till they looked like a bunch of wrinkles with only a pinpoint of light gleaming from them. "You owe me four and tenpence already. Seeing as I cut the cake I'll keep it for you till later on. The agent should come soon."

Thwarted, Daisy drew in a huge breath, savouring for a moment the familiar odours of rancid bacon, ageing cheese and carbolic soap. She blew out her cheeks till she looked as if she might burst. She was not going to walk all the way down the hill to her home and back up again later in the day; yet she did not know how to retreat from the stance she had taken.

Slowly she exhaled, making a most satisfying rude noise. Mrs. Donnelly clamped her thin lips together and busied herself by putting some bacon into the slicer, having first removed the parcel of cake from Daisy's reach.

Muttering sourly to herself, Daisy reached into her skirt pocket. "I got some of Meg's money. I'll pay for it from that."

Mrs. Donnelly thrust out a hand deeply lined with blacking from the daily polishing of her fireplace. Daisy banged two sixpences into it so hard that Mrs. Donnelly's knuckles nearly hit the counter. Mrs. Donnelly silently put the money into her wooden till. Then she put the cake on the counter within reach of Daisy.

Daisy snatched it up, tucked it under her black shawl and stalked out.

Daisy's eldest daughter, Maureen Mary, a faded blonde, arrived in the late afternoon of the day of her grandmother's death, from her home in Princes Park. Carrying her three-year-old daughter, Bridie, she had set out immediately upon receiving word from Meg's little Mary. Knowing the sad state of her mother's home, she brought with her a pair of sheets on which to lay the body, and two candlesticks with long new candles to light the death chamber until the funeral.

She agreed with Daisy that dear Nan looked really beautiful after the ministrations of Great Aunt Mary Devlin.

"She must have looked like that when she was young," Maureen Mary remarked as she dried her eyes with a flowered pocket handkerchief. "I mean, before she had eleven children — and lost six of them."

"Yes," agreed Daisy with a sigh. "We was all young once."

She went on to tell Maureen Mary how she vaguely remembered being taken to say farewell to her own tiny, Irish Nan in the same upstairs bedroom. Nan had been still alive and had blessed her. Three days later she had been carried out of the house in a big box by four of her grandsons, Daisy's cousins.

"Priest told me," she added with a little chuckle, "that Nan would soon be with God; and, you know, it bothered me for ages that people had to be delivered to God in a box!" She chuckled again.

Maureen Mary looked shocked; it was improper to laugh at such a solemn time.

Daisy was immediately sobered by her daughter's disapproval and she said despondently, "It's going to be proper lonely without Nan, seeing as how you don't live here." And she glanced accusingly at her daughter.

Maureen Mary flushed under her heavy makeup. Her bright red lips trembled weakly. She bent over Bridie, to pull up the tot's knickers which had slipped down around her bare knees. Her leaving home after her marriage was a very sore point between Daisy and herself. Good daughters brought their husbands home to live with their mother, just as Daisy had brought her sailor husband, Mike, home; and they had children to cheer up the old house with their squabbles.

"Perhaps Dad could get a shore job next time he comes home," she suggested hopefully.

"Himself? Swallow the anchor? That's not likely. 'Sides I couldn't stand having him under me feet all the time."

Maureen Mary was timidly silent for a moment, then she said, "Well, our Jamie and our Lizzie Ann will finish doing their time and come 'ome one day."

"Humph," grunted her mother. "Lizzie Ann's got at least another eighteen months to do — and Jamie, poor love, has got about another five years."

Silenced, Maureen Mary picked up Bridie and went home.

After she had gone, Daisy thought about this conversation, as she sat in a sagging chair and poked the coal fire in the iron grate, which took up nearly the whole of one wall of her living-room. From time to time she gave a great heaving sigh. Now she would replace her mother as the Nan, the grandmother to whom all the family would look for help and advice; but there was not much pleasure in that if nobody lived with you, she decided. And how was she going to survive sleeping by herself? The idea was scarifying. Whoever had heard of a decent Irish Catholic woman, who kept herself to herself, having to sleep in a house alone? It had been terrible when the district nurse had suggested that Mrs. O'Brien would sleep better if Daisy did not share her bed Daisy had reluctantly removed herself to a bed in the landing bedroom, tucked against the wall of her mother's room. But to be alone was to invite the Devil to come close.

As she sat forlornly by her fire, her plump figure looking somehow deflated in the flickering light, she received the condolences of neighbours and more distant relations. They slipped in from the street, not waiting for a response to their knock, to stand for a moment silently and with pinched lips; then they would say how sorry they were.

"She'll be sorely missed, God rest her," they invariably said. "She was proper kind, she was." Then they shuffled their boots on the stone floor and examined the toes of them, and added, "Maybe it's a blessing, God forgive us, that she had no pain."

Daisy, her throat tight with misery and yet still unable to cry, nodded her head sadly and motioned them to go upstairs, where they would respectfully view the body, under the jealous glare of Great Aunt Devlin. They all came down again weeping softly into the corner of their aprons and assured Daisy, "She looks beautiful — so peaceful, like."

Thankful for their company, Daisy then invited them to the funeral service. They went soberly out, and then rushed up the street to tell their families all about the corpse.

All available members of the family, including Daisy's middle daughter, Sister Margaret of the Little Sisters of the Poor, who travelled from Manchester, came to the funeral. Afterwards, they crammed into Daisy's little living room with some of the neighbours, who had come to pay their respects to the family and get a free drink. Everybody clutched a glass of rum or port in one hand and held a piece of currant cake cupped in the other.

With their mouths full, the members of the family argued in muffled tones about the division of the contents of the house, that being all that Mrs. Mary Ellen O'Brien had to leave.

Daisy was ignored. She downed a welcome glass of rum and listened, hand on hip, to the subdued babble of voices.

Through the conversation, she heard with anxiety the steady coughing of brother George's wife, dear Nellie. She silently poured a bumper glass of port and handed it to seven-year-old iddy Joey, with the request that he pass it to his struggling mother. He winked at his dear Anty Daise, took a quick sip from the glass and passed it over to Nellie.

The argument between the relations grew heated and voices began to rise. Part of the contents of the house belonged to Daisy and her husband, Michael; and when Daisy heard some of these named she would shift her cake to the other side of her toothless mouth and shout, "You can't have that — it belongs to me."

Nobody listened.

17

She was not disturbed by this lack of attention. The excitement of knowing she held a trump card had dulled some of the gnawing unhappiness she had been suffering. Her son-in-law, Freddie, had been brilliantly helpful. For the first time since Maureen Mary had brought home a neat, pin-striped nonentity called Frederick Brown, an English Protestant, and had announced to her enraged mother that she had married him, Daisy was grateful to him. She would never forgive him, she thought darkly, for being a bleeding Prottie or for taking Maureen Mary from her mother's loving arms. He had put his pretty wife into a grand three-bedroomed row house near Princes Park, instead of coming to live with his mother-in-law, Daisy, as was customary; and this was unforgivable. Daisy had, however, voiced to Maureen Mary her fears of being left in an unfurnished house, if Mrs. O'Brien's other children claimed a share of the furnishings. Maureen Mary had consulted Freddie, who, she assured her mother, knew all about laws.

As she watched Freddie standing solitarily with a glass in his hand at the back of the crowd, Daisy began to console herself about Maureen Mary's desertion and to think that perhaps when Elizabeth Ann was released from training school, she would marry and bring her husband to her mother's home, and so make up for Maureen Mary's dereliction.

Grinning maliciously, she snatched up a tin tray and the poker, and banged them together like a gong. The shattering noise in the confined space shocked her relations into silence. Shawls remained half hitched over shoulders, union shirt buttons about to be loosened because of the heat of the room remained buttoned. Children about to shriek in the course of a game of tag round the legs of adults paused with mouths open.

She drew an old butter box out from under the table and stepped up on to it. It creaked threateningly under her weight but did not split. From this elevation she looked even more ferocious than usual to her relations; her head with its neat plaits round each ear moved from side to side like that of a cobra, while she flourished the poker at them.

"Na, then, you pack o' vultures," she addressed them. "Our Mam not more'n an hour in her grave and you wanting to break up her home!" Her handsome face was spoiled by a deep scowl and her blue eyes flashed menacingly.

18

Daisy's younger sister, Agnes, sniffled and rubbed her pug nose with the end of her shawl. "I never said nothin'," she whined.

"Oh, shut your gob, Aggie," ordered Daisy. "Always snivelling about somethin' ".

Agnes burst into tears and turned to her daughter, Winnie, a gangling twelve-year-old, to be comforted. The child put her arms round her mother and glared resentfully at Anty Daise.

Daisy's middle daughter, Sister Margaret of the Little Sisters of the Poor, murmured a gentle remonstration against her mother's sharpness. Daisy silenced her with a heavy frown.

Maureen Mary smiled encouragement at her hefty mother. The last thing she wanted was for her mother to be rendered homeless — she might demand to live with her daughter in Princes Park, something that even patient Freddie would not tolerate.

Daisy's frown vanished. She beamed suddenly at the gathering until her toothless gums showed, and iddy Joey was reminded of the turnip he had made into a jack-o-lantern last All Hallow's E'en.

"I want to tell you that our Nan left a will!"

"A will!" exclaimed Agnes's husband, Joe, an unemployed labourer. "Whatever for?"

Daisy's square chin jutted out belligerently and again she scowled as she replied scornfully, " 'Cos she knew the likes of you. 'Cos I nursed her. 'Cos I'm the eldest daughter and she wanted to make sure I got me rights. 'Cos this's always been Mike's and my home, too." She pointed the poker at him and he flinched. "It's only right."

Meg folded her skinny arms across her flat chest, and asked crossly, "What's right? It was my home, too, remember."

Daisy smiled oversweetly at her sister. "Well, as of yesterday I been tenant of this house. Mam asked the rent collector to arrange it a couple of weeks ago, so it's been passed to me like it's always been passed down." She simpered irritatingly at the other woman. "She didn't mean me to have an empty house, so she left me everything." Daisy crossed her shawl over her chest and the poker waggled suggestively from underneath the garment. "So there, Missus!"

"She never," exclaimed Meg indignantly. "She promised her mirror to me — many a time she did."

Daisy replied primly, "Mirror's in pop. She left you her wedding ring. It's on the mantlepiece by the clock."

The news that the mirror was in pawn did not surprise anyone — so were most of the company's more prized possessions.

Agnes raised her wet face from her daughter's shoulder and asked plaintively, "What about me?"

"You got the photo of her and Dad on their wedding day. We had to sell the frame — but the picture's still good."

Agnes was shaken by a fresh sob. She again flung herself upon her daughter.

Daisy turned to her brother, George, Nellie's husband. "You and brother Gregory, who couldn't come 'cos he's at sea, as we all know, she didn't leave nothing to. She reckoned you could manage. You never came to see her anyway unless she sent for you. It was only your wife, our Nellie, what did." And she bent an approving glance upon her friend, who was looking a little flustered and unsteady after her large glass of wine.

George glowered sullenly at his bossy sister. From long unemployment, his mind and body had become equally flaccid, but he managed to ask, "Where is the bloody will?"

Daisy smirked in triumph. "Our Freddie's got it."

TWO

The company turned wondering eyes upon Freddie. Few had seen him before. As Meg bitingly remarked, in his neat ready-made suit and striped shirt, he stood out like a sore toe.

"Smells like a bloody whore," grumbled George.

Agnes remonstrated, "Now don't you be using such language before the kids!"

George's heavy red face returned to its usual sullenness. He did not reply.

Freddie coughed, partly with shyness and partly from the overwhelming stench of unwashed bodies catching at his throat. A path opened before him so that he could go to stand by Daisy.

Freddie's relationship with his high-smelling mother-in-law was an ambiguous one. He had early in his marriage discovered that it was no good trying to cut Maureen Mary off entirely from her mother; Maureen Mary seemed unable to function at all without the support of regular visits to her. Gradually, mixed with his horror of Daisy had come a reluctant respect for her, and he sought earnestly to please her in the hope of keeping his adored wife with him. Daisy regarded him with contempt mixed with curiosity. She was surprised that anyone could earn as much as he did without getting his hands dirty.

Daisy had only once visited Maureen and Freddie in their home — she had never been invited, and pride kept her from calling again without an invitation.

They had been married in a registry office, because she was a Catholic and he was a Protestant. Neither family had been present, in Maureen's case because she had lacked the courage to inform them until after the fact; and in his case because his parents were outraged at his marrying a poor Irish Catholic girl.

Maureen Mary had been a pert little Nippie waitress at his favourite Lyons' restaurant; he was a traveller for a sweet company. Neither had considered what the other's family might be like.

Daisy beamed toothlessly at him as he turned and stood beside her. "You tell 'em, Freddie," she encouraged.

"Proper fancy pansy," George muttered out of the corner of his mouth to John, Meg's husband. John nodded agreement.

George drained his glass and looked round for another drink. Daisy had, however, whipped the bottles away while there was still something left in them, and they were now reposing under the huge kitchen fender which her great-grandmother had brought from Ireland.

Taking small breaths so as not to be overpowered by the stink from Daisy, Freddie drew a long, narrow envelope from his inside pocket, an envelope which appeared to his experienced audience suspiciously like a summons from the beak.

It was not a missive from the magistrate which he took out, however, but a penny will form from the local stationers.

Though the preamble was almost incomprehensible to Freddie's audience, the bequests were clear. There was a tiny gift for each of her daughters and for her daughter-in-law, Nellie O'Brien. In addition she left her rosary to her granddaughter by Daisy, Elizabeth Ann, who was at that moment scrubbing the dining-hall floor in the training home and was weeping into the grey soapsuds for her dear, dead Nan.

At the mention of Elizabeth Ann, Meg drew in her breath sharply. Her hollow cheeks darkened as she tried to suppress her rising anger.

"Why Lizzie Ann?" she asked. "Why not our Mary?"

Agnes lifted her woebegone face.

"What about our Winnie, if it comes to that?"

Freddie's eyes were watering and his nose was beginning to run from the incredible effluvia emanating from his stout mother-in-law beside him. He took a handkerchief from his pocket and dabbed his eyes before answering Meg.

"Mrs. O'Brien states in her will that Elizabeth always admired the rosary, and was allowed to carry it to her first Communion when she was seven." He thrust his handkerchief back into his pocket, and added with sudden enthusiasm, "It is very beautiful. The beads and the crucifix are hand-carved. I understand Mrs. O'Brien's grandfather made it as a gift to his wife. Perhaps Mrs. O'Brien felt that Elizabeth Ann would take special care of it."

"Humph! So would our Mary."

"Or our Winnie," echoed Agnes.

Meg pointed a thin finger at Freddie and prodded him in the waistcoat. "I don't see why Lizzie Ann should be the only grand-daughter to get anything."

Freddie moved back a step. "Mrs. O'Brien did not have much to leave," he said conciliatorily.

Meg advanced and prodded him again.

"She could have thought of something for Mary," she said savagely.

Daisy here interposed wrathfully and waggled the poker at Meg. "You shut up, Meg, and stop poking Freddie in the stomach." She snorted. "You always was a jealous bitch!"

Meg threw off her shawl and turned angrily upon her sister, ignoring the threatening poker. "Don't you call me names, you fat sow!" she screamed. "Always so bloody stuck up. Now Nan's passed on you needn't think you can throw your weight around, 'cos I won't stand for it." She raised her fist to strike her sister in the stomach, and Daisy teetered on the creaking butter box.

"Meg!" warned her quiet husband, John, shooting forward a fist like a prize fighter and grasping her bony shoulder.

She turned on him like an infuriated ferret, while at the same time Daisy stepped heavily down from the butter box and surged purposefully towards her, eyes flashing, huge arms akimbo, poker still clasped in one hand.

"Na, Daisy, na, Daisy. Meg didn't mean nothing. She's just hot-tempered. Come on, now, you know her." John attempted to clasp his wife firmly round her waist to hold her back. He had a de-spairing feeling that he was going to be caught between two hell-cats.

"Didn't mean nothing!" Daisy paused, and her great bosom swelled. She thrust out her chin and screamed into the face of her small but determined sister. "I'll fat sow yer, yer greedy bitch. Where was you when Ma needed help? Where was you of a night

23

when I was up putting hot poultices on her? When our Lizzie Ann was home she was proper good to her Nan. She earned the rosary, she did."

Daisy dropped the poker, and Agnes squeaked as it hit her ankle. She raised her fist to strike Meg, while John did his best to hold back his kicking, yelling wife.

"Na, Daise," he cried, "Don't you hit her. She didn't mean it. Meg had to look after me Dad. How could she help you?"

The fascinated neighbours began to edge back to form a rough circle and give the combatants room. Iddy Joey climbed on to the table and stood with one foot on a loaf of bread to get a better view. But clear across the squawks of the women and the anxious murmurs of the rest of the family came Freddie's voice, full of long experience of dealing with difficult customers and pathetically anxious to curry favour with his mother-in-law.

"Dear Daisy, restrain yourself."

The crowd reluctantly made way for him as he came towards her with the calmness of the bishop himself. "You must be dreadfully tired. It is time people went home."

Daisy stopped, arm still raised, fist still clenched. Nobody but Freddie had ever called her dear, and it seemed to her that only Freddie, and, of course, Nellie, had her interests at heart.

Meg, who hardly knew him, stopped in mid-shriek as if switched off. For a moment she gazed at him in dumb amazement and then she began to giggle. The giggle became a laugh. She threw herself upon John and howled with laughter. The other adults began to snigger and then to laugh. The children joined in with uncertain tee-hees.

Dumbfounded at the unexpected hilarity, Daisy dropped her threatening fist. She looked at Freddie. Didn't he mind being laughed at? Apparently not, because he was calmly folding up the will and gave no indication that he was perturbed by the mirth he had engendered.

His wife, Maureen Mary, said with brittle brightness to the assembly, "Yes, it's time for home — and I'll take back me sheets and me candlesticks now Nan is laid to rest." A tear trickled down her cheek as she picked up the bundle of linen from the back of a chair and took the candlesticks, encrusted with grease, from between iddy Joey's feet on the table. She gathered up her little daugh-

ter, Bridie, a pretty picture in a pale blue satin dress and bonnet.
She blew a kiss sadly to Daisy across the room and, her arms
loaded with sheets and child, she nudged her aunt towards the
door. "Come on, Anty Meg."

John opened the front door and a still giggling Meg was shepherded into the street. As the other visitors flowed out Maureen
Mary turned and tried to get back in, but it was too difficult, laden
as she was, and she shouted with a little catch in her voice, "I'll
come tomorrow, Mam!"

Daisy who had been watching the sudden exodus with narrowed
eyes, as she considered what she would like to do with Meg, smiled
suddenly and nodded agreement.

When the crowd had thinned, Nellie get up unsteadily from the
chair on which she had been sitting.

"Get down off that table, Joey," she said ineffectually.

Joey danced around, to the further detriment of the loaf of bread.
A few odds and ends fell off the back of the table.

George reached forward and caught his son by the back of his
clothes. He lifted him bodily on to the floor and gave him a sharp
slap across the head. "Gerrout," he said.

Joey howled as if he had been shot and fled to his mother, to
hide his face in her black skirt and bellow like a young bullock.

"You didn't have to do that," Nellie reproached her husband.

"Och, he's spoiled rotten," retorted George. He picked up his
jacket and swung out of the house after John.

Nellie bent over to console Joey. "Never mind, luv," she said.
"Never mind."

Daisy, being more practical, reached over to the plate of cake
still on the mantelpiece. " 'Ere ye are, Joey," she said, as she handed
him a piece.

Joey's wails ceased immediately. He emerged from the folds of
his mother's skirts, stuffed the cake into his mouth and danced
over to the door, through which Daisy could observe him skipping happily across the road to look out over the river.

Nellie embraced Daisy lovingly. "I'll come tomorrow," she promised. Daisy smiled and kissed her, holding the tiny hands with
their terrible, broken nails as if she could not bear to let her go.
She led the frail little woman to the door, where Freddie stood
running his trilby hat uneasily through his fingers.

"Goodbye, Mrs. O'Brien," he said politely to Nellie.

"Goodbye, Freddie. Ta-ra, Daisy. See you tomorrow."

Daisy stood with one hand on the door jamb as Nellie followed the little procession up the street. Freddie watched her uneasily. He knew he should suggest that Maureen Mary stay overnight with her bereaved mother; yet he feared that if he did so she would never return to him. His friends had all warned him how Irish Catholic girls had a tendency to go back to mother once they had a child or two, expecting their husbands to follow uncomplainingly. He knew that he could never live in this rough, bug-ridden home, the very idea made him shudder.

Maureen Mary wanted to stay the night; she had said so over breakfast, and only his argument that the house was so damp that little Bridie might get a chill there had dissuaded her. He had not mentioned that he had a horror of her bringing back vermin from her mother's home. He had been careful not to sit down during the wake, but he was convinced that he had gathered an unwelcome visitor — he itched all over.

"Be all right?" he asked Daisy lamely.

Daisy sighed gustily. "Yes," she replied.

She stood outside the front door to watch the procession of guests and relatives along the road until they turned the corner. Then she stared glumly at the river for a moment. A shaft of sunlight pierced the clouds and gave a soft sheen to the gloomy, heaving water and lit up the Wallasey shore. Then the cloud closed over and the wind nipped playfully at Daisy's loosely pinned-up plaits. She shivered, and stepped back into the deserted house.

Inside, she paused, reluctant to shut the door. The silence was oppressive. For the first time in nearly a hundred years there would be only one resident in the house; for the first time in her life she would be alone overnight. Through the residue of her anger at Meg and her annoyance that Maureen Mary had not stayed with her, loneliness began to penetrate painfully. It seemed to creep through her like a paralysis, and her softly rounded cheeks whitened, making the mauve mottles caused by sitting too close to the fire stand out like scars.

She stood, head bent, in the cold draught and breathed heavily, her shoulders drooping under her black shawl.

"I got to get used to it," she muttered, "till our Lizzie and our

26

Jamie finish doing their time." She did not consider that Michael, her sailor husband, might also return. He was a vague figure in the background of her life who was more nuisance than help when he did have a spell at home. "And I got you, Mog, you old devil," she added forlornly to the cat, which was sitting on the mantelpiece between two dusty china dogs.

She slowly shut the weather-beaten door behind her. "I'm the Nan now, Mog. Only there's nobody here to be Nan over. It's a proper queer life, isn't it?"

27

THREE

Daisy rubbed her tired eyes and then stretched herself. Though stout, she was by no means unhandsome and as she clasped her hands behind her head there was a sensuousness about her, reminiscent of women of an earlier age pictured by Rubens.

She put another shovelful of coal on the fire, and afterwards plonked herself thankfully down on the easy chair her mother had bought at a sale half a century before.

When she was a little rested she took a pad of notepaper and an envelope from the table drawer. Then she hunted impatiently through the rags, paper and ornaments which were piled on the mantelpiece until she found a bottle of Stephens' ink and a wooden penholder. She put everything down on the big, brass fender and sat down again.

To ease the tension within her, she lifted her long black skirt and petticoats up over her fat knees to allow the comforting heat of the fire to reach her thighs, while she considered what she should put in a letter to her husband.

Mike's last post card had been from Accra and had carried his usual message, "Doing fine, love, Mike." It did not inspire Daisy in her reply. Michael had been doing fine as a ship's stoker on tramp steamers, in between bouts of unemployment, through a world war and twenty-nine years of marriage. Scattered through the house were numerous postcards from him carrying cancellation marks of ports all over the world.

Daisy nibbled her wooden penholder thoughtfully. Mike had seen so much and was so good at telling stories about his adventures — after he had downed a couple of pints of bitter, of course

28

— that he had convinced their first-born son, John, that there was no better occupation than that of seaman; and the boy had run away to sea the day he was fourteen. He had never been heard from since. The memory of him made Daisy heave one of her mighty sighs. It was hard on a mother to lose a boy at fourteen, just when he could be sent to work to earn a bit of money.

Now, Mike had been sailing up and down the coasts of Africa for a year and a half. Eighteen bloody cold months, thought Daisy, without a man to warm you occasionally.

She stabbed the pen into the ink and scratched carefully across the lined notepaper, "Nan died on Monday, God rest her. She was laid to rest today — St. Michael's Day." Mike would think his patron saint really cared about him, she reflected acidly. The nib spat suddenly and made a blot as she crossed a t.

"Blast!" she ejaculated, and dabbed the ink dry with the corner of her apron, which was already dingy from many washings. The ink smudged. She clucked irritably and again dipped her pen into the ink.

"The man from the Prue paid her burial money prompt and O'Toole did her funeral real nice. Her burial money will be enough for Bill Donohue to wallpaper her room as well." She stopped and chewed the end of her pen, pressing her toothless gums against it so hard that it cracked. She spat the small sliver of wood into the fire. Mike would resent good money being spent on the redecorating of the room. Slowly and firmly she added in scrawling round letters, "Like he always done it." "Bugger him," she murmured crossly.

She had a fixed belief, handed down through the generations, that nobody should sleep in a room in which someone had died without it first being redecorated. She sighed sadly. So many people had died in the front bedroom of her home — the wallpaper must be inches deep. It was the only room in the house which had ever had anything done to it, as far as she remembered.

"Hope this finds you in the pink as it leaves me, Daisy," she added to her letter. Then she picked up an envelope from the dusty rag rug beneath her feet and put the letter into it. In large capital letters she addressed the letter to Mr. Michael Gallagher, Stoker, s.s. *Heart of Salford,* c/o the shipping company's Liverpool office. She never knew until he came home whether he had re-

29

ceived her letters, but she supposed this one would catch up with him eventually. He had been away such a long time that she had begun to forget him; for weeks at a time she never thought of him.

She heaved herself out of her chair and moved slowly to the oilcloth-covered table. The roses on the cloth stared back at her through a greasy film, where they showed between dirty mugs, wine and rum glasses. Among the glasses lay the sliced white loaf on which iddy Joey had stood, its slices were half out of their wrapping and were scattered and squashed. Beside them lay their inevitable companion, a mangled open package of margarine.

Impatiently she swept the clutter to the back of the table and laid the letter in a prominent position, so that she would not forget to buy a three-halfpenny stamp and post it.

She removed the glass from a small oil lamp, struck a match and lit the wick. Carefully she replaced the glass.

The lamp's weak rays did little to cheer the forlorn room. The walls and ceiling, blackened by a hundred years of coal fires, made it seem even smaller than it was. Generations of spiders had spun thick webs, now laden with dust in every cranny. The window curtain of cheap lace was so tattered and so grey with dust that it looked as if the spiders might have spun it, too. An old chest of drawers stood in one corner, its surface piled with odd sheets of newspaper kept for lighting the fire, and bits of rag which Daisy thought might come in useful for lagging the pipes of the recalcitrant water closet in the yard. Two straight-backed kitchen chairs stood in the middle of the room where they had been abandoned earlier by her visitors, and mechanically she pushed them under the table. Then she stood in silent contemplation of a crumpled newspaper in the hearth on which lay a few lumps of coal. She knew she should get some more coal up from the cellar ready for the morning, but she felt too weary.

The silence and the hollowness of the house made her uneasy. She was normally a cheerful woman, though often aggressive, and her hearty laugh would make her great breasts shake in unison much to the amusement of the male patrons of the Ragged Bear. Deep-set blue eyes looked out at a tough world, but she feared nobody within the confines of the streets she frequented. As far as she was concerned, all wickedness lay outside her own district

— where you never knew what might happen to you, she would sometimes remark darkly to Nellie.

But an empty house was a new phenomenon to her.

"Bloody ghosts in the place," she said to Moggie in a voice that trembled slightly. Then she shrugged her plump shoulders and added with forced firmness, "It's me nairves, Mog. Just me nairves." Even the home's single water tap in the scullery, which had dripped for weeks, had suddenly stopped its irritating tap-tap. A cinder falling from the miserable fire made her jump. There was not even the usual clatter of boots and vehicular traffic in the street; the poor weather must have kept everyone indoors.

She trailed over to the front door and opened it. The night had closed in and solid blackness met her; she could not even see the light at the top of the steps that ran down to the Herculaneum Dock. She peered the other way. The street lamp seemed almost obliterated by fine rain. The dampness carried with it a searing acridity; it caught in her throat and made her cough. Hastily she slammed the door and took her black shawl off the hook at the back of it. She wrapped the garment round her shoulders and tucked it across her breasts. She returned, shivering, to her chair by the fire. From time to time, she coughed and cleared her throat.

The cough bothered her. "Maybe it's T.B.," she thought fearfully, "like our Tommy."

Tommy had coughed himself to death, at the age of twelve, in the room upstairs. The memory still brought a tear to his mother's eye, though it was eight years ago and the cabbage roses on the wallpaper put on after his death were blurred and torn in places.

She sighed lustily. She had had no luck with her boys and very little with her girls. John, born when she was seventeen, had run away. Little Mickey had toddled into Grafton Street when he was three, and had been trampled under the hooves of a pair of Shire horses pulling a wagon of beer up to the Ragged Bear. He was dead, his tiny body mangled and broken, before the carter managed to put on the brake and shout to the rearing horses.

And then there was James, the pride of her heart. There was a lad! How she wished he was with her now. But he was doing seven years for stabbing an Orangeman.

The very thought of the Orangemen made her face darken with venomous wrath. Serve them right if they got stabbed. She reckoned they should know by now that to parade on July 12th was asking for trouble. A pack of bleeding Protties going over the river to New Brighton to celebrate the anniversary of King William winning the Battle of the Boyne, to the ruin of all Catholics. And they carried church banners and all. Enough to make a good Irish Catholic puke.

In a fight with the members of a homeward bound procession, James had broken a beer bottle and accidentally cut the throat of an opponent.

Daisy, a soggy mess of tears, went to see him when he came up for trial for murder.

"I never meant to kill him, Mam," he assured her. "Just a good scratch. But his throat got in the way."

Daisy had been sure that James would hang. Through the trial she had, until she was finally ejected, wept loudly in the Court, beating her breast and exclaiming from time to time, "Jaysus Mary! Me poor boy! God spare him!"

In the depth of despair, she suddenly remembered St. Jude, kind patron saint of lost causes. She fell to her knees on the stone floor of the scullery, and prayed. She promised St. Jude a three-line advertisement in the *Liverpool Echo* if he would only save the life of her beloved son, James.

Apparently, St. Jude heard the impassioned plea, because the charge was reduced to one of manslaughter, and James did not hang. Two days after James went off to serve his sentence, there appeared in the Personal Column of the *Liverpool Echo* an advertisement, which read: "Grateful thanks to St. Jude, patron saint of lost causes, for help in great trouble, D.M.G." It did not make up three lines, but Daisy could not think of anything more to say, and she hoped St. Jude would understand. She would make it up to him some other time.

"Ee, Mog," she addressed the cat, as it climbed on to her knee. "I could use a bit of help now, I could. The house is so empty."

FOUR

The quiet of the house became a miasma which oozed out of the walls and wrapped itself around her. At times she would shiver uncontrollably despite the warmth of the fire. She crouched over the failing flames and wondered what she had done to deserve such desolation.

Despite her feeling of being deserted, she did not grudge Maureen Mary her fancy home with its shiny painted window-sills and brass-edged doorstep — at least the girl seemed to eat plentifully and have more clothes than her mother had ever dreamed of, proper coats instead of a shawl, and rayon stockings instead of cotton or wool. And she was proud that Margaret was a nun. Of course, Elizabeth Ann had been very careless in allowing herself to be caught while shoplifting in Woolworth's; but then all young people were careless, you had to expect it.

She fumed for a little while when she considered that her sisters had also deserted her. It would not have hurt one of them to lend her a daughter to stay with her, she thought bitterly. Winnie or little Mary would have been most welcome guests. But then she remembered that she had had a fight with Meg, which Meg would not easily forgive, and she had reduced placid Agnes to tears, and Nellie, dear frail Nellie, must have taken it for granted that Maureen Mary would keep her company for a few days.

Daisy gave a great trembling sigh, as she stared moodily at the massive collection of Woodbine cigarette butts tossed into the hearth by her guests. A beam in the roof gave a sharp creak and made her jump. She looked fearfully up at the dark shadows at the top of the stairs. Somehow, she had to get up enough courage to

33

go to bed, to clamber into an empty bedstead without even the comfort of knowing that her mother was only on the other side of the wall. She shuddered.

Then she remembered the bottle hidden under the brass fender beneath her feet.

She leaned forward and picked up a glass from the top of the oven. The dregs had dried in it. She felt around under her feet, found one bottle and then slipped down on her knees to reach the three others. She drained all four of them into a tumbler and sipped the mixture of rum and wine. It tasted good to her and warmed her.

The cat cried to be let into the oven, where it usually slept the night. She leaned forward and lifted its heavy latch. Moggie leaped into its womblike darkness.

Daisy got up and lit a stub of candle stuck on a saucer among the debris on the mantelpiece. Then she blew out the oil lamp.

Glass in one hand, candle in the other, she staggered up the hollowed wooden staircase, which led directly from the living room to an open space above which was known as the landing bedroom. From it, a door led into the front bedroom which had been occupied by her mother.

Two double beds took up practically all the floor space in the landing bedroom. One had only a lumpy horse-hair mattress on it, heavily stained by generations of incontinent children; the other bed had lying in the middle of it a mixed pile of old bolsters, a discarded overcoat and an old horse blanket. Daisy did own a pair of blankets but they were in pawn and looked like staying there, unless Michael came home with some money. She had been paying the interest on them to the pawnbroker for months — Michael could use a belt with good effect across her back when he was angry enough; and the loss of the blankets, with the consequential chilly nights he would suffer while home, would be quite enough to raise his Irish temper.

She stood looking round this noisome den while she drained her glass. The chamberpot under the bed had not been emptied for a couple of days and was adding a finishing touch to the stench. The silence was as absolute as that of a church on a Monday.

Slowly she trailed through the door to her mother's room. A shaft of moonlight illuminated the empty, stripped bed. Mixed with the smell of bugs was a faint odour of flowers and of death.

She walked almost fearfully round the bed and put the candle in its saucer down on the mantelpiece. In its dim light she stood looking down at the pillow which still showed the indent of her mother's head.

Suddenly a great bellowing wail came from the bereaved woman. She flung herself on to the bed and, lying spread-eagled upon it, she beat the thin mattress with her fists.

"Oh, Mam!" she shrieked, "Mam!"

FIVE

Daisy was awakened by a steady tapping on the front door and a bright little voice shouting, "Mrs. Gallagher!"

Daisy opened her eyes slowly; the lids were swollen from weeping and felt sore. She became aware that she must have slept for a long time and she turned to look through the undraped window. Though overcast, the sky was light and a wind was rattling at the dormer window, which Great Aunt Mary Devlin had left ajar.

The sharp tap-tap on the door was repeated.

"Come in," shouted Daisy, "Door's open." Then she realised that someone was tapping with a coin or other metal, not with a fist, as would one of the family or a neighbour. "Be down!" she cried.

She rolled slowly off the bed and stood for a second shaking out her skirts and pushing her loosened plaits back from her face. She sighed with a slow sobbing breath and then stumped down the stairs, little jabs of pain going through her head at every step.

She stumbled across the room with its litter of bottles and glasses, opened the door a couple of inches and peered out.

"It's me, Mrs. Gallagher," announced the neat young woman on the doorstep. "I've brought the blanket for Mrs. O'Brien. How is she today?"

The lady from the Welfare! Daisy groaned inwardly, acutely aware of the bottles on the hearth rug. The sight of them would be enough to cut off, for ever, this useful source of creature comforts. The cool wind from the river hit her and she breathed in deeply to help her head to clear.

She longed for the warmth of the blanket in the arms of the

36

Welfare lady. If she was not smart, however, it would be given to another invalid, she was sure.

"Och, she's not so bad. She's sleeping now." She opened the door slightly further, interposing her plump figure so that the Welfare lady could not see into the room, and held out her arms for the parcel.

The lady from the Welfare blinked behind her glasses and held her breath, as the stink from the house and its tenant flowed around her. She dumped the parcel into Daisy's welcoming arms, and stepped back a pace.

Daisy said with suitable subservience, "It's proper kind of you, I'm sure. Please thank the ladies for their help." She gave an old-fashioned half-bob which she had discovered from experience seemed to delight Welfare ladies.

The Welfare lady smiled and gasped in response, "It will be a comfort to Mrs. O'Brien. Since she's sleeping, I won't come in today. Now don't forget, will you, that you have an appointment today to get your teeth from the Dental Hospital?"

Daisy simpered. Jesus! She had forgotten it. "No, I haven't forgotten," she lied glibly.

"I'm sure your health will improve immensely once you have teeth," the kind little woman assured her.

Daisy sighed. The collection of her teeth was the culmination of a long battle between her and the Welfare lady. For such a frail-looking vixen she had a will of pure iron, Daisy had often lamented to Agnes and Nellie. She could press you into anything.

"I'll be there," Daisy promised resignedly. "What time is it now? Me clock's stopped."

The Welfare lady looked at her watch. "Five to eleven," she said brightly. "Your appointment is at four."

Daisy nodded. "Thank you. Me mother will be glad of the blanket." She eased back into her room a little. She would tell the Welfare next week that her mother was dead. They would never take a blanket out of a bug-ridden house like hers once it was unpacked.

The Welfare lady was greatly relieved that she had not to sit in Mrs. O'Brien's fetid bedroom. She promised to come again next week, when she expected Daisy to have a perfect smile.

Daisy smiled faintly and ran her tongue round her gums. No-

37

body expected to have teeth at the age of forty-five, unless they were exceptionally lucky. She glumly closed the door as the Welfare lady started up her tiny car.

There was no room on the table, so she dumped the parcel on the floor and broke the string.

It was a good, thick double blanket. Daisy had never touched such a blanket, and it gave her almost voluptuous pleasure to run her fingers over it. She sat back on her heels looking at its spotless perfection amid the familiar filth of her room. Her head ached excruciatingly and her first thought was to carry the blanket up to her bed and go to sleep again under it.

Moggie leaped down from the kitchen oven and came to nose around the woolly pile. He climbed on to it and began to move languidly round to make himself a nest, while Daisy stared through him, thinking how much her mother would have loved to have such a covering.

In sudden rage she slapped the cat soundly and he went spinning across the room with a frightened yowl.

"Yer — jigger rabbit!" she yelled at him, "Gerroff and stay off."

She got to her feet and picked up the blanket.

"I know what I'll do," she planned. "I'll wait till Mam's room's been done out and then I'll put it on her bed. And I'll have that room, and I can lie in bed and think about her and watch the ships coming up the river."

She was just frying herself a bit of bacon and a leftover potato on the living-room fire when Meg swept into the house. The glasses were still strewn around the room, but the bottles had been removed to the scullery to await a visit from the rag and bone man.

Meg had not bothered to knock. She marched up to Daisy and stood over her, a thin and hungry fury suddenly jealous of Daisy's bacon and potato.

"I come for me ring," she announced, her long thin nose held high, her shawl wrapped tightly round her skimpy frame.

Daisy paused in her cooking long enough to point with a knife. "It's behind the clock," she said. Then she took the frying pan to the table, slapped it down on the oilcloth and looked around for a fork amid the debris. There was a strong smell of sizzling oilcloth.

Meg stood on the fender and felt behind the clock, which was now ticking again. "You're burning the table-cloth, Daise," she reprimanded without looking round, as she searched with her fingers amid the junk on the mantelpiece.

Daisy had found a fork and she said sourly through a mouth full of bacon, "It's *my* table-cloth." The bacon was not very crisp and was hard to masticate without teeth.

Her younger sister got down from the fender and turned. She put on the ring and looked at her hand thus decorated.

"You don't have to tell me," she said crossly as she watched the ring flash from the light of the fire. "Mr. Fancy Pants Freddie told us yesterday and our John's been telling me ever since." She swayed over to Daisy seated at the table.

"Think you're clever, don't you?" she mocked.

Daisy stopped chewing. She shook her knife at her tormentor. "You get out of here, Meg, before I throw you out." Her voice quivered with indignation.

"I'll go when I'm ready. This was my home, too, remember."

"It's mine now." Daisy's eyes gleamed with resentment.

Meg leaned towards her. "Pah! Big cheese, ain't you?"

Slowly Daisy collected the unchewable bits of gristle in her mouth and spat at her sister. Meg received it straight in her face.

She jumped back, wiped her eyes clear with her hand and then with a scream she leaped at Daisy.

"I'll marmalise you, you dirty bugger," she yelled.

Daisy rose swiftly from her chair and with one hand swung the piece of furniture between her and Meg. She pointed the paring knife she had used to cut her bacon at Meg's chest.

Despite her rage, Meg realized that Daisy meant business. The knife was coming slowly closer to her chest, while the chair was grinding painfully against her shins.

She backed a little.

"Get out," whispered Daisy, a world of menace in her voice. "Sling your hook, you bitch. Out!"

Meg was scared now. She backed slowly towards the door, felt the latch behind her and lifted it.

Daisy suddenly flung the chair and the knife away. With a moan of terror, Meg turned and pulled the door open. Daisy moved with the speed of an angry elephant, snatched up her sister by the back of her blouse and skirts and flung her through the doorway, heaving her forward with the toe of her boot in the small woman's buttocks.

Meg shot across the pavement and into the gutter, barely able to keep her feet. She wobbled like a spinning top, then turned and tore back at her sister, face contorted with hatred, hands out-stretched like talons.

Daisy hastily slammed the door and shot the bolt, then leaned her hefty weight against its ancient timbers.

Frustrated, Meg pummelled on its heavy panel and shouted, "I'll larn you, you fat sow." She kicked at the door and Daisy could hear her sobbing. "John'll marmalise *you* for this — you wait till I tell 'im." Daisy grinned at the latter threat. Big John would keep well out of any fight between women.

No amount of screaming would persuade Daisy to open the door again. After a moment or two she went contentedly back to her frying pan. Finally, Meg wiped her face on her shawl, shook her fist at the window, pushed her way through a small group of interested passers-by and marched off home, sobs of hopeless anger mixed with tears of grief for her dead mother making her a small, grey bundle of woe.

As she ran through the back alley to her own home, she mut-tered, "I'll pay her back, I will. Thinks she's the Nan now, does she."

SIX

The row with Meg and the storm of tears the previous night had done much to alleviate Daisy's tense misery. A good fight with Meg was such a normal part of her life — she could not remember when they had not been at war with each other over some trifling detail — that she felt much better.

Fortified by her breakfast she felt strong enough to walk over to Nellie's house to ask her to come with her to the Dental Hospital. To travel such a distance from home without a companion was unthinkable; Daisy could imagine all kinds of terrible things which might happen to her if she went alone.

Nellie, however, was feeling far from well and was still in bed. Looking white and exhausted, she lay curled up on a lumpy mattress in the back, ground floor room which was home to George, Joey and herself.

"I had a bad night, luv," she explained, "Thinking of your dear mother an' all. Your mam was always proper kind to me — I'll never forget her, God rest her."

Daisy felt a lump beginning to rise in her own throat. She fought it down. She must not cry before Nellie; Nellie was sick enough without being reminded of death. Her chest heaved as she considered that she might lose Nellie, as well as her mother. She made the suffering woman a cup of tea and said she would ask Agnes to accompany her. Agnes however, felt that the Public Assistance visitor might call at any time and that she had better be at home, in case he got the idea from her absence that she was working.

"He's worse'n a dose of salts, that man," she told Daisy. "Always wants to know where the kids are, even in school time. Always

41

sayin' 'Where's Joe' as if labourin' jobs were two a penny and he must be bringing home thousands a pounds. Fair demarmalises you, it does."

Daisy sighed and agreed. "I'll ask Mary Foley what lives round the corner if she'll come," she said. "Only I always kept meself to meself, and I don't like asking the neighbours."

"What about Meg? Or Nellie?"

"I'm not speaking to Meg at the moment," replied Daisy primly. "And our Nellie's not well at all." She leaned towards her sister, and added in a whisper, "I got the intuitions something awful about Nell."

Agnes looked startled. "Ee, don't say that," she implored.

A tear welled up in Daisy's eye. She sniffed. "Well, I just hope I'm wrong."

"T.B.?" inquired Agnes, her voice hardly audible as she asked the dread question.

Daisy nodded, her expression lugubrious. The sisters looked at each other in silent horror.

"God have mercy on us," quavered Agnes, flinging her arms heavenward. "Poor dear."

They enjoyed a little weep together, and then Daisy walked homeward, calling at Mary Foley's house on the way.

Mary Foley was out. Great Aunt Devlin was too old to make such a long journey.

Daisy stood tapping a nervous foot on the pavement outside her own front door. Dare she go alone? Dare she not go?

Finally she decided that the dangers of penetrating the centre of Liverpool were less than the danger of losing the goodwill of the Welfare lady, who had so painstakingly collected sixpence a week from her for years to save up for new teeth.

Apart from five shillings put by for the redecorating of her late mother's room, Daisy still had three shillings left from the burial insurance money, so she decided to take a tram down to Lime Street Station and another one out again to the Dental Hospital. She reckoned she would be safer on the tram.

Nellie had accompanied her when she went to have the impression taken for her teeth and they had walked, the appointment having been made for the day before Daisy drew her allotment from her husband's shipping company, a day on which she was always penniless. Michael's allotment was eighteen shillings a week and this, added to her mother's old age pension of ten shillings, had made the two women a shilling or two better off than if they had been dependent upon the Public Assistance Committee. Still, it was not very much.

Now as she sat demurely in the tram, hands folded neatly in her lap, as it trundled through the streets, bell pinging impatiently to make carters move their wagons off the lines, it dawned on her that her mother's pension would have ceased with her death; yet she would be faced with the same need to pay the rent, the same need for a coal fire and oil for the lamp; but she would have only eighteen shillings with which to do it all.

She was aghast. Under her warm shawl her body felt cold, and she trembled. All the small treats that made life bearable would be gone; no twopence for a beer at the Ragged Bear on a Saturday night or an occasional twopence for an afternoon cinema show with Nellie; even paying for a set of teeth at a painful sixpence a week for over three years would have been out of the question on a measly allotment of eighteen shillings.

Because her husband had, by sailing on a boat which never touched Liverpool, kept her off Parish Relief, Daisy had been able to hold her head high in a district where many of the English and Welsh inhabitants looked down upon her — they wore coats and she had only a shawl. But now she knew that though her income was still above the Public Assistance rate for one person, it was not going to be enough.

No more bacon ends from Mrs. Donnelly's! She would soon be as thin as Meg whose family was on relief. A fat lot of good teeth were going to be. For once, a tear of self-pity quivered in the corner of Daisy's deep-set blue eyes and rolled slowly down her plump face, which had been specially wiped with a wet cloth for the benefit of the dentist.

The earnest young dentist who had made her teeth for her awaited her arrival with something approaching agony. He had been unable to forget the interview with her two weeks earlier when he had examined her mouth and taken the impression for her teeth. The fearsome smell of her and of her clothing had been bad enough, the louse which he was sure he had collected from her had been worse. When she opened her mouth, however, he

43

had recoiled like a young soldier going over the top and facing fire for the first time. He had hastily reached for a glass of mouthwash and made her gargle and spit her way through two complete glasses full before trying again.

This time he was prepared. The tall window nearest to him was wide open. In the cupboard rested another clean white coat, together with a large paper bag into which to thrust the one he was wearing immediately Daisy should have left. Neatly lined up by the tiny sink were two glasses of double strength mouthwash. He was ready.

Yet, when she entered not ungracefully with an old-fashioned, respectful half-bob, her plump face beaming in spite of her worries, he felt ashamed. To square his conscience he fussed around her a little, showed her the immaculately white teeth grinning on his side table, explained to her how to keep them clean, warned her that she might feel she was going to vomit when he put them in. He made her rinse her mouth till it stung with the disinfectant.

"Keep taking big breaths and you'll be all right," he advised. "In a few months you'll forget you've got them in your mouth and will be able to eat meat and anything else."

"Humph, meat!" grunted Daisy, her stomach already begining to turn with fear of the apparatus surrounding her. The dentist, however, was treating her as a proper lady and she was enjoying that part of it, so she obediently opened her mouth.

In went the upper and lower teeth and Daisy's stomach began to heave.

"Guggle-guggle," she exclaimed, desperately looking round for the sink.

"Hold it, hold it!" urged the dentist frantically. "Remember, big breaths."

Daisy gasped in the cool autumn air from the open window, and gradually the nausea eased.

"Shlike havin' a golf ball in your mouth," she upbraided the dentist mournfully.

"Smile," he ordered her cheerfully, to take her mind off the nausea.

Blinking miserably she forced her mouth into a cheerful half moon.

The improvement in her looks was so great that the dentist was able to praise her appearance without stint. "Takes years off you," he assured her. "Now don't take them out except at night and to rinse them as necessary."

She nodded sad agreement. Four bloody pounds on teeth when what she was going to need was food to eat.

She heaved herself out of the dentist's chair, bobbed and simpered at him, said 'thank you' and clumped depressedly down the hollowed stone stairs and into the street.

She teetered nervously on the pavement outside the hospital and wished heartily that Nellie was with her to share the perils of the city. Every so often her new teeth would shift slightly and she would hastily breathe deeply to assuage the desire to vomit.

She watched the trams go by. They were packed with people going home and were not stopping except to let passengers down. She would have to walk down to Lime Street, she decided.

She trailed down Pembroke Place until she reached London Road. No one among the scurrying passers-by bothered her, and by the time she had reached the junction of the two thoroughfares she had gained a little confidence. She paused in Monument Place. The brightly lit stores in London Road beckoned her; and when a small group of women shoppers started across the road she went with them, mesmerised by the lights and the cheery bustle of the crowd.

She wandered through two big stores, fingering sheets, caressing shiny furniture and looking open-mouthed at ladies' lingerie of such delicacy as to be shocking. She was pleased to see that they also stocked more sturdy garments, good fleecy cotton bloomers and woollen vests with high necks. She was so highly entertained that she forgot to be afraid; and even the discomfort of her mouth receded.

At closing time she left reluctantly with the other wanderers in the store, and continued her walk towards Lime Street.

"And it was there I went wrong," she told Moggie afterwards. "I shoulda come home. Only I felt comfortable, like, 'cos there was plenty of women like me in shawls, good Irish women, so I took me time."

She was waiting for the traffic to clear so that she could cross a side street, when a delicious aroma of fish and chips was wafted round her. She looked along the mean side street. The pungent

45

smell was being blown towards her from across Islington, where people bearing large newspaper-wrapped packages were emerging from a fish and chip shop. One boy was actually running towards her, his hot parcel balanced carefully on one hand.

She lifted her nose and half closed her eyes. Her mouth was watering; her stomach felt as if it was flapping against her backbone, it was so empty. She forgot about going home and remembered only that she still had money in her apron pocket. She turned and almost ran the short distance to the shop.

The tiny window offered pie and chips, fish and chips, fishcakes and chips, tea and bread and butter, all laid out on thick white plates for passers-by to see. Behind the tiny display were two tables, at one of which a man and woman sat eating. Daisy swallowed and nearly choked on her teeth.

Could she eat with her new teeth? Could she bear to eat in public? It was, after all, not very nice having people watch you eat; eating was a private thing, like going to the privy.

I could carry the parcel home, she thought. She sighed with the effort of making up her mind. But then it would all be cold, she argued, as she paused uncertainly before the tempting display.

The door opened again, as a young woman with a baby wrapped in her shawl came out, bearing an aromatic bundle carefully wrapped in an old copy of the *Liverpool Echo*. Up the steps went Daisy, as if hypnotised, to join the throng of shabby people waiting for their orders to fry. When it was her turn to give her order she hesitated so long that the young man on the other side of the high, tiled counter said, "Hurry up, Ma. What do you want?"

She gulped, smiled nervously and said with difficulty because of her new teeth, "One fish and chips and tea and I'll take it here." She pointed to the vacant table in the bay window.

The young man shook up his huge net basket of chips so that the cauldron of fat spat and bubbled. "O.K. Sit down, Ma. Me Mam'll bring it to you."

Daisy turned and cautiously lowered herself into a chair at the greasy table. She chose a place that would show only her back to the other customers, so that they would not actually see her eat. In front of her the window was totally steamed up by the rapidly increasing damp heat of the shop. By now, the display of food congealed on plates which had tempted her from outside would

46

be almost invisible to passers-by — and so would she be. She took out her teeth and put them in her apron pocket.

In a few seconds a big brown teapot, a chipped milk jug, a thick cup and saucer and an enormous plate of fish and chips joined the grubby sugar basin and the tomato sauce bottle on the table before her.

"Want some bread and butter?"

Afraid of how much it might cost, Daisy refused bread and butter.

"That'll be sixpence," announced Mam, waiting with hand on hip while Daisy counted out the money.

For a moment Daisy contemplated the steaming fish, infinitely appetising in its crisp batter overcoat. Her mouth watered, and then slowly, sensuously she began to eat.

She used the last drop of tea to rinse around her mouth before putting her teeth back in, a task which was easier than she had expected.

Outside, she was surprised to find that it was dark. The lamplighter had already wobbled his way along the street on his bike and the gas lamps gave a friendly glow to the mean neighbourhood. She must have sat longer than she intended, she thought with a little laugh. It was, however, surprising how good food could cheer you up; even her new teeth felt more bearable.

She swung down the steps and without thinking turned left. She turned left again, fully expecting to find herself back in London Road. Instead she faced a narrow dark street. She looked irresolutely along it. There seemed to be no light other than the gleaming lamp above the door of a public house further down. There was a number of people about, however, and this reassured her. Feeling sure that it would lead her into Lime Street, she began to walk along it.

As she passed the public house, the buzz of conversation within made it sound like a beehive with the bees about to swarm. But when she plunged into the gloom beyond it an eerie silence faced her. Where were the surging crowds of Lime Street? The seamen, the prostitutes, the Welsh beggars?

47

SEVEN

The main door of the tavern was on the corner, and Daisy had hardly taken a step towards it when it swung open. Three young sailors in skin-tight naval uniforms rolled unsteadily out of it and came down the street towards her. Although it was early in the evening, they were very merry and, with arms slung round each other's shoulders, they were singing bawdily.

They took up the whole width of the pavement as they staggered towards Daisy, and she stepped back into the mouth of a narrow alleyway to await their passing. She was not particularly scared of them — they were only lads — and she chuckled as she watched them approach.

"Three German officers crossed the line to rape the woman and drink the wine," they roared in cheerful unison.

She knew the song well and began to hum the refrain in tune with them.

Arms over each other's shoulders, round navy blue hats perched precariously on the backs of their heads, they bellowed their way towards her; and, as she watched and waited, she hummed. They gradually became aware that there was a woman singing softly somewhere in the shadows before them, and they slowly staggered to a halt at the alley's entrance. Her white apron showed clearly, and behind it a generous, vaguely definable bulk loomed before them.

" 'Ello, la," said the middle sailor. "Now what nice bit o' fluff have we got 'ere?" He let go of one of his friends, who promptly leaned against the warehouse wall for support.

Daisy took a nervous step backwards, but there was a sudden

rustle as of a rat running behind her, so she hastily stepped forward again.

She gulped. "Aye, lads," she addressed them, her voice pitched uneasily high. "Can you tell me how to get to Lime Street?" She tried to edge her way out of the scant width of the alley but they were blocking it, so she beamed hopefully at their well-scrubbed faces.

"Well, now! Are you lost?" The boy's voice was slightly derisive.

Daisy's heavy-jawed, friendly face with its flashing smile gradually became visible, as the sailors' eyes adjusted to the darkness. They all swayed towards her and leered in true music-hall fashion, as she answered, "Yes, I am." She looked unhappily up and down the street, seeking a peaceful way to pass them.

"Wotcha want to go to Lime Street for?" two of them chortled together. "Isn't here good enough for business?" They winked at each other and dug their elbows into each other's ribs, as they laughed at her.

"Go on with you, you saucy buggers. I want to get a tram from Lime Street."

"Lime Street's got more'n trams in it," announced one of them suggestively. He moved closer to her, till his white vest nearly touched her. She could smell the comfortable beery breath of him. She eased away from him till she was brought up short by the wall of the alley. He put one hand on the dank brick wall behind her and leaned forward confidentially.

This is what happened to you when you went about alone, she reproached herself.

She gathered what courage she could muster and said as cheerfully as she could, "Come on, lad. Tell me which way to Lime Street." She pretended to laugh and tried to duck under his arm. One of the other sailors closed in and teasingly held out his arms, so that she would have sailed right into them. "Come on, luv," he shouted cheerfully.

"Shut up," said the third, who was leaning against the warehouse wall. "You'll bring the cops." He nodded his head towards the pub. "Come on, there's plenty more like her— let's go."

But the other two ignored him. The one who had held out his arms to Daisy whined ingratiatingly at her.

"Come on, Ma. Don't be shy. What about lifting your skirts for us?"

49

Daisy was flustered, her eyes darting up and down the dark road. "Eee, lads. I'm not that kind!" she protested, her heart pounding.

The boy who had first spoken to her and was closest to her let his hand drop from the supporting wall and, with a mischievous grin, curled his fingers round her neck. He pushed his lean body hard against her and rubbed himself against the comfortable rolls of flesh. One hand softly caressed her neck while the other fumbled under her well-formed bosom.

Daisy who had been staunchly faithful for twenty-nine years began to realise that the last eighteen months had been dreadfully bleak. Such a surge of passion ran through her that she found herself beginning to respond, and this shocked her.

"Not here," she panted. "I couldn't — I mustn't!"

Her breath was sweet from the dentist's disinfectant, as hard lips were pressed on hers and long arms were wrapped closely round her generous figure. She fought ineffectually, continuing her protests in ever-weakening whispers, as he eased her away from the wall and down the narrow alley into which she had originally stepped.

She tried to make herself cry out that he must not.

Holy Mother!

Fumbling hands found their way under long black skirt and petticoat, and Daisy was lost while still remonstrating faintly. He needed no caresses from her.

Afterwards, though her head was spinning and her body smarting from making love after such long abstinence, she found herself leaning against the unfriendly wall still holding the boy to her and crooning inarticulately to him as if he had been her lover for years. He rested panting against her, his head on her breast, while in the back of her mind she told herself she should push him off and hit out at him for so misusing her. But when he looked up at her and grinned wickedly, she found herself smiling back.

"Hey, how long you going to be down there?" shouted one of his friends. Cigarette ends flashed brightly in the darkness, as the other sailors leaned against the corners of the alley and smoked.

Daisy's companion shouted back that he was coming. To Daisy he said with a grin, as he buttoned the flap of his trousers, "Ta, Ma."

He put his hand inside his navy blue blouse and brought out half-a-crown. It flashed in the dim light, as he pressed it into her hand. Scarlet and shaken, ashamed of her own feelings, she remained leaning against the wall as he made his way back down the alley to the street whistling cheerfully. He passed one of his friends rolling inwards.

"Any good?"

"Good as you'll get."

A startled Daisy roused herself from her lethargy to find another pair of exploring hands opening her shawl.

"Eee, lad!" she protested. "What is this?" She dropped the half-a-crown down her blouse neck and caught the hands which had descended impatiently to her skirts. "Come on, now, lad. I'm not one o' them."

The lad laughed tipsily and continued. "Tell me another, Ma," he sneered.

Though he looked thin, he was undoubtedly strong and he was by no means as gentle with her as the first boy had been. Daisy became suddenly deathly afraid of what he might do if she refused him — she knew about prostitutes who had been found murdered in just such an alleyway. So, without another word, she straddled herself across the narrow alley, one foot in the gutter, the other resting on the top step leading up to a door into a yard, so that she could accommodate him more easily. He whipped her skirts up over her raised knee, and she silently endured him.

"And there, in no time at all, at all, Mog, I found meself with another half dollar in me hand," she later told her stony-faced cat, "And another one coming up t' jigger at me."

As the third youth approached, it seemed to Daisy that her real self stood outside her body watching in scandalized horror a completely alien Daisy, filled with excited anticipation, await the boy coming towards her.

"Mog, it was as if the divil himself was in me. At first I thought I'd run away up to top of t' entry. But I could hear the rats rustling in the dust bins — and I'm more afraid of rats, as you know, Mog, than I am of any boy. So I waited for him."

As far as Daisy could judge in the gloom, the boy was younger than the other two, and he approached her shyly. Coming in from the lighted street he could hardly see her, though she being more

51

accustomed to the darkness could see him. When his groping hand touched her, he paused.

After a moment's silence, he said, "It's O.K. if you don't want to, Ma."

Driven by forces she did not understand, she said softly, "Come here, luv."

Once more she steadied herself with one foot on the top doorstep beside her and then she opened her shawl and wrapped it round him as if he were a child she wanted to keep warm. To him she felt as cosy and warm as his own mother.

"It's my first time with a woman, Ma," he whispered.

She chuckled, feeling suddenly that she was at last in control of the situation.

"Come close," she ordered, with a surge of pleasure, her fears forgotten, "I'll show you." And she did.

She held him to her for a moment or two afterwards, until his friends, phlegmatically smoking as they waited, started to call him.

"Grinds like the bloody mills of God," one grumbled.

The boy dug around in the small pocket in the front of his sailor's trousers. "How much, Ma?"

Daisy smiled at him warmly and waved a hand negatively. "That's all right," she said.

"Oh, no, Ma! I have to pay." He sounded shocked.

He pressed a handful of small change into her palm and closed her hand over it. She leaned forward and kissed him on the cheek. "Ta," she said, and as he turned and swaggered back down the alley, she called, "Ta-ra, well," in farewell.

After they had gone on their merry way, a very thoughtful Daisy emerged slowly from the alleyway. She straightened her heavy skirts as she considered the deadly sin she had just committed. She could almost hear Father Patrick holding forth on the subject of lust; and a deep flush crept up her neck and over her cheeks. The two coins she had dropped down her chest fell to the pavement with a sharp clink and she bent down and picked them up. Her heart was still pattering unnaturally fast. In the light of the pub she counted the money in her hand. It totalled eight shillings and sixpence. Amongst the change given her by the last sailor were two threepenny bits.

She smiled at the two tiny silver coins. "Two joeys! I'll keep them for luck. He were a proper nice lad."

She sighed. She felt extremely shaky and decided she needed a drink. She went round the side of the pub to the parlour entrance. Over the door was a notice saying, "Ladies with Escorts only."

"Bugger them," she muttered forcefully.

A labourer with his beshawled wife pushed past her. She followed him in smartly and sat down on the same bench as they did. The place was blue with tobacco smoke and the conversation was lively but not noisy.

She sat primly down, hands folded in her lap, her worn wedding ring glinting softly on one swollen finger.

When the barman took her order for a hot rum toddy, he realised that she was without an escort, but she looked so primly respectable that he made no objection to serving her.

As she sat staring at her glass she felt that everybody must know what she had done, and she was thankful for the comforting glow that the rum engendered in her. Nobody spoke to her, however. St. Margaret, her patron saint, did not appear, to upbraid her, and God did not strike her down. Her heart returned to its normal beat and she began to feel clever that she could drink without taking her teeth out. She asked the barman who was easing his way among the crowded tables, a tray of empties poised on four fingers, how to get to Lime Street Station. He told her and she swept out with a great feeling of newfound confidence.

By the time she had boarded the tram for Dingle, her eyelids were drooping. The vehicle's steady swaying and its steamy heat made her doze.

At one stop the driver put his brake on rather abruptly and the shudder that went through the great vehicle awoke her.

Where was she?

She rubbed a spyhole in the steam on the window and peered anxiously through it.

There was the pub with the grocery store next door to it.

She hastily heaved herself off the wooden seat and proceeded unsteadily down the narrow centre aisle, while the driver tapped his foot impatiently. She clambered down the steep steps and wrapped her shawl round her tightly as the wind struck her.

Only when the tram had moved onward and had resumed its rhythmical clang-clang did she realise that she had descended at the Shamrock, instead of at the Ragged Bear.

She shivered in the chilly night wind, and cursed. Holy Mary, it was nearly a mile to her home and rain threatened from a lowering sky. Along the street the gas lamps seemed to march for dismal, frightening miles.

The door of the Shamrock opened and a gust of laughter came out with a patron. It would be at least half an hour before another tram came by, she thought; it would be quicker to walk. But first she would have another drink, to warm her.

The silver in her apron pocket made a happy jingle as she went up the steps, and she grinned ruefully, catching her lower lip with her new teeth.

"Ah'll have a gin, son," she ordered the barman. After all, gin was what you were supposed to drink if you didn't want to get pregnant. Then she remembered that she was past the age when she had to worry about pregnancy.

The gin tasted horrible, so she ordered a rum to follow. The world began to take on a kind of happy haze.

A heavily-built man on his way out paused in front of her. His close-clipped white hair did nothing to soften a wind-hardened red face. His greasy trousers and cap, his jacket ripped under the sweat-soiled armpits suggested a docker.

"Evenin', Mrs. Gallagher," he said. "Sorry to hear from George about your mother."

Daisy smiled dimly through the comfortable mist in which she was floating.

"Evenin', Mr. O'Hara. Thank you."

"Remember your Mam when she was a little girl. We both went to Mrs. Docherty's Sunday school to learn to read afore the Board School was built."

"You did?" Daisy nodded her head.

"Oh, aye." He touched his forelock and with slow, clumping tread went towards the door. "Good night to yez."

Daisy wiped her nose with the back of her hand, finished her rum and, shortly after, followed Mr. O'Hara.

The wind had risen, and the smoke from the rows of chimney pots on the roofs seemed to rest on its side. All the shops were closed, though lights in the windows above them showed that their owners were not yet in bed. The whole street seemed to be relaxing from the clangour of the day. Daisy put her shawl up over her head and held it firmly under her chin, as she bent towards the wind. Her boots clattered noisily over the stone flags.

A woman in a red coat was standing under a lamp post. She was carrying a large handbag and was smoking a cigarette. Daisy recognized her, and pursed her lips.

A proper painted judy, that Violet, picking men up in the streets. Regular trade she did, according to Mrs. Hanlon at the Ragged Bear. Then a slow flush suffused Daisy's neck and crept up her face. What would Mrs. Hanlon say about Daisy's evening?

She'll never find out about it, Daisy argued with herself. Anyway, it was different. Why it was different from what Violet did, she was unable to say. But it was.

At last the brightly-lit doorway of the Ragged Bear came in sight.

"I'll have one more afore I go home," Daisy decided and plunged thankfully into the steaming warmth of the Snug, as the parlour was called.

The seat by the fire which she regarded as her own was occupied by Mrs. Donnelly, the grocer, sitting very correctly upright, black laced-up shoes exactly together, her large black hat straight on top of her piled up grey hair and her matching black coat neatly buttoned. She was delicately sipping a glass of port.

Daisy regarded her sourly as she plumped herself down near the door, a seat which was always draughty. She pushed her shawl back from her hair and smiled and nodded at those people she knew, pointedly ignoring Mrs. Donnelly.

"Half pint o' bitter?" inquired Joe Hanlon, as he pressed past her.

"No. I'll have a hot rum. It's proper cold outside. I'm clemmed." Her voice sounded slightly slurred.

Joe chuckled. "Doing yourself proud, aye?"

Daisy was immediately defensive. Her mind was not yet too clouded to know that even a hot rum mid-week could cause local gossips to wonder where she got the money for it.

"I need it what with me Mam gone," she said, and then added haughtily, "I don't think she'd grudge it me out of her burial money."

"I'm sure she wouldn't," agreed Joe hastily. "I was sorry to hear about her. You gave her a lovely funeral, though. Me wife said she'd never seen a more respectful one."

Daisy's haughtiness vanished. She beamed at the publican as he took the measured glass of rum from his wife's hand and carried it over to the fireplace where the kettle bubbled gently on the hob. As the fragrance of the rum reached her nostrils, Mrs. Donnelly's expression became one of righteous disapproval.

Joe handed Daisy the steaming glass.

Daisy smirked, sipped her rum and gracefully accepted the condolences of two acquaintances sitting nearby. Mrs. Donnelly watched her drink in frigid silence. Daisy Gallagher owed her four shillings and tenpence, had owed it for a month, and there she was drinking rum — at mid-week! Mrs. Donnelly determined that the four and tenpence should be collected tomorrow at the latest, bereavement notwithstanding.

Greatly cheered by Joe's praise of the funeral, Daisy began to hum the song the sailors had been singing. She signalled to Joe Hanlon.

"I'll have another." She beamed beatifically round at her neighbours who, between polite gossiping, regarded her pityingly. Our Daisy was taking her sad loss very hard, they muttered.

"I think you'd better go home, Mrs. Gallagher," Joe said firmly. "Have you finished your drink?"

She stood swaying like a tall jelly pudding. "Yesh," she said. "But I want another. I don't want to go home. Nobody there. Why the hell should I go home?"

Joe put his arm confidentially round her shoulder. "Because I don't want you to become ill, Mrs. Gallagher. I would rather you came in again tomorrow and had another enjoyable evening." He eased her round till she faced the door. "Come on, luv." He pushed her firmly through the door, which his wife had opened, and she stumbled clumsily down the steps, staggered across the pavement and leaned against the gas lamp at the corner. She continued to sniff for a moment and lifted the corner of her apron to wipe her eyes. The clink of money in her apron pocket reminded her of the three sailors. She began to giggle a little ruefully, as she started unsteadily down the slope towards her home. She began to hum to herself, at first sadly and then a little more cheerfully.

Ahead, she could see the river glitter, as a brightly lit liner moved slowly downstream. She stumbled down towards it. Dear, friendly river — it was always there, sometimes scowling, sometimes smiling. Lovely river. She began to sing again.

"Three German officers crossed the line," she shrieked joyfully at the glittering water, as she leaned over the brick wall which separated her from the dock below in which lay a single ship, dark except for the watchman's lantern rising and dipping with the small movement of the water.

She waved drunkenly towards the river. "Hooray to yez, hooray to the bloody Mersey!"

EIGHT

Daisy stood for a long time leaning against the wall and looking out over the river, until she felt steady enough to cross the road again back to her own home. Moggie was complaining loudly on the doorstep and leaped ahead of her, as she stumbled into the dead dark front room.

The fire was out, and she felt around for the box of matches which she kept on the windowsill close to the entrance. The damp breeze from across the river was cold and she hastily closed the door behind her.

"Jaysus!" she exclaimed irritably. Then her fingers closed over the errant box and she fumbled to strike a match to light the lamp. She had not cleaned the lamp that morning and its wick was untrimmed. She took off its funnel awkwardly with one hand. The match sputtered out.

She put down the funnel on the table and got out another match. She paused as she was about to strike it and held her breath. She could distinctly hear heavy breathing behind her.

She had been cold. Now perspiration burst from her in sheer terror. Ghosts come back to haunt you, she knew that. Was her poor mother there? Unable to rest in her grave, unable to go to Purgatory because of what Daisy had done that evening?

She stood, match poised above the box, paralysed with fear. And the rhythmical breathing continued.

She screamed. Moggie brushed against her skirts. She shrieked again and crossed herself. "Holy Mother, help me!"

"That you, Daisy?" asked a woman's voice from the direction of the old easy chair. "What's up?"

58

Daisy did not answer as the fright ebbed out of her and relief flooded in. But her heart was still pounding like a labourer's pick-axe against asphalt, when she answered cautiously, "That you, Nellie?"

"Course it's me. Where you been all this time?"

"My! Did you ever give me a fright." Daisy struck the match, shielded the wick while it caught, put back the funnel and turned, lamp in hand, to survey her visitor with drunken suspicion. "What you come for? You said you wasn't well."

"I wasn't. I was proper bad last night. But when I felt a bit better I come to see if you was all right. Did Mrs. Foley go with you to the Dental?"

"No. I went by myself."

Nellie got up stiffly from the chair and stretched herself slowly. She was a small woman with no flesh on her. Roughly curling grey hair haloed her hollow-cheeked, deeply lined face. Her mouth was tight, the lips hardly showing, partly from her lack of teeth and partly from being clenched when in pain. Daisy noticed that one steel-blue eye was still rimmed with yellow, where George had hit her a couple of weeks earlier.

George had always had the temper of Ould Nick, Daisy ruminated, as she gestured to her friend to be seated again and draw the chair closer to the fire. He and Meg were a right pair when it came to tempers.

She puttered over to the fireplace as steadily as she was able and picked up the poker. In response to vigorous poking the fireplace yielded a few hot cinders and she added a little coal by hand from a small pile on a piece of newspaper in the hearth — the coal scuttle was still in pawn.

She smiled at Nellie over her shoulder. "I'm glad you're feeling better," she said, as she fanned the reluctant coals with another piece of the *Liverpool Echo.* Soon a little warmth began to creep into the room.

Nellie nodded her head. "How do you feel with teeth in?" she asked.

"Not bad. It's hard to talk."

"Oh, aye. Let's see them."

Daisy obligingly put down the paper fan and took the teeth out. They were duly admired and then Daisy set them on the mantelshelf.

"Looks just like a skull grinning at you," remarked Nellie, looking up at them.

Daisy shuddered. "Don't say that. Here, I'll put the kettle on and we'll have a cup of tea. I still got a bit of cake from the funeral."

She took the blackened kettle into the scullery to fill it from the house's single tap.

Nellie held her hands over the struggling fire and rubbed them to get the circulation going again. She pulled the chair even closer, so that her feet were inside the fender, and then wrapped her shawl round herself. "Tea'd be nice. God, it's cold tonight. It's the damp, I suppose?" She started to clear her throat at first slowly and then more rapidly.

"Aye, the damp's got into the house. I forgot to bank up the fire afore I went out." Daisy leaned over her friend, and plonked the kettle on to the hob and pushed it round over the fire. "You should've put some coal on."

"I didn't know if you could spare enough to keep the fire going when you wasn't cooking. And I thought you'd probably be back soon. Where *have* you been all this time?"

Daisy did not answer. She took up a pair of white, earthenware mugs from the table and, after a quick search, found the sticky tin of condensed milk on the chest of drawers, buried beneath an old copy of the *Liverpool Echo*.

"I'm out of sugar," she apologised as she opened a rusty tin box to display the remains of the funeral cake.

"Well, tell me. Did you go anywhere interesting all this time?" asked Nellie doggedly. She cleared her throat and spat accurately into the fire without hitting the kettle. The fire gave a sharp hiss.

"You *know* where I been. I went to the Dental to get me teeth. Then I had fish and chips." She reached up and took her new teeth from the shelf. With some difficulty she put them in again and grimaced at the discomfort.

Nellie looked up sharply from her contemplation of the fire, her own toothless mouth open in wonder. "Yes," she agreed. "But you was such a long time I thought something terrible had happened to yez. Anyway, lemme see them in."

Daisy obligingly grinned.

"My, you look nice! Like I remember you at my wedding!" Nellie's admiration was genuine. She sucked in her lips and then laughed as she teased, "Michael'll have to watch out now."

"What do you mean?" Daisy snapped out the question belligerently. The euphoria of the alcohol was wearing off.

"You know — you look so young, like. I was only joking." Nellie looked Daisy up and down. "You bin drinking?"

"Humph. Had a rum in the Snug on me way home," responded Daisy sulkily. A rum can take any amount of time to drink, so that should satisfy Nellie's nosiness. She poked the fire again, making it flare up, and Nellie nodded understandingly, her shadow on the wall bobbing in unison.

"Rum? Still got a bit of burial money, have yer?"

"I needed a rum after all I been through."

"To be sure," soothed Nellie. "You did so much for your Mam."

Daisy smiled, and swayed unsteadily. She reached down the tea caddy from the mantelpiece, took the lid off the teapot which was standing as always on the top of the oven, and discovered it still had the dregs of earlier brews in it. Muttering imprecations, she went out as steadily as she could to the scullery and opened the back door. The yard was absolutely dark but she emptied the tea leaves accurately on to what had once been a flower bed, which after generations of such treatment consisted largely of decaying tea leaves in which only weeds grew.

She measured out the tea, and, while she waited for the kettle to come to a rolling boil, she gazed reflectively down into the fire which was now burning quite cheerfully.

"If our Meg had been the new Nan, none of us would have got so much as a glass o' beer out of her," she remarked. "What's yours is hers and what's hers is her own."

"Don't be so hard, Daise. She's had a rough life."

"Oh, aye. I wouldn't want to be her. Going to a motherless home to look after a crabby old devil like Fogarty and two brothers-in-law as well as her husband." Daisy sucked at her new teeth. "And now she's got six kids — and might manage another afore the change strikes her."

"At least they're living," Nellie responded in reference to the children. She sighed sadly.

Daisy leaned down and put a compassionate hand on Nellie's

wool-wrapped shoulders. "There, there, luv. The Lord giveth and the Lord taketh away, as Mrs. Temperance Thomas is always saying. And she's right."

Nellie's pinched-in lips trembled. "To take four of ours with the diphtheria — and then to take our Freddie when he fell into the hold of the *Fair Rita* on top of the coal she was unloading." She almost sobbed the last words. "It's no wonder our George gets into a rage at times, with only our iddy-diddy Joey left."

"I know, luv, I know." Daisy turned to rescue the kettle and pour the boiling water over the tea-leaves. Then she put the teapot on the hob to let the fire mash it to a formidable blackness. "Have a cuppa tea, luv. Make you feel better."

With the comforting heat of the mug of tea warming her hands and Daisy's gentleness, Nellie began to feel better. Daisy again filled the kettle with water and set it on the fire.

"What you boiling more water for? You made plenty of tea."

Daisy sat down on a wooden chair which creaked uneasily as it received her weight. She viewed her friend's face cautiously out of the corner of her eye. You couldn't breathe in without somebody noticing, she thought tartly. How could you tell a woman as clean-living and plain good as Nellie that you felt sore underneath because you'd had three sailors?

"Well, I thought as how I had the fire I'd maybe have a wash afore going to bed," she replied carefully. "Bring the bowl in here where it's warm."

Nellie stirred her tea with the single tin spoon which they had been sharing. "Mind you don't get chill," she warned. "Too much washing and you'll feel the cold like anything."

Daisy nodded agreement.

"You finished with blood a couple of years ago, didn't you?"

Daisy again nodded. She understood the import of her friend's inquiry. After a period one washed, but not much otherwise.

Nellie changed the subject.

"When's Bill Donohue coming to do out your Mam's room?"

"Tomorrow." The tea was helping Daisy back to normality. Eagerly she pursued the fresh subject of conversation. "Thought I'd get him to whitewash the ceiling as well."

"It'll cost you another shilling."

Daisy opened her mouth to say she had the money and then

quickly clicked her teeth together again. Blast, she cursed silently. Aloud she said, "You're right. Maybe I can get him to throw it in, anyway. A bit of whitewash can't cost anything like a shilling."

The exchange reminded her forcibly that she must be extremely circumspect about the way in which she spent the eight shillings and sixpence which she had so unexpectedly acquired, or people would begin to surmise about her unaccountable prosperity. Still, it was good to feel the weight of the coins deep in her apron pocket. The money gave her an unexpected feeling of power as if she was now more in command of her life. It would help her over the first week without her mother's pension. She was going to miss that pension nearly as much as her mother. At the thought of her mother the dull pain of loss returned to her.

Nellie slurped comfortably at her mug of tea. "You must be missing Nan," she remarked as if she had read Daisy's thoughts. "What was the cause of her, er. . . ?"

"Doctor said it was the stroke again. Charged me two and six-pence just to say that and write out a certificate to say she'd passed on. I knew she was gone without him telling me!"

Nellie wagged her grizzled head knowingly. "Aye, but them bleeders down at the Prue wouldn't have believed you without a Death Certificate — and without their money how would you have buried her?"

They gossiped a little longer and then Nellie took her departure. The wind hit her as she went through the front door. She began to cough and leaned against the door jamb while she fought to control the spasm.

"Aye, Nellie, luv, you should ask Mr. Williamson up at the chemist's for summat for that cough." Daisy tried to keep the panic she felt out of her voice. "You must take care, Nell."

"Och, it's just me usual winter cough," responded her friend with a confidence which was far from genuine. "It's nothing — it'll pass," she added, as she hitched her heavy shawl over her head. She managed to hold back her cough long enough to kiss Daisy on the cheek. "Tara-well."

Daisy sighed. "Ta-ra, luv."

Holding her shawl across her mouth, Nellie hurried up the street. Daisy shut the door and leaned against it, listening to the diminishing sound of her friend's steady coughing. Dear Virgin Mother, what a cough!

She moved uneasily towards the fire. Nellie really needed a doctor, she thought fearfully. But where would she ever get money for a doctor from?

The kettle was steaming merrily again, so Daisy went immediately into the icy scullery and took from the soapstone sink a battered tin basin and a sliver of coarse laundry soap. She picked up a grey rag of a towel from off an upturned oil drum which served as a table and went back to the living room. She set the basin on the rag rug in front of the fire and emptied the kettle into it. Then she went back to the scullery, filled the kettle with cold water and emptied this into the bowl.

Slowly she took off her serge skirt and black cotton petticoat and then, after a moment's consideration, took off her blouse. To take off her torn vest which was her only other undergarment would be the height of indecency, so she left it on. Her woollen stockings, held up below the knee by a button twisted into each top, were reluctantly discarded. She had not had her clothes off for several weeks, keeping even her serge skirt on at night because the wind off the estuary had been so cold. Now she shivered at the unaccustomed exposure.

It was against her beliefs to use soap on herself except after her monthly periods, now long past; but this time she felt there was a real need and she washed her fat thighs thoroughly and then, after looking down at them cloudily, she washed her feet. She dried herself hurriedly — the draught coming in under the door was bringing her out in goose pimples. The sudden, hard scrubbing made the louse and bug bites on her itch; normally the bites did not swell — she was almost immune to irritation from them — but now they bothered her and she scratched furiously.

She had no other clothes so she put on again those she had taken off. She remembered that, though her mother had had no clothing other than a nightgown provided by the lady from the Welfare, she had clung to her shawl and kept it round her shoulders to ease the winter cold in the frigid room upstairs. The shawl was still up there.

"Come morning I'll take it to the wash house and wash it," Daisy promised herself, "before that Meg wakes up to it being there."

She rinsed out her stockings in the same water in which she had washed and hung them over a piece of string stretched across the front of the mantelpiece, to dry in the heat of the dying fire. She stood contemplating their woolly length steaming at the end nearest to the fire. There were holes in both heels and toes. She decided suddenly that since she did not have to feed her mother any more, sixpence out of her ill-gotten money might be expended on another pair of stockings.

"Nobody'll notice them," she comforted herself. "Black stockings is black stockings — they all look the same."

"And what about a new petticoat then — and a pair of winter bloomers?" inquired an extravagant devil within her.

At the thought of a pair of thick cotton bloomers, brushed to a warm fluff on the inside, she felt a craving for comfort that had never struck her before. She could not remember when she had last worn knickers of any kind. Her mouth watered as if the garment was something good to eat.

"I'll do it," she promised herself exultantly. "Nobody's going to see me bloomers, so they can't ask no questions."

"They'll ask questions if they see you buy them in Parkee Lanee or anywhere hereabouts. You'll have to go down town again to Hughes's in London Road."

This reminder brought her up short. She would have to venture again into the city; and do it alone. While she emptied the basin in which she had washed she thought about this.

Still nervously undecided, she lit a candle and trailed up to bed, but as she laid her head on the lumpy pillow she muttered, "I'll go. Nowt worse could happen to me than happened today."

NINE

Daisy woke with a start. A male voice was shouting "Mrs. Gallagher!" The front door was banged impatiently. "Are you there, Missus?"

"Oh," she groaned, as she swung herself off the bed. Though her head did not ache as it had done the day before, the floor had a curious tendency to come up to meet her. "Bloody so-and-so! Always coming early. Who the hell is it?"

Aloud she shouted, "Coming!"

When she opened the door, she found, fidgeting on the doorstep, Bill Donohue, a small, elderly man with a walrus moustache made ginger by tobacco smoke. He held several rolls of wallpaper tightly to his shabby suit jacket. From his little finger dangled a pail.

"Thought you'd never come," he said irritably as, uninvited, he walked into the living-room and looked around for a place to lay down the wallpaper. Every surface was cluttered from end to end, so he dropped it on to the floor.

"Didn't expect you so soon," replied Daisy sourly. "What colour you brought?"

Mr. Donohue looked affronted. "Same as always, of course — pink roses on a trellis with a white background." He sniffed. "All my customers like pink roses — they're proper pretty."

"I wanted blue for a change," said Daisy, not because she did, but because Bill Donohue was not going to get away with five shillings from her without suffering.

"They don't make it," replied Mr. Donohue loftily. "It's out of fashion. Be back in a minute with me ladder and me paste. I'll need some hot water to mix the paste."

66

"I know that without being told," responded Daisy tartly. "And I don't believe you about the blue — you couldn't have looked."

Bill Donohue was making for the door in an effort to avoid an argument, but was stopped in his attempt to escape by Daisy barking, "And don't go so quick. Wait a minute. I want the ceiling done as well."

He turned slowly round, very surprised. He viewed her with distrustful, watery blue eyes. "It'll cost yer — let me see, it'll cost yer another shilling for plain whitewash."

It was Daisy's turn to be affronted. "Mr. Donohue," she said with huge dignity, "Have I ever failed to pay you?"

Bill teetered slowly back and forth on his heels while he considered this. "No," he agreed. "But it must be all of eight years since I done a room for you."

"You don't need to remind me," Daisy snapped. "I know when our Tommy died."

"Well, have you got enough for the ceiling?" inquired Bill bluntly.

Daisy went to the fireplace where her stockings still dangled like a pair of dried snakes. She reached up and produced two half-crowns from under the clock. She held them up for her visitor to see. Then she plunged her hand into her apron pocket and pulled out another shilling. " 'Ere ye are."

Bill touched his forelock respectfully, took off his cap, scratched his head and replaced the cap. "Have to go and buy some whitewash," he announced. "Back in half an hour." He stopped half way out of the door. "I'll do the ceiling first. Need hot water for the paste later on."

Daisy nodded proudly and put the six shillings back under the clock.

He was back before she had finished eating her breakfast of tea, bread and margarine, in front of the newly made fire. The fire was not burning very well because of the huge pile of cinders under it.

"Room empty?" inquired Bill.

"There's a bed and a chest in it."

"Better get them out afore I start with the whitewash."

Without asking permission, he took his pail and the packet of whitewash into the scullery. After a moment there was the sound of splashing water as he mixed the whitewash, combined with the faltering strains of "The Roses of Picardy". Bill Donohue prided himself on knowing the words of more songs than anybody else in the neighbourhood. He had a radio and he was fond of saying that he listened to it intelligently.

"Holy Mary!" exclaimed Daisy in exasperation as she hastily swallowed the last bit of crust, put her teeth back in and hauled herself out of her chair.

Half-way up the stairs, she stopped to allow a spasm of headache to recede. While it slowly passed she remembered for a second the young sailor who did not know how with a woman, and her irritability vanished. She was chuckling to herself as she entered her mother's room.

The silence of the room struck her forcibly. Her chuckles ceased; the young sailor was forgotten. While she was downstairs she could have the illusion that her mother was quietly sleeping in the bedroom; now, faced with the empty bed and the need to clear it, she had to recognise again that she was alone. Slowly the tears came, accompanied by great hopeless sobs. Instead of having someone to lean on, to advise her, to bully her into staying on her feet when life seemed impossibly hard, she herself would have to be the adviser, the kind helper, the referee of family quarrels; hers would be the knee on to which grandchildren would climb to be comforted, hers would be the shoulder on which the women would weep out their bereavements and all the myriad sorrows of being mams.

"Aye, Mam," she whispered brokenly, "I don't know whether I can do it."

And it seemed to her, as she stood leaning against the door jamb, that she heard again her mother giving her what-for, as she called it, for standing around and not getting on with the job in hand. She almost felt the playful pat on her behind that her mother would give her, to send her back into the street fight she had lost, or to comfort her when there was no bread to assuage her hunger.

Obedient to that sharp, cheerful voice, she sniffed back her tears and surveyed the room to see what she should do first.

Bill Donohue clumped up the stairs with his bucket of whitewash and a brush. He viewed the floor and then the rest of the room with distaste.

"Need some new lino," he remarked.

"I know that," retorted Daisy. "You tell me how to get it out of an eighteen shilling allotment."

Mr. Donohue put down the bucket and rubbed his hands slowly down the sides of his paint-stained trousers. He scuffed a bare piece of board showing through the offending floor covering.

"You got a good oak floor, I reckon." He looked disparagingly at Daisy.

Daisy put her hands on her hips and leaned towards him. "And what good will that do me?"

Bill sniffed so that the dewdrop at the end of his nose wobbled. "If you tore up lino and scrubbed t' floor well — maybe scrape it where the lino's stuck... buy a tin of dark varnish and go over it — it wouldn't look bad at all. Dark varnish'll hide a lot o' marks."

Daisy looked again at the floor. Then she looked across at the window, over the misty river. As a child she had spent many a wet afternoon kneeling on a chair looking out of the window with Nellie, to see the ships go by. She knew the river in all its moods, she knew which company each ship belonged to because her father had taught her the funnel markings of each great company, Cunard, White Star, Ellerman's, and a dozen others, not to speak of strange boats from far away places like China and Russia. She could remember when sailing ships still floated in the Pool of Liverpool. She suddenly envisaged this little window on the world elegantly draped with a pair of Nottingham lace curtains, the sunlight gleaming through on to a shining floor, like an advertisement she had once seen in the *Liverpool Echo*.

She sighed rather hopelessly.

"Varnish is a good idea, Bill," she agreed. "I'll think about it." Then she ordered, "Do the inside of t'cupboard while you're at it."

"Cupboard not included — you know that," replied Bill stonily, as he spread out his step ladder. "Take candlestick off t' mantel. It'll get splashed."

Daisy snatched up the offending candle in its saucer and remembered also the chamber pot under the bed. She picked that up, too. "Come on, Bill," she wheedled, looking at him with eyes slanted under long, black lashes. "You could manage the cupboard with bits of left-over paper — it doesn't have to be perfect."

Bill's moustache bristled. "It's me time as well."

"How much now?" Daisy pouted.

"Cost you another — well, another tanner."

Daisy made a face at his indifferent back. "All right."

Bill dipped his brush into the bucket of whitewash and said placatorily, without looking round, "Room'll look proper nice." He raised a scrawny arm and carefully ran a line of whitewash back and forth across the ceiling.

Daisy hastily unhooked her mother's shawl from the cupboard and, dodging a rain of whitewash drops, took it with the candle and the chamber downstairs.

Moggie emerged from the oven, yawning and stretching first one long, skinny grey leg and then the other. Daisy let him out of the back door. She did not feed him; he hunted for himself and was adept at getting lids off dust bins to get at the contents.

Daisy collected her breakfast dishes and the glasses from the funeral wake, and washed them up in the same basin in which she had washed herself the previous night. One basin was a necessity in a house; two would have been luxurious.

She took a shovel and handleless bucket from under the sink and proceeded with the dusty job of clearing the ashes from the fireplace. She forgot to remove the stockings she had hung up to dry and some of the ash peppered them as well as the rag rug. Suddenly, there was a peremptory knock on the front door. Cursing under her breath, she got up from her knees, wiped her dusty hands on her apron and went and opened the door.

She jumped hastily back from the sill, as the wind from the river playfully blew Mrs. Donnelly's broad-brimmed hat off her head and into the room. It bowled across the floor and came to rest against the fender, its unsullied black collecting cinder dust all the way.

With the loose ends of her hair blown straight upwards by the wind and her red-brimmed blue eyes glaring at a non-plussed Daisy, the grocer looked like a witch who had just landed from her broomstick.

"I want me four and tenpence," announced Mrs. Donnelly frigidly.

"What four and tenpence?" The very sight of the grocer made Daisy's ire rise. Daisy had been wangling credit out of her since she was first sent on a message by her mother when she was five years old and Mrs. Donnelly had been a handsome, newly married woman. Mrs. Donnelly knew very well, argued Daisy to herself as she surveyed the unwelcome visitor, that she never needed to collect in person. She had only to mention the debt to Daisy three or four times while she was in the shop and hint that further credit would be cut off, and the next allotment day after that Daisy would pay.

"You know. You been owing it long enough."

"It's not so long that I've owed it!" Daisy put her hands on her hips and glowered at the grocer.

Undaunted by the scowl, Mrs. Donnelly pursed her lips primly. "Oh, yes, it is. If you can drink rum mid-week, then you can pay your grocery." She sniffed. "And I'd like me hat back, if you don't mind."

Daisy made no move to rescue the hat from the dusty hearth rug. Her eyes blinked and the tears began to rise as she remembered the exhausting days since her mother's death. "I needed a bit of something with me Mam only in her grave a few hours an' all."

Mrs. Donnelly could not have cared less about Daisy's bereavement — Mrs. O'Brien had been a trying customer in her time, too. "A blessed release to her, no doubt," she said icily.

Daisy's tears burst forth genuinely. "That's a cruel thing to say, Mrs. Donnelly," she sobbed, "and me nursing her all these years."

Mrs. Donnelly relented enough to say she was sorry Daisy felt so badly about it, and she would like her four and tenpence and her hat, if Daisy ever expected to get credit again from her.

Bill Donohue had heard the raised voices, and he came slowly down the stairs to see what was happening. He viewed the weeping Daisy with compassion as she turned back into the room. Everybody knew how good Daisy had been with her mother and how she shared what she had with her sisters' children when they came to visit her and were hungry. He watched her stumble round, feeling on the table for her little hoard of silver, then evidently remembering that it was in her apron pocket. She reluctantly came up with the two half crowns she had earned the previous night from the first two sailors.

"Here ye are," she said as, with brimming eyes, she thrust the coins into the scrawny outstretched hand.

Mrs. Donnelly produced twopence change from a small leather

purse with innumerable pockets.

"Me hat," she demanded.

Still sobbing miserably before a silent Bill, Daisy went across to the fireplace to pick up the hat.

She wiped her eyes with a corner of her apron. "Now where is it," she sniffed. "Ah, there," and with a burst of savage rage she trod on it.

She picked up the shattered piece of headgear and carefully brushed the dust it had collected further into its black satin trimmings. The sight of the wreckage restored her aplomb a little, and Mrs. Donnelly's horrified shriek of "What have you done?" was particularly satisfying. Still snuffling, however, she handed the hat to its infuriated owner and slammed the door in her face.

"Bad cess to yez!" she snarled through her tears at the closed door, and still sniffing unhappily she went to the fireplace to warm herself.

Her ample breasts trembled under her thin cotton blouse, as she continued to cry softly, despite the joy of the ruined hat.

"Don't take it too hard." Bill Donohue's ginger moustache quivered in sympathy. "It's proper hard when your husband's away like Mike is." He had a strong desire to take her in his arms to comfort her. So much good womanhood going to waste. He stuck his thumbs in his braces so that his hands would not stray as he went closer to her. "She's a hard-nosed bitch," he said.

"Nearly cleaned me out, she did," confided Daisy between sniffs.

Bill looked alarmed, and the look was not lost on Daisy despite her grief.

"Don't worry. I still got your money. Though what I do till Tuesday when I get me allotment, I don't know."

Bill wagged his head in sad understanding of her predicament. He stood rubbing a bit of whitewash absently into one blue-veined arm, and then said, "I'll do the cupboard for you without extra. After all, I've known you and Michael a long time."

Daisy had put her teeth in immediately after having her breakfast, and now she favoured Bill with a watery smile which set his heart aflutter within his withered frame.

"That's proper kind of you, Mr. Donohue," she said warmly.

Bill bridled. "You're welcome, I'm sure," he said and went shyly back up the stairs.

TEN

While Bill toiled amid the rosy wallpaper. Daisy took her mother's shawl and a few slivers of soap wrapped in a piece of newspaper to the public wash house. Even the brick copper built into the corner of her kitchen was not large enough to hold such a heavy garment, and Daisy's skin rose in goose pimples at the idea of wearing a dead person's shawl without first washing it.

The tide was low and the weak October sun glanced and danced on the tiny waves whipped up by the boisterous wind. Far away, towards the coast of Wallasey, a solitary yacht ran fast before the wind. Daisy watched for a minute as its mast seemed to dip towards the water. She sighed. Michael knew how to sail a boat. As a young boy he had sailed on a clipper all the way to China to fetch tea, and he had always wanted to be rich enough to buy a bit of timber to build himself a rowing boat to take out on the river. Poor Mike. He was a bit feckless and hot-tempered, and once or twice he had given her a good hiding. They had always made up their quarrels, however, and she had usually been pregnant before his next voyage. And he left her an allotment. She told herself she couldn't really complain.

As she passed the Foley home, she said good morning to Mrs. Foley, who was seated on a chair outside her front door peeling potatoes into a piece of newspaper.

Lucky her, Daisy envied. Two married daughters and their husbands and kids to keep her company.

Daisy had for years been so busy trying to keep her children alive and then nursing her mother that she had, like Mrs. Foley, not had much time to miss her sea-going husband. But now as the

73

wind blustered round her wide black skirt, she felt that being the wife of a ship's stoker was no life at all.

Now her mother was dead her loneliness appalled her. Relations she had in plenty, and Nellie was the dearest of friends. But the house was empty and so was her rough and noisome bed.

The wash house loomed before her, a dark and steamy cavern, a cavern equipped, however, with gas-heated boilers, lots of hot water and big sinks. Several women with sleeves rolled back from skinny arms were hard at work with scrubbing boards or were wringing out clothes through huge wooden wringers.

None of Daisy's friends or relations were there because few of them had anything to wash. The children were all stitched into their clothes for the winter, with warm pads of newspaper set between their vests and jerseys.

Daisy whipped up a good lather with her flakes of soap and a little hot water, then ran the thundering cold tap until she had a lukewarm mixture. She carefully lowered the shawl into the water and worked the soapsuds gently through it.

As she dabbled the heavy wool in the water, she felt as if she was slowly pushing her mother down into a watery grave, and she cried silently to herself.

Mrs. Thomas of Temperance fame was using the next sink. She would not normally have acknowledged the existence of the dirty Irish woman next to her. She noticed, however, her neighbour's tightly closed eyes and muffled snivels, and being by nature a kindly woman she touched Daisy's arm with a soap-frothed hand.

"Are you well, Mrs. Gallagher?"

Daisy swallowed a sob, and her eyes shot open at the sound of the inquiry delivered in a high-pitched Welsh sing-song. She hastily pushed her teeth into order with an impatient tongue. God, how sore her gums felt!

"Why, yes, Mrs. Thomas, thanks be. It's me Mam — I was washing her shawl — she passed on last Saturday — and, well..."

"Yes, indeed, I saw the funeral pass by. You must be feeling very bad." Mrs. Thomas seized hold of the hot tap over her sink and set it roaring like a waterfall. Over the frenzied splashing, her voice rose, "I'm very sorry." She leaned over towards Daisy, her face earnest beneath her straight fringe of hair, and patted her wet arm. "Try not to grieve — the Lord giveth and the Lord taketh away," she added piously.

Daisy had often raised a laugh in the Ragged Bear by imitating Mrs. Thomas using her favourite quotation, and now she smiled bleakly.

The Lord could take away a hell of a lot, when he felt like it. He had in the shape of Mrs. Donnelly taken away four shillings and tenpence that morning and, she admitted honestly, given her back sixpence via the kindly Bill Donohue.

She nodded acceptance of the well-meant consolation offered by Mrs. Thomas, rubbed the drip off the end of her nose with wet fingers, and continued to wash.

During the early afternoon, the lady from the Welfare called on Mrs. Thomas with regard to the provision of a wheelchair for her invalid daughter. Mrs. Thomas, feeling that Mrs. Gallagher must be very lonely and in need of consolation, kindly mentioned that old Mrs. O'Brien had died the previous Saturday and no doubt Mrs. Gallagher would be glad of a friendly call.

The Welfare lady understood perfectly the enormous gulf that lay between Welsh Mrs. Thomas, devout Presbyterian and Temperance worker, and Mrs. Gallagher, Irish Roman Catholic, which made it difficult for Mrs. Thomas herself to communicate with the bereaved woman, and she promised to call.

After finishing her business with the Welsh woman, she stood on the well-scrubbed pavement outside Mrs. Thomas's front door, and considered what she could say that would be helpful to Mrs. Gallagher.

She remembered suddenly that only the day before she had called at the Gallagher house to deliver a blanket for Mrs. O'Brien. Daisy had said that her mother was sleeping and had accepted a beautiful blanket squeezed out of precious funds specially for Mrs. O'Brien. She had not said that her mother was already dead.

Really the woman was intolerable. The Welfare lady climbed into her Austin Seven and slammed the door after her. She made a note in her notebook that Mrs. Daisy Gallagher was not to be helped again, except in the most pressing circumstances.

ELEVEN

Because she was feeling so depressed, Daisy did not go directly home from the wash house. She went to call on her younger sister, Agnes.

Agnes was not much help. She burst into a passion of tears within minutes of Daisy's arrival.

"Poor Mam," she whispered, as she took the teapot from in front of the fire and poured a boiling hot, black cup of tea for her sister. After setting the cup conveniently beside Daisy, she sat down herself, threw her apron over her head and wailed miserably into it.

Daisy had once remarked that there was more water in Aggie than in a whole wet week. She could turn on the tears like a tap.

Now Daisy did her best to turn off the tap. Instead of being comforted, she found herself doing the comforting, and this took some time. She spread her mother's shawl over the fireguard and let it steam while she held Agnes's shrouded head to her bosom. She felt like weeping herself, but now that she had taken her mother's place in the family hierarchy she felt she must do as her mother would have done, and lift Aggie's spirits somehow.

She patted Agnes's apron-covered head and held her close until the damp began to penetrate her blouse; then she began to divert her attention by mentioning that her son, Marty, aged five, would be home soon for his dinner and so would Winnie, her daughter. And would Joe, her husband, be home for dinner?

This reminder of her duties made Agnes emerge from her apron

76

and start fluttering about the room like Moggie playing with a screw of paper.

Despite her earlier cry of poverty to Bill, Daisy still had enough money left to buy a pair of bloomers and she was determined to make this purchase. She did not dare buy them at any local store — somebody would be sure to see her and make an awkward comment, so after a friendly cup of tea with Bill Donohue, she took the tram again to the city. She would buy the bloomers in one of the stores in London Road, where she had been the previous day. She felt very brave making this second expedition alone, and she comforted herself about the extravagance with the thought that the next day she would draw her allotment from the shipping office; and this would cover the rent and the cost of some coal and lamp oil. She could at worst pawn the fender again and the new blanket, if she could not manage until the following allotment day.

She spent a couple of happy hours roaming through the big stores and finally found what she wanted. She felt like a princess as she tucked the small parcel under her shawl, and she wondered how she could ever have been afraid of going to town by herself; around London Road there were plenty of Irish women like herself, long hair screwed up in a variety of Victorian styles, black shawls, black skirts, sometimes with aprons, sometimes without. It seemed quite homely.

As she strolled down the crowded pavement, she remembered her glorious repast of the previous day. Her mouth watered uncontrollably, and soon she was digging into a large plate of fish cakes, chips and peas. In the interests of economy, she ordered a cup of tea instead of a pot.

She again sat modestly with her back to the counter, so that she should not be seen eating, and this time she kept her teeth in. She ate slowly and with difficulty, and at times was sorely tempted to take the teeth out and set them by her plate. She was vain enough, however, to wish to keep her lovely new smile, and she finally shovelled in the last pea on the end of her knife with a great sense of achievement. Afterwards, she sat for some time watching the shadowy passers-by through the steamy window.

She was reluctant to go home. Bill Donohue would have finished his work and left, and there would be only Moggie to greet her. It was rather late to call on anybody, except her sisters. She had already seen Agnes and she doubted if Meg would have yet simmered down sufficiently to bury the hatchet. As she had once explained to a neighbour, "Our Meg is proper tempreementil. What you do you wait — maybe a week or two. Then you start up again as if nothing had happened."

It was after eight o'clock when she finally left the little fish and chip shop with a friendly "ta-ra" from the proprietress. Outside she paused, rubbing her arms under her shawl, as she gazed absently across the street.

The side road was quiet. A man in greasy mechanic's overalls whistled as he entered the pub at the corner, two shop girls, chattering in high-pitched voices, tottered by in high-heeled patent leather court shoes.

Daisy grinned to herself as she looked at the bright pub sign; and she hummed almost gleefully the tune the sailors had been singing the previous night. But enough was enough. She must behave herself. She folded her hands primly across her stomach; but still she did not move.

A constable on his beat passed her with only a casual glance. Her shawl and black skirt, her white apron and frowsy hair style were as common and respectable as his own uniform; prostitution was a rare phenomena amongst the Liverpool Irish. His indifference riled her.

"If I'd been decked out like a bloody pro," she fumed, "with furs and feathers and ear-rings an' all, he'd have noticed all right. He'd have stopped and told me to move on." She scowled at the constable's broad back as he turned the corner.

Perversely she began to sway her hips. With an irritable flip, she set her shawl further back on her shoulders in spite of the cool weather, so that the curve of her breasts was better outlined. Slowly, humming the sailor's tune, she swung down the street past the pub and turned round its garish opulence towards the familiar alley. She walked well, and in better circumstances would have been regarded as a fine-looking woman.

Still simmering at the pure indifference of the constable who had passed her, she went down the street without incident. At the end, where it ran into a cross street, she hesitated. The cross street was very dark. She spun round fretfully so that her skirt spread round her and drifted back up the slight rise again towards the pub. When a middle-aged workman approached her, she simpered at him, but he hardly noticed her and continued on his way. This provoked her even more and, as she again approached the pub, she opened the two top buttons of her blouse and tucked the ends in, something no respectable woman would do. She gritted her teeth. She would show them.

She would not have been able to explain who "they" were, except that they were a vague, amorphous cloud of people to whom the name Daisy Margaret Gallagher meant nothing. They employed the police, they were relieving officers, they owned boats that failed to dock in Liverpool, they paid out allotments across shiny mahogany counters, they ignored her when she was sick and found her a nuisance when she was well and wanted something. They surrounded her in ever-widening ripples; there were a lot of theys and thems in courts who put one's sons and daughters in prison. There were even more of them, as Michael had often remarked, in places like London who cared nothing about people who lived north of the River Trent, and yet reckoned they owned the very land you stood on. In short, they were ghostly menaces who threatened the existence of Daisy Margaret Gallagher, who lived down on the waterfront in a cold house where she had been often hungry.

Of course, if your son killed a man, reflected Daisy, as she swaggered slowly up and down, they noticed quick enough. Then you became a screaming biddie to be ejected from the court room while they took your boy away from you. If you dressed in flowers and glittering earrings and walked up and down as she was doing, smiling at every man who passed, then you became a person important enough to be arrested. You might become important enough to have regular clients who knew you, men from outside the tight family world which was normally one's only hope in a wicked universe. You might even find yourself in bed with the beak instead of in the dock in front of him. At this last idea Daisy laughed out loud and forgot for a moment what she was doing.

"Hey, Judy," whispered a voice from the entrance of the alleyway.

She jumped with fright and flung one arm dramatically across her breast. "Holy Mother!" Then as she observed the shadowy figure of a man, her expression changed and she smiled cunningly. " 'Ello, la," she greeted him.

The shadow materialized into a squat, heavily built man in a blue serge suit that was so crumpled it must have been rolled up in a kit bag for months. He grinned knowingly at her.

"What about it, Ma?" He nodded towards the comfortable darkness of the alley.

She looked him up and down, held back by a pang of fear.

"Give you three bob," he promised hopefully. He put out his hand and caressed her bare throat.

She smiled suddenly at him with her flashing white teeth and he almost dragged her into the black lair from which he had emerged, at the same time fumbling in his trouser pocket for the money. She held out her hand and he put three silver shillings into it.

He pressed her hard against the rough stone wall, prepared for only a moment or two's dalliance. Daisy, however, was not sure how much was expected of her. Now she was literally face to face with a client whom she had herself beguiled by flaunting herself in the street, she was nervous about her ability to please. She also feared that he might strike her if she tried to run away. He was solidly built and stronger than she was.

As his hands ran down her back, however, her natural instinct to tease, to caress, took over; and she found herself acting in exactly the same way as she would have done if Michael had caught her in a dark corner. It did not take her long to have him gasping with desire. Afterwards, he did not hurry away, as she had expected, but leaned against the wall by her in a friendly fashion till his breathing returned to normal.

He took out a packet of Woodbines and offered her one. With eyes cast down she shyly refused the cigarette. She was trembling under her shawl and wondering what kind of devil lay within her that she could enjoy a strange man so much.

"What's your name?" he asked her, as he took a closer look at her through a cloud of cigarette smoke.

"Daisy."

"Been in this game long?"

"Well. .. ." She did not know how to reply. She had not con-

80

sidered that a man she picked up might carry on a conversation with her, and she turned her face uneasily away from him.

He saw her shyness, and he laughed softly. The laughter made a plain, hard face suddenly friendly. He flicked the ash off his cigarette. There was many a good woman nowadays who took a man occasionally to help out with the housekeeping, he thought shrewdly.

"Well, Daisy," he said. "See you again." He hitched his belt a notch tighter and rolled with typical seaman's gait back down the alley to the street.

She stood leaning against the wall for a while until she heard voices in a back yard further up the alley. It reminded her that people were closer to her than the deserted entry suggested. She moved slowly along to the street, where she paused uncertainly. Then an impish grin spread over her face and she resumed her promenade up and down the road. She felt young and excited and far from tired.

A negro in a blue suit and trilby hat approached her very diffidently, not certain whether she was a prostitute or just a woman waiting to catch a drunken husband coming out of the Ball and Chain. She stuck her nose in the air and snubbed him soundly. He slunk away.

"Can't stomach them blackies," she muttered. "Don't know how Mike can work with them. Proper scary — black like Old Nick himself."

A chill wind sprang up and she began to feel cold. She bit her lower lip and then tittered to herself as the three shillings in her apron pocket clinked against her. It was as easy as falling off a dock. These men's needs were no different from Michael's and, judging by his friendliness, she had really pleased the man in the rumpled suit.

The street seemed deserted, so she retrieved the parcel of bloomers from the top of the wall on one side of the alley and walked down to Lime Street, where she caught a tram home.

For the first time for years she felt bright and venturesome, as if she had discovered again something of the gaiety of her youth. There was also a feeling of wonderment that something she had done had been appreciated.

"He thought I was worth three bob," she marvelled.

81

TWELVE

Daisy never could decide what drove her yet again to the quiet street at the back of London Road. Perhaps it was the indifference of the clerk at the shipping office who slapped down Mike's eighteen shillings in front of her and made her sign for it — as if he were a bloody relieving officer and the money was public assistance instead of wages from Mike. Maybe it was the dead monotony of Father Patrick's voice granting absolution for the sin of anger against Meg, when Nellie dragged her to confession. The ghost-ridden empty house to which she returned did not help either. Moggie had left a half-devoured mouse on the rag rug. The house was so terrifyingly quiet and the mouse so bloody.

"Fair turns your stomach, it does," she muttered, as she cleaned up the unfortunate mouse and threw it into the fire.

Saturday brought little relief from the loneliness to which had been added a deep boredom. Nellie came for an hour in the afternoon. But her visit only increased Daisy's frightened intuitions about her.

They ate tea together, and after she had gone Daisy lit a candle and wandered up to look at her mother's room. In the uncanny stillness she held the candle high to see what Bill had done.

Frightened by the light, the bugs scattered off the new wallpaper. She grinned. She reckoned she would have to burn the house down to get rid of the vermin.

Bill had left the cupboard door open so that she could see the inside of it. He had filled up an old rat hole with balls of paper and then put wallpaper over it as he had explained to her, and it looked much neater. He had also cleared up the worst of the splashes of

82

whitewash from the floor. She decided that if no one came to see her on Sunday, she would take up the old linoleum and scrub the floor.

She went to the undraped window and looked out over the dock. It was a fine evening with a thin rind of moon gleaming softly above the river. She pushed open the dormer window. It was stiff and gave reluctantly and she got a bit of damp paint on her hand. The candle flickered in the draught. She could hear men shouting to each other in a boat in the dock. Their voices in the night made her feel lonelier than ever.

She clumped down the stairs again and lit the lamp from the candle. Then she took down a bit of comb from the mantelpiece, pulled out her hair pins and put them in her aproned lap while she combed and rebraided her hair, two braids to the front and two to the back; the two at the back were wound into a neat bun and the two at the front were draped back under each ear and pinned to the bun, leaving the bare ears neatly circled by plaits in a fashion the young Queen Victoria had once favoured. Her grandson, King George, was on the throne and women now had their hair cut and permanently waved, but such far-out fashions had not reached women of Daisy's ilk. She put on her shawl and went up to the Ragged Bear for her usual Saturday night half pint of bitter.

The pub was busy and a frail old man in a cloth cap occupied her usual seat by the fire.

"Evenin', Mrs. Gallagher. Glass of bitter?" asked Mrs. Hanlon, as Daisy, frowning petulantly, plonked herself down in another seat. The man she sat down by was a steward on a passenger liner when in work, and he fancied himself a bit too much, according to Daisy. She said a short "Evenin'" to him and he gave her a pained smile, while he edged away from her to avoid the smell emanating from her. She sensed his distaste, and this irritated her even more.

Two acquaintances in their best black shawls were hedged in by other patrons on the far side of the room. They waved and smiled at her but there was no room for her to join them, so she shrugged hopelessly, making a wry mouth at them. To make them laugh, she raised her eyebrows comically and pointed a derisive thumb surreptitiously at the steward beside her, who had turned away from her to talk to a youth on the other side of him. The women cackled with laughter and the steward looked up suspiciously. Daisy's nose was in her glass, however, and she looked the picture of respectable innocence.

She glanced round at the groups close to her. They were mostly men absorbed in their own arguments. It was going to be a hopeless evening. She finished her drink and left.

Half an hour later, she was again swaying up and down the street which had proved so fruitful on the two previous evenings. This evening, being Saturday, there were more people going and coming from the Ball and Chain, and Daisy was glad that her dress was so sober that most passers-by would not realise what she was about. She did not want them telling the scuffer about her.

She loitered for a good three-quarters of an hour, stepping hastily into the alley when the police constable on the beat ran up the steps of the pub, presumably to check that all was well, and then crossed over to continue his orderly preambulation along the side of a warehouse. At each door he stopped to try the lock; and each time he paused Daisy wondered nervously if he would suddenly turn around and come back. She could be accused of loitering, never mind anything else. He continued straight on, however, and was soon lost in the night. She emerged thankfully from the mouth of the alley and stood quietly with hands crossed over her stomach, feeling that she must be out of her mind to have come there at all.

Two young merchant sailors came laughing out of the pub. They saw her white apron gleaming in the poor light and rolled up to her. They winked at each other and then stared at her knowingly with hard, experienced eyes. Both of them smirked.

"What you doin' out so late, Ma? Without your old man?" one of them teased, while the other broke into a guffaw.

She fluttered her long black eyelashes at them and, with hands still clasped across her stomach, swayed a little towards them and tittered, "What do you think?"

"Hm, hm, that's the way the land lies, is it?" They leered at each other, clowning to make her laugh, which she did. She put her hands on her hips so that her shawl fell open, flung back her head and gurgled appreciatively. Her huge chest looked round and pillow cosy.

84

"What's your name, duck?"

"Daisy."

"Ha!" The seaman who had first spoken nudged his friend.

"See, we can't have Shanghai Lil — but we got Liverpool Daisy." He almost sang the last words.

The second man chortled and asked hopefully, "Like to make a trick, Daise?"

"Cost you half a crown and you got to put it in me hand first," she told him, looking very coy.

"Aw come on, Al, it's too early," the first man protested.

"It's never too early for me. Come on, Daise. See you in a few minutes, Joe," and he whisked Daisy up the alleyway as fast as anyone of her tonnage could be whisked.

She was leaning against the corner of the alleyway, breathless after the energetic attentions of Joe and Al, when an indignant female voice assailed her ears.

"What you doing on my beat? You get outter here!"

Daisy gulped, and turned to face a woman in a veiled hat, a pale blue coat and high-heeled shoes. A pair of malevolent eyes glared at her from behind the veiling.

Daisy slowly straightened herself and pulled her shawl around her. "What yer mean? Your beat?"

"You know what I mean," the voice was scornful. "I work this bit. You get to hell outter here."

Daisy looked the woman up and down. Her breath had returned to her and she stuck out her chest like a courting frog and thrust her chin forward aggressively. "You mind what you're saying," she ordered in a growl. "You mind your own business and get away home!"

"I am minding my own business — and you'd better get home afore I tell Jim about you."

"Go on with yez," snarled Daisy. "I'm not doing you any harm or your Jim, whoever he might be."

The other woman snorted. "I been here for months. This is my beat, do y'hear, and I'm not standing for anyone else." The voice rose. "If you don't beat it quick, I'll fetch Jim." She pushed her face close to Daisy's and her voice descended menacingly. "You don't want your face slashed, do you, luv?"

"Pah!" Daisy almost spat. "You get going afore I call t' scuffer."

"Cops!" the woman sneered and tossed her head. "Since when have cops been on our side, ducks? You make me laugh." And she screeched with high-pitched laughter.

"Having trouble, Maisie?" inquired a deceptively quiet male voice.

The laughter stopped abruptly. Maisie turned to the new arrival and said in ingratiating tones, sniffing as if close to tears, "Jim, I'm glad you come. This bloody biddie took a couple of men from under me very nose, she did."

The man was a foot shorter than Daisy and seemed curiously anonymous beneath a wide-brimmed trilby hat. He turned towards Daisy who would have bolted, had she not been hemmed in by the wall behind her and Maisie in front.

Jim's voice was low and even, though very threatening. "Get out!"

This order made Daisy angry enough to forget her fears.

"Nobody's going to tell me to get out, you little runt! This is a public street. *You* get out before I clout you into next week!"

She shook a hefty fist under the brim of his hat.

He hastily stepped back a pace and slipped his hand into his pocket. Daisy saw the movement.

"And you keep that knife in your pocket, you bleeder, or I'll start screaming right now. T' scuffer'll come. I saw him not more'n a minute back."

But Jim recovered his aplomb, though he did not take his hand out of his pocket. "And where will that get you? Up before the Old Man, I can tell you. I'll see to that, you dirty git."

Daisy's temper was up now. Slowly swinging her arms she advanced towards the pimp. He backed. "You shut your bleeding gob," she hissed at him. "I'll larn yer to interfere with a respectable woman, I will. I'll larn yer."

Maisie quickly got out of the way. She paid half her earnings to Jim. He had set her up. Let him take the punishment.

Jim felt as if he had taken on an elephant, an elephant which was slowly but firmly pushing him towards the revealing lights of the pub. The more he could see of Daisy the more he wished himself several streets away, where his other girl worked in comparative peace. He was going to have to really use his knife or lose his credibility with Maisie.

86

He whipped the knife out. Daisy heard the blade snick open. With all her strength she kicked out and with a howl of pain he doubled up and fell to the pavement. She brought her boot down heavily on his right wrist.

"Leggo," she roared. "Leggo o' that knife — or I'll jump on yer."

The weight on his wrist was agonising. He scrabbled frantically at her ankles with his left hand. The stench from her was overwhelming. He brought his feet up suddenly and tried to kick her in her stomach. He was not too well balanced on his shoulders and she knocked him forcibly to one side. This wrenched the pinned-down wrist and made him moan. She ground harder on it with her foot and he screamed.

The door of the pub swung open, as a customer who had heard the scream looked out.

"You bloody bastard!" yelled Daisy, stamping harder on the wrist. "I'm going to jump on you."

He saw her tense herself and with a violent effort he again rolled himself up on his shoulders and tried to kick her, but his feet got entangled with her skirt and he fought to free them, while she hit out at his legs with her hands.

A man came running down the steps of the pub.

"Wot you doing to our Daisy?" he shouted. Another man, laughing, followed him down the steps. They were both in a merry state of drunkenness, but still steady on their feet.

Poised to jump, Daisy was frozen into immobility at the sound of her name. She looked, to the approaching men, like a triumphant prize-fighter standing over his fallen opponent. Jim tried again to push her boot off his wrist with his left hand. She automatically renewed the pressure and he yelped and lay still, since the sound of pounding feet indicated some kind of help was coming.

Maisie fled.

"Wot's up, Daise?" asked one of the seamen who had enjoyed her favours only a short time earlier. "Yeah, Daisy, wot's to do?" inquired the other breathlessly. Several patrons from the pub crowded on to the steps to watch.

Daisy recognised her customers with great relief. "This bleeder tried to knife me," she told them, her voice shrill and suddenly shaky. "See, there's his knife."

Al picked up the switchblade.

"You dirty son of a dirty noseless mother!" He peered down at Jim, still pinned by Daisy's iron foot. "It'd serve you right if I carved her name on your face, you bloody git."

Jim whimpered. "I didn't mean nothing. She was upsetting my girl."

"Bloody pimp," added Bert. "What *shall* we do to him, Al?" He viewed Jim's ashen face with such joyful anticipation of the vengeance they could wreak that Jim nearly passed out. Daisy was suddenly afraid that murder might ensue. She was intensely grateful to Bert and Al and was, at the same time, astonished at their coming to her aid. Maybe I'm better than I know, she told herself. Aloud, she said, as she slowly removed her foot from Jim's wrist. "Let him go, lads. If he knows you're around he isn't going to bother me any more."

The pimp scrambled to his feet, holding the injured member close to his chest to ease the pain. The two seamen were longing for a good fight. They were enjoying themselves hugely in the role of heroes, and they hunched their shoulders and swung their arms as they crowded in on the man.

"Sure we're going to be around," Al grunted. His fist shot forward and he nearly lifted Jim off his feet with the force of the punch on the side of the jaw. Jim staggered, turned to run and received a kick in the rear from the pointed toe of Al's best shoe. He cried out, and ran zigzagging along the gutter into the darkness at the bottom of the street.

Al brushed imaginary dust off the sleeves of his jacket. "He'll not bother you again, Daise, will 'e, Bert?"

"Not he," Bert assured her. He looked at her face which had blenched. "Come on and have a drink, luv."

Daise accepted the invitation in a wavery voice.

The customers returned to their seats, talking loudly about how the streets were no longer safe for respectable folks, and Daise and her two friends followed them in.

The waiter had watched the encounter from the pub window and had told the landlord.

The landlord himself brought Bert's order. He looked Daisy over and decided there was no accounting for taste. As he put a tot of rum in front of her, he whispered, "If you solicit in here, I'll call a cop straight off, d'yer understand? This is a respectable house."

Daisy folded her hands neatly across her stomach and looked the landlord straight in the eye. "And what might you mean by that?" she inquired and pursed her lips till she looked like a model of injured virtue.

Though the landlord looked calmly back at her, as he put a clean ash tray in front of her and removed one overflowing with cigarette butts, he doubted suddenly the accuracy of his waiter's assumption about Daisy. However, he nodded his head up and down like a toy Buddha Daisy had once seen in Bunney's gift shop. "You know what I mean," he said firmly, and moved quietly away.

The two seamen had downed their shots of rum and were following them with glasses of stout as chasers, and they asked above their foaming glasses, "What did he say?"

Daisy scowled, but shrugged her shoulders. "It were nothin' ".

She took a big sip of rum and grinned suddenly at her rescuers, her eyes dancing with malicious glee. "It was proper nice of you boys to come. You give him a proper doing over."

Bert dug her in the ribs with his elbow. "Go on, now. Got to look after our Liverpool Daisy. We'll need you again." He chortled as he looked knowingly at Al, and Al lifted his glass to Daisy.

The rum was warm, the company comforting and Daisy was filled with a surge of happiness. She shoved each man in turn with a plump shoulder.

"Go on with you, you impudent buggers," she said lovingly.

THIRTEEN

Bert and Al returned to their boat on Monday morning, back to the steady rhythm of greasing engines and trimming lamps. They sailed on the morning tide, and while they worked they told the story of their rescue of Liverpool Daisy. It lost nothing in the telling; and when they arrived at Lagos they met, apart from strangers, other Merseyside men; and in humid wharfside bars the tale was told all over again. The history of this female elephant, as they described her, made men laugh; and when they docked in Liverpool they remembered it and inquired for Liverpool Daisy. Soon everybody in the Legs o' Man and the other pubs near Lime Street knew where Liverpool Daisy was to be found.

Unaware of this free publicity, Daisy went one wet Sunday to Mass with Nellie, in the black neo-Gothic church they had both attended since childhood. Meg and Agnes were both there. Agnes spoke to Daisy, and Meg killed her with a look, as Daisy remarked to Nellie afterwards.

Daisy enjoyed a visit from Maureen Mary that Sunday afternoon; and little Bridie enjoyed the dried remains of the cake bought for her great-grandmother's funeral. She was a whey-faced little girl, with straggling blonde hair held off her face by a blue hair slide set with rhinestones, a birthday present from Daisy. While Daisy held her lovingly in her lap, she chewed the stone-hard currants in the cake very carefully, to avoid the caries with which her teeth already abounded.

Maureen watched her child's obvious pleasure at the fuss her grandmother made of her, and worried that she would surely pick up vermin from Daisy. She knew, however, that no amount of nagging would make Daisy concerned about such minor details as bugs and lice. Maureen Mary had been so impressed by her late employer's rigid standards of cleanliness that her own home was spotless; and yet, she felt as she looked around it, the rumpled, smelly familiarity of her childhood home was far more comforting to her than the carbolic sterility of her own house. Anyway, cleanliness cost a lot of money, and she knew that her father never left much of an allotment to his wife. He liked to come home at the end of a voyage with his money in his own pocket, to treat family and friends to drinks and extra food before he vanished off again. A fat lot he had ever cared about her mother's struggle to keep her children fed. Freddie might be pernickety, but Bridie and she were well fed and clothed, she thought. Her father had been away so long this time that she wondered if he would ever get back to Liverpool — you never knew with tramp steamers.

After tea they went to inspect the newly decorated bedroom.

"Eee, it's awful quiet now your Nan's gone," lamented Daisy. "I wish they'd let our Lizzie or our Jamie out — real hard it is for him. And me not able to afford to visit either of them and all."

"What about having a boarder in here?" suggested Maureen Mary. "It'd be company. Some young girl by herself, like?"

Daisy looked down at the top of Bridie's shining head cradled against her chest, and sighed. While she considered Maureen Mary's suggestion, she got up and gently set the little girl down in her place on the easy chair. The rain had stopped but the day was overcast and the room was full of shadows. She lit the oil lamp and the room immediately looked cosier. Then she took down the two china dogs from the mantelpiece and gave them to Bridie to play with. This was one of the treats of visiting grandma, and Bridie slipped joyfully down on to the hearth rug with them. Daisy smiled down at her; however hard-pressed, she had never pawned the china dogs since Bridie had taken a fancy to them.

"Aye, it's not a bad idea, that," she said heavily, in response to Maureen Mary's suggestion.

"You could put a notice in Mrs. Donnelly's shop window it's — twopence for a week, if I remember right — and you can have as many words as you like."

Daisy nodded, and bent forward to turn little Bridie's coat which had been hung over the oven door to dry. Maureen Mary's coat hung steaming from the back of a straight chair crowded with them near the fire. Winter was setting in, thought Daisy, and in the rain she would not be able to carry on her new-found lucrative trade. "I got a new blanket from the Welfare that I could put on the bed," she said finally. "If I could get a cheque from the club man I could buy some sheets and things. Last time I arst they wouldn't give me, 'cos I don't always have the money ready every week when the club man come to collect. Worse'n the rent collector, they are." She sniffed. "Got to pay it off every week, or you don't get another, he tells me."

The next day, the kettle was refilled and boiled most of the day, while Daisy scraped and cleaned the bedroom floor, after she had heaved out the rotten linoleum and stowed it in a corner of the yard.

Afterwards, she lay on her bed in the landing bedroom. Her mouth was sore, so she took her teeth out and laid them on the bed beside her, where they grinned at her in the half-light.

She thought wistfully how nice it would be to have a proper bed for herself, with blankets and sheets and a bedspread. Next time, maybe. This time she had to give the best bed to a lodger — at least for the winter.

FOURTEEN

The rain came down intermittently for most of the following week and put a temporary end to Daisy's street-walking. She managed to obtain a cheque from the finance company, and she bought a pair of sheets, two pillowcases, a small blanket and a cotton bedspread. Maureen Mary contributed a pair of curtains for the bedroom from her own house. She also helped her mother to stain and varnish the oak floor, while Bridie played with Moggie and the china dogs. There was a little varnish left over, so they did the chest of drawers as well.

Mrs. Donnelly put the advertisement, written on an envelope, in the window, amongst a dog-eared collection offering old furniture for sale, the services of Bill Donohue, painter, and Mary Devlin, sitter, kittens to give away and rooms for rent.

There was no response. Nobody came to see the room, except Nellie and Mary, Meg's daughter, who arrived together. Mary had retreated to the safety of her Aunty Daisy's house while a family row raged in her own home. Both visitors declared the room lovely, nicer than a hotel. Mary thought of the misery she suffered from sharing a bed with two younger brothers and a restless sister.

"I wish I could live with you, Antie Daise," she said wistfully.

"Yer Ma'd never let you," replied Daisy frankly, as she stroked her niece's lank brown hair. "There'll be a bit more room in your house when your Uncle Albert gets married — and maybe your Emily and her husband'll get a council house and move out soon."

"Yes," Mary agreed, and leaned lovingly against her aunt's comforting bulk.

"You're really lucky to have such a big house all to yourself,"

93

remarked Nellie, "A bedroom, a landing bedroom and all."

"Oh, aye, But this house's been crowded in its time. Remember when you and George was still here with your first two babies? God rest their little souls. There was me other older brother and Meg and Agnes and me — and me father and me Mam — and me father's sister what was single and had a flower basket outside of Central Station of a Saturday. Then Meg married and went to old Fogarty's house, and I married Mike and we had Maureen Mary here."

Nellie nodded her curly head over her tea mug. "Aye. It was fun sometimes. But your poor Mam thought she would go daft."

Daisy chuckled. "We had some good times and some good laughs, for all that." She leaned over, teapot in hand to fill up Nellie's mug, and then continued, "I'm going to get a lodger — to help me through the winter. Mike's allotment wouldn't keep a cat in fish — I'm hoping to find somebody who's workin'."

"Working?" inquired Nelly scornfully.

Daisy grinned. "There's still a few in work, though you might not think it. Those working on the big tunnel under the river is working."

Nellie shrugged. "Wish you luck."

In the evening the rain finally drifted out to sea and the moon rose clear and serene. Daisy thankfully flung her shawl over her shoulders and went up to the Ragged Bear for her Saturday half pint.

She got her usual seat on the bench by the fire, and spent a happy hour with two cronies from a few streets away, hearing all the latest tittle-tattle of births and deaths, all of which appeared to have been gruesome in the extreme.

She managed to make the half pint last until closing time at ten o'clock; then, after standing talking under the lamp post at the corner for a few more minutes, she made her way leisurely down to the river. There was a hint of frost in the air, and the nostrils of her strong straight nose dilated as she enjoyed the freshness of the breeze. She walked for a little while along silent Grafton Street, savouring the air. On her return, she paused to lean against the wall, to look out over the dock to the placid river, where the lights of Birkenhead and Rock Ferry twinkled back at her. Cigarette smoke had wafted round her for several minutes before she realised that a solitary man a few feet away was similarly engaged.

Normally, she would have quickly recrossed the road to avoid him — that's what a woman who kept herself to herself would have done, she told herself. But instead, she said cheerfully to him, "Nice night."

"It is," replied an Irish voice, with a brogue so thick that Daisy ventured to inquire if he was newly come from Dublin.

"Aye."

"Looking for work?"

"No. Me brother got me a job down there." He pointed to the dock below them. "Watchman."

Daisy clucked. If her brother, George, had had his wits about him he might have got that job. Then dear Nellie might have had the money for a doctor.

The stranger moved a little closer during her silence. She could see the friendly glow of his cigarette, as he flicked the ash over the wall.

"You're lucky," she said with a friendly grin.

He chuckled. "Luck of the Irish!"

A ship's bell rang the half-hour. The man heaved himself straight. He was a tall, thin man, with long, lanky arms. In the gloom, under a flat cap, she could just make out the handsome, though saturnine, face of a man in his early thirties.

"That must be ten-thirty," he remarked, in reference to the bell. "Don't have to be there till midnight."

A silence fell between them and they contemplated the river, until Daisy said cautiously, "That's a long wait."

"It is indeed."

Daisy sighed. "I must get home."

She moved from the wall, and the stranger turned with her towards the entry to the Herculaneum Dock. "You live round here?" he inquired.

"Aye, up past the Hercy."

They paced along together, Daisy with her arms folded under her shawl, he smoking his cigarette. She could feel herself beginning to shiver with a kind of joyful anticipation which by her standards no decent woman should feel.

"Your old man will be wonderin' where you got to?" ventured the watchman.

95

Daisy laughed. "Not he. He's been at sea for months." She looked slyly at her companion from out of the corners of her eyes. "I ain't got nobody at home at present." She sighed. "It's proper lonely o' nights."

The man agreed that it was proper lonely, and proceeded to make himself agreeable to the sufferer.

Daisy suddenly realised that she had a use for the newly decorated bedroom.

FIFTEEN

Daisy leaned over a faded collection of packets of biscuits, bottles of liniment and dusty imitation chocolate bars in order to retrieve her advertisement from Mrs. Donnelly's window. She screwed up the little envelope and threw it into the street.

"You got a lodger already?" inquired Mrs. Donnelly, as she put a side of bacon through the slicer. The slicer whirred with an ominous sibilance as if to warn of its sharpness.

"Yes," lied Daisy glibly. A lodger would explain away a man entering her house; and her new-found acquaintance had promised to come again. Three shillings from him was nestling comfortably in her apron pocket at that moment.

"Who yer got?"

You nosy so-and-so, thought Daisy. Aloud, she said, "He told me he's a night watchman at the Hercy. He's a quiet type — he'll be no trouble."

"Humph," grunted Mrs. Donnelly. "Will yer husband mind?"

"I haven't asked him," replied Daisy tartly. "I'll thank you for a pound of that bacon, Mrs. Donnelly."

Mrs. Donnelly slapped a handful of bacon on the scale. The indicator danced away below the pound sign. Daisy pointed accusingly at it. "Put it on slow," she ordered. "That's no pound."

With tight lips, Mrs. Donnelly put a finger on the scale to steady it, let it come to rest and then added another couple of rashers. "I can't be right all the time," she argued.

"You're always on the right side of right — your side," snarled Daisy.

Mrs. Donnelly rolled the bacon into a piece of paper and slammed it on the worn counter. Daisy scooped it up.

"That'll be tenpence." Mrs. Donnelly clenched her teeth together. She would not allow herself to be drawn into another fight with Daisy. She was still smarting over her ruined hat, and she shuddered when she considered what damage a rampaging Daisy might wreak in her store.

To her surprise, Daisy did not ask for the tenpence to be put on the slate at the back of the counter, where customers' indebtedness was recorded for all to see. She produced the money.

Mrs. Donnelly took the coins and put them into the wooden till. She was still staring at the open till drawer when Daisy wheeled round and marched out.

"Nosy bugger," muttered Daisy.

Daisy fell into a routine which was comfortable to her. On fine nights she worked the small street behind London Road. When the weather threatened rain or frost, she would meander along Grafton Street and occasionally pick up a man there. Her house being the only one which faced the river gave her a high degree of privacy; and women rarely ventured along the dock road at night, not because it was dangerous but because there was nothing to attract them to it; so all she had to do was to be careful not to approach a local man. Sometimes she did well, sometimes she was out of luck, as she put it.

Money which she dared not spend locally began to accumulate in an old tobacco tin. She tucked the tin away at the back of the shelf in the cupboard in the front bedroom and covered it with two extra petticoats she had bought herself in the town. Nobody sees petticoats, she had told herself, as she bought them.

Christmas Eve was a fine night and London Road was thronged with eager last-minute shoppers, despite the amount of unemployment in the city. The pub near Daisy's beat was very busy with rubicund men and pale, shadowy women standing glass in hand even in the parlour.

Daisy had just come to the conclusion that everyone was too busy with family or friends to bother with a woman, when she was accosted by a small, shabby man in a bowler hat. They retired up the narrow alleyway.

Because Daisy was so plump and the man was so small in stature, matters did not proceed very satisfactorily and he demanded his money back.

"Go on with yez," retorted Daisy roundly. "You've had your bit of fun. Now piss off." She glowered at him as she buttoned her blouse.

"You give me that money back or I'll call the cops, you thieving bitch." He leaned towards her and seizing the neckline of her blouse ripped it open.

"Gerroff. What do you think you're doin'?" demanded Daisy furiously, hastily clasping her blouse together with one hand while she gave him a sharp push with the other.

He was surprisingly strong for his size and came back at her, one fist raised. "Give me me money," he snarled. He brought his fist heavily down on her half bare breast. She felt a sharp prick and looked down in sudden terror. Blood was welling up from a small wound.

She went white with fear and backed to the wall; the alley was so narrow that it offered her little room for manoeuvre.

"Want it in yer face?" He raised his hand again. There was a glint of steel in the faint light.

Her heart beat violently as she stared at him. Her panic was so great that she could not make herself either answer him or produce the money. If he wounded her, she had no one to turn to and if he murdered her, who would know or care?

"Well?" he asked, flourishing the weapon.

Her bleeding chest rose and fell with the big breaths she took as she continued to goggle at him.

She began to whine. "You had some fun. I didn't mean no harm. What you so fussy about?" With every show of reluctance, she felt around in the deep pocket she had made in her black skirt to hold her money.

The hand holding the razor seemed to relax a little, and, as a sense of outrage took over from panic, she took her time looking for his half-a-crown.

"Come on!" The blade moved closer despite the slight relaxation of his hand.

"I'm getting it! I'm getting it," she said testily. She sniffed, and drew out the coin.

Holding it up between forefinger and thumb, she gritted her teeth and sidled up close to him until the blade nearly touched her. She put her free arm round him and slid her hand suggestively down his back. The blouse released from her hold fell open. "Like to try again?"

"No, you filthy git." He snatched the coin from her fingers.

She backed away from him towards the further end of the alley, clutching her shawl over her nakedness. He laughed at her as he pocketed her money. "That'll teach you," he sneered.

"Ya, you gutter scum," she jeered back.

She whipped around and ran up the alley to where it joined a cross entry. In a few seconds she was panting along Lime Street, cursing under her breath.

She flung into her house as if the whole of the Liverpool Police Force was after her. She shot the bolt on the front door — it was stiff from infrequent use — and leaned against the inside, as if she had run all the way home instead of having sat on a tram for twenty minutes.

She felt her way to the table, found her matches and lit the lamp. Then, still holding her shawl round her she climbed the stairs to the bedroom, it being the most secret place she could think of. She put the lamp down on the brightly varnished chest of drawers and went over to the window and hastily flicked the curtains shut.

She sat down on the bed feeling overwhelmed with weakness. The bed creaked complainingly. Very slowly she let her shawl slip off her and looked down at the cut on her breast. Blood had trickled down to the waistband of her skirt and then dried, though the cut itself was still damp. She dabbed fearfully at the wound with her torn blouse, but it was no longer oozing and she let out a sigh of relief. Then she let drop from her other hand the wallet she had been clutching all the way home.

She was nearly as scared at the sight of the wallet as she had been of the cut on her chest. Pinching from Woollies or Lewis's was one thing; stealing from a man who might come back for revenge was another. And yet the bugger had asked for it, she told herself, and she had been smart enough to get it out of his hip pocket without his realising it had gone. With a bit of Irish luck he might not discover its loss for a little while, and then he could not be sure where he lost it.

It was an old, oil-stained pocket book, covered with a worn

100

design of camels and pyramids. She opened it cautiously and with trembling fingers drew out its contents. She counted out seventeen pound notes and three ten shilling ones. She gazed in amazement at the pile of money. He must have just been paid off, she assumed. She looked through the papers it also contained. There was an identity card made out in the name of Thomas Ward by a shipping company in Liberia, a receipt or two, a snap of a group of negroes and another of a fat woman sitting in a deck chair on a beach.

The trembling of her hands spread to the rest of her body and she sat shivering helplessly for a few minutes. She had been bent on revenge and now she wondered fearfully what would happen to her if she were caught with the wallet.

Still shivering, she got up and went to the cupboard and took down the tobacco tin from under her petticoats. It was heavy with about five pounds' worth of silver in it. She added the notes to it.

"Serve the bastard right," she said savagely, though there was a tremor of misgiving in her voice.

She picked up the lamp to go downstairs to the kitchen to bathe her wound. She wondered if she should go to a doctor; the scratch was deep and might be infected by the knife.

"And he'll want to know how you came by a knife wound," she warned herself, and then shrugged. "Och, it'll heal itself, it will."

The word 'doctor' reminded her of Nellie and how sick she was. Poor Nellie, she needed a doctor all right.

If you can afford a doctor for yourself, you dumb cluck, you can afford one for Nellie, her conscience reminded her.

She stood transfixed, lamp in hand. What a fool she had been. She would pay for Nellie to see a doctor, maybe even one of those in Rodney Street, specialists they were called. "Oh, Nellie, luv," she cried out joyously. "We'll have you better, we will."

She'll ask where you got the money from.

Daisy grinned. "I'll tell her Mike sent it."

There was a knock on the front door and she jumped in guilty fright.

"Are ye there, Daise?" her sister, Agnes, called. "Coom on, lemme in. It's bloody cold out here."

"Holy Mary!" Daisy swore. "Coming," she shouted.

She looked hastily round the room and then quickly put down the lamp and stuffed the wallet under the bed mattress.

101

SIXTEEN

"What you want to lock up for?" asked Agnes petulantly, as she pushed through the door the moment it was unbolted. "I'm fair clemmed." She shook out her shawl like a flapping raven and blinked in the lamp light. Then as her eyes became accustomed to its radiance and Daisy moved to one side to let her enter, she asked, "And what's up? Your blouse is torn and you're all bloody." Her protruding blue eyes popped wide, "And you're as white as a sheet."

"Eee, I-er-um," faltered Daisy, making a quick grab at her torn blouse to cover herself. She must give some explanation.

"I was just down the yard a few minutes back," she improvised hastily. "I caught me blouse on the latch of the privy and it tore." She gained a little confidence, and went on, "It caught me, too — it hurt proper sharp for a moment — that's what took me colour out. I was upstairs when you come, looking for something else to put on."

Agnes was shivering with cold and made impolite haste towards the fire, without commiserating with her sister. Cuts and bangs were nothing — they healed or they went septic and had to be poulticed with hot water till they were clean. She seized the poker and quickly broke up the damp slack with which Daisy had banked the fire before going out. "Are you short of coal that you bank up your fire so early?"

"Not specially," said Daisy. "I let it go out at night like always. But I went out a bit earlier to buy a Christmas present for your Marty, and I thought it could stay banked till morning." She sighed. What was one more lie on top of so many? "I've got an old blouse upstairs — I'll just put it on. Be back in a seccie."

Agnes rubbed her hands over the flames. "I'll put on the kettle," she offered hopefully.

"You do that," agreed Daisy, and escaped upstairs. She looked again at the cut but it seemed to be drying, so she put an aged blouse on over it.

She looked anxiously at the bed, and cursed that she had not been able to burn the wallet before Agnes came. It would have to wait now until she went.

When she came downstairs again the fire was blazing cheerfully and the kettle was singing on it.

"You oughtta write to Mike and make him send you some money," advised Agnes, as she viewed the washed-out, threadbare blouse Daisy was wearing. "He must have lots in his pocket by now." There was a hint of jealousy in her tone — other than Freddie, who did not count, Mike was the only man in the whole family who was in work. "Your allotment is proper mean, I think."

Daisy opened her mouth to retort that asking Mike for money was like asking one of Lewis's for it, but she hastily swallowed this reference to a dummy in Lewis's store window. Agnes, bless her, had confirmed her own idea of a perfect explanation for the presence of any small extras that she had bought with her ill-gotten gains. Mike had sent her some money — real generous, he was.

She beamed with the relief she felt. "I already done that. I'm hoping he'll reply soon."

"You don't have to spend money on our Marty," Agnes reproved her absently, in reference to the present Daisy said she had bought.

"Och, it's not much," Daisy replied, hoping that Agnes would not demand to see the present.

But Agnes's attention had wandered, as she looked round the room over the rim of her tea mug. "You been doing some work here?"

Daisy had indeed been doing some work. With all the time in the world and no one to gossip to unless she walked at least as far as the Ragged Bear, she had slowly been cleaning up the long neglected house. To Mrs. Donnelly's surprise, she had purchased some Brasso.

"To clean t' fender," Daisy had explained sullenly.

Agnes looked down at the fender on which her feet rested, and

103

remarked admiringly, "Whole room looks lovely."

Daisy heaved another of her long sighs. "Aye, I'd no time with our Mam in bed." She could not say that the saturnine watchman who had been her first customer in the house had remarked that it looked like a pig sty. They had joked about it but she had taken the remark to heart. She had no intention of bringing very many clients to the house — just a few to assuage that long, lonely hour before she went to bed — because, as she explained to Moggie, some interfering biddie will notice them if I do. She never considered that Mike might return home — that was something which might happen in the distant future — too far ahead to even be thought about.

"Are you going to Maureen Mary's for Christmas dinner — after Mass?" asked Agnes.

"Are you kidding? Only been to her house once and that was when I heard she was expecting Bridie, and I went and told her I didn't like her marrying a Prottie; but she should still come and see me. She never even asked me in — but I could see she had a proper nice home."

"She got real stuck up working in Lyon's."

Daisy grimaced. "Well, I know where I'm not welcome." She glowered resentfully, and then added, "They could be living with me, they could! It hurts, it really does."

"I'm sure," agreed Agnes. Then she giggled. "That Freddie! He makes me laugh."

"Aye, he's a proper panse. But he knows a lot — and he treats me like a lady when he comes."

Agnes forebore from reminding her sister again that he never asked her to his home, even at Christmas. She told herself she was not a troublemaker like Meg.

"Is Lizzie Ann being let out for Christmas?"

Daisy's voice was despondent as she answered. "No. I posted a present to Jamie — don't know whether the bastards'll let him have it — and some scent to Lizzie Ann. I wish I could go and see them, but it's an awful long way and it costs a lot."

Agnes nodded her flaxen head.

"Maureen Mary'll come on Christmas afternoon. She allus brings a present."

"You come along and have dinner with us," ordered Agnes. "I

104

raised a pair of hens along with our Joe's fighting cocks. Got some eggs out of them first and now they're hanging in the cellar. Feathered they are and all ready to go into the oven first thing tomorrow."

"Ta, ever so. I'll come. You was lucky not to have them stop you having them hens — and the cocks. Mary Ellen up the road — she tried it and her neighbours complained, bloody canting Presbyterians; they said they smelled."

Agnes laughed. "I got a couple of rabbits, too, ready for New Year's. Joe made a hutch for them out of a butter box."

For some weeks, Daisy had been collecting small gifts for her nephews and nieces, for her children and for dear little Bridie. They were all stacked together in a paper carrier bag in a corner of the living-room. She promised herself that, after dinner with Agnes she would walk round the various homes of the family and distribute her presents. She would even go to Meg's house, though Meg had continued to ignore her whenever they met.

She had a rewarding Christmas Day, putting little presents into small, grubby fists. All the parents except Meg, remarked upon her generosity and expressed the hope that she had not left herself short. She was home in time for tea with Maureen Mary and Bridie, and in the late evening she finished up at George and Nellie's house. She presented Nellie with three boxes of the best snuff. Nellie put her arms round her friend and kissed her ecstatically. Her thin body felt hot to Daisy and her eyes glistened with fever.

"I don't know how you do it," Nellie half wept. "You manage your money so much better than I do."

George gruffly thanked Daisy for the tobacco she had brought him and gratefully lit up his blackened pipe which had perforce been empty for several days while his wife scrimped to give their last surviving child, Joey, "a bit o' Christmas". She had knitted the skimpy lad a pullover out of old wool retrieved from a garment she had picked up for a penny in a rummage sale, and he was wearing it with great delight. He showed it off with pride to his admiring Auntie Daisy. Nellie had also made a large toffee apple for him; the remains of it were plastered like a moustache along his upper lip. His father had over the previous month carved him a wooden horse and cart from a piece of driftwood and this also had to be shown to Daisy. The fine detail of the horse showed how well George knew the animals with which he had spent his life, until the firm for which he had worked had gone bankrupt.

When Daisy presented the boy with six tin soldiers wrapped in old tissue paper his day was complete.

"Thanks, Anty Daise," he breathed through a stuffed-up nose, and skipped off to show the present to his friends in the street. The adults sat silently listening for a minute to the clatter of his boots and his shouts to the other boys.

"I don't know how you managed to get them," said George with reference to the tin soldiers. He looked suspiciously at Daisy. "Our Nellie can't even feed us properly." He scowled at his wife.

Daisy did not want to point out that he spent too much of their Public Assistance allowance on beer and horses. It was not nice to start a fight at Christmas. Yet she saw the need to rescue Nellie from bitter recriminations breaking out the moment she left the house, so she lied gaily to help her friend.

"Nan and me were in old Donnelly's Christmas tontine before she died, so I had quite a bit to draw — and then I got a club cheque not long back for some bedding, and I used some of that for Christmas things."

"Humph," grunted George. "The tontine payments must have strapped yez?"

"Well, I written to Mike to ask for some money to help out," replied Daisy firmly. She stuck her chin up in the air as if defying him to ask any further questions. "Mike must have lots in his pocket by now."

George's response was acidulous.

"Money burns holes in Mike's pockets faster'n anybody I know."

Daisy's response was prompt. "Don't you criticise Mike. I know some others what wouldn't bear looking at." Then she realised that this would be the beginning of a quarrel; and Nellie was already looking alarmed. "Och, you're right," she said placatingly. "He does spend a lot at times. But there's no harm in asking him for some."

George cleared his throat and spat into the fire.

She glanced at her brother, and then went on cheerfully, "He'll send this time for sure."

106

SEVENTEEN

January brought another post card from Mike. It was pushed under the door by the postman, picture side up, and Daisy picked it up and looked at the highly coloured print of the port of Accra.

"He must have bought a dozen all the same," she thought as she stuck it up on the mantelpiece, along with two other identical cards received the previous year. She did not bother to turn it over to read it. Mike never said anything, except, "Doing fine."

She went out to collect her allotment from the shipping office.

On her return, she dropped off the tram outside the soot-blackened row house where Nellie and George rented the back room and a scullery. The front door led into a room occupied by a large family, so Daisy went down the back entry and came in through the tiny, walled back yard. She slammed the wooden door behind her and marched past a dustbin, out of which a cat scrambled hastily, and past the privy which was doorless and stank.

A dog within the house barked a warning.

She opened the door to the tiled scullery. It was empty except for an old terrier gnawing at a bone. He knew her and his tail flapped lazily in welcome, though he did not get up.

A dirty saucepan and the remains of a loaf of bread lay on a wooden table. Otherwise the room was as bleak as her own back kitchen.

"Hey, Nellie!" she shouted.

"*I'm* in here. Come in," responded a muffled voice from the other room.

Daisy opened the inner door into what had once been the kitchen

107

of the house. Now it was home to Nellie.

The afternoon light filtered through a torn lace curtain which masked a tall, narrow window where cardboard inadequately covered a broken windowpane. In the large, iron fireplace a few cinders gleamed. On the far side another door led to the front part of the house. Daisy knew that the door was locked and that the key had been thrown away, to discourage a procession of people going through from the rest of the house to use the privy in the back yard; the tenants fumed and complained and walked down the street and up the alley to get to the lavatory. The atmosphere of the room was foetid despite the draught from the broken window. A double bed reached from the wall to the fireplace, and in the middle of the bed Daisy could see the small curled-up figure of Nellie.

In the poor light Nellie seemed no bigger than a ten-year-old girl, and her black shawl covered her completely.

"That you, Daise?" she whispered, without bothering to lift her head.

Daisy laughed. "No, it's me ghost," she replied cheerily. She crossed to the bed and looked down at the tiny form on it. The laughter went out of her voice and she asked apprehensively, "What's up? You ill?"

Nellie slowly turned her head and opened her eyes. She made an effort to smile.

" 'Allo, la. Sit down." A hand that was practically all bone patted the bed beside her.

Daisy sat down, and the sudden advent of her weight caused the bed to bounce. Nellie started to cough, and Daisy viewed her with alarm as the spasm continued.

"I got to spit," Nellie announced suddenly between spasms. Daisy got up hastily and assisted her friend off the bed. She spat into the fire but partially missed and, even in the poor light, a long streak of blood was clearly visible across the hearth. The spittle on Nellie's chin was also streaked.

"Mother of God!" Daisy exclaimed in horror.

Very gently she helped the suffering woman on to the bed, the coughing having eased for a moment. With tender hands she wrapped the shawl again round Nellie.

"Nellie, you're proper sick. You got to see a doctor. I got some

108

money from Mike and I can pay." This latter remark was literally true since she had Mike's allotment in her pocket.

She leaned over Nellie and gently patted her shoulder. "But never you fret. I'm going to ask t' quack to come to you."

Nellie gasped for breath and made weak negative gestures with her hands. "No — oh, no, Daise! He'll put me into the infirmary and I'll die. And what would happen to iddy Joey — and our George." She clutched at her friend's arm as if to save herself from falling into a crevasse. "I couldn't bear it, Daise, I couldn't!"

Daisy's face was white, the mottles from fire burns on her cheeks standing out like a design for lace. "Aye, Nellie, luv, we got to do something. You can't go on like this." She knelt down by the bed and put her arm comfortingly over Nellie's shoulders. "You're spitting blood and you can't go on doing that."

Nellie took a labouring breath. "Been spitting for ages."

"Jaysus! Look, I'm going to get t' doctor. Lots of people with T.B. don't go into hospital. I know our Tommy did for a while — but I had him home most of the time."

A slow tear fell from Nellie's tightly clenched eyes on to the coverless pillow, which had several ominous dark stains on it. "Yes, he died at home."

The words were like an arrow shot into Daisy. The pain of the inference was so terrible she did not know how to bear it. She gasped for breath, while she tried to gather up her courage. Then she said, "Come on, now, Nell. You're not going to die — not if we get a doctor quick."

Nellie smiled but it was not a cheerful smile, rather it conveyed that she knew secrets hidden from Daisy, far away, unearthly secrets.

Daisy felt as cornered as she had done when she was threatened with a knife in the narrow alleyway she now knew so well. "Aye, Nell, come on," she rallied the other woman. "I'll get that doctor from Park Road to come down — he's proper nice, real kind. He'll know what to do."

"No, Daise!" The sick woman forced herself to raise herself on her elbow.

"Now, look here, Nell." Daisy's expression was grim. "I promise I won't let him put you in the infirmary or anywhere else, unless you change your mind. Hear me? We'll manage somehow. If you stay in bed you'll get better. Our Meg and our Agnes and me — we'll help you." She grasped her friend's hand. "You got to get better!" she cried in anguish.

EIGHTEEN

Daisy returned from the doctor's house feeling tired and thirsty. Nellie's tea caddy was empty, however, so she put some fresh water on the old leaves in the battered tin teapot and set it on the fire to heat. She had, before leaving, sifted the cinders from the accumulation under the grate and put them on the embers to burn. The result was not a very good fire but sufficient to warm the water.

"Got any conny-onny, luv?" she inquired of Nellie.

"On the kitchen shelf."

Daisy fetched the sticky tin of condensed milk, which was half glued to the shelf by its own drips.

Joey clattered in from school. He wore the pullover his mother had knitted for him for Christmas — it was already stained down the front — and a pair of shorts too small for him. His thin legs, grey with grime, were chapped in places. His boots were good, having come from the Public Assistance Committee; they were marked so that no pawnbroker would accept them. He had no socks.

He went straight to the fireplace and stood with his back to it.

" 'Lo, Anty Daisy. How's yourself?"

He grinned up at her. The thinness of his face made his teeth look too big for his mouth and his nose was running like candle grease in a draught.

Daisy ruffled his hair. "Not bad, luv."

The boy turned to his mother. "I want a conny-onny sandwich, Mam," he whined. "I'm hungry."

His mother nodded and made as if to rise.

"I'll make you one," offered Daisy. "Your Mam's not feeling very well."

111

Joey was much more interested in the piece of bread spread with condensed milk than he was in his mother's indisposition. Mothers were always complaining about headaches or nerves. He snatched the sandwich out of his aunt's hand and ran off to play in the back entry, where the boys got up a game to see who could urinate highest up the wall.

"Doctor's missus said he'd come later on — afore he starts his surgery," Daisy reported to Nellie, after Joey had gone. She helped Nellie to sit up and drink a cup of the wishy-washy tea she had made. "Me side hurts," the invalid moaned as she tried to find an easy position.

"I got a brick heating in the oven," Daisy comforted her. "It'll take the pain out a bit."

Nellie sipped her tea.

"Where's George?" asked Daisy suddenly. Though she had been in the house some time she had not seen her brother, and she fully expected that he would be furious at her going to get the doctor without asking him first.

Nellie shrugged. "He won three bob on the 2.30 yesterday." Her mouth took on bitter lines. "He'll be bevvied when he comes in."

Daisy agreed. George got as drunk as he possibly could on his infrequent betting wins. That was the way men were. The coal hole was empty and so was the tea caddy; the only food in the house was the tin of condensed milk and half a loaf of bread; yet both women knew that to remonstrate with George would be a waste of time and might mean a beating for his wife.

She poked up the cinders to encourage them to burn. "I'll bring you some tea, after t' doctor's been," she promised, "and I'll ask t'coalman to drop by tomorrer."

"I won't have any money till afternoon," Nellie sighed. "George goes down to the Parish in the afternoon."

"I'll pay for it and you can pay me back later."

"Ta." Nellie's affection and gratitude burst out of her. "You're a proper friend, Daise."

"Known you a long time — it's a habit," chipped Daisy with a loving grin.

It was dark by the time the doctor finally arrived. He went to the front door, and was met by a surprised denial of need of him

112

by the father of the family living there. Fortunately, Daisy heard the exchange rumbling through the locked door. She hammered on the door and put her mouth to the wood.

"Tell him to come round back," she yelled.

She could hear this message being relayed to the doctor, and she then whipped out of the back door and along the entry. She caught the doctor standing uncertainly on the doorstep, bag in hand, just as the front door was shut on him.

"Y' have to come up jigger, Doctor," she explained. "It's me sister-in-law. She lives in t'back. She's proper sick."

The doctor glanced nervously at his shabby Austin Seven parked in front of the house. Already a couple of urchins were looking it over.

Daisy appreciated the doctor's reluctance to leave his car out of his sight. She knew how her Jamie could strip a car within a few minutes. She shouted to Joey who was seated on the pavement playing a flicking game with cigarette cards.

"Aye, Joey, you and your mates watch doctor's car. Don't you let nobody near it or I'll clobber yez." She shook her fist playfully at him.

Joey grinned, and he and his two small friends moved over to the car to lean in a proprietary way against the doors.

Daisy jerked her head towards the alley. "He'll watch it all right."

The darkness made the alley look very menacing to the physician and he was not averse to having such a hefty person as Daisy precede him down it. He sighed as he glanced round the empty scullery and then entered Nellie's bare room.

Daisy had put a penny in the gas meter and had lit the gas lamp hanging from the centre of the ceiling. Though the mantle was damaged there was enough light to see in painful detail two wooden chairs and an older rocker with a battered copy of a racing paper on the seat, an orange crate set on end to act as shelves to hold a few dishes and cooking utensils, a candlestick with a nub of candle in it on the mantelpiece, a teapot and mugs in the hearth and over all the smelly grime of poverty.

Making a sharp clicking sound with it, Daisy put down on the top of the orange box the half-a-crown she had been holding in her hand, so that the doctor could see that she had his fee for the visit.

The doctor laid his bag on one of the wooden chairs. He smiled down at Nellie who was regarding him with the bright, scared eyes of a cornered animal.

"Good evening, Mrs. er—"

"Nellie O'Brien, sir," whispered Nellie.

"Ah, yes. I don't think I've seen you before, have I?"

"No, sir."

"And this lady?" he turned gentle questioning eyes upon Daisy.

"She's me sister-in-law, Mrs. Gallagher."

"I see." He did not sit down for fear of picking up vermin in his clothes, but leaned over the patient to take a closer look at her. "What's the trouble?"

"It's me cough," said Nellie falteringly.

"She's bin spitting blood," interposed Daisy.

Gradually the story came out and Nellie's shrunken body was carefully examined as far as her sense of modesty permitted. The dried trail of blood in the hearth was pointed out by Daisy with a dramatic sweep of her arm.

The doctor slowly put his stethoscope back into his bag and straightened up. His face looked pinched and tired. He glanced around the pitiful room and then back at his patient who lay staring at him with unblinking, terrified eyes.

"Mrs. O'Brien," he addressed her, "I would like to have your chest X-rayed. You need hospital treatment, that is certain. I can try to get you a bed in the sanatorium, where they will probably be able to help you."

"I'm not going to no hospital!" Nellie's voice was surprisingly firm considering how ill she was. "It's T.B., isn't it, Doctor?"

The doctor did not answer. His brow wrinkled in a worried frown. Again and again he came upon patients with an almost superstitious horror of hospitals. Death and hospital seemed to be synonymous to them.

Nellie saw his hesitation. "You can tell me," she said baldly. "Am I going to die?"

Her piercing gaze allowed of no prevarication and he reluctantly replied. "It is tuberculosis, Mrs. O'Brien — but you are not necessarily going to die of it. The sanatorium has performed wonders of recent years."

The soft pink of Nellie's cheeks drained to an ivory white as her

114

worst fears were confirmed. Daisy, too, blenched at the naming of the dread killer.

The women instinctively turned to each other and Daisy went down on her knees by the bed to put a protective arm around Nellie. Despite the doctor's words, they both felt it was a sentence of death.

Nellie put her hand into Daisy's strong grasp. Her breath was laboured, as she tried to conquer the panic which surged through her.

"I'll die for sure if I go to hospital," she murmured to Daisy through trembling lips. "Don't let them put me in hospital, Daise. You promised, remember!"

Daisy looked up at the doctor who had hastily stepped back from the bedside when Daisy had darted forward to comfort her friend. "Couldn't I nurse her at home?" she implored.

The doctor gestured helplessly with his hand at the poverty-stricken room. "She needs more than you can provide — warmth, fresh air, a good diet. Has she any children?"

"One lad."

"He should not sleep in the same room as her. She would have every care in the sanatorium. If she were at home I would have to visit frequently — and that would mean more expense — and drugs."

Daisy remembered again the big tobacco tin full of silver and stolen pound notes stowed away in the clean, airy room which had been her mother's. She squeezed her friend's hand. "Nellie!" she exclaimed passionately. "You could have Nan's room." She turned to the doctor. "I got a nice room with a fireplace. It looks straight out on to the river. She could have the windows open and a good fire." The words tumbled out of her. "I nursed our Tommy through T.B. I got a good new blanket and I could borrow some more." Her eyes pleaded with him.

"The expense would be quite high, Mrs. Gallagher. You could, of course, have the Parish doctor."

Nellie slowly withdrew her hand. She turned her head wearily from side to side on her pillow. Her whole expression was one of blank despair.

Daisy bent over her and wrapped her shawl close around her.

"Now, you rest, ducks," she ordered briskly. "I'm going to talk outside with doctor. You ain't going to have no Parish vet." She stroked the sick woman's white cheek with a tender hand. "You stop worrying. I'll fix it."

She turned swiftly, picked up the coin from the orange crate and put it on top of the doctor's bag.

"Can I talk to yez outside?"

"Of course." The doctor picked up his bag and the half-a-crown, which he slipped into the pocket of his shabby overcoat. He smiled down at Nellie. "Don't lose heart, Mrs. O'Brien. Stay in bed, keep warm. I want you to consider going into the sanatorium, and I will come to see you again tomorrow morning."

She nodded, her eyes closed. When she was alone, she took her rosary out from under her pillow and lay with it held to her chest for comfort.

In the scullery Daisy addressed the doctor urgently. "Me sisters will help me nurse her," she assured him, recklessly committing Meg and Agnes to the job. "She's proper ill, isn't she? I seen it so often."

"One should never give up hope, Mrs. Gallagher. The treatment of tuberculosis has improved greatly of latter years." In the almost empty scullery the pomposity of his voice was echoed from the walls, and he felt suddenly weak and inadequate before this forceful woman's shrewd gaze.

"They said that about our Tommy, but he died anyway, God rest his poor little soul." Daisy laid her hand on the doctor's threadbare sleeve. "I'll take great care of her, I will. I can afford to buy her anything she needs. Maybe I can get her better."

The doctor looked down at the muddy floor. "I presume she is a widow?"

"No. Me brother is out.. ." she was going to say at the pub, "That is, getting his P.A.C. money," she corrected herself hastily.

"Well, talk it over with him. I shall be here again tomorrow. In the meantime, I will give you a prescription which will help her. Get it made up tonight." He took his prescription pad out of his breast pocket and scribbled on it. He handed the slip of paper to Daisy, and went on, rather hopelessly, "Feed her lightly. Eggs, milk, oranges."

"Whatever you say, Doctor," Daisy assured him. The fortune in the tobacco tin would provide it all.

NINETEEN

After the doctor had gone, Daisy went out to get the prescription made up at the chemist's, a magical shop filled with the delicate odours of lavender, naphtha balls and cough mixture and presided over by an elderly druggist, who often provided the only medical advice his neighbours received.

Daisy stood impatiently tapping her foot amid the mahogany and glass showcases. While inwardly she screamed, "Hurry, hurry!" she examined the clutter of soaps, perfumes, nailbrushes and patent medicines, and the chemist behind a frosted-glass screen carefully compounded the medicine. He soon presented her with a neat white parcel, sealed at either end with a drop of red sealing-wax. She paid him and, carrying it gingerly under her shawl, she ran to the dairy for milk and then to Mrs. Donnelly's for tea and sugar. The cows at the back of the dairy had not long been milked, and the milk was still warm when it was poured into Daisy's can.

By the time George stumbled through the darkness of the back yard to his home, Daisy had fed Nellie and Joey with bread and milk, dosed the invalid with the bright pink medicine, and had settled down by the dead fire to wait for George's return. Nellie was snoring gently; Daisy had tucked her up in her shawl and the old eiderdown which was the bed's only other covering.

Joey was rocking himself in the rocker. He had hauled Rex, the terrier, on to his lap to keep him warm.

Though George was not drunk he was not particularly sober either. His heavily lined face was an unhealthy yellow and he stood in the doorway of the room blinking stupidly in the gaslight.

"What's up?" he asked, after silently taking in the scene. Women-

117

folk did not usually visit each other so late.

"Shush," warned Daisy, turning to look up at him with a scowl of disapproval. "Nellie's proper sick."

George ambled over to take a closer look at the invalid. He swayed uncertainly over her.

Daisy caught his arm. "Come in t' scullery," she commanded, with a knowing look towards Joey. The boy had ignored his father's arrival and was busy investigating the inside of the patient dog's left ear.

"Come on, now, I got something to tell yer."

George allowed himself to be guided into the icy scullery.

Daisy shut the door. This left them in darkness except for a shaft of moonlight across the floor.

"Listen, George," Daisy whispered urgently. "I had the doctor to her this afternoon. He wanted to put her in a sanatorium, but she won't go!"

"Sanatorium?"

"Yes. And you know what that means."

George considered the matter laboriously. Then his voice came lugubriously out of the darkness. "Yes. I know. She's got T.B. Always coughing, she is. Christ! What'll I do?"

Daisy explained her idea of nursing Nellie in her own home by the river.

"Oh, Daise!" George began to weep drunkenly.

"Now, you shut up. You and Joey could come, too, except I don't have time to look after everybody 'cos I'm working, see. You could take care of Joey here — then he won't know too much about the trouble with his Mam — and you could come and help me in the daytime a bit — or maybe in the evening when I'm working."

"I didn't know you was working. Where you working?"

Daisy was silent for a moment and then she flashed out, "That's none of your business."

George cleared his nose with a large sniff. "I only asked."

"Well — I'm working evening shift in t' bottle factory downtown. Mike's allotment isn't enough. And you listen to me, George." She shook a finger at him. "We're going to have to pay doctor and chemist and coalman and everything — so no more getting bevvied every time you get a few shillings. Hear me? You got to buckle to and help me."

All this was more than George's fogged brain could take in. Never bright at best, it seemed to him that his world had been in chaos ever since he had come home from the third Battle of Ypres in 1917 to spend a year in hospital while the quacks dug pieces of shell splinter out of him. Now Nellie was sick to the point of death — that much he understood. Beyond that he could only think about lying down before he fell down.

Finally, Daisy snapped at him, "Och, go and sleep it off — but don't you dare wake Nellie. I'll come over in the morning."

She opened the door and called softly to Joey. "I'm going home, Joey. Watch you don't wake your Ma when you get into bed. And mind you get off to school in the morning."

Joey grinned at her over Rex's rough back and nodded.

George pushed past Daisy and shambled into the room. "I'll take a strap to yez if you don't behave," he mouthed thickly.

Back in her own home, though the hour was late, Daisy built up her fire with extravagant hands, till it roared up the chimney and the room was bright with dancing flames and glowing coals. The room was more cheerful looking than it had been. Articles that had lain for months at the pawnbroker's were now returned to their proper place. A black enamel coal hod stood resplendently full of coal by the fireplace; a shabby red cloth with a fringe of pompons round its edge covered the table again. A pair of brass candlesticks, a wedding present from an aunt of Mike's, kept the china dogs company on the littered mantelpiece. From the oven came a fragrant odour of meat, potatoes and onions simmering in a casserole in the oven. Under a chair rested Daisy's best high-heeled, black patent shoes, which had been in pawn almost constantly ever since little Tommy's funeral.

The heat of the fire soothed Daisy as she sat down and baked in front of it. Her shins and her cheeks gathered new burn mottles. When some of her weariness and worry had seeped out of her, she took the casserole out of the oven and ate the contents with a battered tin spoon, while the heat of the basin in her lap added to her contentment. But when the casserole was empty and she had settled back in her chair, while the fire reduced to a rosy glow, a huge wave of fresh grief about Nellie rose in her.

She remembered how they had skipped in the street together,
wandered on the Cassy shore and gone to stare at the Chinese
inhabitants of Parkee Lanee. They had shared every treat, taking
turns, at times, to suck a single sweet.

Slowly she began to weep, at first quietly and then noisily. They
had lain in bed together and talked about that mysterious thing
called 'blood' and had giggled about boys, while an irate Meg and
Agnes, who had also slept in the same bed and found a visitor
added to their number too much of a crowd, had kicked them and
told them to shut their gobs.

Nobody heard her lamentations and gradually they dimin-
ished to an occasional dry sob. She blew her nose through her
fingers into the fire and then wiped her face slowly with her apron.
Drained and exhausted, she stared into the embers.

Nellie! She must wake up and think what was best for the girl.
She would have to break the icy silence which existed between
Meg and her. Great Aunt Devlin might be persuaded to help, too,
though she might have to be paid. Her mouth twisted wryly. She
was going to need all the money she could make. She was going to
have to work much harder. Like a judgement on her, it was. Served
her right for going on the streets like a common tart.

It was after midnight when a knock came on the door.

Daisy jerked awake and tumbled Moggie off her lap.

She did not know the young man at the door. A merchant seaman, she judged, by the way he stood swaying on his heels as if to
keep his balance on a heaving deck.

"Yes, lad?" she inquired, her hand still on the heavy door.

"You Daisy?" The voice was rich and deep.

"Yes."

"Pat — the watchman at the Hercy — sent me up. Said you
were very obliging, like."

Daisy simpered. "Come in, lad," she said, her voice oily with
friendliness.

After closing the door behind him, she sidled round him and
with a knowing smile, announced, "It's five bob for an hour."

She stood saucily in front of him, hands on hips, head thrown
back, so that he could examine the goods, as she put it to herself.

He looked her up and down slyly, and then said, "O.K."

She held out her hand and he pressed two half-crowns into it.

She lit a candle and led him up to the bedroom, which was not quite as cold as usual, some of the heat having percolated from the living-room. She stood watching him leisurely take off his jacket.

"Well, what about taking your clothes off?" he asked, when she had made no move.

"Me! I never take all me clothes off!" The idea of exposing all of her body to anyone shocked her. She doubted if Mike had ever seen her naked. " 'Sides, it's too bloody cold."

"Aw, come on, Ma," he cajoled, as he continued to strip himself. "We'll warm each other soon enough."

She put down the candle and reluctantly began to unbutton her blouse.

"Come on. I'll help you."

His idea of how to undress her was so caressing that she found herself kicking off her boots and nearly leaping into bed.

Her satin skin and luxuriously long hair showed to advantage in the candlelight and they did warm each other. Daisy learned more in an hour than she had ever known before, and it was with a feeling of tired pleasure that she added the five shillings to the tobacco tin which was going to save Nellie's life.

After the stranger had gone, she stood with one of her long petticoats wrapped round her like a cloak, thinking that if she could get a bed under her every time, life could be a lot more pleasant — and she could earn more.

TWENTY

Daisy woke late and lay languidly looking out of the bedroom window at a pure blue sky, until remembrance of Nellie's terrible need forced her to move.

She tidied the bed ready for Nellie, made a cup of tea and drank it quickly and, thus fortified, walked round to see Agnes, who received her with pleasure and more cups of tea.

"Agnes is easy," ruminated Daisy. "You can sell her anything. When she gets in a panic, though, it's pure mairder."

There was no panic that morning, however. The news about Nellie only confirmed Agnes's own long held opinion. She was glad, she said, to hear about Daisy's job in the bottle factory and wondered if she could get a job there herself.

"Not a hope in hell," Daisy assured her hastily. "There's queues of them trying to get in every day."

It did not strike Agnes to ask Daisy how she got in; she accepted everything that Daisy said as gospel truth. Old Daise had always been straight with her — always traded under a lamp post, she did, never under a tree.

Daisy warned Agnes that sometimes she did an extra half shift, which meant that she would come home on the first tram in the morning, rather than on the last tram at night. Agnes assured her that she would never leave poor Nellie alone.

Meg was different, thought Daisy, as she hurried over to her other sister's home. Meg could argufy like a scuffer in front of the beak, and yet she was the best bet for real help with Nellie.

Meg's father-in-law, Mr. Fogarty, was the true head of Meg's household. The three-bedroom row house sheltered him, his son,

John, who was Meg's husband, six of John and Meg's children, aged from thirteen to seven, his second son, Tom, and his wife, Emily, and their six-month-old baby, and lastly his youngest son, Albert, when he was not in gaol. Meg remarked bitterly from time to time that she did not believe that Albert could be guilty of all the thefts for which he had at different times served sentences, because when he was at home he did nothing but eat and doze comfortably on the sofa in the living room.

As Daisy rolled into the scullery, her arms neatly crossed under her shawl, Meg looked up from the greasy dishes she was trying to wash clean without benefit of soap or hot water.

"Why, look what the cat's brought in!" she exclaimed acidly. "And what brings you here, Missus?"

"Oh, stow it, Meg," Daisy responded crossly, as she subsided, panting, on to the only chair in the scullery.

"Who's there?" inquired a cracked, male voice from the living room.

"It's only me, Daisy, Mr. Fogarty. How are you?" She rose and went to the door of the other room.

A very thin, old man, his white hair ruffled up like a cockscomb, was sitting in a straight, wooden armchair. His clean union shirt was open at the neck and the sleeves were rolled up as if ready for work. He regarded Daisy with bloodshot blue eyes.

"How do you think?" he replied disagreeably to her inquiry.

"Well, I was hoping the pain wasn't so bad," she said brightly.

He looked down at his cruelly twisted fingers. "With arthritis? Less pain? It's a bloody pain in the neck, I can tell you," he growled, and then cackled with laughter at his own joke. He raised his voice to shout to his daughter-in-law. "Meg, when you going to give me me aspirins?"

There was the sound of the tap running, and then Meg appeared with a nearly empty bottle of aspirin and a cup of water.

"You never remember on your own, do you?" he berated her. He opened his mouth and she set an aspirin on his tongue and then held the cup so that he could drink. "I'll have another," he said. "It's bad this morning."

"You won't have enough for the night if you do," replied Meg dully.

"I'll worry about the night when I get to it. I may be dead by then, and that would make you happy, wouldn't it now?" He gestured impatiently towards the bottle. "Well, shake a leg, girl, and give me another."

Meg obediently gave him another tablet.

"Cover me. I'm cold," he ordered.

Meg brought an old overcoat and tucked it round his knees. He looked cunningly at Daisy. "Our Albert'll get me another bottle out of Boots. Proper nimble fingers he's got. Nothing like having a croppy head in the family, eh, Daisy?"

Daisy had no doubt that Albert could lift a bottle of aspirins out of Boot's Cash Chemists in Lime Street, so she nodded agreement.

Meg silently returned to her saucepan washing in the scullery, and Daisy followed her. The house was quiet, except for a baby crying upstairs. "Meg's little nevvie letting everybody know," thought Daisy with a soft smile.

All Meg's own children were in school, and her husband John had gone down to the docks to sign on as being available for work. He had to do this twice a day and stand around, rain or shine, in case he was needed. It was an empty charade. There was rarely any work for him, and he often returned at night sopping wet and frozen.

"Well, what do you want?" Meg pinched her mouth tight, as she rubbed away at a soot-blackened saucepan.

Daisy cast a stabbing look at Meg's thin back and then said in honeyed tones, "Listen, Meg. Nellie is terribly ill. The doctor come to her yesterday. Meg, she isn't going to live unless we do summat about it."

Meg paused in her work and let the saucepan slowly sink into the grey dish water. She watched the concentric rings of grease eddy out from it. "Going to die?"

Daisy fought back a desire to weep. She said, "It's T.B., Meg. She's spitting blood often now, and she can cough like you'd never believe."

Meg's narrow shoulders slumped even more as she slowly ran the dishrag round the pan. She liked Nellie — everybody did — but she did not like Daisy very much, so she asked sarcastically, "What am I supposed to do about it?"

"Well, I'm going to put her in our Mam's bed and nurse her.

124

The quack wanted her to go into the sannie. But she won't go and I don't blame her — heartless bloody place."

Meg shrugged. "Well, she's *your* friend."

"I know. She's your sister-in-law, too, remember." Daisy sighed. "And it's going to cost a bit for medicine and things." Meg was smart and she must be careful what she said. "Maybe Agnes told you I got an evening job — and I don't want to give it up seeing as how I'll have to pay the doctor, 'cos George can't do it."

"Ho-ho, hum-hum!" exclaimed Meg in surprise, and half turned to look at her sister. "Working, are yez? Since when may I ask?"

"I been doing it off and on ever since our Mam died. Don't get her pension no more and me allotment isn't enough."

"Where you workin'?"

"In t' bottle factory down town."

Meg stared at her fat sister doubtfully.

"What do you do there?"

Daisy floundered for a moment, then said, "Wash bottles and pack them in straw in cardboard boxes."

"And what do you expect me to do — on top of the ould fella an' all."

"Well, I was hoping you would come and sit with Nellie some nights. Keep the fire going and help her if she coughs up." Daisy rubbed her arms under her shawl, and added uneasily, "Sometimes I don't get home till early morning — doing overtime, like."

"What about George — can't he wake up long enough to do a bit?"

"You know our George. He allus was the dumb one and he ain't never been the same since he was in the hospital all that time. 'Sides he hits her sometimes."

Mr. Fogarty suddenly bawled from the next room, "Meg, come 'ere. I want to pee."

"Old bastard," muttered Meg. She turned on Daisy savagely. "I got enough to do. I can't do no more." She pointed an angry finger at the door to the other room. "He can't do nothing for himself now."

"Your Emily from upstairs could help you," Daisy suggested, a dark mantle rising up her neck. "Nell's your sister-in-law too, isn't she?" she added with asperity. "Make Emily do something."

"Ha," Meg sniffed. "She's expecting again and the baby only six months old," she flared. "Always whining. Wait till she's got six. I'll thank all the Saints if she gets a Council house and gets to hell out of here."

Daisy wagged an admonishing finger at her. "You got Mary to help you, anyways — and your husband   John is handy — and Tom and Albert is your brothers-in-law — they owe you something. You could find some time to help me with Nellie — I haven't got nobody."

Meg's thin nostrils expanded as she drew in a breath. She was tired beyond endurance, frantic that she would not be able to feed the brood which depended upon her, grief-stricken as she watched her husband's fine body deteriorate from lack of employment and poor food. She felt her sister to be grossly unfair.

"I can't do no more!" she cried with a half sob. "You got nobody to think about except yourself. Do you good to help our Nellie."

"Meg!" came an urgent voice from the other room. "Bring the pot, quick!"

Daisy got up and flounced towards the door as Meg whipped a jam jar from under the kitchen sink and made for the other room.

"Albert could do that for his father," said Daisy furiously.

Meg paused. Her mouth twisted in a sneer. "You ask him!"

"Oh, go jump off the dock," shouted Daisy in return.

She threw open the back door and went grumbling down the back alley like a wood down a ninepins lane. Behind her anger the tears welled up. Where *was* she to get help? Nellie had no sisters or parents. She had lost one brother in the same Battle of Ypres that George had been wounded in, and her other brother had taken his wife and family and gone south to find work only a year before. "Holy Mother," prayed Daisy, "help me. Dear Holy Mary."

Meg bent again to her saucepan washing. For a while her wrath at her sister sustained her, and then she began to feel a qualm of conscience about Nellie. Such a good woman deserved help, she knew. But I'm so tired, she cried silently to herself. I'm so tired.

After the saucepans had been neatly arranged on their shelf, she took a bucket of rubbish and Mr. Fogarty's filled jam jar out to the rubbish bin and the lavatory respectively, to empty. When the repulsive jobs were done, she leaned against the door jamb to look up over the smoke-blackened brick walls of the yard to the sky, a pale, limpid winter blue through which two gulls sailed and swooped. She watched through half-closed eyes as their raucous cries came down to her. For a moment she shared their freedom of the upper air. Then from the house she heard the petulant cry, "Meg! Meg! What about a cup of tea? Where are you, Meg?"

She closed her eyes in exhaustion and lifted herself away from the door jamb. The latch of the door into the back entry clicked and her husband, John, come slowly in. He was a tall, lanky man and his long hatchet face was shaded by a flat cap. He had his hands clenched in the pockets of an old cloth jacket stained with oil and grease on the back and shoulders. He looked as exhausted as his wife felt, but his face softened when he saw Meg.

" 'Lo, luv. What you doin' out here? It's cold."

"Emptying the ould fella's pot." She put the jar down on the stone step and went to her husband.

He hastily took his hands out of his pockets and, with a quick glance round to see if anyone was looking, he enfolded her in his arms.

She laid her head on his chest and her arms crept up round his neck. He bent and kissed the top of her tidy braided head.

"No luck?"

"No. Maybe tomorrer."

TWENTY-ONE

Still smarting from Meg's rebuff, Daisy marched down the windy street to see George and Nellie. Her boots scuffed along the stone paving, as she muttered under her breath, "She's nothin' but a bloody bitch. No heart to her."

She found Nellie puttering slowly round her room, a coal shovel in her hand. A sober and obviously worried George was watching her from the rocking-chair. On his lap was a back copy of a pink racing paper.

"Jesus!" exclaimed Daisy. "Couldn't you make up the fire for her, George?"

She snatched the coal shovel from Nellie and added a few lumps of coal to the fire. She had gone round to the coal merchant the previous evening and paid him to deliver a hundredweight of the precious fuel to Nellie first thing in the morning.

George clamped his lips together sulkily.

Nellie intervened. "It's all right, Daise. I don't feel so bad to-day."

"Good. But you get back on that bed again," ordered Daisy. "Have you had any breakfast?"

"Just a cup a tea. That's all I ever take."

Daisy accepted this statement with a nod and plunked herself down on a chair, while Nellie obediently lay down on the bed.

Daisy then turned a malevolent blue eye upon the luckless George.

"Na, George. I don't know how much you remember about last night," she commenced bitingly.

George glared at her. " 'Course I remember," he snapped indignantly.

Daisy grunted and looked round as if she had a large audience. "Humph, now that's remarkable, ain't it?"

"Don't be eggy, Daise. He knows," Nellie pleaded.

"Well, then, George, tell me. How are we going to get Nell to my house?"

Nellie half rose on her elbow and interposed hastily. "I don't need to go, Daise. I'll be all right here."

Daise swung round towards her. Her voice took on a cooing note, as she said, "Na, look, Nell. We got to get you well somehow. And I haven't time to come down here every day."

"George'll look after me."

"You haven't got the money to buy what's needed, eggs an' all. And he's got to sign on for work and go to the P.A.C."

"If she stays with you, the Relieving Officer will stop the allowance I get for her, t' bloody bastard," said George heavily.

"Not if you don't say nothing, you stupid bugger. You stay here and look after Joey, and if the P.A. visitor asks where Nellie is, tell him — well, tell him she's nursing me! So she's over at my place most days." Daisy chortled at this idea and Nellie giggled and began to cough. Even George grinned sheepishly.

"Our Aggie will come and sit with you of an evening some nights," said Daisy, turning to Nellie who was trying desperately to control her coughing. "But Meg has got too much to do with old Fogarty an' all, so George and Joey'll have to come some nights. Great Aunt Mary Devlin'll come, o' course, sometimes, but we got to pay her, 'cos she can't be sitting with other people if she's sitting with you — and she needs the money."

Nellie and George agreed about Great Aunt Devlin.

"Meg's got too much on her shoulders already," remarked Nellie, clearing her throat and managing to stop her coughing spasm.

"Pah!" snorted Daisy. "She should get that Emily off her ass and make her help. And John, too."

"Emily's bloody useless," said George with unexpected warmth. "And John's got to sign on twice a day, you know that."

"If Ellen hadn't gone to live in Southampton, she'd have helped," sighed Nellie, in reference to her brother's wife.

George ignored this remark, and continued, "Best way to move you, Nell, 'd be to borrow a handcart and lay you on it."

"Ha, using your brains at last," sneered his unloving sister. She turned to Nellie. "He's right, you know. Wrap you up warm. You'd be like Queen Mary in her carriage, you would." She cackled with laughter.

"Taffy might lend us his," said George, steadily pursuing a single line of thought.

Nellie raised her tousled head from her pillow. "Ah couldn't, Daise! What'd people think? Me sitting on a rag and bone man's handcart, like!"

"They won't see you," replied Daisy comfortingly. "We'll do it after it's dark, won't we, George?" She fixed George with a stony stare. "You get the handcart and ask John to help yer. And I'll get the fire going in our Mam's room and have it real warm by the time you come after tea."

George let the newspaper slip off his lap and nodded in a bewildered fashion at Daisy. Even if he had not agreed with her he would not have dared to argue. Arguing with Daisy was like arguing with a tank in Flanders. He wished suddenly that he was a seaman like Mike and could sail away from his troubles ashore for months at a time.

He got up slowly to go to see Taffy about the handcart.

Daisy got up, too. She took a half-crown piece out of her skirt pocket and stuck it on the mantelpiece. When she saw the movement, Nellie immediately protested.

"Daise! We can pay the doctor. George gets his dole today."

Daisy laughed down at her anxious friend. "Come on. I feel rich today. Me American uncle been and left me a thousand pounds." She laughed again at her own joke. She felt like a monarch, as she bent to kiss Nellie gently on the forehead.

"Oh, Daise! You sure?"

" 'Course I'm sure. While I work I got money enough."

Nellie sighed, then smiled at her friend. She laid her head down on her lumpy, stained pillow and closed her eyes. For once, the room was warm. It felt good to rest, to drift for a while. She could be certain that Daisy would look after iddy Joey — and George. She put out her tiny hand towards Daisy. Daisy took it and squeezed it passionately, as if to pass some of her own strength to her.

When the room was empty, Nellie took her rosary from under her pillow, found the cross on it and, with her lips against its comforting presence, she fell asleep.

Daisy's first attempt at kindling a blaze in her late mother's bed-room went out, so she got a broomstick and poked around up the chimney. Clumps of soot tumbled down and covered her arms with fine black powder. She cursed, and shoved the broomstick up again. This time part of a bird's nest descended with a thud, as well as more soot.

She looked at the offending bundle of clay and fine twigs. "Must have built the bloody thing right in the chimney," she fumed.

She inserted her arm as high as it would go and felt around. She could find no more of the nest, so she swept up the soot and started a fresh fire. This time it burned well.

Clucking with irritation, she washed the soot off herself and changed her ruined blouse. Then she spread over the bed the new blanket intended for her mother and two others she had redeemed from pawn. Between the sheets she slipped two bricks which she had heated in the downstairs oven and wrapped up in newspaper. She emptied the chamber pot and replaced it under the bed.

The room smelled strongly of soot, so she opened the window and leaned out and took a big breath. Though the night was damp, the air from the estuary smelled sweet and fresh. Daisy smiled. With clean, damp air like that Nellie would find her breathing much easier.

When she tidied up her living-room, she found a post card under the door mat. Mike, as usual, was doing fine, it said, so she tossed it on to the mantelpiece to join the other ones already there. She was tired of pictures of Accra.

The card reminded her of Elizabeth Ann's last letter, which had said that her sentence might be shortened because she had behaved so well. "Bless her iddy-biddy heart!" murmured her mother, as she leaned back in her chair and stared into the fire. A nice-looking girl who might bring a husband home to live with her mother, not like Maureen Mary. Let him be a man who smelled like a man, of sweat and dust or oil or coal, so as you knew he'd been working for you. She felt she could not endure another son-in-law who smelled of talcum powder.

With her stockinged feet on the fender, she began to doze. The young man of the previous night had tired her more than she cared to admit. As soon as Nellie had been put to bed, however,

131

she would instruct George to sit with her, while she herself went out to turn an honest dollar. "You're a born tart, Daise," she told herself with a laugh.

Then her eyes sprang open with horror. With Nellie in the house, she could not bring a man home. Yet money in large sums would be needed. She would squeeze a bit of George's allowance out of him, of course. But it would not be nearly enough. An anxious frown creased her usually smooth forehead, as she tussled with the problem.

The rattle of the handcart over the stone sets of the street made her leap out of her chair to answer the door.

Nellie was curled up on a pile of newspapers and her old eiderdown. She was covered by John's overcoat. The bumpy journey through the night chill had shaken her, and she lay exhausted with eyes closed.

"Maybe she's dead already," agonised Daisy, as she hurried out.

But Nellie opened her eyes and smiled weakly. "The boys were proper careful of me," she assured Daisy in response to anxious inquiries.

The two great clumsy men grinned sheepishly. They stood uncertainly, watching the women while Nellie slowly raised herself.

"Na, George. Don't just stand there. Lift Nellie out and carry her upstairs." She turned briskly back to Nellie. "Room's lovely and warm, luv, and waiting for yez."

Obediently George lifted his wife and carefully carried her in. She was so light that blind terror struck him that she might really die and he would be left with only iddy Joey. He paused on the doorstep, as memories of his ill-treatment of her rushed into his mind. If she died, the devil would take him for his wickedness, he was sure of that.

Nellie felt his chest heave under her and sensed the fear in him. She lifted one tired hand and stroked his face, just as she had had the habit of doing when they were first married. He looked down at her sharply and saw for a second the young, saucy Irish girl he had married, and not a dying woman.

"Nell!" he muttered, "Aye, Nell!"

Her hand closed gently round his neck under the band of his rough cotton shirt. She smiled at him very sweetly.

"Don't be afraid, Georgie, luv. Daise'll help us."

132

He nodded dumbly.

"Come on, George! She'll catch her death! Take her in," ordered Daisy, pushing impatiently from behind.

Like one of the cart horses he had tended in the past, George braced himself for the steep rise of the stairs, and then climbed them slowly and passed through to his late mother's room.

Daisy was right. It was beautifully warm, though it smelled strongly of soot. The fire glowed a welcome, and two candles flickered extravagantly on the little mantelpiece.

He laid his wife down on the bed, while John and Daisy crowded into the room. John looked around him with surprised interest at the new wallpaper and Maureen Mary's white curtains drawn over the window. The bed, too, looked lovely with two clean white pillows and a white sheet turned down over good blankets. He thought longingly how he would like to give Meg a room like this, with a fire in it and no children sharing it, so that they could relax in sensuous luxury like in a film.

His wistfulness was rudely broken by Daisy.

"You boys get outta here. I'm going to put Nellie to bed. Then I'm going to make her some bread and milk afore I go to work." She nodded at John. "You go down and put the kettle on the fire for some tea for her."

John clomped down the stairs with a "Ta-ra, Nell" as a good-bye to the invalid.

"Ta-ra, well," responded Nellie. "Thanks, John." She was still holding her husband's hand as if afraid to release it. Daisy went to her and slipped her boots off her feet and put them in the hearth.

"I can do for meself, after I've rested a bit," Nellie protested.

"Nay," said George suddenly. "You let Daisy help you."

Daisy nodded approvingly. "That's right. Now you get out of the way and I'll help her off with her skirt. She'd better keep 'er stockings on for warmth." She began to untie the tape which held up Nellie's gathered skirt. "I haven't got a nightie for you yet, luv. I thought I'd ask the Welfare lady for one — and a coat or something to go over you when you get out of bed. It'd be more comfy."

Nellie had never owned a nightgown and thought that Daisy was taking too much trouble on her behalf but, when she protested, Daisy pointed out practically that nighties were soon washed through and with the fevers she got she could become sweaty and

133

then she would get cold.

Soon the little woman was laid in bed, the blankets tucked round her, a hot brick at her feet and another at her aching side. "I'll get some new bags of sand, tomorrow," promised Daisy. "I threw out the ones I had for Nan 'cos they was leakin'. Sand does keep the heat better, there's no doubt."

George was again holding his wife's hand and Daisy grinned at him knowingly. "Three's a crowd. I'll go and make the bread and milk." And she bustled out with a speed and determination that surprised George, who had always regarded her as a lazy, gossiping bitch.

"Best get back to Joey, George."

He nodded. He felt bewildered and at a loss in this women's world of sickness, where the wings of death seemed literally to beat down at him from the shadowy ceiling.

"He's all right with Mrs. Higgins for now." The grip on Nellie's hand tightened. He wanted to get into bed with her and hold her closely as he had done in happier days, without fear that she would shrink from him because she did not want to carry another child.

"George," whispered Nellie. "Take care of iddy Joey. Bring him to see me tomorrow."

He roused himself with an effort. "Surely," he agreed. "He'll be over on his own in the morning."

"No." Nellie's voice was sharp. "See he goes to school. He can come after school."

George dropped her hand. "O.K.," he agreed irritably. An old wound in his back was aching and he moved towards the door sullenly. His wife watched him, her perception heightened by the fear of death.

"Aye, Georgie, come back here a mo'."

He paused, his hand on the doorknob.

"Come 'ere, now."

With a face as droopy as that of a basset hound, he came sulkily back to the bedside.

Nellie lifted her arms. "Come 'ere."

He bent over her, stark fear of her dying breaking through his churlishness. She wrapped her arms around his neck and pulled him to her. She patted his back as if he was a child and kissed his cheek. "And you take care of yourself, Georgie, lad." She held him

134

to her tightly for a moment. "There's nothing to be afraid of, do you hear."

"Aye, Nell," he whispered brokenly, as he returned her embrace, "I'm so scared. What have we come to, you and me?"

TWENTY-TWO

The January night felt dank, and the wind coming through the dampness seemed more chilling than usual. The few people about hurried along with coat collars turned up or with shawls held tightly across their chests. Even the Ball and Chain, with all its lights gleaming through steamed-up windows, seemed to huddle miserably against the blackened walls of the boarded-up warehouse next to it.

And Daisy could not find a client. She hummed her favourite obscene song hopefully in the shadows, every time a male figure hastened by. Then she moved closer to the lights of the pub and flashed her bright white smile. "Like to make a trick, dearie?" she whispered.

Most shook her off impatiently. One who knew her muttered querulously, "In this cold?" and made a rude gesture.

The general dampness turned to light rain, and Daisy cursed the weather roundly under her breath. She told herself despairingly that even a blackie would have been welcome on a night like this.

"You won't do much tonight, duck," remarked a feminine voice behind her, as she moved into a doorway of the warehouse to shelter. The voice was soft and carried a subdued giggle in it, as if the owner was permanently trying to suppress her laughter.

A figure nearly as plump as herself squeezed into the doorway of the warehouse at the same time as Daisy sought shelter there. She brought with her an overwhelming cloud of violet perfume; and Daisy felt her hackles slowly rise. She eased herself round, to look at what she sensed was an intruding competitor.

Competition it certainly was.

Daisy's lips tightened as she viewed the cheerfully overpainted face surveying her from under a cheeky-looking veiled hat. A mangy fox fur encircled the woman's neck and she carried a large, light-coloured handbag in which she was now digging absently while she stared back at Daisy.

"Like a cigarette?" asked the intruder, bringing out a battered packet of Woodbines.

Daisy scowled.

"No." The single word came out as sharply as a pebble from iddy Joey's catapult. "And you get off my beat!"

"Aa, stow it!" responded the other woman, as she tore a match out of a folder and lit her cigarette. "I don't trade in t'streets. I got me own apartment, I have. Got me regulars." She blew out cigarette smoke which wreathed round Daisy's head, much to her discomfort. "Once you got some regulars, they tell the other boys and you don't have to go out that often."

Daisy blinked her eyes against the tobacco smoke. Then she inquired loftily, "And what may I ask, are you doin' here if you've got everything sewn up so bloody comfortable, like?"

The unwelcome intruder's voice was gleeful, as she replied. "Been to the pictures. Proper nice film at the Forum." She sighed blissfully. "Ronald Coleman is a bloody marvel. Have you seen it?" Without waiting for Daisy to reply, she went on, "Got pissed off with the whole bloody issue, so I took meself to the pictures." She laughed richly. "And I got a man when I come out — proper funny, it was." Her voice sobered suddenly. "But it isn't safe in Lime Street if you ain't got a pimp. You got a pimp?"

"None o' your business," snapped Daisy. She stuck out her hand to see if the rain had stopped. It had not.

"Well, I'm telling you, they got Lime Street so tightly laid out they're on you in a second. Bloody great switchblades, they got. One girl got proper beat up only a couple of weeks ago. I was sweatin' they'd catch me tonight."

"I never go there," replied Daisy, shrugging her damp shawl more tightly round her shoulders.

It was quiet for a moment, while the smoke round Daisy increased rapidly, despite the encroaching rain. The uncrushable sharer of her shelter looked Daisy up and down, "How do yer

137

ever make out in them clothes?" she asked.

"What's the matter with me clothes? You mind your own bloody business and I'll mind mine."

The other woman laughed. "We're both in the same business, luv. Seen you several times when I been going into the Ball for a quick one."

Daisy snorted. She was so incensed that she considered plunging out into the icy rain and going home. Then she realised that as far as Nellie and George were concerned, she was at work — and could not go home until a reasonable work period had elapsed.

"Bugger everything!" she growled.

The constable on the beat came slowly down the deserted street. The rain dripped unhappily off his helmet and his waterproof cape. Occasionally, he stopped and flashed his torch while he tried a door lock or checked a window.

When he reached the two sheltering women, he stopped and flashed a torch over both of them. The light rested only cursorily on Daisy, noting the unpainted face, the pursed up mouth and belligerent chin stuck up in the air as if daring him to ask her a question. The torchlight, however, ran thoroughly up and down her companion and came to rest on the heavily rouged face and the merry mascara-rimmed eyes.

"Na, ladies," he said, not unkindly, "Loiterin' ain't allowed. Move along, please."

"Come on, Officer," wheedled the painted female. "I'm only sheltering."

Daisy murmured agreement. This was the first time to her knowledge that the constable on the beat had seen her and she was desperately anxious that he should not remember her in any way. Her well rounded throat quivered, as she tried to keep calm and look like a respectable Irish woman on her way home from St. John's Market.

The constable inclined his head towards the public house. "What about going to have a drink until it gives over?" he suggested.

The bright-faced female gurgled, "You going to stand us, Officer?"

The constable's voice hardened at this impudence. "Now you get moving, Missus Woman!" His eyes flashed in the shadow of his helmet. He gestured with his torch. "Out!" he ordered.

Daisy did not wait for any more. Like Moggie on the prowl, she slunk silently past the constable while his light was still on the other prostitute, and started up the street.

The other woman prepared to move also. She arranged her fox fur tighter round her chin.

"Bad cess to you," she muttered angrily at the irate constable.

"Want me to take you in?" he asked fiercely.

Her answer was lost, as she tottered out on very high heels, which were so worn down that she looked bow-legged as she wobbled up the street after Daisy.

The rain was hissing down now, penetrating Daisy's thick shawl and running down her back. What a night!

She paused at the corner, wondering what she should do. Nellie certainly made life complicated. Not for one moment did she regret taking in her dear friend — somehow Nellie was going to be fed and nursed back to health. But money had to be found to do it.

"Wait for me," shouted the gurgly voice again from further down the street. Daisy half turned and watched the woman totter up to her on her uncomfortable heels.

"Like to come and have a cuppa tea with me? You can't do nothing in this weather." A wicked grin was flashed at her from behind the wilted veil. "Don't often have a woman to talk to now me sister's dead. It's all fellas around the place." The rich laugh came again and she cupped Daisy's elbow with her hand to guide her across the street.

"There's a couple of other women in our house, up on the second floor. Proper bitches, they are. Take the bread out of your mouth, they would."

Daisy glanced up and down the cross street. Cars swished behind them as they made their way over, and her skirt was splashed with mud from them. There was not a pedestrian in sight. And she could not go home yet.

"O.K.," she agreed — any port in a storm, she thought ruefully. "What's your name?"

"Ivy. What's yours?"

"Daisy."

"Daisy? I heard tell from a fella not long back about a woman called Liverpool Daisy." She scrutinized Daisy with new interest

139

as she propelled her towards the side door of a small tobacconist's shop. "See, I wasn't far from home — Liverpool Daisy, now?"

"Some of the boys calls me that."

Ivy paused, her key extended towards the door lock, and glanced up again at Daisy. "You're bloody lucky. That young fella was proper nice about you. You're getting yourself a good reputation!" And again a surge of laughter rocked her, as she unlocked the door.

They entered a dingy hall lit by a single low watt bulb without a shade. A door, which Daisy assumed led into the tobacco shop, occupied one side wall, and straight ahead of her was a flight of stairs covered with shabby linoleum.

"Come on up," invited Ivy.

At the head of the stairs was a small landing with two doors facing them, while on Daisy's left the staircase continued upwards into darkness.

One of the doors had a grubby card pinned to it on which the name "Ivy Le Fleur" had been crudely printed in red pencil. Ivy unlocked this door and kicked her shoes off into the room which lay before her. She took off her hat and examined the sopping ruin regretfully.

She saw Daisy glance at the card on the door and her eyes twinkled, as she said, "Me real name's Ivy Brown — that's me name from when I was a dancer — it's Frenchy — good for me business."

Daisy was impressed by this display of business acumen and allowed herself to be led into the apartment which seemed to her to be very luxurious. It consisted of a single room stuffed with furniture. A large rumpled bed with numerous pillows and a bright green eiderdown dominated the room. On the other side of it a cage on a stand held a disconsolate-looking canary. Behind the bird, the window was covered by shiny green curtains. An easy chair, faded to near grey, faced a large gas fire which Ivy immediately lit. The pop it made as the gas flamed made Daisy jump, and Ivy chuckled.

"I got coal fires — more healthy 'n gas," said Daisy defensively.

"Too much work," replied Ivy, as she got up off her knees. "Make yourself at home while I fill up the kettle." She took off her coat, shook it out and hung it over the back of a chair, then laid the dripping fox fur over a line strung across the corner above an ancient gas cooker. She picked up a tin kettle from the stove and hurried out of the room. The gas stove had two shelves above it and these were crammed with a dusty assortment of dishes, small saucepans, packets of salt and sugar, all mixed up with a full ash tray, several boxes of matches, a tin of talcum powder and some greasy bottles.

Daisy strolled round the tiny space not committed to furniture. Behind an old hospital screen with faded cretonne curtains was a wash-hand stand, complete with jug and basin and a slop bucket underneath. The stand was also tightly packed, with odds and ends, tooth brushes, a soap dish, a sticky pot of vaseline, aspirins and liver pills.

A small dressing-table, with a mirror suffering from smallpox, was equally littered with powder boxes, a hair tidy, pin cushions, broken combs, hairpins, pots of cream, and a gadget which Daisy did not recognise. She picked it up and was examining it when Ivy came back into the room.

"That's me eyelash curler," she explained in answer to Daisy's query.

"Curl your eyelashes?" exclaimed Daisy in disbelief. She stared incredulously at the tiny contrivance and then burst into sudden laughter.

Ivy lit the gas jet under the kettle. "Aye," she said, looking up from her task, "That's better. You look real pretty when you laugh. Reminds me of me mother — she wore a shawl, too. Take your shawl off and put it on the fender in front of the gas fire. You're dripping." She bustled round, clearing a table and laying two cups and saucers on it. Then she quickly slipped off her damp dress, hung it on a hanger and put on a crumpled wrapper over her bright pink underslip. She snatched up a towel from behind the hospital screen and handed it to Daisy.

"Here. Here's a towel for your hair."

Daisy thankfully accepted this kind hospitality. The room was rapidly becoming deliciously warm and, as the chill went out of her, she began to relax.

She took off her shawl and laid it on the fender. Her thin cotton blouse was also sodden, as was the shift under it. The garments clung to her large breasts and Ivy eyed them enviously.

"You got a fine pair o' bristols," she remarked.

141

"Suckled all me kids," Daisy informed her. She sat down on the easy chair, and ran her hand round the neck of her blouse to loosen it from her skin.

Ivy sloshed hot water into a small brown teapot.

"Surprisin' how many men like fat women," she remarked, "Seein' as how the fashion is always for thin ones."

"Oh, aye," agreed Ivy.

Daisy took the pins out of her hair and began to rub it with the towel. She felt around for a piece of comb in the pocket of her wet apron and after she had found it she took the apron off and set it to steam beside the shawl.

Ivy sat down on a small straight bedroom chair and poured out the tea, ladling in spoonsful of sugar with a generous hand, while Daisy patted the front of her blouse with the towel.

Ivy handed her a cup of tea and she laid the towel across her knee while she took it gratefully.

"Ta," she said.

Ivy drew her chair closer to the fire.

"You don't wear no makeup?"

Daisy was shocked. "Never!" she spluttered into her teacup.

Ivy laughed at the strong denial. Her own makeup had run in the rain and she had grey rivulets of mascara down each cheek, giving her a clownlike appearance. Daisy eyed her resentfully over the steaming teacup. In her small world, only real whores like Ivy wore makeup. Of course, girls put lipstick on nowadays like their mothers would never have dared.

"Aaa, you should paint your face. It'd do a lot for you."

"Humph," grunted Daisy. She stirred uneasily in her chair. She wasn't a whore like this woman and she didn't want to look like one. She was unable to think why what she was doing for a living was different from what Ivy was engaged in; but to her it was not the same thing at all, at all, it wasn't. Further, she had realized instinctively that the normality of her dress was an advantage to her. If she was seen with a man he could pass her off as an acquaintance, a neighbour, a relation.

"You really should buy some makeup."

"I dunno. I dunno as it is a good idea. T' scuffer looked at you tonight — he hardly noticed me."

"A lot of men wouldn't notice you neither."

142

"To hell with her," thought Daisy. "I wish I hadn't come." Aloud, she said stiffly, "I do all right." She leaned over and helped herself to another spoonful of sugar. She whirled the spoon fretfully round her cup while she wondered if the rain had stopped.

Ivy picked up the sugar bowl and sat with it in her hand, as if to protect it from further raids by Daisy. She felt that Daisy was smarter than she was; yet, she suspected, Daisy did not know her own value.

"How much do you get?" she inquired.

"Half a dollar. If I don't like the look o' them, I try for five shillun." Daisy clapped her spoon into her saucer noisily. The woman was a proper Nosy Parker, she was.

"You could do better'n that if you had a room. Ever been to a hotel?"

"Me? In a shawl? Na." She reflected for a moment. Ivy's face expressed only honest interest, so she confided, "I got a house of me own. But I got someone living with me, so I can't take fellas there. Not now, anyway."

"Your ould fella there?"

"No. He's at sea."

"Don't he ever come home?"

"He's been away for ages this time. He don't touch Liverpool. He could be gone for years." She had not given any thought to the possibility of Mike's return, and Ivy's question introduced the disturbing idea that he might indeed come home.

Ivy took a tin of broken biscuits from the shelf under the table. She took off the lid and proffered the contents.

"Have a bickie," she invited and at the same time put the sugar basin back on the table.

Daisy took several pieces of biscuit and popped them into her mouth one after another. One piece got stuck in the top of her dentures and she had a bad moment getting it off her plate with her tongue. "Ta," she said.

"You married?" asked Daisy after she had downed the biscuits.

"Yes. Married to a comic. I used to be on the stage. He left me years ago with a couple of kids to feed. Me Mam looked after them while I was dancing — choruses — in panto mostly. Then it got hard to find jobs — they like you thin as a rake so I began to take fellas home." The merry look went out of her face for a minute and she looked old and haggard. "Me boy's in the army — he sends me an allotment — a few shillings, bless 'im. Gloria, me girl, went to London. She writes at Christmas. Says she's workin'."

The conversation passed to Daisy's progeny; and Ivy was fascinated as a few sorrows over children were shared, including a tear shed for James doing time for dispatching a bloody Prottie, for little Michael, killed by a brewer's dray, and for Tommy who had coughed himself to death and even for John who had run away to sea so long ago that it was doubtful if his mother could have recognised him if he ever returned. The high drama of James's and Lizzie Ann's arrests was gone over to their mutual enjoyment.

Daisy was just beginning to feel that she had found a friend, and the tin alarm clock on the mantelpiece said ten past ten, when suddenly there was the sound of the outside door being opened and the clomp of heavy feet on the stairs. Raucous, drunken voices shouted bawdy jokes to each other, and one loud male voice bayed, "Hey, Ivy, hey Doris. Open up there. Your loved ones has come in from the rain."

TWENTY-THREE

In a matter of seconds, after opening the door and seeing the jocular crowd coming up the stairs, Daisy had been offered and had accepted Ivy's late sister's room next door, a noisome den still cluttered with the dead woman's belongings. She snatched up her shawl and apron from in front of Ivy's gas fire and followed her hostess into the dark room.

Ivy lit the gas jet and then the gas fire. "There you are," she said, as Daisy blinked in the doorway at the sudden light. "Landlord'll never know. Friend of mine has rented it as of next week." She gave Daisy a playful push in the stomach, as she turned back into the hall, where the first men were shaking the rain off their bare heads like collie dogs. One of them slapped a bewildered Daisy on the bottom, and this had the effect of propelling her into the room; the man followed so closely that she could feel his breath on her bare neck. Ivy slipped off her wrapper and wriggled her pink satin-covered bottom. "Come on, lads, it's five bob. Who's first?"

A bear of a man clasped her round the waist from the rear, and they danced a conga into her room. The door was left ajar.

A shaken Daisy took the first tram home in the morning. She was bruised, bitten and in pain. She felt filthy and degraded. All the buttons were off her blouse, which had been nearly torn off her back. Her first client, a man so big and so drunk that she had been afraid of him, had demanded that she strip and she had hastily abandoned even her shift.

For the first time she learned what her trade could really be like.

" 'Twas a judgement in the eyes of God," she thought bitterly.

Her mind had got muzzy as one drunk after another came slinking through the half shut door. Only one clear thought had stayed with her, that for Nellie's sake she must collect the money first. This she had done, shoving the precious shillings under the mattress as each man gave it to her. How many men could one take, she wondered? A goodly number judging by the happy shouts and yelps from Ivy's room. Must have been a bloody ship's crew, she told herself resentfully.

The two girls upstairs had opened their doors and screeched over the banisters, and this had led to a clatter of boots climbing to the upper floor amid cheerful whoops from the steaming mob packed into the tiny hall and staircase.

"How could men be such beasts?" Daisy asked herself as the tram trundled homeward. Now she had seen it all, for sure. She had been pushed around by men all her life, but never had she felt so helpless before them as she had done on this obscene night. Near to tears, she tried to console herself with the thought of the clinking contents of her skirt pocket. With that much money added to her present hoard she need not go out for several nights.

Sore discomfort had rapidly become sharp pain and she had begun to wonder wildly how she could shut out the still clamouring men, who leaned against the door jamb shouting encouragement to whoever was with her. She finally rebelled when a young stalwart demanded a service of her which she felt was unnatural. Horrified fury took possession of her, and the surprised youngster found himself propelled back through the door by a stark naked amazon mouthing language that surprised even him. He stumbled against the next man in the queue and for a second they were out of the doorway. Daisy slammed the door on them and shot the bolts at the top and bottom. Since she had already taken the money of her last would-be client, this led to a lot of bad language in return and much hammering on the old oak panels.

Terrified, Daisy glanced around her. She snatched up her skirt and petticoats and struggled into them, pushed her arms into her buttonless blouse, scooped up the money from between the mattresses and stuffed it, with her stockings, into her skirt pocket. With her shawl, apron and shoes tight under one arm, she ran to the window.

"Hi, open up," came a chorus from beyond the door.

146

"Holy Angels, preserve me," sobbed Daisy, as she flung back the tattered curtains to reveal a big sash window.

She turned the latch and with one hand tried to heave open the long unused bottom half. It would not budge. She put down her shoes and shawl and tried with two hands. There was a lot of laughter from the hallway and a heavy thud suggested that someone had put his shoulder to the door in an effort to break it.

"Holy Mary, pray for me now," implored Daisy as she tugged at the recalcitrant window. "Let there be a fire escape! Let there be one!"

The window gave suddenly and the rain blew cold on Daisy's flushed face. She leaned out.

There was an iron veranda running across both her window and that of Ivy's room. She could not see in the darkness whether it had a staircase at the end of it or whether it was enclosed. She crawled out and cautiously let her weight on to it. It shook uneasily but it held. She leaned back in and rescued her shoes, apron and shawl and then shut the window after her.

The wet iron hurt her feet and she put down her shoes and eased her feet into them. Then she flung her shawl over her hair which was tumbling down her back and wrapped it close across her naked chest. She put a shaky hand on the veranda railing and edged slowly along the complaining wrought iron beneath her feet.

She was numb with fear and sudden cold.

A shaft of light from between Ivy's curtains lay across her path. Beyond that she could see nothing. She paused at the light to peer ahead and then turned to look through the chink in the curtains into Ivy's room. She caught a horrifying glimpse of Ivy standing stark naked astride a tin bowl. She was swaying like a dervish and flourishing an old towel round her head. Daisy could clearly hear her shout, "Come on, lads! Ivy's waiting!"

Daisy moaned under her breath and put out an exploratory toe past the line of light. The veranda appeared to continue, so she eased herself past Ivy's window. She put out her foot again and there was nothing under it. Daisy froze.

Afraid of what might be ahead and even more fearful of what lay behind her, she quivered with indecision.

"Perhaps I'm turned the wrong way," she managed to think. "Staircase could be from the other end."

Desperately she peered ahead of her. Below her she saw the sudden flash of a torch. The constable on the beat must be checking the back of the building, she decided. From the direction in which the torch moved it appeared that there was an open courtyard below instead of the usual tiny back yard. The light ran up the wall and illuminated for a second an iron staircase ahead of her. She nearly fainted with relief.

She waited until the torchlight had moved away and then edged herself carefully down the welcome stairs.

Careless of rats, she ran like an alley cat along the side of the building until she found an entry which led into a deserted side street. From there she found her way into Lime Street which was still quite busy, despite the rain. She huddled for a minute or two in the doorway of the Empire Theatre, until the sound of shunting in the nearby railway station penetrated her numbed brain. The familiar noise comforted her a little and reminded her that the station had a ladies' lavatory where she might tidy herself. She sneaked up the side of the station and darted quickly through the Victorian archway which led into the platform nearest the waiting rooms. She ran the last few yards, at the same time hunting through her pockets for a penny. For a dreadful second she thought that she had only silver, then her fingers closed over one at the bottom of her pocket. She thrust the coin into the slot on a lavatory door and nipped inside. Quickly she shot the bolt, despite the fact that both station and waiting room appeared deserted.

She leaned, panting and shivering, against the door for a long time. Then she combed her hair and rebraided it. She put on her blouse and tied the front of it together. Since nobody else seemed to be using the cloakroom, and she feared that she had missed the last tram to Dingle, she sat down on the edge of the lavatory until, through her dozing, she heard the first morning tram rumble by.

At home, she found an anxious Agnes, who had taken over the care of Nellie from George. It did not take much persuasion to get her to go home, and Daisy sank thankfully into her own armchair before the roaring fire which Agnes had kept up for her. Nellie was sleeping well, Agnes had assured her.

Daisy started to shake again from head to foot. She put her head down on her knees to stop herself fainting and let the tears come in floods.

148

TWENTY-FOUR

A lorry rumbling along the street warned Daisy that morning had come. She raised her head and shook it, as if to rid herself of some of her wretchedness.

"Smarten up, Daise," she told herself, "Nell will be awake soon — and what'll she think if she sees you lookin' like a wet week?"

She was painfully sore, and she ached from head to foot. But she forced herself to remake the fire, which had fallen low while she wept, and to put a kettle of water on to boil. When the water was hot she took it into the scullery and washed herself.

Never in her life had she had such a desire to scrub herself all over; the scullery was so intensely cold, however, that she compromised by washing her face and those parts of herself which were most uncomfortable. Afterwards she took out her teeth and rinsed her mouth again and again. She was covered with goose pimples by the time she returned to the living-room, to stand by the fire and dress herself in her two petticoats. With needle and thread garnered from the crowded mantelpiece and some buttons taken out of a spoutless teapot she managed to make her blouse useable again. From a dresser drawer she took out one of her precious pairs of bloomers — which she never wore during her trips down town. Their softness was comforting.

"When t' pedlar comes, I'll buy meself a couple of blouses," she muttered with a watery sniff.

A piece of broken mirror was propped up on the scullery window and she lifted it down in order to examine herself. She was marked quite badly round the neck and her eyes were red-rimmed from crying.

If Nellie or anybody sees them hickies the game's up, she decided. She mentally sorted through the little house for something to put round her neck. "Pretend I got a sore throat," she advised herself. "Ee, I know, now."

She went to the dresser and took out two old stockings and carefully wound these round her neck, pinning them in place with a safety pin.

She put the kettle on again for tea and spread her shawl and skirt over the oven door to dry. Though she was swaying with fatigue, tea and a bit of bread and margarine seemed urgent necessities before she slept. She hoped passionately that Nellie would sleep late.

After eating, she dragged her humiliated, weary body on to her bed in the landing room, heaved over herself the collection of old coats which formed her covering and fell into a deep sleep.

She was awakened by Nellie, who had pottered out of her room feeling stronger than she had done for some time. A warm bed and a warm supper had given her sounder sleep than she had known for weeks.

"You was sleeping the sleep o' the dead," chuckled Nellie. "What you doing with the stocking round your neck?"

Daisy heaved herself over to face the questioner and forced herself into consciousness. Every bone in her body cried out for more rest. Nellie, however, had to be cared for, so slowly she got herself up on to her feet. She was very cold.

"How are you, Nell, luv?" She rubbed her arms to restore their warmth. "Me throat seemed sore last night — that's why I put the stockings round it."

"Oh, I'm feelin' much better." Nellie looked concernedly at Daisy. "You must have got chilled. Your eyes is all red and your lips is swollen."

"Och, I'm not so bad." She grinned at her friend. "Now you get back into bed till I get the fire going again or you'll be the one with a chill. I'll bring you some breakfast. Did doctor say you should stay in bed all the time?"

"No. Said I could do what I fancied. To keep warm but have the window open. He's coming here today, he said, anyways."

"The devil he did. I'd better hurry up."

She got Nellie back into bed and crawled downstairs. The doctor would not be the only visitor, she was sure. The place would be like a bloody tram terminus, she told herself. "I'll need the patience of a martyred saint."

Daisy's forecast proved accurate. Visitors trickled in and out all day. Sickness held a morbid fascination for the community, and, when the doctor arrived, the bedroom was already overcrowded with three beshawled, high-smelling visitors sitting cawing round the bed like carrion crows. The invalid was looking exhausted, and the doctor instructed that there should be only one visitor at a time and only when Nellie felt like receiving them.

He had been shocked at the miserable state of the living-room through which he had passed, and sickened by the sight of the landing bedroom. Nellie's bedroom came as a welcome surprise; it was basically clean and comfortable, and the fire gave plenty of warmth to the tiny room.

Seeing that Daisy seemed quite intelligent, he spent some time teaching her how to manage Nellie's illness. It was apparent to him that she was herself, for some reason, exhausted, and he warned her to watch her own health.

"Och, I'm fine," Daisy assured him, "except for a bit of a sore throat."

Iddy Joey came to see his mother after school. He stood uneasily by her bed, shifting from one foot to another.

"When you comin' home, Mam?" he asked her.

Nellie smiled adoringly at him. "Soon," she assured him. "You missin' your old Mam?"

"Yep." He went to stand by the fire to warm his backside.

"Yer Dad make your breakfast all right?"

Yes, the ould fella had made his breakfast O.K. and they had had chips for lunch and a boiled egg for tea. Dad would be over later. Yes, he had been to school, and the teacher had given him a pair of socks from the lost and found box. He exhibited these to his mother — they did not match but, yes, they were warm.

When his mother ran out of questions and leaned back on her pillow, he waited for a moment and then edged to the door.

"Ta-ra, Mam."

"Ta-ra, luv." Nellie longed to call him back and kiss him but dared not. To pass T.B. to Joey would be the end, she told herself sadly.

Relieved that his visiting duties were over, Joey bounced down the stairs. Moggie saw him coming, and retreated under the table, his back arched. Joey went down on his knees and crept towards him, growling menacingly as he advanced. The cat spat as it found itself cornered. Joey seized its swishing tail and dragged the animal out from its retreat. The maddened cat scratched him soundly, as he swung it exultantly into the air. Joey howled in sudden pain, and let go. The cat fled into the scullery.

Nellie called out in fright at Joey's sharp cry, and Daisy sped in from the back yard.

"What ails you?"

Wailing, Joey exhibited a thin wrist with a long scratch welling with blood.

"Och, you stupid git." Daisy bent down, picked the child up and carried him lovingly to the kitchen tap to have his wound washed. Then she gave him a penny and sent him up to Mrs. Donnelly's to buy a lollipop.

The postman brought another card from Mike. Daisy was so busy that she just stuck it up against the clock and forgot about it.

Maureen Mary, anxious about her gentle aunt, arrived in the afternoon. When she let herself in, she found her mother boiling eggs. She greeted her daughter absently.

As Maureen Mary eased off her blue felt hat, she noticed the brightly coloured post card, and picked it up and read it.

"Our Dad's coming home! You never told me!"

Daisy was throwing the eggshells into the fire and raking them into the coals to drown the awful odour they made. For a moment, she stood transfixed as the blood ebbed from her face. Mike home? Saints in Heaven preserve us! She felt Mike's belt across her back as surely as if she had actually been struck; she felt his boot hit her bottom as he kicked her into the street.

Her hand shook as, with her back still turned to Maureen Mary, she dropped the shelled eggs into a cup and broke them up with a spoon. "Yes, isn't it grand?" she finally managed to gasp.

Maureen Mary stared at her mother's broad back. "You sound proper queer. Aren't you glad?"

" 'Course, I am. It's me throat being sore that makes me sound funny." She hastily put down her spoon and caressed her stocking-wrapped neck. Then she balanced a couple of slices of bread and margarine on top of the cup, picked up the salt packet and tucked it under her arm, took up a clean spoon and the cup, and thus laden, turned and said to her daughter, "I'll just take these up to your Anty Nell. I'll be back in a tick. You could go up and sit with her while she eats."

Maureen Mary nodded agreement, as she hung her coat on the back of the front door, and then watched her mother slowly climb the stairs. She seemed to find the climb hard, and Maureen Mary thought uneasily that her mother did not seem to be her usual brisk self. A twinge of fear went through her, as she realized that the elder woman might find the care of yet another invalid too much for her health. Even mothers were not indestructible.

Daisy herself was having the greatest difficulty in avoiding falling into hysterics.

"I'm demolished," she wheezed, as she stopped in the landing bedroom to catch her breath. "What in the Name of God am I going to do?"

TWENTY-FIVE

Scarified at the news of Mike's return, Daisy sought with flustered fingers through her collection of old newspapers for the latest copy she had of the *Liverpool Echo*. Did the dreaded words "home soon" mean a month hence or next week or tomorrow?

A Shipping List in a copy of the paper which was two days old did not list the *Heart of Salford* under 'Vessels Due Soon.' With a sigh of relief, Daisy flung the paper on to the floor and sank down into her easy chair. Slowly the beat of her heart returned to normal. Jaysus Christ! What a predicament.

Mike would have money in his pocket when he returned. But most of it would end up in the Ragged Bear in payment for rounds of drinks for his friends. He would never give a thought to the cost of nursing an invalid, though certainly he would make no objection to Nellie's being cared for in his home.

"And you can tell him forever and he won't hear," grumbled Daisy sourly to herself, as she leaned forward to stir the contents of a large blackened saucepan on the back of the fire. She was making stew with plenty of meat in it for Nellie and herself. And meat cost money.

She wondered if Mike would swallow the story of the bottle factory and, after much vacillation and rubbing of her tired face with her hands, she decided that he might do so.

But she must have a room, like Ivy. She'd be safer from chance encounters with Mike's friends, if she had her regulars in a room.

When she thought about the room next to Ivy's she shuddered. Not even for Nellie could she again go through the nightmare of the previous evening. Men by ones and twos she could manage; a horde like last night's was a terrible thing to happen to a law-abiding woman. It had been like the tales that Agnes's husband, Joe, had told them about the Germans in Belgium during the war, awful tales of kitchen tables dragged into the streets and girls held down on them and raped until they died. Them bleeding Jerries had a lot to answer for. Her mind wandered back to the day during the war when she had helped to smash up a German's butcher shop in Parkee Lanee. Bloody Bosche. She and the kids had eaten meat every day for a week after that.

The sound of the chair scraping across the bedroom floor, as Maureen rose, brought her back to the present with a jolt. Where could she find a room? A place where the landlord would turn a blind eye? A place close to the Ball and Chain.

Hands clasped between her knees, she rocked herself backwards and forwards, while she endeavoured frantically to find an answer. Finally, as Maureen Mary, came slowly back down the stairs, she decided that she had no one to turn to for advice except Ivy.

With nothing on but a faded wrapper, a very bleary-eyed Ivy answered Daisy's knock. Her breath smelled strongly of spirits and her room stank, even to Daisy's tolerant nose.

Ivy groaned and swayed on her feet, as she let her new-found friend in. "Ugh, I feel like somethin' the cat brought in. How's yourself?"

"I'd hate to tell yez," responded Daisy. She sat down gingerly on a chair by the roaring gas fire.

"What happened to you last night? T'door was bolted when I come in atterwards, but you didn't answer."

"Couldn't stand any more," confessed Daisy, and she went on to explain her escape along the veranda.

Ivy took a tin teapot off the gas stove and poured out two cups of the boiling liquid, and while they sipped tea together Daisy broached the subject of a room.

Ivy eyed her silently. It was bad enough having two younger girls upstairs and a dear friend moving in next door very shortly.

Daisy sensed Ivy's reluctance to have her nearby, and she said conciliatorily, "We take different kinds — most of mine is young boys — just occasionally an older man. You must get those as likes a more Frenchy type."

155

The flattering suggestion that she was more sophisticated made Ivy unbend slightly. She tucked her wrapper more modestly over her thighs. "Trouble is, I don't know anywhere. Not many houses round here — mostly businesses."

Daisy felt a qualm of anxiety that this last resort might fail her, while Ivy hummed and haaed and sipped her tea.

She finally remembered a tailor who had, until recently, lived over his shop. He had now moved out of this apartment, while retaining the shop beneath.

The tailor was still working in the back of his shop, sitting cross-legged on his table and sewing button holes. It was some time before he answered Daisy's persistent rattle at his door.

He opened the door a mere slit.

"I'm closed," he snapped. Then, when he saw that a shawl woman stood on his step, he snarled, "What do you want?"

"Ivy sent me — about the rooms over your shop."

A thin, lascivious grin split a cadaverous face. "Come in, Missus," he invited oilily.

At first he demanded a shilling for every man she brought in, but Daisy's language at this suggestion was so explicit that he paled. "What I want a room for is me own business and none o' yours," she roared. "What a way to talk to a plain, decent woman what keeps herself to herself." She looked around his workroom so fiercely that he feared for a moment that she might begin to ransack it.

Finally, a bargain was struck. Daisy could have the room at the top of the side stairs and the use of the bathroom. The other two rooms he wanted as storage and workrooms.

A rent book was found. Old entries were torn out and Daisy's name and the first week's rent were entered in it.

After she had handed over the money, she realised she had not yet seen the room and demanded to do so.

Grumbling, the tailor led her out of his shop, locked the front door, and then unlocked the side door and took her up a narrow, dark staircase.

"T' room's got furniture in it," he said. "Stuff I didn't want to put in me new house." He unlocked the door, took a box of matches out of his pocket, struck a match and lit a single gas light near the fireplace. He then bent down and lit a gas fire.

Daisy looked around primly. To her, the place was princely. There was a double bed with a mattress, a dressing-table, a table with two chairs tucked under it, and a small easy chair in a corner. There were cheap chintz curtains over the window, and clean, flowered linoleum covered the floor. A door on the opposite wall indicated that there was a storage cupboard.

She sniffed. "I suppose it'll do," she said.

The bathroom was next door. It was a small Victorian washroom with a single cold water tap, a wash basin and a cracked lavatory.

"Lock up everything when you go out," the tailor instructed, "And any damage you got to put right, understand?"

"Och, you're getting enough rent to cover the whole army marchin' through," replied Daisy. "What you worrying about?"

"Friends of Ivy has lots o' visitors," responded the tailor grimly.

Daisy had a strong desire to lift a fist and clout him down the stairs. She restrained herself, however, with the thought that the place was ideally isolated once the little shops in the street closed; and if she allowed that the constable on the beat might try the door once in the night, she was likely to be undisturbed. She decided that she must at all costs remember to lock the outside door when a man was with her; otherwise the constable might enter to check for intruders.

"I'll move in tomorrer," she told her hunched, ungainly landlord, as he put his matches back into his waistcoat pocket.

He looked the big, comely woman up and down in the gleam of light from the hallway and decided he might have a go himself one day. He contented himself for the moment by saying, "I'm gonna get a gas meter put in."

Daisy had taken for granted that somewhere in the room there was already a meter into which she would have to feed pennies to obtain gas, so she just nodded, and turned away.

He watched her as, with black skirts swaying, she walked smartly up the street. With a bit of luck, he would set the gas meter in such a way that he would make as much out of that as out of the rent itself. That would teach her.

157

TWENTY- SIX

The wind was wailing through the streets, carrying an occasional flake of snow with it, so Daisy decided to go home. "I'll tell George and Nell there was no work for me tonight," she decided, as she clambered laboriously on to a tram. Mother of Christ, every bone in her body ached and her eyelids dropped with lack of sleep. She sighed heavily, as she rocked with the motion of the vehicle and watched the street lamps flick by.

At home, she found George asleep beside his wife, and little Joey was dozing in the easy chair by a fading living-room fire.

George looked like a stuck pig, with his mouth wide open. But Nellie admonished her, "Himself is proper tired. Let him sleep."

"There was no work for me tonight," Daisy yawned. "I'll make us all some supper and we'll get into bed."

As she trailed up and downstairs, distributing bread, cheese and tea to her guests, she worried about where she could hide her newly-acquired rent book and also her precious hoard of savings. George would be in most nights, and iddy Joey was as nosy as a hungry cur, not to mention the possibility that sharp, observant Meg might arrive.

"And there'll be all the old biddies from round about come avisiting, every bloody cousin we've got, and Christ knows who," she muttered. "I got to get that money out of Nellie's room yet — it ain't safe there."

She thought fleetingly of opening a banking account. Then, despite her fatigue, she could not help laughing at the idea. Even if she was allowed by the commissionaire to walk in, she would face a supercilious probing of her business; someone dressed in a shawl and boots did not fit in with gilt, marble and mahogany. She decided she couldn't face it.

"I can put rent book under me mattress in me new room," she concluded. "Money's a different matter."

If Mike discovered what she was doing, he would go through the roof with the force of the self-righteous explosion that would ensue. But, far worse than that, he would almost certainly demand the money she had made.

The problem was still not resolved when, the next evening, she toiled up the narrow, dark staircase to her new room. She knew now what kind of a trade she wished to carry on and she was anxious that the room look pleasant for those who wanted to stay an hour or so. She was laden with a bedspread and bedding, a fringed cloth for the table and a flowered china candlestick and candles.

She arranged the bed, and afterwards pulled one of the chairs out and sat down. She looked round her domain with satisfaction. The night at Ivy's had at least paid for all that she had bought.

The sound of her own breathing seemed unnaturally loud in the still room. Gradually the unearthly quietness of the place became overwhelming, and she jumped when a piece of furniture gave a sudden creak. She found herself listening with abnormal intensity. But through the thick walls no sound of distant traffic penetrated, no human voice or footstep came from the deserted street below.

She looked slowly round the room as if she expected that someone or something would surely spring at her. But the sparse furniture remained in its place, the cupboard door remained shut.

She shuddered.

"Ee, I could be mairdered and lie here for a week before anybody found me — and they wouldn't know who I was when they did find me," she said out loud, and the sound of her own voice made her jump.

Then she laughed with a hint of hysteria. "Get out and find yourself somebody to bring in, you bloody fool. Only be a bit careful, like."

She got up and shook out her skirts, smoothed her hair in front of a small mirror on the wall, and smiled with artificial gaiety at her reflection. "Get moving, Liverpool Daisy!"

TWENTY-SEVEN

When next Daisy went down to the shipping office to collect Mike's allotment, she inquired about the arrival of the *Heart of Salford*.

She was assured that the ship was indeed coming home. She should watch the "Due Soon" column in the *Echo* for the exact date of arrival.

She forgot all about Mike immediately she lifted the latch of her front door. She could hear Nellie coughing frantically.

The invalid had crawled downstairs and the effort had set off a fit of coughing. She was sitting in the easy chair with her head on her knee, when Daisy entered.

"Holy Mary!" exclaimed Daisy. "What you been doing?" She ran to Nellie and eased her back till she rested against the cushion. "Nell, luv, ah thought you'd be all right in bed till I come. You should have stayed in yer bed, dear."

The coughing began to ease, and Nellie gasped, "I was fed up — thought I'd come down for a change." She sounded fretful, not her usual patient self.

"Well, never mind," said Daisy. "I'll get a cloth and wipe your face, and then we'll have a nice cuppa tea to clear your throat."

Never argue with them as has T.B., was one of Daisy's favourite adages. They're just plain bad-tempered. She soon had Nellie in a better frame of mind, when, after a dose of medicine, she was tucked up in the easy chair, her feet on the brass fender. Over their tea, they reminisced about the funny things they had done when they were young together. Finally, the conversation turned to the man of the house.

" 'E won't want me here," said Nellie apprehensively.

"Och, never give it a thought," replied Daisy. "He'll just be thankful it isn't me Mam that's up there."

Nellie chuckled at the memory of Mike's dislike of his sharp little mother-in-law, and then as if suddenly very tired she leaned back in the chair and closed her eyes.

Daisy viewed compassionately her friend's worn face. The firelight cast shadows in the hollow cheeks and darkened the eye sockets, till Daisy felt with a sense of panic that she was already looking at a dead skull. Her stomach muscles clenched. She could not endure the thought of losing Nellie and she wondered agonisedly what more she could do to help her. Food, medicine, warmth, all these had been provided with a lavish hand. What more?

Then with sudden inspiration, she asked, "Would you like to see Father Patrick, Nell? 'Cos you can't go to church at present, like."

Nellie's eyes shot open. Their expression was one of pure terror. When your relations started to think about sending for the priest, you were a sure gonner. It was one thing to feel that you were going to die, another to be brought face to face with other people's confirmation of it. She seemed to shrink into herself and become an even smaller lump beneath her enveloping shawl.

"Am I that sick, Daise?"

"Ee, na, Nellie, luv. You're not fit to go to Mass, so I thought you might like to see him."

Last time she and Nellie had gone to Confession, Daisy had, after prevaricating her way through a garbled admission of the sin of avarice, fully expected to be struck dead by lightning bolts. But nothing had happened, and she wondered now, as she waited for Nellie's reply, if perhaps God and His Holy Mother understood better than men what dire things could happen to a woman.

Nellie clasped and unclasped her hands, which looked like misshaped, blue-veined claws. She looked around the crowded, homely room where she had spent so many youthful, contented hours with Daisy and her brothers and sisters.

"Yes," she finally sighed unhappily. "Yes, I'd better see 'im. I want to ask him to help keep an eye on iddy Joey."

A couple of days later Father Patrick came to visit. Daisy left him with the invalid so that Nellie could, if she wished, make her confession.

161

The old priest conversed with Nellie for some time and promised to visit George and iddy Joey.

"Mrs. Gallagher seems to have made you very comfortable here," he remarked.

"Oh, aye," whispered Nellie. "She's proper kind. She's a wonder. She even works Saturdays and Sundays at her job, so as to get time and a half to help pay for everything. And then she comes home and takes care o' me. She's a true friend."

Father Patrick went slowly and thoughtfully down the stairs. Sometimes the manifestation of pure, self-sacrificing human love in his poverty-stricken parish was so humbling that it blotted out the remembrance of the drunkenness, the family quarrels, the street fights, the endless petty theft, of which he was painfully aware.

He blessed a flushed, embarrassed Daisy as he went out into the street.

Daisy began to use her new room each evening. She acquired a regular client, which pleased her. He was a young labourer working on the new tunnel under the River Mersey. He came in each Friday night, after the Ball and Chain closed.

She learned the timing of the police constable on his beat, and slipped her clients in and out circumspectly, so that his attention was never particularly drawn to the door beside the tailor's shop. She paid her rent promptly and maintained a stiff-lipped silence, when the tailor jeered at her with obscene remarks, though she sometimes longed to strike him.

She bought an old alarm clock to help her with the timing of the constable's beat and the length of her clients' visits. She nearly yielded to the temptation of paying for some additional bed sheets out of her earnings. But her earnings were for Nellie's needs, for bowls, soap, towels, nightgowns.

One morning, she went to see her old antagonist, the Welfare lady.

The moment the Welfare lady saw Daisy's file she remembered how Daisy had accepted a blanket for her invalid mother's use when that lady was already dead.

Daisy, seated suitably humbly on a wooden chair beside the desk, saw her stiffen with disapproval. Undaunted, she launched into a long description of Nellie's illness and the need for extra bedding in case she haemorrhaged unexpectedly.

"Why hasn't the doctor put her in the sanatorium?"

Daisy sighed. How to explain how frightening it was to be put in a hospital? That's where you went to die, if you had no one to care for you.

She shook her head negatively. "She didn't want to go. T' doctor didn't press her, 'cos she's got me to look after her."

"Humph. Terminal, I suppose?"

Daisy went white and there was a singing in her ears. You don't say things like that about a woman's best friend.

"No," she gasped out. "She's going to get better." She wiped a genuine tear from her eye.

The Welfare lady saw the tear and her manner softened. "I'll visit you tomorrow," she promised.

When the next morning her little car drew up outside Daisy's front door and a beaming Daisy let her in, she noticed immediately the improvement in the little home. She remembered it clearly as one of the more neglected and poverty-stricken in her district. In a thousand subtle ways it indicated to her experienced eyes either a great change of heart or a great improvement in circumstances. She began to wonder suspiciously if her help was truly needed.

She looked round doubtfully, at the glowing fire, the glittering fender, the new pat of margarine on the table. The comfortable smell of kippers outweighed the usual odour of vermin, and on the clothes line stretched along the mantelpiece some white, recently washed, underwear steamed in the fire's heat.

Mrs. Gallagher had declared her income as eighteen shillings a week allotment and Nellie's part of the allowance George drew from the Public Assistance Committee, out of which she paid seven shillings' rent. The woman must be a better manager than most were.

She asked to see Nellie and, again, was agreeably surprised. By her personal standards the house was still dirty and comfortless, but in comparison with others in the district Mrs. O'Brien's bedroom, where a good fire also blazed, was much superior.

If the Welfare Lady had expected to get any information out of Nellie as to how the transformation had been achieved, she was disappointed. Not even simple Nellie would discuss with a welfare worker what money one had — one discussed only what money was needed.

Downstairs, the Welfare worker asked Daisy, "Would you be prepared to pay, say, a shilling a week towards the cost?"

Daisy looked horror-stricken. "With less'n thirty bob a week coming in, and me with a sick woman to feed?" she asked, with a dramatic flourish of a hand across her heart. The thought of having to take a shilling each week to the woman's office or, alternatively, have a voluntary worker collect it, filled her with repugnance. More bloody nosy-parkers round the place.

A week later, Daisy received with real gratitude two pairs of sheets and a fine wool blanket. The blanket was made from small, brightly coloured hand-knitted squares stitched together, and she immediately spread it over Nellie's bed.

"Aye!" Nellie exclaimed, "It's proper pretty to look at when you feel low."

Daisy took the sheets down to her room in the city.

It seemed to Daisy that she was walking a narrow tightrope and that any moment she might, from sheer fatigue, lose her balance and go spinning to the floor. What little sleep she managed to get was frequently broken by a fretful cry from Nellie, who needed help now even to use the rose-wreathed chamber pot under the bed.

And the visitors trickled into the house steadily. Even Freddie came one evening, with Maureen Mary, just before Daisy departed for work.

Daisy had not seen her son-in-law since her mother's funeral, and she greeted him with rough good humour. Maureen Mary kissed her mother and then went upstairs to see her aunt, leaving Daisy alone with Freddie for a few minutes.

He stood with his back to the fire, giving no hint that the heavy stuffiness of the room made him feel nauseated. This was his wife's mother, and he knew that her influence on Maureen Mary was so strong that the slightest upset might culminate in Maureen Mary and little Bridie finishing up in Daisy's house.

He watched Daisy arrange her plaits carefully round her ears and add a couple of hairpins to the back of her head. She looked quite graceful, standing in front of the tiny wall mirror, and he realised suddenly where Maureen Mary had got her charm from.

164

She turned and picked up her shawl from the back of a chair and flung it over her shoulders. She smiled at him a little mischievously, and then said hesitatingly, "I got to go to work. You know I'm workin', Freddie?"

"Yes."

"Well, I'm trying to save a bit." Her smile faded and she looked suddenly terribly sad, the generous mouth drooping as if she might start to cry. "It's in case our Nell dies — she hasn't got any insurance — no burial club. And I won't have her with a pauper's funeral." She bit her lower lip. "I don't know how to keep the money safe. I mean, banks aren't for the likes o' me — they'd laugh at me. And what with me husband coming home soon, and our George ... What could I do with it, Fred?"

The implied trust of the confidence made Freddie swell out his chest a little and rock himself confidently backwards and forwards on his heels. He put his hands in his trouser pockets while he considered the matter.

"Well," he replied judiciously. "The best thing would be to open a Post Office Savings account. Everybody goes to the post office." He grinned at her. "Just watch you don't lose the book."

"Aaah!" breathed Daisy. She relaxed, and some of the distress went out of her expression. "That's the gear! What would I do without you, Fred?"

She opened an account at the huge central post office, where it was practically certain that no one would recognise her. A deposit such as she made, if handed over in the local store which doubled as a post office, would have caused a sensation.

On the tram returning home, she smiled a little grimly to herself, as she felt the savings book through the thickness of her skirt. "I'll hide book in me room — with the rent book." Then she sighed heavily. All that money would have bought a lot of glasses of beer at the Ragged Bear, a lot of seats to see the pictures in the "Flea Pit", the local cinema. It was as well she could not spend much locally without drawing comment from her neighbours; otherwise, she might not have felt so strongly about saving for a funeral that she kept assuring herself would not take place. Nellie had to get better, not buried.

"Holy Angels from the Throne of Light, let her live," she muttered suddenly.

165

TWENTY-EIGHT

It was fluttery Agnes's turn to watch Nellie. She spent hour after hour of the dark winter evening sitting nervously by the sick woman's bed, gnawing her nails and muttering, "What'll I do if she dies while Daisy is out?" Every time Nellie, beset by fever, burst into incoherent speech, Agnes would half rise from her seat in panic and mutter, "Holy Mother, save us!" while she patted Nellie's shoulder to comfort her.

She was further unnerved when a strange man came to the door and asked for Daisy.

"Daisy's at work at the bottle factory," she said timidly, holding the door open only a crack.

The man sniggered unpleasantly. "Tell her Pat from the Hercy Dock came."

She nodded, and quickly shut the door.

When Daisy came home about three in the morning, she told her about the Irishman. Relief at Daisy's return overwhelmed her initial curiosity, and she failed to notice how white Daisy went at the news.

Good God and the angels! she thought frantically, I must tell those I know not to come to the house any more. She continued to worry as she and Agnes lay down together on one of the landing-room beds, since Agnes was much too scared to go home in the dark.

Both women awoke to the violent coughing of Nellie, from the front bedroom.

"Jaysus!" Daisy muttered as she stumbled out of bed and ran to help her friend.

Agnes leaned out of bed and felt frantically for the candle and matches. Not even for Nellie could she persuade herself to get out of bed without a light.

In Nellie's room the candle had gutted and only a faint glimmer from the fire gave any light. It bathed the suffering woman in a dim, unearthly glow as, half raised on her elbow, she struggled for breath.

"Bring a basin, Aggie, and a towel," shouted Daisy, "and be quick about it." She put her arm around Nellie and eased her to a more upright position. "It's all right, luv, you'll be all right in a minute," she assured Nellie, as she stroked back the straggling hair from the woman's face.

Agnes fumbled with the matches and finally got a light. She tumbled out of bed and, shielding the precious candle flame with one hand, she fled to the kitchen for the towel and basin. The spasm of coughing seemed to get worse and she could hear Nellie's mourning sobs of pain in between the coughs. Tears burst from her eyes.

"Holy Mary, Mother of God," she prayed, as she ran into the bedroom, the candle flame lying flat and threatening to go out. "Dear St. Jude, hear me."

But Nellie did not die that night. The two women struggled to ease her as she haemorrhaged, then cleaned her tenderly and propped her up as comfortably as they could. The kitchen fire was stoked up, the hot water bottle was filled and salt bags heated to ease her pain.

As she emptied the basin, Agnes vomited uncontrollably into the kitchen sink. She turned on the tap, and, while she waited for the water to cleanse the sink, she cried bitterly, partly from fear of death and partly because her bare feet were icy on the stone floor.

She had left the candle with Daisy, but the faint light of early dawn gave some small illumination. Shakily she crept back upstairs in order to be close to Daisy.

She stood shivering by the fire in her petticoats while Daisy made soft crooning sounds to Nellie and stroked her forehead.

Daisy said irritably, "Go and get your clothes on and see if you can find a boy in t' street to go up to the doctor. Tell him to come soon."

A boy on his way to fetch milk from the dairy promised to get the doctor as soon as he had finished his message. Agnes pressed twopence in his hand and told him to hurry because somebody might die if he did not. Suitably impressed, he broke into a fast jog trot, his milk can jiggling madly on its handle.

The doctor again pressed Nellie to enter hospital.

Nellie clutched at Daisy's hand with what poor strength she had and kept nodding her head negatively throughout the discussion, and Daisy said flatly, "Our Nell's not going if she don't want to. I'll get our Meg to help me, too."

Resignedly, the doctor wrote another prescription and said he would come again the next morning.

Since neither woman wanted to be left alone with Nellie, they deferred taking the prescription to the chemist, in the hope that they could find a messenger to take it in the course of the morning. Agnes made some breakfast for them all. Nellie refused everything but tea. For the most part she lay quiet, but at times her mind seemed to wander and she would make some inconsequential remark as if she was talking to George during their courtship. This set Agnes fluttering like an autumn leaf in the wind and, with almost hysterical relief, she pounced on Joey when he arrived near lunch time.

"Take this to Mr. Williamson and wait while he makes it up," she said, thrusting the prescription into his hand. Then she shouted up to Daisy, "Can you give me some money for the medicine?"

"Aye," said Daisy and came down to get her purse, to which she had transferred her earnings of the previous night.

"Your Mam isn't too well, at all," she said to Joey. "Hurry."

Joey looked fearfully up at his aunt. Without a word he took the slip of paper and ran out of the house. He was back in five minutes. "He's makin' the stuff, but he wants another half-a-crown." He was white and panting.

Daisy looked at him with compassion. "You stay with your Anty Aggie and go up to see your Ma. I'll go for the meddie." She sighed. "Then maybe Antie Aggie'll make you summat to eat."

It took her a few minutes to walk up the sloping street to the chemist. Her boot heels dragged along the pavement and her shoulders slumped under her shawl. What a night! Still, street-walking was better than working in the laundry or the sack factory, she told herself. You can have a good laugh with t' men — and they're

168

proper grateful when you give 'em a good time.

After leaving the chemist's, she went next door to the bakery and bought some fancy cakes in the hope of tempting Nellie to eat something.

Iddy Joey, looking a little less scared, was ensconced in her easy chair, a piece of bread and jam in his hand. "Cousin Winnie come to see if her Mam was still here. She says me Dad's just gone in to the Ragged Bear," he informed her. Over his hunk of bread, he glanced quickly round the room. "Where's Moggie?"

Nellie saw the gleam of the cat's eyes peeping down at the boy from the back of the mantelpiece. "Dunno," she said to him.

Blast George! She had forgotten that this was the day on which he drew his public assistance; he'd probably be too drunk to watch Nellie tonight. She pondered on the wisdom of asking Great Aunt Devlin to do a turn. But if, after her last spasm, Nellie saw her Great Aunt leaning over her, she might think she was near to death. "I'll have to ask Meg to help me tonight," she remarked dismally to Agnes, "George may be bevvied."

Agnes made a rude face. "You could send Joey up to ask her," she suggested.

Iddy Joey was surreptitiously opening the white paper bag of cakes to see what was in it. Daisy leaned over and gave his wrist a sharp slap. "Have you been up to see your Ma?"

"No," he said sulkily, as he rubbed his sore wrist.

"Well, I'll go and give her her medicine and you can come with me."

Nellie was awake and staring silently into the fire. She smiled weakly at her son, as he reluctantly sidled round the bed. "You all right, luv?" she asked tenderly.

He nodded dumbly, while he stared wide-eyed at her and rubbed the back of his leg with one boot-shod foot.

"You should be in school," she reproved him.

"No — it's some old saint's day."

She nodded. When she put out a thin hand to touch him, he retreated from her. The hurt look on her face, however, shamed him, and he came up close again and put his arm clumsily round her head, as it rested on the pillow.

Her smile was beatific. "That's my lad. Now you be a good boy and do whatever your Auntie Daise tells you."

169

Back downstairs with Agnes, he crammed a mass of bacon and potatoes into his mouth, prior to going up to ask his Auntie Meg to come.

"You can have a cake, when you've finished your bacon, luv. And another one after you been to Aunt Meg's."

Joey sighed blissfully at the thought of the cakes. Then said, "I don't want to go. I'd rather stay with you."

"Nay, you go. She'll come if you ask. She'd not refuse you."

TWENTY-NINE

On the morning of desperate Daisy's capitulation to Meg, the m.v. *Heart of Salford* slid slowly over the bar. Salt-caked and rusted, it chugged up-river and docked at the north end. It was, however, late afternoon before Mike Gallagher was finally paid off and came sauntering down the gangplank, followed closely by his friend, Peter O'Shea, trimmer. Opposite the dock entrance, the lights of a pub shone out across the damp sets of the street, as a barman flicked them on, ready for the evening trade.

"Let's have a quick one," said Mike, reluctant to leave his friend and face the re-adjustment to his bleak home and formidable wife. The blast of warm air and the bright glitter of mirrors and well-polished brass welcomed them, as they entered, and there they remained until closing time.

Meg was delighted to receive a token of surrender from Daisy, in the shape of iddy Joey begging for help. She patted the child's head and assured him she would come as soon as she had given her family their tea. She ran upstairs and ordered her whining, protesting sister-in-law, Emily, to get the children and Mr. Fogarty to bed before ten o'clock. She moved through the house like light; and slow John had to hold her against the scullery wall, while he fondled her hopefully through her skirts.

"For the love of Christ, let me be, Johnnie boy," she cried fretfully. "I got enough to do, without you botherin' me."

But he would not let her go, and swung her out of the back door and into the absolute blackness of a corner of the tiny backyard, the only private place they had ever known.

171

She responded to him, despite her hurry, and clung to him, loving him dumbly, unable to communicate with him very well except sexually.

She entered her sister's house like a gust of wind, just as Daisy was wrapping a shawl round herself, preparatory to going to work.

Daisy had on a clean apron, which she had ironed with a huge flat iron now standing on the mantelpiece, next to one of the precious china dogs. The iron was a recent purchase from Hannigan's Second Hand Furniture Emporium. Her hair was neatly combed and plaited and her face scrubbed in cold water until it was rosy. Her gold keeper earrings which her grandfather had bought her, gleamed in her ears, having been rescued after a long sojourn in the pawnbroker's shop; Meg could not remember when she had last seen them. Her black stockings were for once neatly pulled up and secured by elastic garters below her knees; on her feet were her best patent leather shoes, bought originally for little Tommy's funeral. She wiggled her feet uncomfortably, because the shoes had become tight after the soaking they had received on the night that she had met Ivy.

"Well, isn't that the gear," remarked Meg, as she swept off her shawl and circled slowly round her sister.

Daisy flushed with embarrassment, and her teeth flashed as she muttered defensively, "Well, I got to look nice for work, somehow. Proper fussy, they are." By this time she had managed to build up in her mind a world in a bottle factory, for the benefit of Nellie who was naturally interested in her friend's occupation, so this statement came out without a moment's hesitation in response to Meg's sneer.

Meg shrugged and sniffed, then went to the fire to warm her hands. "How's our Nellie tonight?"

"She isn't well at all." There was a break in Daisy's voice. "Aye, I hate to leave her." She paused, and then went on heavily, "I need the money, though — her meddie this morning cost the earth and the doctor an' all. And she gets pain, Meg — give her two spoonsful of meddie if it's real bad — and there's some salt bags in the oven to put by her side if she needs them."

Meg bit her lower lip and her voice was gentle as she replied, "Never you mind. I'll take care of her. It'll be a pleasure after old Fogarty. Is she eating?"

172

"A bit. Make her some tea."

"Where's Joey?"

"Upstairs, asleep."

Meg sat down in a straight chair and began to unlace her boots. "It wouldn't hurt your Maureen Mary to come down and give you a hand."

Daisy's face flushed. That was Meg all over. First, all kindness and light, and the next minute hitting you on a real sore spot. She controlled the retort that rose to her lips. She said carefully, "She hasn't anyone to leave Bridie with."

"Humph," grunted Meg, and dropped her boots into the hearth as if Maureen Mary was under them.

Daisy made haste to the door, lest she be provoked into saying something she would afterwards regret. "Be back about one, all being well."

"Christ!" exclaimed Meg, her round eyes wide, "That's late! How'll I get home?"

"Och, go in the morning when it's light. If they want overtime, I'll do it."

"You *are* after the money."

"And do you think as I would be going out in the middle of the night, if I didn't need it?" Daisy flipped the latch open impatiently.

"Is George up with Nellie?"

"No. He's bevvied. Joey says he's asleep in their old room." She clicked her tongue. "He gets his Public Assistance of a Thursday."

At least on the subject of George the two sisters were united in their disapproval, so Meg said, "What else would you be expecting him to do?" She wrinkled her nose in distaste.

Daisy sighed gustily. "Ta-ra," she said in farewell and slammed the door after her, remembering a fraction too late poor Nellie in the room above.

Meg ran lightly up the stairs in her stockinged feet.

The bed was rumpled by the sick woman's tossing and turning. She was muttering to herself as if she had fever.

When Meg laid her hand on her brow to check her temperature, Nellie opened her eyes and stared at her without recognition for a moment. Then she said with a faint smile, "It's our Meg. Aye, Meg, the pain is bad and I'm so hot." Her mind seemed to wander, and after a pause, she asked, "Has the baby come yet?"

The inconsequential question made Meg jump. Poor Nellie must be unhinged. She peered closely at her patient.

"Pain's real bad this time," Nellie whimpered. Her lips drew back over her gums, and she gasped. "How long do you think it'll be?" Her back arched suddenly as if she was indeed in childbirth. "Give me summat to hold."

Meg glanced quickly round the room in search of some object that Nellie might clutch to help her bear the pain. There was nothing suitable. She leaned over Nellie to straighten the bedclothes. "There, there, Nellie, luv. There's no baby; you're sick, that's all. But you lie still a mo' and I'll get the rolling-pin for yez."

Nellie seemed to understand, and Meg sped down to the scullery, where a candle burned in generous waste. Aided by its flickering light, Meg searched hastily along the cluttered shelves. Daise had more stuff on one long kitchen shelf than Meg had on half a dozen. For the love of Christ, where was the rolling-pin?

She found it between a meat tin with a good inch of fat in it and a large Quaker Oats box, and snatched it up thankfully. Then she went to the kitchen oven, hauled Moggie out and found, behind the spitting cat's resting place, a fresh, hot salt bag.

Nellie had tossed the bedding off again.

"Here, Nellie, dear, you hold this," and she thrust the rolling-pin into Nellie's hands. Then she tucked the hot bag close to Nellie's side.

Nellie clasped the pin and seemed comforted by it. It was the same pin that Daisy had held through all the births and miscarriages she had endured. She lay still, while Meg straightened the bottom sheet and smoothed the edges under the mattress. When she tucked in the side furthest from where Nellie was lying, her fingers touched something between slats and mattress. She pulled it out. It was an old wallet, and she laid it on the floor while she finished her bedmaking.

When Nellie was well wrapped up again and had swallowed a dose of medicine, she seemed more herself, and Meg asked, "Shall I put your wallet under your pillow, luv? You might forget it under the mattress."

"Eh?"

"Your wallet. Where do you want to keep it?"

Nellie smiled dimly. "I don't have no wallet. I got a little purse

174

at home. I didn't bring it 'cos there's nothin' in it." She gave a little laugh which hurt her, and she winced and closed her eyes.

"Must be one o' Mike's old ones or one o' Daisy's," Meg said. She took it close to the candle on the mantelpiece and idly opened it. She ran her fingers round its compartments. There was no money in it. There was, however, a card in it — a kind of identity card. She held it up to the candle flame so that she could read it. It was a seaman's card, made out in the name of a Liberian shipping company; and it carried the photograph of a middle-aged man. A signature identified him as Thomas Ward. She turned the card over in her hand. She was mystified.

Nellie's eyes were closed. The medicine and the warmth seemed to have soothed her, so Meg tiptoed from the room. In the landing bedroom Joey snuffled and turned over. Meg threw an old coat lying on the floor over his shoulders.

Downstairs, she pulled the easy chair up to the fireplace and sat down. Very thoughtfully, she opened the wallet again. Further exploration yielded three receipts, which she glanced at without much interest, and two photographs. One photo was of a fat woman sitting in a deck chair on a beach; the other was of a group of negroes in long, flapping costumes. She examined both pictures intently in the light of the paraffin lamp. She decided that she had never seen the woman in the picture; the picture of the negroes had palm trees in the background and she presumed that it had been taken in Liberia.

While the wind whined around the house, sometimes sending a gust down the chimney to blow puffs of smoke into the room, she toasted her toes in the hearth and thought about her find.

Had Mike or Daisy found it in the street, say? She pondered this idea and dismissed it. Who was going to push a found wallet under a mattress? It would be left lying around in the living-room.

Had Mike stolen it from another crew member? Meg nodded her head negatively at this idea. Mike would not risk a beating up from an enraged victim, who would almost certainly be bigger than Mike's miserable five foot two inches. Besides, he had not been home since Nan's death; and, as she had observed when she went to tend Nellie, the room had been done up since then, and the bed would have been stripped.

While the soot-encrusted kettle sang over the fire, she thoughtfully ran her fingers over the worn design of camels and palm trees on the outside of the wallet. She smiled grimly to herself.

Mike had been away a long time, far longer than he ever had before; and, though in Meg's opinion, he was a miserable runt of a man compared to her own John, Daisy probably missed him. She might have found herself a boy friend. Daisy had never been short of admirers when she was young, and why she had chosen to marry Mike was a mystery to Meg. Now, of course, she was old and as plump as a cottage loaf. Just that bit older than Meg that she did not have to worry about being pregnant, thought her sister savagely. Not too old to enjoy a bit of slap and tickle, though.

Meg caressed the wallet in her hand. She began to glow all over. "God give me a good vengeance," she said out loud.

THIRTY

Mike kicked his kitbag to one side of the room and dumped his tin suitcase down by it. He flung his cap on to the chest of drawers, where it landed with a rustle amid copies of the *Liverpool Echo*, which Daisy had forgotten to check over during the previous few days. He wiped his yellow-white face on his sleeve and advanced towards the fire, to rub his hands over it. He had travelled across the city on the swaying overhead railway and, on arrival at Dingle Station, his outraged stomach had rebelled and he had vomited.

"Where's Daise?" he inquired of Meg, who had hastily risen from her chair as he entered the front door. She was staring at him, as if he was a ghost, her round eyes barely able to assimilate the fact that the man she had been thinking about was suddenly standing before her.

"Workin'," she said, as she slipped the wallet hastily into her apron pocket.

"Her? What for?"

"Money, of course." Meg unexpectedly felt the need to defend her sister's absence, and she added with asperity, "She needed the money — the allotment wasn't enough after Nan died and took her pension with her."

Mike's mouth twisted sulkily. "She'd only herself to keep."

"Och, you men! She'd rent to pay and fire to keep just the same," retorted Meg. She took the teapot out of the oven, where she had been keeping it warm. "She's on night shift, according to Joey, so I don't know when she'll be home. Will you have a cup of tea? Or would you like me to make you a bite to eat?"

Mike closed his eyes. He felt sick again. "Tea'll do," he said. He

177

sat down suddenly on a kitchen chair.

She poured the tea for him and he took a slurpy gulp of the well-boiled liquid, and shuddered. "What's Daise workin' at?" he asked.

"In t' bottle factory downtown, so Agnes says."

"Why didn't she go to t' sack place? It's closer."

"Dunno. More money probably. Beggars can't be choosers. Now she's got Nell to look after, she needs money."

Nellie's illness was explained to him, and her presence and that of iddy Joey upstairs. He accepted this as a natural happening, after which silence fell.

While Mike drew out a cigarette and lit it, Meg surreptitiously slipped her feet into her boots. It was not seemly, she felt, to be observed without footwear by one's brother-in-law.

She tried to think of something to say to him. But women did not gossip much with men in her small world and nothing suggested itself, except a desire to ask him if he knew a man called Thomas Ward. She cleared her throat nervously, and this roused Mike from the warm stupor into which he had fallen.

"I'll not wait for Daisy," he announced. "I was workin' all night and we was docking today — it was a long day."

Meg jumped up, and said with relief, "I'll tell Daise you're here. Nellie is in the front room and Joey is on one of the beds in the back."

"Humph. I'll find a place."

He was soon snoring irregularly beside Joey. His booted feet, sticking out at the bottom, twitched occasionally as he dreamed.

Joey, half-wakened, assumed his father had arrived and cuddled down again, to add his modest snuffles to his uncle's stentorian performance.

Meg came up, slipping past the sleepers like a mouse, and made up the fire in Nellie's room. Daisy must be going through coal like an ocean liner, she decided.

She poked up the fire in the living-room. She was so accustomed to having too much to do that to sit for long was difficult to her. Once again she took out the wallet and fingered its worn surface. What *had* Daisy been up to? There wasn't much opportunity to be unfaithful in a place where everybody knew everybody else. Gossip went round too fast.

She was still musing over the mystery when a footsore, worn-out Daisy arrived home soon after three.

She entered slowly, dragging one foot after another, and Meg yawned and jumped up. She glanced at the clock. "My God, you're late!" she exclaimed. She sounded almost compassionate, when, after viewing Daisy's bedraggled appearance, she added, "You look real tired."

"I am, b' Jaysus. Missed the bloody tram. Had to walk." She slumped down on to the straight chair on which, earlier, Mike had sat.

"I'll make some fresh tea."

"Ta, Meg."

A spark of real gratitude went through Daisy. Thank goodness, Meg seemed willing to bury the hatchet at last. She heaved herself close to the fire, put her feet on the fender and pulled her skirts back over her knees.

This evening she had not had to walk the streets at all and she had over a pound in her skirt pocket. But sharp-eyed Meg was here. She must be careful. She pulled her black shawl up round her neck. Lord, how cold she was. If it had not been for Nellie, she would have put a shilling in the gas meter and stayed the night in her secret room.

"Mike come home," Meg informed her cheerfully, as she put a fresh kettle on the fire.

Daisy swivelled round on her wooden chair as if she had been struck.

Meg looked up from ladling more tea into the pot. Her sister's face had drained to an unearthly white, except for the burn mottles on either cheek. She stared at Meg, her mouth agape.

Meg stood with a teaspoonful of tea poised over the pot and stared back at Daisy's horrified expression.

"What's up?" she asked. "Wasn't you expectin' him?"

Daisy's bosom heaved as she sought for breath to enable her to answer Meg. Her terror was so great that the words would not come.

The tea spilled from the overfilled spoon. Meg looked down at the fallen leaves and swore. She hastily dropped the remaining leaves into the pot.

The diversion gave Daisy a moment in which to control her

panting.

Meg kneeled down to brush up the dry leaves from the hearth with a piece of newspaper. "Didn't you know?" she inquired.

"No. Well, yes. He said he'd be home soon," Daisy floundered. "I didn't expect him yet, though. I forgot to watch the shipping list in the *Echo* — and them bloody shipping clerks down at the office, they never tell you nothin'. Ee, what'll I do?"

Meg sat back on her heels. "Well, I'd have thought you would have been glad after all this time." She tittered as she got up off the rag rug. "What you so upset about? He'll keep you warm at night. He's been away a long time." Her voice was heavy with innuendo.

Daisy rubbed her face wearily with her hands. "Mike?" she gasped derisively, as colour began to come back into her cheeks. "Him?" She clapped her hands down on to her knees and looked up at Meg. "Naught left by the time he comes home. Where is he?"

"Gone to bed. He's bevvied." Meg made a face. "Smelled as if he'd coughed up."

"Humph."

"I must get home meself."

Daisy was recovering from her first panic; Mike's coming home drunk put him in the wrong immediately — which was very convenient if you looked like being in trouble yourself. She said kindly to Meg, "You might as well stay till daylight. You can kip down with me. How's our Nell?"

Meg sighed, then stretched herself and yawned. She swung her arms hopelessly down to her sides.

"She's sinking, Daise, to my way of thinking."

"No, she isn't," snapped Daisy. She sniffed, and wriggled her shoulders unhappily under her shawl. "She's going to get better. I'm giving her everything so as she can, poor dear." Daisy's voice rose in protest, "She's got to get better."

"Well, I don't like the look of her at all, I don't."

"You're welcome to your opinion." Daisy leaned forward and spread her cold hands to the fire for a moment; then she took her teeth out of her mouth and slipped them into her apron pocket.

"Tush," said Meg irritably. Daisy was the most provoking bitch she had ever had to deal with. She could never agree with you for

180

more than two minutes together. And she'd taken over their mother's home without so much as a by your leave. Meg's nostrils distended and her mouth compressed. She stuffed her hands into her apron pockets and touched the wallet.

Her eyes gleamed with sudden malice. She pulled out the wallet and sidled towards her unsuspecting sister, who was trying to fight down a fear that Meg was right about Nellie being close to dying.

"I found this, Missus, while I was making Nellie's bed — and I'm wondering who is Tom Ward."

Daisy turned from contemplation of the fire to look at Meg's face, and did not at first notice what she had drawn out of her pocket. Her own expression showed genuine bewilderment.

"Tom Ward?" she queried, as she considered the name. "I don't know no Tom Ward."

Meg thrust the wallet under her nose. "This!"

Slowly Daisy's deep-set eyes widened until Meg thought they would pop out of their sockets. For the second time, her face drained of blood. She flung one hand dramatically across her heart. "Saints in Heaven, save us!" she cried hysterically, and fainted.

The sudden slackening of her buxom body made her roll off her wooden chair and on to the rag hearth rug. She struck her head against the brass fender as she slipped. She lay still, her shawl flung back from her slack flesh.

Meg dropped the wallet and flung herself on her knees beside Daisy.

"Daise!" she cried. "Daise, I didn't mean nothing. Daise!"

Meg tried to lift her sister but the weight was too great for her. She slipped her skinny arm round Daisy's neck and held her lolling head close to her chest. She looked down appalled at the white face with the sharp red mark on the forehead where Daisy had hit herself on the fender.

Frantically Meg patted the icy cheeks. There was no response. Daisy, already exhausted, had been terrified out of her wits and was also partially stunned by the blow she had received.

"Holy angels, help me," pleaded Meg desperately.

She laid her sister's head carefully down on the rug again. She leaned over and undid the buttons of her blouse, with the idea of loosening her brassiere or any other tight garment she might be wearing underneath; it would help her to breathe, she reasoned.

181

But Daisy had only a shift on underneath. It had been partially ripped down the front and the marks on the heavy, creamy white breasts made Meg lean back on her heels with a soft whistle. So Tom Ward did exist — and he was the mauling kind, she thought grimly, judging by the savage marks. Heaven help Daisy if Mike saw those. Though Mike was small and easy-going, Meg had seen him wield a belt with surprising viciousness; he might find consolation among his shipmates or with women ashore, but he would not tolerate his wife straying, that was certain. Very carefully Meg turned her sister's head so that she could look at her neck. Even in the poor light of the paraffin lamp she could see that she had been marked there, too, though the scars were only faint and were nearly healed.

Very thoughtfully, Meg began to chafe Daisy's hands and call her back to consciousness.

"What's up, Meg?" The whispering voice from the top of the stairs nearly caused Meg to faint, too.

Meg whipped Daisy's shawl over her bare chest.

"Aye, Nell," she protested, looking upwards at the dark staircase. "You didn't ought to be out of bed. It's naught. Daisy's fainted, that's all. She'll come round in a minute, don't worry. You get back into bed. I'll be up in a minute to see yez."

The faint shadow of her sister-in-law's nightgown fluttered; and, as if she had not heard Meg, Nellie sat down on the top stair and slowly and carefully began to ease herself down the stairs. One thin hand moved slowly down from one baluster to the next, as she progressed; the other hand she kept pressed to her side as if to ease her pain.

"Blast!" muttered Meg. She hastily began to pat Daisy's cheeks again, while she continued to urge Nellie to return to her bed.

Nellie took no notice of her. "Poor Daisy," the invalid gasped, as she rested for a moment near the bottom of the staircase. She looked like a wispy ghost, her grey curls roughed out like a halo, one hand on the newel post, the other clutching the front of the flannel nightgown which Daisy had bought her.

Nellie closed her eyes as a spasm of pain rolled over her. Then she asked, "Is it George upstairs? You could get him to lift Daisy up."

"It's Mike up there — he's drunk."

Meg jumped to her feet. She felt for a moment like the heroine of a Hollywood film, the centre of a great drama. "I'll get some water. You go back to bed, dear."

Nellie ignored Meg's order. Balancing herself by holding on to the table and then the easy chair, she advanced shakily to the hearth rug.

Daisy stirred.

"Poor Daisy. Why did she faint? Did Mike hit her?"

"No, he come in drunk," Meg's voice floated in from the scullery where she was filling a mug with water, "He went to bed afore she come in."

"Daisy, luv." Nellie's trembling voice reached Daisy through folds of darkness which she felt too tired and too exhausted to part.

Very carefully, with the aid of a hand on the wooden chair, Nellie went down on her knees beside her friend. The world whirled around her for a moment and the pain in her side was excruciating. Tears of weakness sprang to her eyes. "Daisy, luv. Say something."

Keeping one hand on the seat of the chair, to steady herself, Nellie reached forward and ran her hand round Daisy's waxen face. There was no response. Nellie began to shake with pain and fever.

Meg hastened in with the mug of water. She, too, knelt down on the rug. She dipped her fingers in the mug and began to flick the water over Daisy's face.

Daisy felt the cold droplets trickling over her cheeks and stirred again. Faintly she could hear Nellie's heavy, laboured breathing near her.

"That's better, duck," cooed Nellie.

Meg lifted Daisy's head and forced a little water between her lips. Most of it trickled down her neck, and Meg put down the mug and mopped the wetness with the end of Daisy's shawl.

Daisy tried to raise herself on her elbow and then fell back. The weak movement was, however, enough for the shawl to fall away from her chest.

Bared for Nellie to see were the fine white breasts, now marred by a series of cruel bites and red blotches. Between the breasts was a fresh bruise, and other scars in various stages of healing were scattered on both chest and throat.

Meg held her breath, expecting an immediate outcry from Nellie. But Nellie was too heavy with drugs and too anxious about her friend's fainting to realise at that point the import of the marks;

183

and the crisis passed.

Mechanically Nellie reached over to Daisy's shawl end and folded it over her nakedness. Then she closed her eyes as she herself felt faintness stealing over her.

"Go back to bed, Nellie," implored Meg, afraid she might have a second woman collapse on the overcrowded hearth rug. "I'll get Daise round. She had to walk from town and it was too much for her."

Nellie opened her eyes and looked blearily at Meg. A tear welled from one eye. She said clearly, "Aye, she's doin' too much — an' all for me, poor dear." Then her mind seemed to wander again. She began to rock herself slowly backwards and forwards and to keen softly to herself as if Daisy were dead.

"Now, Nell, don't upset yourself. She's got a bit of colour in her cheeks now — she's coming round." Meg laid Daisy's head carefully down on the dusty rug. She got to her feet and gently lifted Nellie up. She was shocked as she felt how wasted Nellie's frame was.

With many backward glances, the invalid allowed herself to be half carried upstairs again.

Meg hastily flipped the bedclothes over Nellie and rushed back downstairs.

As Meg approached her, Daisy opened her eyes. "Where am I?" she asked, and then, as her strength returned, "What happened?"

Meg stood over Daisy, arms akimbo. "You fainted," she said shortly, fuming irritation replacing her earlier fears.

Daisy raised herself on her elbow and put her hand to her bumped head.

She remembered the wallet, and again she felt as if she would faint. She flopped back on to the rug and instinctively pulled her shawl over herself. She closed her eyes again and, while her senses swam, she tried frantically to find a likely-sounding explanation for the presence of the wallet.

Meg picked up the wallet. Her eyes were hard now, as she observed a return of more natural colour to Daisy's face. She's faking, she thought, as she lovingly rubbed her fingers over the old wallet. And now I've got you, she addressed her thoughts to Daisy, and I can make you crawl like a dog that's been kicked. I'll shut your gob for you for ever.

THIRTY-ONE

Daisy had no illusions about Meg's ability to use the finding of the wallet as a tool to discredit her, both with family and neighbours. Meg would enjoy succeeding her as the Nan.

Slowly, as her senses returned, and she felt the warmth from the fire penetrating her cold body, inspiration came to her. She wanted to laugh. She glanced at Meg through the shadow of her lashes. Meg had sat down on the easy chair and her face was creased in a thin, satisfied smile. She held the wallet in her hand.

I'll wipe that grin off your bloody face, Daisy promised herself.

"Help me up, Meg," she ordered with deceptive quietness.

Meg was startled out of her daydreams. She put the wallet down on the floor, sprang up from the chair and, making every movement very warily, she helped to raise Daisy to her feet.

Daisy flopped into the chair that Meg had vacated. Meg righted the wooden chair which had fallen over when Daisy slipped off it; she did not sit down on it, however, but watched Daisy with narrow, distrustful eyes, one hand clenching the chair back.

Daisy took her time. She rested for a moment with her head leaning against the aged upholstery. Then she bent slowly down and retrieved the wallet from the floor.

"You was showing me me wallet," she remarked in dulcet tones. "I'm sorry I fainted on yez. It was the long walk home what did it."

At the sweetness of the voice, Meg felt like taking off like a coursing greyhound. She stood poised half on her toes, unsure from which direction the attack would come. *Your* wallet!" she exclaimed, her voice pitched high with nervous strain. "It's got

185

papers belonging to a man called Tom Ward in it."

"I know. Iddy Joey found it a long time ago and gave it to me. I kept the photos and such to show to Mike. There was no money in it, so I thought I might as well keep it and put me own savings in it." With elaborate nonchalance she opened the wallet, looked surprised and ran her fingers round the various pockets.

"Where's me money? Me savings?"

"What money? There wasn't any money in it."

"Yes, there was, Missus." Daisy raised an accusing finger and stabbed at Meg with it. "What you done with it?"

A frightened cry of inquiry from Nellie above stairs was ignored by both sisters.

It was the turn of Meg's face to drain of colour.

"There wasn't any money," she declared stoutly. "You're just saying there was to make trouble." She put her hands on her hips and stuck her nose in the air defiantly.

Daisy was feeling stronger now. She got up slowly and threateningly from the chair. "Oh, yes, there was," she declared. "I got over five pound in there — in ten shilling notes," she added, to give an air of veracity to her accusation.

Meg leaned forward, so that her face was within a foot of Daisy's.

"Well, there wasn't when I found it," she retorted hotly. "You're just trying to get out of telling me how you come by that wallet." She snatched up her shawl from the back of a chair and began a retreat to the door. "Maybe iddy Joey or George knows where it is," she insinuated cunningly.

"Not they. How would they know it was under the mattress?"

As Meg retreated, Daisy advanced towards her, chin thrust out, arms swinging, until Meg was pinned against the closed front door.

"I want me money back," hissed Daisy, feeling strength surge back into her.

Upstairs, Nellie began to cough, but neither sister heeded it. They were engaged in a test which went beyond the matter of the wallet; the real dispute between them was about who would rule the family, who would be the Nan in place of their late mother.

Frightened though she was, Meg had no intention of giving up the fight. With her back against the door, she endeavoured to push her stout sister away from her.

"I haven't got your bloody money. I don't believe you had any. Lemme go."

"You calling me a liar?" Daisy raised her clenched fist to strike.

"No!" She struggled with her hands on her sister's shoulders to push her away. "Yes, I mean..."

Daisy's fist caught her on her cheek, and Meg's head swung to one side with the force of the blow. She clapped one hand to her face. "You stinking bitch!" she screamed, and kicked her sister's shins with two fast movements.

Though muffled by her thick skirt, the kicks from such heavy boots hurt; and Daisy, mouthing curses, seized Meg's bun of hair and twisted it painfully, meanwhile taking a battering on her chest from Meg's fists.

Shawls fell off and blouses burst at the armpits.

Joey woke suddenly to the sound of female combat and with a sob of dismay hid his head under the filthy bolster. Long experience had taught him not to intervene in adult disputes; you could end up being beaten yourself.

In her room, Nellie wept silently.

Daisy hauled hard on Meg's hair. It came loose from its few hairpins, and Meg clawed at her sister's face to make her lose her hold. Struggling and screaming obscenities, they staggered round the tiny room, as Meg fought to get free. With a quick lunge she gave Daisy a wicked scratch on the face.

Daisy let go, and instinctively put her hands to her face to protect herself from another quick rip. She jumped back and seized a chipped enamel plate from the crowded table. She flung it like a boomerang at Meg. It missed and crashed against the fireplace.

Meg whipped round to look for a suitable missile. Another plate zoomed over her head. She ducked towards the hearth, picked up the poker and sent it flying murderously in Daisy's direction. A tin mug flew back at her and caught her on the shoulder.

In a paroxysm of rage, Meg lifted one of the china dogs from the mantelpiece and raised it to take careful aim at Daisy.

Daisy, a chair lifted above her head, stopped dead.

"You throw that, y' divil, and I'll kill yez!" The snarl was so intense, the threat so forceful, that it penetrated through the fog of Meg's hysterical rage.

"And why not, you great fat turd?"

"It's our Bridie's and she loves it."

"No, it isn't. It was Nan's."

Meg began slowly to skirt round the easy chair, swinging the china dog maddeningly between two fingers.

"I won't stand for it!" screamed Daisy, and lunged towards her. She tripped over Mike's kitbag, stumbled and fell. Sprawled on her stomach, she pounded the ancient flag stones with her fists. "I won't stand for it! I won't! I'll tell your John, I will."

The original reason for the fight was forgotten in this new threat to her grandchild's plaything. In total hysteria she flung herself over on to her back. Then pounding her heels on the floor like an outraged child and her fists flaying in a similar tattoo, she screamed again and again.

Joey whimpered in terror, and Mike snored on.

Meg ran forward, picking up her shawl as she ran.

With great care she held the dog over Daisy's face, as, with eyes close shut, Daisy yelled on. Then she dropped the prized possession on the gaping mouth. It was sufficiently heavy to bring a trickle of blood from Daisy's nose and to bruise her already sore mouth. It bounced off her and smashed on to the stone floor.

Daisy stopped in mid-stream at the sound of breakage. She rolled on to her side, saw the scattered pieces of china, and nearly blind with rage, she shot out a hand to catch Meg by the ankle as she made for the door. Meg was quicker. She grasped the latch, kicked out at her sister, opened the door and fled into the silent night.

THIRTY-TWO

Nellie lay helpless upon her bed, slow tears welling from half closed eyes. Daisy and Meg had been fighting all their lives and Nellie had regarded the spates of rage and jealousy with humorous exasperation, something to be borne patiently till they wore themselves out, like the sudden rainstorms that sometimes swept up the river to soak a pile of washing newly pegged out in the back yard. Tonight, however, the turmoil seemed almost unbearable. Her fever seemed to have left her temporarily and her senses seemed unnaturally acute; even the sound of a bug falling off the wall came to her with irritating clarity. She sobbed silently to herself.

Meg's sudden exit silenced Daisy. There is no pleasure in enacting a great drama without an audience. And with the loss of the treasured china dog, real tragedy had suddenly entered the scene. She lay still on the stone floor, her nose running with blood. Then she wiped the gory trickle with the back of her hand. The blood thus revealed to her would have caused her to faint again, if she had not still been boiling with a terrible, cold fury.

"I'd like to feed her powdered glass, I would," she hissed.

It was anger which gave her the strength to get up in response to a nervous cry from Nellie.

She staggered to the foot of the stairs.

"I'll be up in a minute, ducks," she called softly. Her breath came in gasps, and she was still raging inwardly while she ran the kitchen tap and splashed water on her face to clean the blood off it and ease the pain of her swollen lip. Every bone in her body ached, every muscle seemed to have its own peculiar pain; yet the

189

excitement of her fury gave her the energy to move swiftly.

She lit a candle and, with bodice still unbuttoned, she climbed the stairs, and passed through to Nellie's room, without so much as a glance at her inebriated spouse or iddy Joey, who was cowering under his bolster.

Nellie was lying on her bed, with the blankets flung off her, as if she had tried to get up again and had failed. She sighed with relief at the sight of Daisy.

"Daise, whatever happened between you and Meg?" Her voice, though weak, was clearer than it had been for several days.

Daisy made herself laugh. "Me and Meg got into a fight — as usual. She's got a filthy temper, as you well know." She put the candlestick down on a large paint drum which George had brought in for use as a bedside table. "It's proper late — you should be asleep, luv."

"Aye, I know. Sit down with me a bit, Daise. I got fair shook up by the noise — and I couldn't come down again. We can sleep a bit in the morning." She shivered. "And I've gone and got meself cold, like a mug, pushin' off the blankets."

Daisy nodded soberly. Her anger left her as she lifted the bedclothes and covered Nellie. She glanced hastily at the fire grate — the fire was still quite good.

"Sit with me, Daise." Nellie struggled to get one hand free; and Daisy loosened the covers so that she could do this, and then sat down on the side of the bed. Her weight was sufficient to make the bed dip; and Nellie rolled half on her side towards her.

The glow of the fire lit up Nellie's tiny hand, mis-shapen by rheumatism and work, as she lifted it to stroke Daisy's ruffled hair. The candle on the oil drum flickered and flared in the breeze from the window.

Nellie let her swollen forefinger travel down the line of Daisy's neck till it pointed to the marks on her breasts. She tried to lift her head to peer closely.

"Daise," she cried incredulously. "What you been doing? You're marked all over." Her eyes twinkled suddenly. "Mike been busy with you?"

The twinkle faded. Nellie's eyes widened as if with shock. "Mike only come home a little while back. I heard him. You won't have seen him yet — he's never stirred from his bed since he come up."

She stopped to cough and then swallowed hard. Her head fell back on the pillow. "Daise, what *have* you been up to?"

"Oh, nothin'." Daisy yawned heavily and hastily closed the blouse with its hooks and eyes. "You get all kinds of bruises when you're workin'. Movin' a lot of bloody bottles around, you get clumsy by the end of the shift."

Nellie was not convinced. She slipped her hand into Daisy's, while with apprehensive, honest eyes, she appraised Daisy's weary, scratched face and swollen lips. Daisy's hand was remarkably soft, considering she was supposed to have been washing bottles for nights on end.

"You should get to sleep," repeated Daisy. Her own fatigue was so great that she could hardly mouth the words coherently. Her muddled mind could hold only the idea that she would never forgive Meg as long as she lived for breaking the china dog; she'd learn her who was boss, if it took her till the end of time.

Nellie's feeble voice forced her to attend. Nellie was saying, "Them's love bites on you. I seen 'em when I was downstairs, but I was proper confused and I didn't think I was seeing right." She touched one deep red imprint gently with a finger. "And not one man did all that, Daise."

The shock of this deduction made Daisy jump, and Nellie felt the tremor through her friend's hand. No! O Holy Virgin say it's not true, Nellie silently implored. But with the clarity of vision sometimes granted to the dying, she looked into Daisy's deep-set eyes, as Daisy sought frantically for a feasible explanation to give to Nellie; and she saw that it was true.

"You're on the streets? It's true, isn't it, Daise? There ain't no bottle factory." The whispering voice gathered horror, "Daise! You done it for me."

"Nah. Me? What chance would I have on the streets? I'm too fat. You don't have to worry about me. You just go to sleep and sleep yourself better. I'm O.K." She turned her face away from Nellie's intent gaze and sought to release her hand, but Nellie's grasp tightened.

"Stay a bit, Daise. I got to know. I'm not long for this world, Daise, and I got a lot to say as well as a lot to know." The long sentence took her strength and she closed her eyes and winced in pain. Then she said gently, "We never had secrets from each other from the time we was little kids playing on the Cassie and watching the tide come in, now did we?"

At this recollection of their shared childhood, Daisy's eyes began to fill with tears. She said firmly, despite her desire to cry, "You ain't going to die yet. Doctor says so."

"Don't try to kid me, Daise. I know. Sometimes I think I see the Holy Angels from the Throne of Light waiting for me." She gestured towards the open window, and Daisy instinctively turned round to look out. She almost expected to see a Heavenly Host fluttering in the darkness outside.

Nellie sighed, and said, "It's just a little while now."

Daisy's lips trembled. "No," she muttered vehemently, "No!"

She flung her arms round the invalid and laid her head on her shoulder, but there was not enough room on the bed for her to lie beside Nellie and she slid to her knees on the floor. She clasped her friend to her and tears poured down her scratched face. "Don't say that, Nell."

Her face was close to Nellie's and Nellie gently touched the wet cheeks with her free hand. "Don't cry, Daise. You done so much for me . . . and I'm afraid what else you done."

Daisy sobbed softly, her face half hidden by her loosened hair in which a few white hairs glinted in the candle light. The room was silent, except for Daisy's lament, and Nellie could clearly hear Mike's steady snores from the other room. In Nellie's mind, the snores boded ill for Daisy. If Mike saw those marks he would beat the daylights out of her; not, thought Nellie cynically, because he really cared much, but he would feel that he was supposed to do something. It would express his continuing authority over his wife without much permanent damage being done; he could then forgive her magnanimously. But he would never fail to bring the matter up whenever they quarrelled again — and this would drive Daisy mad with rage.

"Daisy, lovie," she said weakly. "Listen to me, Daise. Why did you go on the streets?"

Daisy half lifted her head from Nellie's shoulder. Her voice was muffled by the folds of her friend's flannel nightgown. "I never."

"You must have done 'cos of the hickies and that."

"No, I never."

But Nellie pressed, and finally Daisy sniffed, "Well, what if I did?"

"Oh, Daise — and for my sake?"

Daisy turned her wet face towards Nellie, and wagged her head negatively. "No, not just for you."

"Well, how come?"

Daisy hung her head. She was so tired and she longed to sleep. But again Nellie asked.

"It were an accident," she said dully, and she went on to tell the story of her new teeth and how she had met the three young sailors and how lonely she had been. "I needed the money as well," she said sulkily, " 'Cos our Mam took her pension with her when she died."

"God save us," breathed Nellie, "And Meg atop of that."

"Aye, Meg. She was set on being the Nan, though she's younger'n me."

Poor Daisy, with her own children scattered or dead. It was against nature, reflected Nellie. And Maureen Mary never lifting a finger to help her mother. It was too hard.

Tenderly she stroked Daisy's hair.

"You might have caught the pox," she said suddenly.

Daisy jumped. She had not seriously considered this danger, except to heed Ivy's warning to avoid Americans. She shrugged her aching shoulders, however, while weary sobs ran through her plump body. Then she whispered sadly, "Lots o' people got it, anyway. Wouldn't be so many blind kids if it wasn't so." She paused, and then said heavily, "Suppose I could get it from Mike, anyway. He's got an eye for the girls, he has."

Nellie ignored this last remark; there was no point in adding to matrimonial strife. "The scuffer might have caught you and then in gaol you'd be for sure."

"Och, no. Just one night and the next day the beak fines you. I got enough money to pay, if I ever have to."

"That's bad enough, on top of everything else. Listen, Daise, I got to ask you something."

Nellie sighed, and a spasm of coughing which she did her best to suppress bothered her painfully for a minute or two. Daisy bestirred herself. Still on her knees, she measured out a dose of medicine into a sticky spoon and gave it to Nellie. It seemed to relieve the coughing, and Nellie continued, "Daisy, when I die will you take iddy Joey and be a mother to him?"

"Well, you're not going to die." The response was mechanical and did not carry conviction.

"Well, if I do?"

"Of course, I will. You know that."

"Would Mike mind if George came back here, too?"

"Not if I say so."

"Well, take care of him, too, Daise. He's a good carter — he knows horses — and he'll get work again one of these days and maybe stop drinking — he never drank, as you well know, until he'd been out of work so long that he lost hope. And the pain from his old wound in his back hurts real bad sometimes. Nobody'd take care of him like you would, Daise — putting hot poultices on, like."

Daisy gave a weak, affirmative nod.

"And he'll bring a bit of money into the house even if it's only a bit of relief — you must say he's a lodger, not your brother — so the Relieving Officer don't cut it down 'cos you've got money coming in from Mike. What with him and Mike together, you might be able to manage for all of you and not have to go on the streets — oh, Daise, that was proper awful." She made a clucking sound of disapproval, and then said, "And one of these days Elizabeth Ann and Jamie will finish their time and come 'ome — and they'll bring money in — and a husband or wife, maybe, to help out."

Daisy had ceased to sob. She lay almost in a coma while Nellie slowly built her a family over which to rule. Nellie was right. Even if she did not die and Daisy did not inherit her family, Elizabeth Ann would undoubtedly come home to her mother one day. And maybe Maureen Mary, too, for all her swanky husband and fancy house, if Daisy played her cards right. And little Bridie — there was still one china dog for her to play with. At the memory of the broken ornament, some of her lethargy left her and she nearly choked as her ire rose in her.

"You're a dear, Nell," she burst out passionately. "You've got to get better."

But Nellie only smiled enigmatically and continued to stroke her friend's hair. Then the immense effort she had made to soothe Daisy became too much for her. Her hand fell to her stomach and she closed her eyes. Daisy started uneasily to get to her feet.

194

Nellie's eyes shot open; they were twinkling faintly.

"And there's one thing, Daise. You know that high-necked blouse you got?"

"Yes?"

"You wear it for the next few weeks. Mike never makes love with a light on, does he?"

"Oh, no." Daisy was shocked at the idea, though many of her clients had demanded that the candle be left lit. But they were not her husband.

"Then if you're careful, he don't need to know about anything, and you'll be all right, won't you now?"

Slowly Daisy nodded agreement, and the friends smiled at each other.

THIRTY-THREE

Mike staggered out of bed the next morning. The house was still enough for him to hear Moggie scratching his flea bites, while he waited by the front door to be let out. A bit bewildered because there was not a heaving deck under his feet, he teetered downstairs as quietly as possible so that he did not wake Joey. The boy was asleep on his back, mouth wide open, a bolster clasped to him as if it were a teddy bear.

The living-room fire was out, and on the floor near the front door were scattered pieces of broken china. He unbuttoned his shirt and scratched his chest while he contemplated the scene. Moggie continued to scratch, too, as if he knew that no male of the house was going to be bothered opening a door for a cat.

Where is Daisy? Mike fretted.

Thinking that she might have gone to the privy, he went to the back door, peered into the brick-lined yard, and called, "Daise! Are you there?"

There was no reply. Moggie shot between his feet and through the door, and he cursed the impatient animal. From over the high yard wall came the sounds of the city waking up, a rumble of lorries, a clanging of trams, screeches of children on their way to school, the slow squeal of a bridge being swung across a dock.

"Bugger everything," he snarled.

He stumped back into the living-room. It felt cold and dank, and he shivered. Where was the bloody woman? What a welcome home! He was clemmed and needed his breakfast. He reckoned she must have gone out to borrow something from a neighbour or to Mrs. Donnelly's shop.

He inspected the grate. It was choked with cinders, so he sought in the hearth for the poker in order to rake it out.

There was no poker.

Bloody Jaysus! He turned to go into the kitchen to look for something else to poke out the dead fire with; and suddenly spotted the missing tool lying on the table across an opened packet of sliced bread, its point buried in a lump of margarine.

"Well, I'll be buggered," he muttered, as he went over to get it. He stood looking at its greasy point for a moment before he started to clean out the grate; but the poker offered no clue as to how it had managed to arrive in such a peculiar place. He shrugged, and then raked out the cinders. He found a bundle of wood chips lying above the oven, and the coal hod was full. He soon had a fire going and then filled the kettle and put it on to heat.

While the kettle sang, he stripped off his shirt in the scullery and washed himself under the running tap, the icy water splashing out at him from the old, soapstone sink. This cleared his head and removed the smell of vomit from him. He took a piece of towel from a nail on the back of the door, and, rubbing himself vigorously, he went back into the living-room to warm himself by the newly made blaze. He put on his shirt and slicked his thin, black hair with a pocket comb he took from his jacket pocket.

Where was Daise? He opened the front door. The street was empty. A weak sun was making the river's heaving, grey waters almost silver, and a morning mist was dissipating rapidly. He stood outside and stretched himself, thankful for the moment to be away from a boat's cramped quarters and a weary, quarrelsome crew. It would be good to have a wife to sleep with; Daisy had always been obliging in bed — bed was the only place in which he was king, he thought irritably, in a home which had always been his mother-in-law's. But where, in the Name of God, was the girl?

He turned back in, his eyes dazzled by the daylight. It seemed uncanny that Daisy should be in the room, standing over the fire warming her hands. It was as if she had materialised out of nothing, like a bloody ghost.

She looked like a ghost, too, when she glanced up at him. Her face was like paper, the eyes two black rings drawn with ink.

" 'Lo, Daise. Where you bin? I bin lookin' for yez." He advanced towards her. She shivered and held her shawl closer. I bet you've

197

been looking, she thought; you'll have but one idea now you're home.

"I was with Nell. Did Meg tell you about her?"

"She did. It was so quiet I didn't think of you being in there." He went, with a hopeful smile, to put his arms round Daisy, but she pushed him off mechanically, her thoughts elsewhere.

She shivered again and looked at him with such despair that he felt for the first time in his married life a real concern for her.

"What's to do?" he asked.

"It's Nell, Mike. You'll have to go up for the doctor." She glanced up at the clock. "Before his surgery that's at half-past nine." Her voice had a sob in it. "She's terrible ill this morning."

He drew in his breath exasperatedly. To be sent for the bloody doctor, when you haven't been with your old woman for months, even before you've had your breakfast.

He scowled.

Daisy looked at him imploringly. "I can't help it, Mike. She's dying, I think. I'd go myself, only I don't want to leave her." A great sob wracked her.

Without another word, he reached for his jacket, his face suddenly blenched at the idea of a death in his own age group.

"Where's George?"

"At their house, I think."

"Right. I won't be long. Put some tea on — I'll get George at the same time."

"Ta, Mike." Her gratitude was so apparent that he immediately forgot his impatience and felt like a hero.

While he was out, Daisy ran upstairs again, took the high-necked blouse out of the chest of drawers in Nellie's room and hastily hooked herself into it. Nellie seemed to be in a coma and was breathing with slow, shallow inhalations as if to avoid further pain.

Daisy took the dirty bowl into which Nellie had spat her life blood down to the scullery and washed it out. A reluctant iddy Joey was hauled out of bed and hurried off to school. He paused on his way out of the front door to kick a piece of the china dog cautiously with his toe. He took a bite out of the jam sandwich he was carrying, and asked, "How did you break your china dog, Anty Daise?"

Daisy had done her best not to show any distress while she

198

hastened him off to school, but now she snapped, "It got dropped last night. Now away with you. Go on, now, duck, or you'll be late." Her pain at the breakage of the ornament for a second obliterated her grief over Nellie. I'll kill that Meg; I'll kill her, she promised herself savagely. By God I will.

Joey grinned at her wickedly, took a bite from his sandwich again, slammed the door after him and ran happily up the street.

During that terrible day, Daisy held Nellie in her arms practically the whole time. The doctor, Father Patrick and a truly concerned Mike seemed to Daisy to float on the periphery of a world which held only Nellie and herself, a world which Nellie was preparing to quit. In the late afternoon, under pressure from Great Aunt Devlin, she yielded Nellie's wasted body to a distraught George. But she would not go further away than the top of the stairs, where she sat with her head on her knees in an agony of misery. Mike brought her a strong, hot cup of tea, but she would not raise her head and he set it down by her on the stairs, where it went cold. When, with rough concern, he put an arm round her shoulders, she shook it off, and he slunk away.

Around four o'clock, while iddy Joey played in the side street under the kindly eye of Mrs. Foley, his mother slipped quietly out of a life which had held little but sorrow; and Great Aunt Devlin led a weeping George out of the room.

When she saw them emerge, Daisy leapt to her feet, her hand to her mouth as if to hold back a scream.

"She's gone," announced Great Aunt Devlin.

"Oh, Mother of God, no," mourned Daisy, and she pushed past them and rushed into the bedroom.

Great Aunt Devlin had lifted the sheet up over Nellie's face, and when Daisy saw this she began to scream. She flung herself passionately on her knees beside the corpse and rocked herself backwards and forwards before it, her forehead touching the bed with the forward movement. Scream after scream came from her in hopeless hysteria.

Mrs. Foley heard the first shriek, borne by the wind, and with considerable presence of mind called iddy Joey in to share her children's tea.

Mike sat George down by the fire and let Daisy shriek on, while he poured a glass of gin out for him from a bottle proffered by

Great Aunt Devlin. Then, whistling under his breath, he ran upstairs with the quick short steps of a sailor, head tucked down
between shoulders as if traversing a narrow companionway.

"Daise," he called her firmly.

She ignored him and shrieked again.

He strode round the bed. Though smaller than her, he shovelled coal for a living and was a bundle of muscle. He seized her by
one shoulder, half swung her round and administered the hardest
slap he could on her face. It stung so sharply that she stopped
immediately, gazing up at him with appalled, black-ringed eyes,
her toothless mouth another black shadow on a white face where
the mark of his hand was already apparent in bright scarlet.

"Come on, Daisy. There's nothing you can do for her. Come
on, now. She's at peace."

She allowed herself to be helped to her feet and Mike put his
arm round her ample waist and led her downstairs. He persuaded
her to sit with George to comfort him.

While Great Aunt Devlin laid out the body, Mike, feeling the
need for more female support, called Mrs. Foley from her seat on
the front step of her house. She dispatched her eldest boy to call
the rest of Daisy's family.

Agnes arrived, streaming with tears, accompanied by her lugu-
brious-looking husband, Joe. Mike immediately sent Joe up to the
Ragged Bear for a large bottle of whisky.

John came soon afterwards. Instead of Meg, he brought with
him his eldest daughter, Mary, who was whimpering quietly to
herself.

George sat, elbows on knees, his face buried in his huge hands;
his great shoulders heaved with his stifled sobs. From time to
time, Daisy would give a little sob and lean forward to pat his
knee. He did not look up at the arrival of his relations.

John did not tell him of the fight he had just had with his sister,
Meg. She had said, "There's nowt I can do for our Nell. God rest
her soul, poor dear. And George deserves to lose her. And as for
our Daise, she can rot in hell for all I care."

Nothing would persuade her to enter Daisy's house again, she
had announced in final defiance.

Nobody wanted to tell iddy Joey, still playing with Mrs. Foley's
children in their kitchen, that he was now motherless. Finally, Daisy

said, between little, quivering sobs, "I'll tell 'im. I promised Nell I'd be a Mam to 'im." She mopped her face with her apron and sobbed more loudly into it, while the menfolk stood round uneasily. "I'll come up to your house, if you don't mind, Mrs. Foley?"

"To be sure, Mrs. Gallagher." She put her arm round Daisy's shoulders and, thus supported, Daisy went round the corner and up the street to fulfil her promise to Nellie.

Holy Mother, she wondered as she went, how long can you go without sleep? How long can you bear a pain like this?

A terrified iddy Joey, howling like a dog left out in the rain, came back to Daisy's house, clinging close to her, his head on her hip under her shawl. He was rocked on Daisy's knee by the fire until the howls became sobs, the sobs became sniffs, and he began to doze.

In response to a command from Daisy, Mike carried the little boy up to the landing bedroom and laid him on one of the beds. The child began to whimper again, so Daisy said soothingly, "I'll stay with you a bit, luv." The candle light shone on her own tear-stained face, and Joey began to cry again in real earnest.

Daisy turned to Mike. "You go down and do what you can for George, you and John together." She heaved herself on to the bed beside Joey and covered him tenderly with an old coat. "Now, luv, you're safe with your Anty Daise." She took no more notice of Mike, but put her arm protectively over the child and in a second was asleep herself.

Mike glanced sardonically at George. A fat lot of good he had ever been to Nellie. Maybe he was weeping because his conscience was hurting him at last.

But George's grief was genuine. It seemed to him that Nellie's death was the final culmination of all the terrible things that had happened to him since the first piercing agony of the shrapnel wounds he had acquired in Flanders; he had lived, but in that moment his youth, his hope, had died. Now he felt that nothing much more could happen to him. He had no work, his strength was gone from lack of exercise, all his children, except iddy Joey, were dead from the diphtheria; and Nellie, on whom he had vented his frustration, had slipped away; and he realised that with her had gone all that he knew of love and faithfulness.

THIRTY-FOUR

Exhausted in mind and body, Daisy slept until noon the next day. When she woke, the house was very quiet, and she lay for a little while, staring up at the water-stained ceiling. A spider was swinging from one of the beams, and a weak ray of sunshine turned its thread to silver. At first she felt completely emptied of feeling; and then, with painful clarity, memory of the happenings of the previous day swept back into her mind.

She turned her face into her pillow and bit at the material with toothless gums, to stem the anguish within her.

"Oh, Nell!" she mourned.

Great Aunt Devlin heard her turn over and the little cry. She floated out of Nellie's room and over to Daisy's bedside, like a black wraith.

"Ye awake, Daise?" she whispered. "Our Agnes come just now and took iddy Joey over to her house. We thought we'd let you sleep."

"Ta, Anty," Daisy said into the pillow. Holy Angels at the feet of God, care for our Nell.

"T' undertaker come," Aunt Devlin said; and to Daisy the words seemed like a kick in the side from a steel-toed boot.

"George and me fixed the funeral for tomorrer," the old sitter went on. "T' undertaker asked if there was any burial money. George didn't know. Do you know? Proper upset George was. He thinks she might have to be buried by the Parish."

Daisy turned her tear-sodden face towards her aunt. Suddenly her street-walking seemed worthwhile in every respect. She turned over and swung herself into a sitting position, as she said pridefully. "She ain't going to be buried by no Parish. I got enough money to give her a real funeral — with black plumes and flowers an' all."

Followed by Aunt Devlin's murmurs of approbation, she walked with new-found dignity down the stairs, her bootlaces making small tapping sounds on each step as she descended.

George was seated by the fire, exactly as she had left him the night before. He had, however, shared with Mike the second bed in the landing bedroom and had had enough whisky poured into him to make him sleep heavily.

He lifted his face from his hands, in response to Daisy's kindly, " 'allo, la."

" 'Lo, Daise," he responded glumly, his eyes vacant. Then, as if to avoid further conversation, he picked up a racing paper brought in by Joe and began to read it.

As Daisy went to the scullery for bacon, a frying-pan and some plates, in order to prepare a meal for him and for Great Aunt Devlin, she asked, "Where's Mike?"

"He went down to see the Second on his boat — see if there was any news about her, like. Wants to sail on her again when she's ready."

Daisy nodded, and began to fry bacon on the open fire. Presumably, iddy Joey would have his dinner with Agnes. Already her brow was acquiring the two anxious furrows across it, which seem to mark all harassed Mams with their calling.

George broke into her reverie by unexpectedly remarking, "I'll put a bob each way on Hairpin Bend in t' two-thirty tomorrow."

Daisy turned a rasher of bacon, and sniffed. She opened her mouth to tick him off about wasting money. Then she thought sadly that today she should not add to his misery. She said instead, with artificial brightness, "Do you allus bet both ways?"

"Aye. You're proper daft if you don't. Win or place is always best."

That afternoon a very quiet Daisy walked round to see the undertaker, to choose a coffin and pay a deposit. She wore with pride her patent leather shoes and her keeper earrings. Her fresh white apron and neatly plaited hair gave her an air of elegance, and the wind whipped a little colour into her face. She had washed her teeth and put them in, so that altogether the undertaker would be able to deduce that he was dealing with a woman of substance, a woman with money in the Savings Bank.

She wept copiously as she chose the coffin — one with a proper polish, she insisted, and good brass handles. Afterwards, she walked slowly back along Park Road. Her mind was beginning to work again now, and she pondered on how best to organise her new family — and cope with Mike, who was sure to be put out by the arrival of George to join his household.

She paused to look at the chocolate boxes in a newsvendor's shop window. "I'll get a box for Nell," she murmured, and then remembered that Nellie was not there any more. She stood very still, while she allowed a surge of grief in her to subside. You've just ordered the last box she'll ever need, she upbraided herself bitterly.

When a small boy pushed past her to enter the shop, she went in with him, anyway, and bought a small box of chocolates for iddy Joey and the latest racing paper for George. She blinked back her tears, as she came back into the bustling street again. George and his racing. Always bet both ways, he had said.

She continued to make her way homeward. Then suddenly she remembered her secret room. The rent was due today. What should she do about it?

She stopped in the middle of the pavement, as if transfixed. Women in shawls, old men in cloth caps, girls carrying grubby babies, pushed past her like grey waves down either side of a battleship, a tattered battered crew carrying with them the stench of poverty.

Mike was home. Could she get away with what she was doing, with him around?

He might sail again in a week, or he might be under her feet for months, unemployed like George. Two unemployed men and iddy Joey to feed, not to speak of herself, on unemployment pay or public assistance; hunger would be laying desolation between them all.

Forced to make way for a woman wheeling a pram load of coal, she moved slowly along the edge of the pavement. Good St. Margaret, help me.

Cyclists zipping along in the gutter tinged their bells. The rumble of drays and the steady clump of horses' hooves belaboured her ears. She hardly heard the noise, as she fought with her fear of Mike and struggled to come to a decision.

If a scuffer caught me, I suppose I could say I was a poor widow woman. There must be thousands of Margaret Gallaghers in Liverpool. Who would care which one I was? And the ould fella on the bench ought to have pity on a widow. That way they wouldn't find Mike, to charge him with living off the avails of prostitution.

The open window of a butcher's shop caught her eye and mechanically she moved across the pavement, to look at the chops and liver, roasts and kidneys, all neatly laid out with bits of parsley between them. Behind the display huge links of pale pink sausages hung from a bar, like delicate flower wreaths. She leaned over the meat to take a close look at them. Mike loved a bit of sausage with a black pudding, and she really fancied some herself.

Unworried by the cost, she went in and demanded two pounds of the best beef sausages and four black puddings. She watched with a satisfied smile, as the butcher dexterously whipped them into a neat, brown paper parcel. Afterwards, she teetered uncertainly on the sawdust-strewn step.

Keeping that room meant having sausages for tea, like the old song said. It meant having twopence left for a glass of beer at the Ragged Bear on a Saturday evening — or for a matinee at the cinema; when she thought of the latter, she realised that there was no Nellie to accompany her any more, and a great lump rose in her throat. She rubbed her hand across her eyes. She mustn't think of Nellie for a while — it hurt too much.

But if she worked, iddy Joey could have socks to wear and a blazing fire to come home to, and something better to eat than conney-onney butties. She could be a real mother to the poor little lad.

And what if Mike finds out? First thing is, she argued, he's not likely to find out. Nobody we know ever goes past Park Road — I would never have gone meself, if it hadn't have been for me teeth. And if he *did* by a fluke find out, he'd say everything but his prayers, till I was fed up with him. And he'd use his belt till me back was sore. And then he'd ask what I'd done with the money. And I'd tell him he'd eaten it! She laughed at the thought.

There's no reason for him to connect me with Liverpool Daisy, even if other men talk. If he ever came in search of her himself,

I'd have him nailed better'n on the cross. But I'll take care of him. I've learned a lot while he's been away in that bloody boat. I'll keep him in such a state he won't have the strength to so much as look at anybody else. She stepped out into the street, laughing so hard, that a passing chimney sweep, pushing his barrow of brushes, laughed back at her.

She ran out into the street, almost under the nose of the leader of a team pulling a wagon loaded with bales of raw cotton. Nimbly she jumped on to a tram temporarily halted by a police constable on point duty. The conductor caught her arm and heaved her up the second step.

She grinned at him. "Ta, lad." As she sat down on the bench by the back entrance, she produced two pennies from her placket pocket, and handed them to him. "Lime Street, lad. Nearest stop to the Legs o' Man."

The conductor laughed, and punched a ticket for her. "Goin' down to Lime Street to find yourself a boy friend, Ma?" he teased.

She looked up at him quite cheerfully. "Go on with yez, you cheeky bugger. I'm goin' down to pay me rent."

THREE WOMEN OF LIVERPOOL

Author's Note

The author would like to thank very much the Institute of Oceanographic Sciences, Bidston Observatory, Birkenhead, the Liverpool Record Office of the Brown, Picton and Hornby Libraries, her brothers and sister, and many friends and acquaintances for supplying her with much useful information on the subject of the great May blitz on Liverpool.

It should be pointed out that this is a novel, and the sailors' canteen, the situations and the characters are imaginary. Whatever similarity there may be of name, no reference is made or intended to any person living or dead.

In the spring of 1941, Admiral Erich Raeder wrote a memo to the Führer of the German Reich, Adolf Hitler. It said:

"An early concentrated attack on Britain is necessary, on Liverpool, for example, so that the whole nation will feel the effect."

THURSDAY 1 MAY 1941

I

He felt better, more sure of himself, now he was back in Liverpool and had a ship again. He had a new identity card safely tucked into the old wallet his father had found for him; it was surprising how naked you felt without a piece of paper to say who you were. Robert Owen, deckhand and fiancé of Emma Thomas, once more officially existed.

The clothing the Red Cross lady had found for him, to replace his lost kit, fitted well; the brown leather jacket would keep the wind out like nothing else would. He had had his faded blond hair cut in honour of his date with Emmie and he had a present for her in the brown paper carrier he was holding. His legs had stopped shaking.

Panic had, once more, struck him when, earlier that morning, he had entered the crowded Mercantile Marine office in search of a new set of papers and a new ship. At the thought of going to sea again, he had for a moment turned to jelly. He had not really walked to the huge mahogany counter; he had been nearly lifted off his damaged feet and edged towards it by the heaving, shouting mass of drunken seamen, all trying to get attention.

The clerk on the other side of the wide counter, a pimpled youth young enough to be his son, had been unexpectedly understanding of the tall, drained-looking deckhand in front of him.

"Two days on a raft, floating around in the Channel?" he had queried incredulously. "I'd have thought there was enough shipping down there that they would have spotted you in a few minutes."

215

"It's a lot o' water." Robert had tried to sound nonchalant. "Corvette out of Southampton picked me up." Again, he felt the ghastly fear that his hands would lose their grip on the raft and he would slide off and drown. "I were the only survivor." Try as he would, his voice still held a quiver.

"You were lucky."

"Aye, I suppose. Anyway, t' doctor says me feet'll be all right now. He signed me off yesterday. It were the cold water that affected 'em."

"Cold can do some rotten things to you," agreed the clerk. He chewed the end of his stub of pencil and ran his finger down a list. "There's the *Marakand* loading in No. 2 Huskisson. They're short a deckhand. How about it?"

To a fisherman who, until his last disastrous voyage, had always worked in his father's smack, one ship was as good as another, so he took the clerk's proffered fountain pen and shakily applied his signature where the boy pointed with his finger. A ship was a ship, and if he were going to marry Emmie he needed the money. If he did not go to sea, he would be called up for the army — at fourteen shillings a week. Better the devil you knew than the one that you did not.

Afterwards, until he got a better grip on himself, he stood on the handsome steps of the old Customs House, his hands in his pockets, the brown carrier bag swinging from his wrist. Beside him, legs astride, hands behind his back, stood the huge policeman who kept order amongst the tough clientele of the Mercantile Marine office. The sun lit up the long row of medal ribbons on his chest, but failed to soften a face with an expression that could have quelled an angry regimental sergeant-major. However, he said very cordially to Robert, "Nice mornin'. Ready for off agen?"

As Robert nodded affirmatively, the nervous twitch of his right eye was not lost on the constable and his expression returned to its usual grimness. Poor devil. Sent to sea again before he's fit, I'll bet me life. Just like the last war. He turned again to Robert and added, as if to offer some comfort, "You know, you're sometimes safer at sea than you are in Liverpool, these days, what with the air raids and all."

"Could be," Robert agreed, and then plunged down the steps,

216

head bent to the wind, to make his way towards the gangway of the floating dock from which the ferry boats sailed across the river Mersey. There, he would meet Emmie.

With subs as numerous as cockroaches waiting for you once you'd crossed the bar, any minute could be your last. But this was also true of the hapless civilian. Air raids had been uncomfortably frequent all winter, and it worried him deeply that Emmie lived in Toxteth, within a half a mile of the much pounded dock area.

This was no way of thinking, he told himself crossly. He began to whistle firmly and winked at a very pregnant girl with a small child wrapped in her shawl. She sniffed and turned her face away from him. He grinned. Nothing like a Merseyside woman. As pretty as they come, like his Emmie with her soft voice with its Welsh inflections — and her warm body, surprisingly flexible for a middle-aged woman.

She was waiting, her face turned towards the multitude of shipping on the glittering river. A plain navy skirt flapped against thin legs and she hugged a heavy blue cardigan against her chest, while the breeze whipped at her brown curls.

"It'll ruin me set before he ever comes," she muttered despondently and tried to smooth her ruffled locks. With her long, thin face and straight, determined-looking nose made pink by the fresh air, she appeared to the casual observer to be a nondescript woman approaching middle age. But Robert Owen was certain that she was the best thing that had happened to him in his entire life.

His mother, who wholly approved of her, said that the best thing that had ever happened to Emmie was that both her parents had finally died and had thus set her free.

"Like livin' in a box all her life, poor lass," she had told her son. "Now mind you give her some freedom, share with her, like. Too many women are nought but slaveys."

He had grinned and kissed her plump rosy cheek and had promised.

While Emmie waited, she thought again of the spate of wrath which she had, that morning, suffered from her sister-in-law, Gwen Thomas; and she wondered how much longer she could endure living with her. The moment she was married she would move out and find a room on the other side of the river, a room which she could make into a little home for Robert between voyages,

217

until the war was over and they could hope for a better place.

Gwen had been furious that Patrick, the eldest of the family which lived next door, had shot an arrow through the glass of the Thomases' back bedroom window. Then, instead of being suitably apologetic, he had calmly asked for his arrow back. Emmie had burst into laughter at the sheer nerve of the lad, and this had set Gwen off on one of her lectures about responsibility and morality, which Emmie had endured with gritted teeth. What on earth had her brother, David, ever seen in the woman? A skinny, nagging ferret, she was.

She suddenly caught sight of Robert. Gwen was immediately forgotten and she ran towards him along the gently heaving dock, her whole body aching to hold him and be held by him.

Later, when he broke it to her that he would be sailing again in a day or two, she stroked the side of his face, as if to imprint on her memory every line of it. She touched the heavy blond brows and the tobacco-stained moustache. "Dearest Robbie," she whispered, "come back safe. I can't live without you." She snuggled closer. "You know, I never had a proper sweetheart before — I never had the time or the chance."

His lips curved mischievously under his moustache. "I know," he replied. "It were the biggest shock of me life when I realised it. Did I hurt you?"

Her thin white face was suddenly scarlet. "No — well, not much." She bit her lips, and then asked shyly, "Did you mind? Me not being at all experienced, like?"

"Nay, luv." He stood up suddenly from their seat on the top deck of the ferry and pulled her to her feet. "It were the nicest thing that ever happened to me — as if you'd been waiting for me." He held her closer. "But I can tell you, my girl, you were a real fast learner, you were."

"Well, at least I'm clean — no disease, I mean." She laughed self-consciously, her lower lip between her teeth. Then she looked at him wickedly out of the corner of her eyes, a plain woman suddenly made pretty.

II

Emmie mechanically handed twopence to the plump, untidy clippie and received her tram ticket. Now Robert was about to sail, she felt deserted, unbelievably alone. At 39, she had never expected to marry; at that age one was on the shelf. She had many times told herself that such things were not for everyone; and she had done her best to ignore her inward longings, which could make nights a sleepless misery. She had had to try to be happy that she had nursed both her parents until they died. Then, when suddenly she was free of them, she had believed that she was too old for anything but more work. Domestic work, at that.

As she sat down on the slatted wooden seat of the tram, she asked herself bewilderedly whether it was really only four months since her father had died of heart failure. He had been a regular soldier, injured in the First World War, during army manoeuvres in 1915, and subsequently confined to a wheelchair for the rest of his life. And then, within a week, her mother, who had been bedridden with arthritis for twenty-three years, had followed him, as if her reason for living had gone.

With both of them to nurse, no wonder I hadn't even time to wink at the milkman or gossip with the neighbours, thought Emmie. No time — and no money, to make myself look nice enough to find a husband. She closed her eyes, as she remembered all the lifting of them, the washing for them, the repulsive tasks of caring for people well-nigh helpless. And her father forever filthy-tempered and her mother so fretful and in such dire pain.

Being Mrs Forster-Harrington's daily cleaning lady and cook had been rough, too, though her grand Victorian house had been very conveniently close to Emmie's tiny row house. Every morning, since the age of thirteen, she had run backwards and forwards from it and thus earned a little to augment her father's army pension, worried all the time that while she was away her father might fall out of his chair by the window or her mother might need her chamber pot. For twenty-six years she had stoically polished and scrubbed the house, through wars and Depression, until she knew every niche in the carved newel posts, every crack between the slate kitchen tiles. She did it while kind old Mrs Forster-Harrington, dressed in black silk, sat in her drawing room like Queen Victoria and mourned the death in 1918 of General Sir Alfred Forster-Harrington.

"Gone a bit soft in the head, she had, but proper kind for all that," Emmie had confided to Robert. "When I think on it, I were real lucky to have a job — so many didn't have one. But it were all work, Robbie. I never had a minute for meself. I never been to the pictures till you took me."

"Didn't they have any friends?" asked Robert incredulously. "To visit them, while you went out?"

"Not they. Me mam always said as soldiers often don't make many friends 'cos they move so much. Years ago, one or two serving men come to see me dad for a little while — but, you know, they went away — and some of them was killed in the war." She paused, and then added, "And they was both so short-tempered, they put people off, like."

After her mother's funeral, her brother, David, his wife, Gwen, and their sly, gangling 13-year-old daughter, Mari, all decorously clothed in black, had come back to Emmie's house. They had sat drinking tea in the living room, while Emmie wept out to David her fears for herself She was panic-stricken that she did not earn enough to pay the rent and keep herself.

Gwen had sat silently sizing up the furniture in the tiny room. It's good, she had reflected. Can't buy that kind of stuff nowadays, particularly since the war began. Me best dishes would look great on the Welsh dresser. Young Mari, who had occasionally visited her grandparents in the front bedroom, had told her that there, also, the furniture was big and shiny and, therefore, probably good; David had said that the dead couple had inherited practically all of it from their parents. Now, David should inherit it, since he was the eldest; but if Emmie continued to live in her father's house, Gwen knew that David would never take the furniture from her.

While he listened to his sister's woes, David Thomas had stirred his tea with slow turns of the tin spoon. He felt tense and tired in his black Sunday suit and stiff white collar, and curiously breathless. He felt little sense of loss at his parents' death. His father had bullied him and his mother had been a nagger, though he felt sorry that she had had so much pain. Their death had, however, reawakened a strong sense of guilt regarding Emmie. He had berated himself that she had carried the whole load of his parents' invalidism, and Gwen, here, had done nothing whatever for them. He ought to have pushed Gwen harder, to take an occasional turn, so that Emmie could have gone out a bit. Emmie wasn't a bad looking woman and she had a real sweet manner with her — maybe got it from that Forster-Harrington woman. Given a chance, she might have married, and then he would not have had her on his hands now — though how any husband of hers would have put up with his parents, he could not imagine. Anyway, on his hands she was, and he knew he had to do something to get her started again.

With a slow ponderous movement, he put his spoon down in the saucer and rubbed the dark jowls of his face, while he looked out of the corner of his eye at his virago of a wife.

"Maybe I could go into service — Mrs Forster-Harrington might be glad to have me live in, now she's so old," Emmie sobbed, her pointed nose red from weeping.

"Nay. You're free now. You can do better'n that," her brother replied heavily. He was not going to see her thrown into the kind of jail that living-in domestic service could be. She'd had enough. She deserved better. "With the war on, there's a lot more work around for women now." He took a large breath and steeled himself, as he turned to Gwen. "She could have our middle bedroom for a while — till she got settled, like," he suggested.

Gwen sucked her teeth and turned a scornful glance at the dishevelled Emmie. Who wanted a plaster saint in the house? Another person to cook for?

But her husband's face reflected a stubbornness which had defeated her many a time in their married life, a woodenness which sometimes reminded her of his father. She stared back at him uneasily.

David added, "She'll get work soon enough and then she can pay her shot, couldn't you, Emmie?"

Emmie gave a long shivering sigh and glanced uncertainly at Gwen. Gwen had, for the moment, put on her chapel expression, as Mari called it, a thoroughly virtuous look. It had suddenly been made clear to her how she could acquire her parents-in-law's furniture with a minimum of infighting.

"Aye," she agreed. "She can have the middle room — and there's space enough in the house, if I move our furniture round a bit, for the furniture from here."

221

Though very suspicious of Gwen's sudden acquiescence, Emmie said thankfully that, of course, she would pay. "And I could help you in the house," she added, as she wiped her eyes with the backs of her hands. Until she got on her feet, any company would be good company. And there was little Mari — she liked Mari.

Mari stopped munching seed-cake and unexpectedly interjected, "It would be nice if you could live with us, Auntie Emmie."

Emmie smiled waterily at her. From time to time, the child had come on her own, or with David, to see her grandparents, and Emmie had always spoiled her with a bit of cake or a sweet biscuit and a loving hug. To Mari, her aunt was easier to gossip with than her mother was. Mothers had a way of jumping on you, Mari had always thought, if you so much as said a word out of place.

With a satisfied smirk, Gwen rose, to indicate that they should leave. Once the furniture had been moved into her house, she would hold on to it; possession was nine points of the law. And if, in order to do this, she had to put up with a paying sister-in-law in the house for a while, it was cheap at the price; very different from having a couple of invalids wished on you, a fear which had haunted her all of her married life.

She sniffed. Despite the local gossips' accusations of neglect, David *had* visited his acerbic parents occasionally, and had spent good money on winter clothes and coal for them. Only Emmie had said thank you, according to David. And, she recollected bitterly, no one seemed to have ever given *her* any credit for getting by with that much less money.

III

It proved simple to obtain work. After asking what experience she had, the employment exchange sent her to a sailors' canteen, set up in Paradise Street by a church group.

Stout, beaming Mrs Robinson, a volunteer who managed the place, was delighted to have an applicant willing to do washing up, clean lavatories and scrub floors. Furthermore, she liked the well-mannered, grey-eyed woman with a face as innocent as a nun's, yet old enough to keep young seafarers at bay.

"We have a lot of volunteers on the staff, but occasionally they don't turn up," she explained to Emmie. "Then we have to manage somehow, so we have four full-time paid people, two for each shift."

Emmie smiled and said she could cook, too. Mrs Robinson looked at the marvellous reference from the Honourable Mrs Forster-Harrington — and increased the wage offered by five shillings a week.

At seven the next morning Emmie was given a white overall and the prettiest flowered apron she had ever worn, and was sent across a small back yard to scrub two very dirty lavatories.

The yard was cobbled and was obviously much older than the buildings surrounding it; it had been adapted as a light well and was lined overhead with office windows. Little of the spring sunshine penetrated it; only a small square patch of sky far above hinted at the beauty of the day.

With her long, straight nose wrinkled in disgust, Emmie used up four pails of hot water and a whole bottle of pine disinfectant and, to the relief of the other members of the staff who had to use the ancient thrones, as well as the seamen, she had left them cleaner than they had been for half a century.

When she returned to the canteen itself, she saw that the front door was hospitably open, though round the entrance stood a wall of sandbags to protect it from blast. The two big windows facing the street had been pushed up; their panes had been crisscrossed with black tape, to minimise the danger of flying glass, and on either side big, old-fashioned shutters, their hinges well oiled, hung ready to be folded across the windows at night.

Two volunteers were wiping down the tables and chairs. They were both dressed in matching sweaters and cardigans, one in pink, the other in green. Over their tweed skirts they had tied flowered aprons similar to Emmie's. One had a string of pearls round her neck, the other a gold chain with a cross hanging from it. Though they were about the same age as Emmie, Emmie thought she had never seen two more beautiful young ladies. They greeted her cheerfully and asked her name; she did not dare to ask them their names.

Bringing with her a strong smell of sausages grilling, Mrs Robinson rushed in from the kitchen carrying a pile of clean ashtrays. "Put one of these on each table, Emmie," she ordered briskly.

"It's funny-peculiar how small things change your life," Emmie remarked to Mari later on. "All the happiness I've got came because I had to put an ashtray on a certain table. Proper queer, when you think on it."

As Emmie put down the last ashtray, two men, anxious for a late breakfast, swung themselves into chairs at the table. Both wore navy-blue turtleneck sweaters and shabby jackets over them. They grinned up at Emmie.

"Mornin', duck. What you got for brekkie?" The speaker must have been in his sixties, judging by his almost bald head fringed by tightly clipped white hair. Black eyes, like a friendly magpie's, surveyed her.

Emmie blushed slightly. "I don't know. I can smell sausages."

The other man was younger, fair-haired, with a full moustache tinged orange by tobacco smoke. He laughed, and Emmie's blush grew redder, because she felt she had given a stupid answer. Her fingers fidgeted with a corner of her flowered apron. After a second, he said to his companion, "It doesn't matter what it is, Dickie. I'm that hungry, I could eat an elephant. Had to wait hours at the bloody hospital, in spite o' being so early."

"Aye. Bring two plates of whatever's cooking," agreed his companion, taking a well-charred pipe out of his pocket and then opening up an oilskin tobacco pouch from another pocket.

Emmie flashed them a shy smile and fled to the kitchen. She reported anxiously to Mrs Robinson.

Mrs Robinson paused, a half-open packet of dried eggs in her hand. Then she chuckled. "Here, take a pencil and notebook from over there, and ask them whether they want tea or coffee, bread or toast, and would they like porridge to start with."

Flustered, Emmie snatched up the notebook, while Mrs Robinson called after her, "We've got scrambled eggs, sausages and baked beans."

Emmie waited, pencil poised, until the men looked up from their conversation. Behind her, other men rolled in with the typical sailor's gait, each man's head bent slightly forward, chin tucked in, from years of living in boats' confining spaces, where heads could be easily bumped. Coughing, hawking, talking, they scraped chairs back from the tables, while the volunteers advanced purposefully, notebooks in hand.

The man with the moustache watched her curiously, as she took his friend's order; when she turned to him she found herself facing rich blue eyes, narrowed as though used to staring into sunlight. The face was weatherbeaten, lined and filled with strain. He smiled at her and she lowered her eyes modestly, as she wrote the order down. Her mother had been warning her since the First World War about being forward with men. Not that she need have worried, thought Emmie. When you're keeping house you live in a daytime world of women, children and very old men. Even the tiny shops she had patronised had been largely run by women, and her parents had never allowed her to go out at night; when she had once or twice protested at this, her father had, in a tremendous rage, shouted her down, threatened her with his stick and told her that it was bad enough that they were left alone in the mornings while she was with Mrs Forster-Harrington and went for the groceries. Many of her neighbours were equally tied to their homes, she knew, by a horde of children, the sick or the old, and by sheer lack of a penny of their own. She submitted.

This morning, she was being rapidly surrounded by an ever increasing crowd of lively, talkative men. It felt very strange, nervously exciting.

"Tea or coffee?" she inquired of her younger customer, forcing herself to look at him. He grinned, a slow, friendly smile, which made all the sun wrinkles on his face stand out. Her heart gave an uncomfortable bounce. "Tea," he replied, and then asked, "You new here?"

"Yes," she said shyly, smiled briefly and hurried back to the safety of the kitchen. A whole lot of questions about men tumbled into her mind. Here, this very morning, she was going to meet more men than she believed she had met in the whole of her desperately narrow existence, and she really knew very little about them.

When she was a young girl and her mother was still able to move around the house a little, she had not dreamed of being tied to her parents for the rest of her life. She had hoped for a handsome sweetheart in soldier's uniform, with fine legs bound up in puttees; but her parents had kept her rigidly reined in and, very soon afterwards, the horrible battles of the First World War had taken nearly all the young men of the district, and hardly any of them returned. "Round us, there must have been three girls to every man," she guessed, as through the day she trotted patiently backwards and forwards to the tables; and once she suddenly felt sick, as she realised that the same thing was going to happen to the young girls now hoping for a husband. The young lads were again going out to die. And for what? How many men in this very room would be alive twelve months hence?

The man with the moustache came again the next morning, this time for a cup of coffee and a bun. He sat at the same table. Dickie was not with him.

Emmie snatched her notebook out of her apron pocket and scuttled across the crowded room to take his order, afraid that one of the volunteers would get there first.

"Mornin'," she greeted him shyly, wondering what had brought her to him at a run. He was sitting with his elbows on the small round table, chin resting on clasped hands. At her voice, he glanced up quickly and smiled. Despite the smile, he looked drawn and very tired.

"We got a bit o' bacon," she whispered conspiratorially. "Would you like some?"

He had already had breakfast with his parents, out at Hoylake, but he was delighted to be specially favoured. "Ah would," he said, the smile broadening into a grin.

When he took his cup of coffee from her instead of allowing her to lay it on the table, she noticed that his hand was not too steady. The cup wobbled in the ill-fitting saucer and then tipped over. He was deluged in coffee.

She whipped a tea towel from the belt of her apron and gave it to him to wipe himself down, while they had a rueful laugh together. "Lucky your trousers is navy blue," she told him. "Stain won't show."

When she brought his bill, he asked her rather diffidently if she would like to go to the cinema with him the following night.

Gwen was scandalized. "At your age!" she exclaimed. "Lettin' yourself be picked up."

Mari had giggled, and said, "It's exciting for her, Mam." Her mother's look was sufficient to freeze her into silence and, with tight lips, the 13-year-old again bent her head over her knitting.

Shaken by a series of emotions she had never expected to be able to give range to, Emmie had turned appealingly to David.

"I'm free now," she said to him, a little break in her voice. "I'm goin' to enjoy meself as much as I can."

226

David folded his newspaper up carefully. "And so you should," he said, regardless of his wife's grim disapproval. "Be careful who you're with, that's all."

"He's a real nice fella," responded Emmie, looking defiantly at Gwen. Inwardly, she wondered what kind of a man she had drawn out of the pack. He was certainly nothing like her father. She was trembling with nervous anticipation, as, after tea, she washed her face and did her hair. Instead of her usual bun, she rolled her long hair over a shoelace tied round her head and the result was a smooth, neat roll which framed her face; she had got the idea from a women's magazine which Gwen subscribed to. As she tucked in a few precious hairpins to make sure the roll did not slip, she wondered frantically if he were married.

Now, homeward bound on the clanging tram, she reflected fondly on the memory of that first date. There had not been an air raid and they had laughed together as they stumbled round in the blacked out city. He had insisted on bringing her all the way home to her brother's house and he had actually kissed her before leaving her. With joy mixed with fear for his safety, she once more felt under her glove the small garnet-and-pearl ring which a couple of weeks back he had given her.

He had produced it shyly and had confessed when he had slipped it on to her finger, "I never thought much about getting married before — always seemed to be too much to do, fishing with me father. Prices was so bad we never made much — not enough for me to keep a wife as well. Being Methodists, me and me brothers didn't drink and we didn't dance, so we didn't meet too many womenfolk — a few neighbouring girls — but never anyone like you, Emmie. You're beautiful and I want you so bad."

They had lain in the damp April grass, amid the Meols sand-dunes, not too far from his home. Great rolls of barbed wire stretched along the beach, to protect it from possible invasion. The Home Guard, keeping their nightly watch, had left them undisturbed. Rumour had it that both the beach and the dunes were mined, but they forgot everything in their need for each other. While the sound of the waves rolling softly up the shore, and a silent sea mist drifting inland, cut them off for a little while from a world in torment, two gentle, deprived people found an ecstasy granted to few.

They lay for a long time in each other's arms, until Emmie giggled suddenly.

"I was thinkin'. Supposing I have a baby! It *could* happen, even at my age."

Robert had lifted his head and kissed her again. "Not to worry. It'll have a proper father. I wouldn't let you down, luv." He held her tightly, and then said, "If anything should happen to me before we can be married, and you're in trouble, go to me mam and dad. They'll take care of you."

"Oh, Robbie," she whispered with a sigh. "You have to come back safe."

"I'll do me best," he said, with a forced laugh. "But don't you forget. Me dad's earning enough now to keep you for a while."

She lay quiet for a moment, and then she said in a puzzled voice, "It's funny that it's taken a war to give us decent wages, isn't it?" She rolled over him until she was lying on top of him, her head on his shoulder, and then she sighed. "But I'd rather manage on poor wages and know you was safe." She felt him stir under her again and scrambled hastily to her feet. "Enough, luv, enough. I got to go to work on the morning. And you got to have the hospital check your feet again. The cold and wet you suffered on that raft must've been proper awful." She dusted down her skirt and buttoned up her blouse, looking down at him impishly. "But, you know, I wish your feet were still just a bit bad, so as we could have more time together before you have to go to sea again."

He had swung himself to his feet and caught her in his arms and kissed her long and hard. "Aye, luv, I don't want to go either."

Another time, while they sat on a bench underneath a chestnut tree in Sefton Park, she had told him about her life with her parents. He had marvelled at her patience and endurance. She had shrugged her shoulders and said, "I only did what a lot of single daughters have to do — who else will look after people like that? Couldn't let them go into the workhouse. We could just manage if we all three lived together. But there wasn't nothin' left over for going to the pictures or suchlike, even if I'd had the time. We was lucky to have a low rent and something to eat each day. We'd have fair frozen to death some winters, if David hadn't bought some coal."

"It'll be easier from now on, luv," he had promised her. And

228

she had felt indeed that a new life was unfurling for her as surely as the tiny leaves sprouting on the chestnut tree.

"Rialto Cinema," shouted the clippie, and Emmie came sharply back to the present.

IV

Gwen Thomas always averred that her life was never the same again after that young scoundrel, Patrick Donnelly from next door, had at dinnertime on Wednesday shot an arrow through the back bedroom window of their small row house.

"There was broken glass all over our Mari's bedspread. Ruined, it was," she complained angrily to Emmie and to her husband, David.

She was sick to death of her new, Irish next-door neighbours. A pack of sloths, she fumed. She had nearly choked when the 13-year-old boy had calmly knocked at her back door and had asked for his arrow back.

A small bundle of outrage, thin lips drawn back over blackened broken teeth, she had hissed back, "Arrow? You ain't gettin' no arrow from me, young man. You're goin' to get a bill for seven bob for puttin' t'glass back, and I hope your dad gives you a good beatin'."

Large, calculating blue eyes, fringed with long black eyelashes, looked calmly back at her. "It were an accident, Mrs Thomas — and you could say it were blown out in the last air raid and get it mended easy." He grinned at her beguilingly, a grin that usually worked wonders with middle-aged lady teachers.

It did not work on Gwen Thomas. She wanted to strike him with the broom she was holding; but he was as tall as she was and heavily built for his age. She felt uneasily that he might hit her back. She shook a bony finger at him.

"And what good would that do me, beyond makin' a liar of meself?"

"T' city might do it for free."

She slammed the door in his face.

Bow in hand, he stood staring at the cracked black paint on the back door. All that fuss about a window, when any night the Jerries raided Liverpool hundreds of windows got broken. Old bitch.

229

On the way out of the tiny brick-lined yard, he gave the cages holding David Thomas's racing pigeons an angry shake. The pigeons fluttered madly round and round their prison in alarm. Next time he shot at a cat, he reckoned crossly, he should take a look at what else was in the line of flight. As his father often said, you live and learn.

"Patrick! Patrick! Coom 'ere. I want yer to go a message, afore you go back to school," he could hear his mother shouting from their kitchen. "Coom 'ere, afore I come after yez. Where are you?"

He dropped his bow into a corner behind the lavatory in the yard and slunk uneasily into the kitchen.

In her living room, Gwen sank on to the sofa, leaned back and flung a skinny arm across her chest. "He's started me palpitations, he has. Mari, luv, pour me another cuppa tea and bring the aspirin bottle."

Mari was just putting on her school blazer, preparatory to returning to school, but she obediently ran upstairs to her mother's bedroom to get the aspirin bottle and, on her return, poured a cup of tea from the aluminium teapot keeping warm on the hob in front of the fire.

"I don't suppose he meant to break the window, Mam," she pleaded, turning a thin, well-scrubbed face towards her mother who was lying back with her eyes closed.

Gwen ignored her plea. She shook a couple of aspirins out of the bottle, popped them into her mouth and swallowed them down with a gulp of tea. "Mind you come straight home," she told her daughter, without opening her eyes. The girl slowly buttoned her blazer and, with a sour grimace towards her mother, she left for school. Palpitations! How come every time her mother fell into a fit of rage, it was called palpitations, and when she, Mari, was angry, it was called a sinful paddywack.

As she kicked a stone down the road towards school — her mother hated her to do anything so vulgar — she ruminated on the subject of Patrick. Though she was scared of him, she found him a fascinating subject for thought. Her school friends thought he was the handsomest boy in the neighbourhood and he was so excitingly wild — and a wicked Catholic, too. Only last week, at the end of the street, he had fought off three Protestant boys and left them all with bleeding noses. Cock of the walk, he was, thought

Mari a trifle wistfully. But her mother's warnings about men had been drummed into her ever since she could stand, and while the other girls, Protestant and Catholic alike, giggled hopefully whenever they passed him, she held back and passed with eyes cast down, her satchel carried neatly on her back, to cover her long black plait so that boys could not pull it.

V

Emmie descended from the tram and walked briskly down a side street towards her brother's house. The wind sent bits of paper skittering before her, and a red-faced baby, which seemed to have got dust in its eyes, was wailing unhappily in a pram set outside one of the front doors. In a gutter, two small boys in brown woollen jerseys were quarrelling loudly over their coloured glass marbles.

"Evenin', Miss Thomas."

At the sound of the deep Irish voice, Emmie's lips clamped together. She half turned towards the lanky man in blue air raid warden's overalls, who had fallen into step with her. His battered old retriever, Sarge, nosed between them as if anxious not to be ignored, and she bent to stroke his dusty muzzle. "Evening, Mr Donnelly," she replied a little stiffly, uncertain how to treat him.

Patrick's father, with his shrieking wife and bevy of unwashed children, had been, according to Gwen, a no-good out-of-work until he had been made a warden. "Keeps fighting cocks, if you please. Says a bad shoulder keeps him out of the army, ha! For ever shouting at you to 'put that light out'. Never seems to miss the slightest chink in your blackout curtains. Thinks you're signalling to the Jerries if you so much as carry a candle down the yard when you got to go to the lavvie. Work? He lives the life of Riley."

For his part, Conor Donnelly regarded Gwen and David Thomas as worse than a packet of starch, with their highly polished and scrubbed house front, their ritual of Sunday clothes and chapel-going, their disapproval of little boys who sometimes got caught short and piddled on the pavement, and ate conny-onny butties while sitting on their adjacent front doorstep. Ellen Donnelly had expressed the opinion that, "Them holier-than-thou types is the worst. That Mari'll be in trouble with the boys in no time at all, at all."

231

Conor Donnelly could not imagine how anybody could endure such a regimented life, without even an occasional bout of drinking or fighting to break the monotony. Of course, since he had become an air raid warden he had had to mind himself a bit. He had to stay sober while on duty and be a bit careful when he was carrying stolen goods for a small group of friends who preyed on lorries serving the docks.

When he and his family had been bombed out in the previous autumn, the city had rehoused him in the empty row house next door to Mr High and Mighty David Thomas, plumber. That bombing had been a basketful, that had. Poor little Ruby, his eldest daughter, and old Sarge had been buried for nearly four hours. A bloody miracle that the rest of them had been at the pictures at the time.

Miss Thomas, now she was different. She was polite to his wife and sometimes she made jokes with the kids. On Easter morning she had filled Ruby's hands with toffees — must have given her most of her ration — to share with the other kids. She was a very quiet woman, he mused, but with a bit of encouragement from the right fella she might be more lively than she appeared. His face crinkled up in a grin, as she glanced up at him. He ventured a mild joke and was rewarded by a shy laugh.

Emmie forced herself to attend to what he was saying. With his face a polished mahogany from years of inadequate washing and his long, yellow teeth, he was an oddity to her; yet his sheer bouncing gaiety was infectious and she could understand why he had been chosen as an air raid warden — he would be a real tonic if you were in trouble.

They turned towards their adjoining front doorsteps. Conor pushed open his unlocked door, while she inserted her key into her brother's carefully burnished Yale lock. Before he entered, Conor turned to point up to the sky, where a few clouds were building and a slight haze was dulling the sunshine.

"Bit o' luck and them clouds'll form a nice cover afore midnight. Should mean no raid."

"Aye. It's been over quiet lately, hasn't it? Makes you wonder what's brewing."

Conor nodded agreement. "Well, keep yer fingers crossed."

"I got to work the late shift at the canteen tonight, so I'll be up and about anyways," Emmie confided.

232

VI

As usual, the slam of the Donnellys' front door caused a slight shudder to pass through the Thomases' house and rattled the wooden signboard nailed to their door. The faded board announced *David Thomas, plumber, est. 1914. Prompt attention.*

The noise immediately brought Gwen Thomas out of the back kitchen. She clucked fussily, as clearly through the dividing wall came the sound of Ellen Donnelly's strident voice above the shriek of a child. Conor's voice rumbled back.

"Really! Slammin' t' door like that! Brings all the dust down. And me just finished cleaning." Red-ringed, faded blue eyes looked impatiently up at Emmie, as Gwen licked her finger and ran it along a ledge to pick up an offending grain of dust.

Emmie hung up her coat, gas mask and handbag on the hall peg. While she nerved herself to deal with Gwen, she picked up the floppy, brown carrier bag given to her by Robert. She was always anxious not to break up her tenuous housing arrangement by letting her bitter, pent-up resentment burst forth at Gwen's never having given her the slightest help with her parents. She was grateful for David's protection and did not want to move until she was married. Though she was now paying very adequately for her lodgings and she also helped Gwen in the house, Gwen never considered it necessary to thank her and was often barely civil.

Nothing annoyed Gwen more than dust and dirt and untidiness, and her shining, neat house indicated how successfully she dealt with them. Almost invariably wrapped in a black cross-over overall dotted with blue forget-me-nots, she was a bundle of muscles. Because she kept running her fingers through her greying red hair with its tight natural curl, it tended to stand up in a wild bush. Tonight it was in particular disarray, indicating a trying day's battle with her household gods.

"T' glazier hasn't got no glass for Mari's bedroom window," she grumbled, as she followed Emmie into the living room, where a cheerful fire blazed in an old-fashioned cooking range gleaming with blackleading; at its side, the brass tap of the hot water tank winked in the light of the darting flames.

David Thomas was seated in his armchair beside the fire, and he looked up from his perusal of the *Liverpool Echo*. " 'Allo, la," he greeted Emmie, and then he said to his wife. "I'll nail a bit o' plywood over t' window when I've had me tea. It'll be safer for Mari than glass."

"Where *is* Mari?" inquired Emmie, smiling down at her brother.

"She's away out to tea with her friend, Dorothy." Gwen clicked her tongue and reverted to her grievance. "I'll teach that lad, even if his mam won't. He'll not get his arrow back." She continued to grumble, as she went through to the back kitchen. Emmie followed her with the carrier bag.

She interrupted Gwen's tirade, by saying, "Robbie set a line while the tide was out yesterday. He caught ten whiting and he's sent you two. They feel real heavy."

"That's proper kind of him, I'm sure," replied Gwen coldly. She seized a pot of boiled potatoes and deftly drained the water from them into the sink. Through the ensuing steam, she added with a sniff, "Being engaged to a fisherman has its advantages, I suppose. T' fishmonger didn't have so much as a cod's head left today, by the time he got to me. Ever so long, the queue was."

"Well, there's the makin's of a nice dinner here," Emmie soothed.

"Humph," grunted Gwen. "Here, take the potatoes and put them on the table for me." She sighed. Provided Emmie could be prevented from taking her parents' furniture with her, she would be thankful when the woman got married and left. When the pieces had been moved into the house, nothing had been said as to the ownership; but Gwen burnished them determinedly; they were hers, because David was the eldest and should inherit.

What little Emmie said about the furniture indicated that she took it for granted that, since she had lived with it all her life, the furniture belonged to her. Besides, in the middle of a war, where else would she get furniture from for a home?

She had brought Robert home for tea one Sunday and Gwen had made it clear that she strongly disapproved of a woman of sober years suddenly marrying a man she had known less than four months. It did not occur to Emmie that Gwen had been smitten by a lingering envy of her blatant happiness, her obvious contentment.

"I must hurry," said Emmie, as they sat down to their meal. "I got to be in the canteen by seven. Mrs Robinson and the others were ever so kind about me engagement, giving me a bit of time

234

off when Robbie was free."

Gwen responded tartly, "Well, I hope you're doing the right thing." She stirred her tea hard, in the hope of making half a teaspoonful of her sugar ration sweeten it adequately. She made a face when she sipped it. "Picking up a man like that don't seem like a good start to me."

Emmie ached to slap her.

"Now, Gwen," her husband warned. "Emmie got to know him in the canteen. That's not picking up. And he took her home to Hoylake to meet his mum and dad — quite proper. He's given her a nice ring, too."

Gwen shrugged her shoulders slightly and poured another cup of tea. Emmie kept her eyelids down and wondered if Gwen had ever been in love with poor David — or with anything except the shiny aspidistra in the front room or the bronze soldiers looking down at them from the living room mantelpiece.

To distract Gwen, David said, "I'll get me tools and do Mari's window."

That brought Gwen back to her favourite complaint — the Donnellys. "We ought to have moved from here years ago — the whole of Toxteth's gone to pot. The minute Mrs Tasker died next door I knew we'd never get decent neighbours again."

"House were empty for months. T' landlord held out for too high a rent." David gritted his teeth as he pushed away his empty plate.

"Oh, aye. And how does he pay seventeen shillings a week on an air raid warden's wages, I'd like to know. Maybe it's true that he's hand in hand with a gang o' dock thieves."

"Gwen!" David was shocked. "That's just idle gossip. Because he sometimes has lipsticks or silk stockings for sale? He could buy 'em easy from a merchant seaman on the New York run. It don't make 'im a thief."

VII

The sharp wail of the air raid siren made David jump. He had been washing himself in the kitchen sink, in preparation for going to bed, and he stood in his under vest and trousers while he dried the back of his neck. He was numb with fatigue after a long day working on the intricacies of the plumbing of the Royal Infirmary, and he felt again a small, choking pain in the middle of his chest, a pain that had been bothering him occasionally for a couple of weeks.

"Blow them," he muttered, and hastily finished drying himself.

He leaned over the sink to pull back the blackout curtain and look out of the window. There was enough moonlight to cast a shadow of the house across the back yard. Behind the neighbouring chimneys, searchlights suddenly sent seeking fingers across a starry sky. It was much too light for safety. He dropped the curtain into place, making the flame of the candle on the drainboard dance, as Gwen came hurrying from the living room. She carried a steaming kettle in one hand, and the warning had obviously flustered her.

"For goodness' sake, get your dressing-gown on and something on your feet. We'll have tea on the cellar steps. What a nuisance they are."

As she flung two teaspoonsful of tea into the pot, she went on anxiously, "Our Mari's not in yet, from Dorothy's. She's real late. I'll have to have a word with that young lady."

"I could go and fetch her," David offered, without much conviction.

"No. It'd just mean two of you out in the flak. You get out the blankets and cushions and take them on to the cellar steps, while I do the tea tray." She jumped suddenly, as the steady boom-boom of anti-aircraft fire made the windows rattle. Sometimes the guns sounded more menacing than the bombs did.

David would have been thankful to crawl into bed and risk being blown out of it. He did not feel, however, that he could go to bed while Mari was still not home, so he obediently arranged the cushions on the cellar steps, for them to sit on. With the slope of the staircase overhead, this spot offered good protection and the least likelihood of being crushed.

With a sigh, he sat down and arranged a blanket over his knees. While Gwen held the tea tray a little high, he tucked another blanket round her. He took the candle from the tray and set it on a small shelf above their heads. Gwen scolded, "Be careful, stupid. You'll upset the tray." She stirred the pot balanced uncertainly on the tray on her lap, while he listened for the battery to start firing in nearby Princes Park; the sound would indicate to him how close

236

the raiders were. Beyond the rumble of more distant guns, how-ever, all he heard was Donnelly's front door slam. Likely, Donnelly was in for a busy night.

Gwen's lips curled. "That'll be him goin' down to the wardens' post. Bangin' the door, as usual. No manners, that man."

Their own front door slammed. Quick footsteps ran along the narrow, linoleumed passage, then stumbled through the dark liv-ing room and into the kitchen.

"That you, Mari? Come on down, quick now."

Mari was panting, as she whipped a cushion off the shelf and almost slithered down the concrete steps, her long bare legs flash-ing white in the candlelight.

She sat down close to her mother. Like many families seeking refuge in this safest corner of the house, they always sat very tightly together, so that if the building was hit they either died or survived together.

Gwen felt her trembling and lifted down the candle to have a closer look at her. The girl's face was blenched and her eyes stared unblinkingly at her mother from behind the candle flame.

"There, there, luv. No need to be scared. You're safe home now," she told the girl quite gently.

Her father turned towards her and added reassuringly, "It don't sound as if they're interested in the south end of the town to-night."

Above them, a number of aeroplane engines throbbed increas-ingly loudly.

"They'll be some of ours," David declared authoritatively. "Al-ways know the difference by the sound o' the engines."

His words were immediately belied by a shrieking whistle pass-ing over them. Instinctively, they ducked and flung their hands over their heads for protection. The tea tray on Gwen 's lap rocked perilously. There was a moment of silence: then a deafening ex-plosion which shook the whole house above them. They waited, like rabbits hiding in a thorn bush from a fox. A piece of plaster plopped from the ceiling on to the tray, and a cloud of thin dust enveloped them.

Mari buried her face against her mother's bony legs and whim-pered in terror. The next bomb in the rack would hit them; she knew it. It would be a judgment on her for what she had allowed

Patrick Donnelly to do to her.

He had been bothering her for weeks, touching her when she passed him, holding her against the wall of the alley one day, when she had run down it to visit Dorothy; not hurting her, just making her feel funny when he pressed himself against her. It had been most funny-peculiar, because, despite all her mother's warning about not letting a man come near her, she had wanted him to remain close. Perhaps the warning didn't apply to boys, she argued to herself.

Tonight, he had pushed her into a street air raid shelter, which nobody used except as a urinal. He had held her tightly against the wall and her silent struggles had been of no avail against his considerable weight. When in scared despair, she had stopped wriggling, he had lifted her skirt and gently stroked between her legs. And she knew now that she was on her way to hell. It had felt wonderful, incredible; and he had laughed when, not understanding the driving impulse, she had put her arms round him. He had said it was nothing to what he could do. If that was nothing, she decided without really knowing why, it was a good thing that the air raid warning had begun to shriek and that they had both run for home.

Now the bombs were falling all around her. God must be very angry with her.

"Incendiaries! Incendiaries!" Conor Donnelly could be heard, calling his firewatchers to the street.

Despite his wife's protests, David insisted on going out in his dressing-gown to check his roof, back and front. He came back very soberly and hauled the blanket round himself again. "Looks like the whole town's alight. Hope our Emmie's all right." Then to his crouching daughter, he said, "Don't take on so, Mari. Everything's going to be all right. We're quite safe here on the steps."

You don't know what a wicked daughter you've got, thought Mari, not lifting her head from her mother's knee. God could do anything to us tonight.

VIII

As the guns in Princes Park began to roar, Ellen Donnelly finished spreading the washing on her wooden airer in her living room and

238

then heaved the heavy rack up to the ceiling again and tied the rope firmly to hold it there. The clothes began to drip depressingly onto the rag rug below and onto the otherwise bare floor. A few droplets reached baby Michael asleep in a battered easy chair. She edged the chair away from under the rack and flung her black woollen shawl over the sleeping child.

There was a quick patter of bare feet on the stairs, and her eldest daughter, Ruby, still in her clothes, dashed into the room. She was brought up short by the sight of her mother seating herself calmly on a wooden chair in front of the fire.

"Mam, shall I bring Brendy and Nora down? The guns sound awful." Her voice was tightly constricted, as she tried to control her panic. After the dreadful experience of being buried in the ruins of their former home, the sound of the air raid warning always brought her close to a bout of hysterics. Her breath came in tight gasps and, from under a fringe like a Skye terrier's, eyes gleamed with tears.

"Aye, luv. Coom 'ere." Her mother held out a stout red arm to her and thankfully the skinny 12-year-old cuddled close to her heavy breast. "It ain't likely we'll be bombed again."

The guns continued to growl and, after a minute, Ellen said, "Let's have a look-see outside. Then we'll decide if we should bring t' kids down." She rose, and went to the front door, Ruby trotting closely behind her for comfort.

With a strong, red hand on either door-post, she leaned out as far as she could. The wind caught her untidy mop of shoulder-length hair and flapped her long black skirt. Metronomic search-lights flicked back and forth across the sky as if to time the drumming guns, and high in the heavens a bright flare floated gently; it silvered the slate roofs of the close-packed houses, gave a halo to a church spire and outlined the solid mass of a nearby tenement building.

"Reckon they're doin' Wallasey and Birkenhead tonight," she opined comfortingly. "Quite away from us. We'll let the kids rest for a bit. You come and sit by the fire with me and we'll have a drop of your dad's whiskey."

Ruby did not like the taste of whiskey, but since the disastrous raid which had robbed them of their home, her mother had often given her a teaspoonful of it, and it made her feel better. Now, she

239

went to the dying fire to warm her bare feet, while her mother tried to guess where Donnelly's latest hiding-place for the bottle might be. In such an empty home there were not many places to look.

She found it on the window-sill, behind the blackout curtain, and she sat down while she eased out the cork. Ruby came to lean against her. The glow from the fire lit up their faces, as they solemnly took a sip each from the bottle. Then Ellen took a good gulp, and gasped as it caught her throat. She laughed and set down the bottle under her chair and again put her arm round Ruby.

The front door was flung open. Patrick strolled slowly in, determined to show that he was not afraid of air raids. A cool breeze followed him in.

"What you bin up to?" Ellen inquired truculently. "You're lookin' too pleased with yourself by far."

"Haven't bin doin' nothin'." The satisfied grin on his face belied his words, but she knew from experience that she would get no more out of him.

A screaming whistle overhead wiped the grin from Patrick's face, but, hands in pockets, he stood his ground, while Ruby clung shrieking to her mother. Blast swung the front door hard open and shook the old house. The blackout curtains billowed like sails in a sudden gust. A mass of soot descended the chimney, obliterated the fire and covered all of them in black dust. Little Michael, covered by his mother's thick shawl, continued to sleep, but from upstairs came frightened howls.

Ellen wiped the soot off her mouth. "God's curse upon the buggers!" she cried, and bent down to reach for the whiskey bottle.

A piece of debris landed on the roof with a sharp crump; then, for a moment, unearthly quiet.

A nerve-racking clatter in the street and the familiar sound of her husband's running feet caused Ellen to burst out again, "Incendiaries, blast 'em!"

Patrick went to the door. The darkness was broken all along the street by sparks hissing from the small, vicious fire bombs. Dark shadows carrying sandbags ran to dowse the scary, sizzling devils, and one or two bravely tried to put them out by holding dustbin lids over them. Patrick seized one of the sandbags in the hall and ran gleefully out to help.

Opposite, a furious Bridget Mahoney flung up the empty frames of her bedroom window, sat out on the sill with her back to the street and struck out with a broom at an incendiary which had lodged in the gutter of her home. She managed, after a few wild shots, to hook it out and it fell into the street, where Patrick pounced on it happily and covered it with sand. Bridget eased herself back into her bedroom.

"Ow!" she exclaimed, as she caught her arm on a jagged piece of glass left in the window-frame. The blood gushing out looked black in the moonlight. Hastily she picked up her discarded apron from the bedroom chair and wrapped it tightly round the wound.

Early the next morning, a sympathetic Ellen Donnelly bathed off the apron stuck on the deep, ugly cut and rebandaged it tightly with a bit of an old pillowslip brought by Bridget. Afterwards, they finished the rest of Conor Donnelly's whiskey and, despite the pain, a fulminating Bridget went off to work in a large garage, where she spent her days sewing aeroplane canvas. As usual, her little boys went to school with clean hands and faces, and stomachs full of porridge.

About ten o'clock, an exhausted Conor arrived home. He was covered in dust from working on the results of a direct hit on a dairy three streets away. "Three dead — and twelve cows spattered all over," he informed his sleepy wife. He went straight to the window and flicked back the half-drawn blackout curtains. "Where's me whiskey?"

"Me and Bridget Mahoney drank it," his wife said dully. "She were hurt." She was holding Michael to her breast and he was sucking eagerly. She did not look up.

In two strides her husband reached her. He struck her hard across her plump face. Then he stumbled upstairs to their bed and flung himself on to it.

IX

To alleviate the excruciating boredom of raidless nights, the clerks and shop assistants on fire guard duty in the buildings near the sailors' canteen would take it in turns to nip into the canteen for coffee. Mrs Robinson had once remarked that they complained when nothing happened and then they complained when there was a raid. "Then they're scared stiff, poor souls," she added.

Emmie had looked up at some of the steeply sloping roofs along which a firewatcher might have to clamber to get at a fire, and had been thankful that up to now the regular canteen staff had been excused from fire-watching.

Tonight, she entered the canteen through the narrow side passage which led into the light well at the rear. The light well was already shadowing and she fingered the long hat pin she kept under her coat lapel, until she had slipped through the kitchen door. You never knew who might be lurking at night in such a gloomy place as a light well, she told herself. A hat pin was a girl's best defence.

She greeted Doris, another paid member of the staff, who was shaking up a huge basket of potato chips above a vat of fat. Near her, with a bulging sack between them, sat two volunteers patiently peeling and slicing further supplies for her. One lady dropped a handful of irregularly sliced chips into a bucket of water, and moaned, "This must be the most unromantic job in the whole war."

Emmie had lost some of her awe of these well-dressed ladies, and she teased them. "Now what would the boys out there do without chips? They couldn't go on without your chips. Proper miserable they'd be."

The volunteer nodded her head in rueful agreement and picked up another potato between her beautifully manicured nails. Then she chuckled. "You're quite right — they all seem to keep going on chips."

Emmie took her new lipstick from her handbag and clumsily outlined her lips in front of the kitchen mirror. She grimaced at the uncertain result. "Painted women are the devil's children," Gwen had told her. She smiled at herself in the mirror.

After years of having only Mrs Forster-Harrington to talk to, Emmie was happy in the company of the canteen staff. The customers were usually fun, too, she thought, though she did not always understand the jokes they made; and she was sure that to many she was only a pair of chapped hands bringing plates of food.

As she closed the wooden shutters over the big kitchen window

242

looking out at the light well and then slotted the iron bar across them, she thought wistfully of Robert in his new ship. Perhaps after the war, when he could go back to being an inshore fisherman again, he could be at home more often, depending only on the time of the tides for his trips in and out.

She went to attend to a small window on the same wall. Carefully she drew a pair of old grey velvet curtains over it. Then she lifted the telephone off the table nearby and tucked it tightly against them, so that cracks of light would not show at the curtain hem. She had never in her life used a telephone and regarded it with some deference; Mrs Forster-Harrington had felt it unnecessary to have such an intrusion upon her privacy.

Despite the wail of the air raid siren, a steady buzz of conversation came through the thick tobacco smoke. Liverpudlians are not easily stopped in mid-argument, she reflected with a little smile. The men's aplomb lessened her own fear, and she bustled round her tables as if nothing unusual was happening outside.

In the kitchen, Doris stood clutching the edge of the pig bin in which all the kitchen scraps were kept for feeding pigs. She was trembling violently, her lined face as white as the tiles on the walls. She had lost home, husband and children in the Christmas air raids the previous year and the memory was still agonisedly fresh.

Lady Mentmore, a countess, lifted her beringed hands from the washing-up water and went to comfort her. Not by even the flicker of an eyelid did she show her own nervousness.

The gunfire was heavy and the quick thump-thump of bombs hastily discharged was unnervingly close. From a table in the corner near the kitchen door came the piercing sweet sound of a mouth organ. Almost immediately a strong tenor voice joined in with the words, *She'll be comin' round the mountain when she comes.* There was a general roar of voices raised to sing what she would be wearing when she came, and Emmie tut-tutted to herself, as she dried dinner plates at record speed for the countess. What would Lady Mentmore think of such naughty words, worse than anything she had heard since she left school? Proper wicked little boys' words they were. Through the open door, she glimpsed the men's faces, red from exposure or yellow from too much confinement below decks. They glowed with pure mischief as they thought up new verses, each bawdier than the last. Doris gave the countess a watery

243

smile and the countess unexpectedly chuckled.

The canteen closed at midnight, but most people there stayed on until the All Clear sounded about one o'clock. The volunteers murmured that they hoped all the ferry boats had not been sunk. "You can't walk on water," one laughingly remarked. Doris hoped the trams out to Bootle would still be running, and Emmie, who could walk home, hoped fervently that she would not be accosted by thieves, because she had just been paid. She transferred her pay packet from her handbag to her coat pocket and checked that her hat pin was still under her lapel; too many petty thieves, either singly or in small gangs, haunted the ill-lit streets and she was always nervous.

The light of the fires in the city made the shadows of the buildings still standing look even blacker than usual. She glanced at the sky. It was flushed in several directions and the smell of burning tobacco and smouldering rubber was thick in the air. Service vehicles of various kinds, with shaded headlamps, moved like dark ghosts. Except for two drunks helping each other along, there seemed to be no pedestrians. She began to run.

FRIDAY, 2nd MAY 1941

I

At half-past one on Friday morning, when Emmie let herself into her brother's house, an overwhelming smell of soot greeted her, but when she had lit a candle in the hallway, she was thankful to see that everything looked much as usual. She went straight upstairs, undressed and crept thankfully into bed.

At six o'clock the sound of Gwen's alarm jerked her awake, and she heard Mari next door clamber out of her creaky bed. Yawning, she crawled out herself, poured water from her ewer into a hand-basin on the wash-stand and splashed her face with it.

As she dried herself with a worn white towel, she whipped back the blackout curtains and saw a cheerful sun in a pale blue sky. Behind the houses across the back alley, the sky was flushed, but she argued hopefully to herself that it could be because the sun had not long risen. She hurried into an old cotton frock.

In the living room, the curtains were already drawn back, and David Thomas was kneeling on the hearth rug, clearing the ashes and soot from the hearth. " 'allo, la," he greeted her amiably, between small, persistent coughs. "Proper mess, eh? Soon get t' fire goin', though."

Emmie agreed. Every stick of furniture was covered with a fine film of soot. It clung to the bronze Roman soldiers ornamenting each end of the high mantelpiece; it had coated the net curtains at the window and the fancywork runner across the middle of the table; even the four precious oranges in the fruit bowl on the sideboard were black. Gwen was going to be hard to live with

247

today, she thought wryly.

David gave a sudden enormous sneeze and little puffs of soot rose round him.

Emmie clicked her tongue. "I'll get the floor cloth and wipe down the table and chairs, so as we can have brekkie," she said briskly. "Has the milk come?"

"I haven't looked."

Emmie went to the front door and peeped out. No milk bottle sat on the doorstep. "Well, I'm blowed," she exclaimed. "He's never missed before, not even in the Christmas blitz. I'll have to open a tin. Gwen's not going to like that."

Where the dairy once had stood, the milkman and his twelve cows lay neatly shovelled into bags, awaiting transport.

As she worked the tin-opener into a tiny tin of Nestlé's milk, Emmie asked, "Did you have any incendiaries up here?"

"Aye. Had to put 'em out with sand. Woman who stores the stirrup-pump wouldn't open her door. Keeping the pump for herself, she was, in case her own house caught fire."

"That's proper awful."

"It was. I hope the warden gives her what for, today."

David, in clean overalls, was dispatched on time to the Royal Infirmary, where he was still repairing the plumbing damaged in the Christmas raids. A dreamy Mari was slapped by Gwen for not getting on with washing herself at the kitchen sink, scolded for not eating her cornflakes and was sent to school comparatively free of soot smudges.

With endless buckets of hot water and small amounts of the irreplaceable, rationed soap, Emmie spent the morning washing down every nook and cranny of the living room and Gwen's bedroom, which was the only bedroom with a fireplace. The blackout curtains were taken into the back yard, put over the clothes-line and beaten, the net ones were washed and hung out to dry. The fireplaces were blackleaded and the oranges carefully scrubbed with a nail brush. Gwen herself sprinkled tea leaves over the red, Belgian carpet in the sitting room and solicitously brushed it, remembering sadly the number of weeks it had taken her to pay for it, shilling by shilling. The china ornaments on the mantelpiece were lovingly bathed in the kitchen sink, the various messages printed on them in gilt twinkling A *present from Blackpool* or *Greet-*

ings from Llandudno through the soapsuds. Gwen nearly cried. Lovely holidays those had been. She wondered when they would be able to go to the seaside again.

One of the whiting which Robert had caught made a consolingly large fish pie, some of which Gwen, Emmie and Mari ate at lunchtime. The rest was put away for David's tea.

Gwen reminded Emmie that she was due at Blackler's Store at one o'clock, to help in Dress Materials. She was very proud that she went to work two afternoons a week. Just before lunch, she changed into her best black dress, with its neat white lace collar, and her Sunday black stockings and shoes.

After she had left and Mari had returned to school, Emmie filled the kitchen bowl with hot water dipped from the oven tank beside the living room fire, stripped herself in the back kitchen and washed herself all over, in an effort to remove streaks of soot. Gwen did not encourage such scrubbings in the bedrooms — it made too many splashes on the polished linoleum.

II

Next door, a sullen, resentful Ellen fried up some boiled potatoes and an egg and shoved them in front of her husband seated at the table. Conor was unusually quiet as he ate the food. When Ellen sat down by the fire, picked up 3-year-old Michael and gave him her breast, he stared past her, as if he were looking at something behind her.

The youngster suckled contentedly and Ellen enjoyed the physical pleasure of it, but finally her husband's oppressive silence became too much for her.

"What's to do with yez?" she asked sulkily.

He poked listlessly at his fried egg and sighed heavily. "It were a bad night, last night. The dairy were a shambles — blood everywhere — from the cows mostly. And them two women in Plum Street — bits of one of 'em hanging from the tree out front."

"Jesus Mary!" exclaimed Ellen. She shuddered, and Michael lost her nipple and complained fretfully. Her anger at Conor's striking her was forgotten in fascinated contemplation of this horror. She pushed her nipple back into Michael's mouth. "Maybe t' Nazis won't come again," she tried to comfort.

249

"There's nuthin' to stop 'em, 'specially at night. Play ducks and drakes they can." He contemplated a piece of grey potato on the end of his fork. "'T' kid at the corner house 'as got a broken arm and bruises all over — part of the roof fell in on 'im. His dumb cluck of a mother left him in bed 'stead of bringing 'im down to the cellar."

"Poor little divil." She hugged her child closer and remembered, with a tremor, how close she had come to losing Ruby. What an evening that had been. The rest of the family had returned from a Christmas visit to the local cinema, to find the rescue men just hauling her out, unscratched, from under the kitchen table, which her grandfather had fashioned from oak fifty years before. She wondered idly if, when he had made it so solidly, he had had an intimation that it would save a life. Bless the sainted man. And God preserve her from another night like that.

III

When Emmie descended from the tram, at her usual Church Street stop, on her way to work that afternoon, the traffic seemed nearly as busy as usual, though everywhere there was a strong smell of burning, and there was a general haze in the sky.

At the door of the canteen, she bumped into Doris, who promptly complained, "Me pore feet. Had to walk all the way to Bootle last night. Not a tram working. Bloody miles."

When Mrs Robinson and two volunteers arrived, they also looked tired after being up half the night, though all three were immaculately dressed. One of the volunteers, Mrs Starr, said, "I thought I was going to be late. We lost all our windows and I've been hammering old rugs over the downstairs ones ever since daybreak. First time I've ever used a hammer!"

Emmie listened to the lament. Did the stupid woman imagine that they had all been able to spend the morning in bed? In her opinion, complaining never did any good. You just took what life threw at you and did the best you could.

When the siren went, Emmie was busy serving a surge of men who had just come in after the closing of the public houses.

"Blow it," she exclaimed irritably, and some of the men made obscene gestures towards the ceiling. They were none of them drunk — publicans spread their meagre consignments of beer and spirits too thinly for anyone to achieve that happy state — but they were loquacious. Some of the language they used, as they consigned all Germans to Kingdom Come, made Emmie wonder innocently to Doris how Robert managed not to pick up such words.

Doris, trying to be brave, laughed shakily. "There never was a sea-going man what couldn't swear — your Robbie knows his manners, that's what it is."

While she doled out fish and chips — a little fish and a lot of chips — Emmie meditated on Doris's remark and realised that there was a side of her beloved which she did not know much about. For a minute or two, the sickening loneliness she had felt when her mother's coffin had been lowered into her grave was revived; and her new world of Robert Owen and the canteen seemed suddenly distant and alien.

As she cleared a table hastily evacuated by the buildings' firewatchers when they had fled back to their posts, there was a high-pitched swish-swish overhead.

Emmie froze. For a second all conversation stopped. The tiny silence was succeeded by a tremendous roar. The room shook and the electric lights dipped. Everyone looked towards the ceiling.

A tumbling rumble announced the descent of the debris flung up by the explosion. Another roar, another series of rumbles.

Emmie stood terrified, the crockery rattling on her tray, as the guns began to answer the challenge of the planes.

"Put your tray down, luv, or you'll break everything." Deckie Dick, the friend of Robert's who had breakfasted with him on the morning he had first met Emmie, took the tray from her and put it back on the table. "Those two was away over ..." he began.

His voice was drowned by a crash that numbed her ears. His arms went round her and she was clamped against an old navy sweater that reeked of perspiration, as he sought to protect her face and head. In the kitchen, Doris screamed.

"Phew! That was near." Deckie Dick slowly let her go and she giggled nervously. As the guns continued their steady tattoo, a man at the next table chipped Dick, "You never misses a chance with the girls, do you?" Dick gave him a playful punch on the head, and Emmie slipped away to continue her clearing of tables.

Another crash, somewhere at the back of the building, brought Mrs Robinson running from the kitchen. "Gentlemen, there is a shelter downstairs. Take the staircase to the left of the front door. I think it would be a good idea ..." She was cut off by a series of appalling crashes, when again all faces automatically looked up at the ceiling. A crack zipped across it, but it held.

"Come on, lads. Everybody downstairs. Come on." Deckie Dick began to move amongst the tables, touching men on their shoulders and pointing to the staircase. He turned to Mrs Robinson. "Get your ladies down, missus. It's going to be a bad night."

Without a word, she hastened back to the kitchen, where Doris was trying not to have hysterics in front of a pile of fish which she had been flouring. The fish was now covered with heavy dust.

Outside, fire engines raced pell-mell through the darkness, amid the shrill blare of burglar alarms set going in the shaken buildings opposite. Boots pounded past the front door, as rescue crews and air raid wardens ran by.

The customers no longer felt the need to look brave; the pandemonium outside was bad enough to justify a retreat, and they followed the volunteers down to the basement as fleetly as they would have abandoned a sinking vessel. Mrs Robinson, white-faced captain of her little ship, refused to descend until everyone was safely down. Then she quietly followed her crew.

At the foot of the stairs, she closed a very ancient, heavy door, bound with iron, hung there, presumably, to keep out eighteenth-century thieves and rioters. As she lowered the iron latch, she heard the upstairs front windows and shutters blow in, and the tinkle of slivers of glass sweeping across the canteen, to bury themselves in walls and tables. The blast reversed itself and blew outwards, causing a resounding crash of crockery from the tables. There was a muffled bang, when the shutters hit the empty window-frames again.

"Pooh!" she exclaimed. "Just in time." She sank down thankfully on one of the timeworn school benches which had been provided as seating.

The shelter was a windowless cellar, used for years for the storage of coal to heat the building. Its only entrance, other than the stairs, was a pavement light of heavy glass set in an iron frame.

This could be swung upwards to facilitate the delivery of sacks of coal; in the construction of the shelter, it had been left as it was. A simple bolt on the inside held it down and it would form a convenient escape hatch from the basement to the street in the event of fire. Though the walls had been freshly whitewashed and the floor well swept, there was still a smell of coal. As a first line of defence against fire, a stirrup-pump with several buckets of water stood in a corner. In another corner was a small table; on it lay an electric ring and a clutter of much used tea-making apparatus. A single bulb hanging, unshaded, from the centre of the ceiling provided the only light.

Some of the men stood around smoking, while others slouched on the benches. Four of them sat cross-legged on the floor and prepared for a long wait by dealing out a pack of cards. The two volunteers sat primly together, backs straight; two middle-class women determined to be stoical.

A shivering Emmie sat by Doris with her arm round her. The bombed-out woman was sobbing quietly to herself, tears glistening on her rouged cheeks.

"Have a cigarette, me duck. It'll calm you."

A tall, thin seaman, a cigarette wobbling at the corner of his mouth, squatted down in front of Doris and generously proffered a precious packet of Player's. "You like one, luv?" he asked Emmie.

Doris smiled wanly, but made no move to take a cigarette. "Neither of us smoke," Emmie responded for both of them. "Ta, all the same."

The man turned back to Doris. "Well, you start. You're the woman that was bombed out, wasn't yez?"

Doris's eyes clenched shut. She nodded agreement.

"You should smoke. It helps. See, I'll show you how."

Her mind diverted, Doris opened her eyes. He was not a young man and bore all the marks of years of seagoing, of rotten food and working in cramped spaces. He grinned and lit a cigarette for her, drew the first breath on it and handed it to her. "There y'are, luv," he said, his sallow, hollow-cheeked face compassionate.

Emmie watched him wonderingly, captivated by his easy goodwill. Really, she thought, men *can* be kind; and she remembered, for a second, her father's unremitted bad temper. Who else, of the male sex, had she really known, other than him — and stolid, dull

253

David? They had been no particular recommendation for their sex. She had taken Robert purely on trust; and how lucky she had been. The squatting seaman wondered why she suddenly smiled so sweetly.

While Doris cautiously puffed at her first cigarette, the barrage of noise persisted, as in steady waves the Luftwaffe swept over the doomed port. They were guided, at first, by the fires started the previous night and then by huge conflagrations which now began to flare in every direction. Far down the river, the flames' reflection danced on the water, lit up the rooms of suburban homes and warned ships at sea not to cross the bar. Forty miles away, in the Isle of Man, residents peeped between their bedroom curtains, to watch the blaze on the horizon mount higher and higher. "Liverpool's getting it again," they told each other in shocked whispers, so as not to wake the children.

In the shelter, two young deckhands who had drunk a lot of beer decided that they must go to the lavatory. In a brief lull in the noise outside, they ran up the stairs, across the littered canteen, out through the kitchen door to the cobbled light well, where stood the ancient loos. As they relieved themselves, they looked fearfully back over their shoulders through the open doors. What had once been, long ago before the offices had been built round it, the courtyard of a rich merchant's house now seemed to be a deadly funnel, down which bits of debris, shrapnel and occasional sparks travelled with unnerving rapidity. After a quick peek through the empty window facing the street, they were thankful to get back to the shelter.

"Proper shambles out front," one of them reported. "Beams and wires and stones scattered all over. Them last ones must've hit real close."

One of the card players looked up from his seat on the floor, pushed his plug of tobacco into one cheek and said, with a faint sneer, "Don't need a crystal ball to know they're close. Listen to em now."

"Ah, shut yer gob," retorted the returned youngster, hitching his braces up under his jacket.

"Now, gentlemen, this is no time to get upset," Mrs Robinson interjected hastily, having no illusions regarding the shortness of tempers amongst her usually overwrought, seagoing customers.

The young man made a wry face at Mrs Robinson and drifted over to the other side of the room, while the man on the floor muttered irritably, "Think they're bloody heroes every time they go to pee."

The second young man had kept his mouth shut, but now he said, with a tinge of wonderment in his voice, "There's a WVS canteen parked at the corner. T' women's doling out tea and sandwiches as if they was in their parlours at home. Feedin' the firemen, I think they are. Ordinary women just like me mam. And the flak flying round 'em like confetti."

A fast salvo of bombs nearly deafened them. Everybody crouched, hands over heads, fully expecting to be buried. When they found they had survived, they ruefully rubbed piercingly painful ears. From the ceiling, whitewash snowed gently.

Suddenly, all heads were raised; all noses sniffed. Smoke. The smell of burning wood was unmistakable. Fear jumped from one face to another. Some people rose quickly to their feet. Doris whimpered, and Emmie felt a rising panic.

"Hold it. No point in getting scared." Deckie Dick got up and put his pipe into his trouser pocket. "I'll nip upstairs and take a dekko for you. If I call, you come up orderly, mind."

The men quickly made a passage for him. Elderly, well-known and with forty years of seagoing experience spanning the First World War, he commanded respect. He ran swiftly up the stairs, the deck of cards which gave him his nickname bulging in his back trouser pocket.

The crowd relaxed slightly as, above the now more distant rumbles from outside, they could hear him working his way through the tumbled furniture of the canteen overhead. The back door slammed, indicating that it was still on its hinges.

Nothing was burning in the light well, though it was smoky. In the flickering light of fire reflected in the remaining windows of the offices across the street, he made his way to the front door with its protective sandbags. He flattened himself against the battered wall of sandbags, as a whistle sounded overhead. A huge explosion from South Castle Street sent shock waves running, and his ears rang. He listened, as intently as his hurt ears allowed. The throb of engines seemed to come from a greater distance, but in the street the smoke was thickening rapidly. Taking a big

255

breath, he ran across the street and looked back up at the roof of the building housing the canteen. There was no sign of its being on fire, though it was outlined against a scarlet sky. The buildings on either side also showed no hint of fire.

He raced back across the road and down the steps again to the shelter. He reported, panting, "T' smoke's nothing, as far as we're concerned," and then paused to get his breath while another series of detonations drowned him out. Emmie felt her courage draining from her and she and Doris clung to each other. He continued, "There's some big fires not far away — and I could hear machine guns for a minute. Bloody Boche going for the firemen." He looked at the anxious faces surrounding him. "If we try to move, like as not we'll walk into more trouble. I'd say stay here." He sat down suddenly on a bench, aware that he was no longer as young as he had been. He looked down at his shabby boots, while men slowly resumed their seats.

When his heart had stopped racing, he said diffidently, "Think I'll walk up Lord Street and see what's to do. T' rescue squads must be hard-pressed at the back there. Anybody want to come?"

The men stopped their subdued gossiping and looked uneasily at Dick, and Dick said, "Them as has wives and kids, maybe you shouldn't. A couple of you is perhaps like me — you can please yourselves."

"My family is killed in Antwerp," said a melancholy Dutch voice from the far end of the room. "Who to rescue? This is shops and offices round here. Nobody here." He got up, a big, handsome blond man towering over most of those present.

"There's firewatchers and caretakers in every building," replied Dick simply. "Young girls, some of them watchers is."

Two men in naval uniform stood up and the four of them, without a further word, eased their way through to the staircase. Not to be outdone by the Royal Navy, two merchant seamen followed them.

Mrs Robinson said brightly, "As soon as the raid is over, we'll see if we can clean the canteen up, ready for business tomorrow."

The women nodded tired agreement. Emmie was stiff with fatigue and the enforced idleness; the worst thing about air raids was, she thought, that you couldn't hit back.

The electric light went out. Emmie gave a frightened squeak

and Doris drew in her breath quickly. The glowing ends of lighted cigarettes looked like red eyes staring in the darkness. A man laughed shakily. A voice from the gloom said bitterly, "If that isn't the bottom!"

There was a jingle of keys and change, as Mrs Robinson rummaged in the depths of her shabby crocodile-skin handbag. "I've got a match somewhere. There should be some candles in the drawer of the table."

Someone lit a match and a male voice from near the floor said, "I've got a torch, Missus."

The beam seemed as brilliant as a searchlight.

"Oh, thank you," she cried, stumbling over feet as, guided by the torch, she went to the table. She snapped the drawer open. "Really!" she exclaimed. "This is too bad. Somebody has stolen both the candles and the matches. There's not even a stump here."

There was an angry murmur through the room. Petty theft was a way of life in Liverpool. Now, with everything in short supply, it could cause real problems. The owner of the torch, however, said magnanimously, "Anybody as needs to move, tell me and I put me torch on."

Batteries were harder to obtain than candles, so when a young voice said, "Thanks, friend," it expressed the feelings of everybody.

Listening to the clamour outside while sitting in total darkness was far worse, thought Emmie. The minutes seemed longer; the noise wrapped one closer. People tended not to talk; instead they huddled together for comfort.

Gwen had told her of a woman in the next street, who had clung to a perfect stranger in the street's unlighted shelter, while they sat out the Christmas Eve raid, the year before. In their terrible fear, they had become sexually aroused, and now she was pregnant by a man she had never seen. Shocking, Gwen called it; but David, with unexpected understanding, had said that it was Mother Nature's way of seeing that people who had died in a disaster were replaced.

Gwen had responded tartly, "More likely they didn't know right from wrong."

As she hugged Doris, Emmie wondered if she herself were pregnant, or whether the change of life was making its presence felt.

Though frightened, in her secret heart she hoped that she was still young enough for a bun to be in the oven, Robert's little one.

"I hope Robbie's sailed and out of this rumpus," she whispered to Doris.

"You might get a letter tomorrer," Doris suggested. Her own heart ached at the thought; even the letters her dead husband had written to her when they were courting had been lost, with him, in their burned-out home.

The racket outside seemed to be slackening, the explosions further away. "Sounds like they might be doin' Bootle or Seaforth," suggested a disembodied voice.

"God spare us," exploded Doris. "Haven't we had enough up there?"

IV

The women stood forlornly at the top of the shelter stairs. The All Clear had sounded; the noise abated. Through the gaping front windows, the whole town seemed to glow, the shattered room lighted up as if a good coal fire was burning in the old-fashioned grate. As they moved forward, glass and china crunched beneath their feet. The counter, which normally held the tea and coffee samovars, flanked by plates of buns and sandwiches, had been swept clear. Both samovars lay on their sides on the floor, silent humps in pools of black liquid, their copper exteriors reflecting the dancing light from outside.

The light from outside did not penetrate the kitchen, so Mrs Starr struck a match. "Ah, that's better," she cried.

Though very dusty, the kitchen was practically undisturbed. The telephone, which Emmie had put on the sill to hold down the blackout curtains of the small window, had fallen on to the table beneath the window. Emmie lifted the curtain to peer out and was surprised that, at least there, there was still glass to look through.

Mrs Starr, one of the volunteers, asked Mrs Robinson a little diffidently, "Would you mind if I phoned my son to say I am all right?"

Mrs Robinson looked up from her task of setting out candles and lighting them. "Of course not," she replied.

The phone was dead. Mrs Starr sighed, and looked at her watch.

It was nearly 3 a.m.

An air raid warden paused by the open front door. "Anybody here?" he shouted. Drawn by the sudden flare of the candles, he clumped towards the kitchen. His face was gaunt, eyes burning with fatigue. A striped pyjama collar stuck out untidily from the neck of his uniform.

"Are we safe from the fires?" Mrs Robinson asked, after greeting him.

"Aye. There's a firewatcher on the roof — young Dolly — she'll tell you if fires out t' back are spreading this side."

"What's burning?" Mrs Starr asked.

"Church House. It'll be gutted. Too far gone to save. And the Corn Exchange and the White Star building — God knows how many others. Bootle's calling for fire-engines out there, but they can't spare none from here." He heaved a sigh. "Must go check next door. Ta-ra." He crunched his way back across the strewn canteen floor and they heard him curse as he caught his boot against one of the recumbent samovars and it clanged like a bell.

V

While Emmie and Gwen cleaned up their home and David laid new waterpipes in the Royal Infirmary, Conor walked round his district to assess the damage of the previous night.

"Rain'll do more damage than t'bombs," he told the already very depressed families, who a few streets away from his own home had lost their roofs. "I'll get you some tarps to lay over the rafters."

He returned to the post and put in a request for tarpaulin. Then he retrieved the front and back doors of the oldest couple affected, and helped the old man hang them again.

From nearby homes still comparatively undamaged, older women, silent, hands clasped over their stomachs, drifted over to watch and then to help their stricken neighbours shovel plaster and soot out of their chaotic little homes. Children, too small for school, found jam butties thrust into their hands by strange, smiling women. Buckets of water and trays of tea were lugged from several streets away, where water was still available. Friendships which were to last a lifetime were made between tearful outbursts

259

from women beginning to quiver from delayed shock. The acute shortage of young, strong men to help was remarked upon and an extra tear was shed for those of them fighting in Greece or on a warship somewhere in the Mediterranean. And slowly, painfully slowly, some order was restored.

While he munched a very dry sandwich, back at the post, Conor wrote out his reports. After that, seething with rage, he went to see the bitch who had refused to produce the street's stirrup-pump, at a time when the whole road had been littered with incendiaries.

God, how he needed a drink. He seemed to be floating, rather than walking. Light-headed, that was the word. And what a fool he had been to put at the back of the cellar of the post the half-dozen bottles of whiskey he had lifted from a lorry unwise enough to park in the district a couple of days before. Now, the post was as busy as a tram terminus and he could not retrieve them without its being noticed. If he had found a better place for them, he could have had a drink right now and flogged the rest for good money.

He slammed down his fountain pen and went home.

With one side of her face still slightly swollen from the blow he had given her, Ellen was in no mood to be conciliatory. Practically the whole of the family's bacon ration piled on his plate, however, suggested that the storm might be passing. He was too tired, too overwhelmed by other people's troubles laid upon his shoulders, to make an effort to break the silence between them, and as soon as he had mopped up the last bit of grease from his plate with a piece of bread, he announced that he was going to bed.

Within minutes, he was sound asleep, and did not hear Ellen shouting exasperatedly at Patrick's back, as he went out of the front door.

"I'm not going to bed at seven o' clock, no matter how many raids there are," he had said obstinately. "I'm goin' to see a pal." And he had wandered out into the deserted street, with a lazy grin at her over his shoulder.

He slipped through the soft spring evening, to the unfinished, roofless air raid shelter where he had taken Mari and where she had reluctantly promised to meet him again. He hung around outside it for nearly an hour, but Mari did not come.

A thoroughly scared Mari was certain that the previous night's raid had been arranged by God particularly to punish her.

He walked back home, clenched fists in trouser pockets, shoulders hunched, muttering angrily under his breath. Nothing but a stuck-up Judy, that's her. Wait till he caught her again. Yet, beneath his rage, he felt no true desire to harm her; only a craven fear that she would not come again; a young Romeo who had not yet managed to persuade his Juliet to fall in love with him. Wait till he was a Spitfire pilot, he reassured himself, with embroidered wings on his tunic; then she'd come crawling, and he might just condescend to take her to a dance.

At half-past ten, he was sitting despondently on the basement steps, listening to the guns and whistling to himself, while a fearful Ruby crouched close to him, pulling nervously at her thick, black fringe. Their sleepy father had tumbled back into his overalls and gone down to the post.

VI

Dress Materials at Blackler's had, that Friday afternoon, been busy. Women were buying dress lengths, in anticipation of clothes being rationed; Gwen herself had several such lengths stored away in the mahogany chest of drawers brought from Emmie's home. Out of her wages, she was also holding a little money in order to buy two pairs of silk stockings, which a girl from Hosiery had told her, during her tea break, had at last arrived.

She was surprised when her supervisor sent her over to the Dress Department to help out.

"They're rushed off their feet," she explained. "People wanting mourning clothes."

When, homeward bound, she descended from the tram at the corner of her street, her feet ached abominably. She had sold so many black dresses that she felt deeply dispirited. At one point, she had been positively thankful to be faced with a giggling 15-year-old who wanted a pale blue bridesmaid's dress.

"Me sister's boy friend's got a forty-eight-hour pass. Comin' 'ome Tuesday night. Me mam's nearly out of her mind tryin' to get everything ready for a wedding on Wednesday mornin'."

The girl's flippant elation had made several sad-faced women turn on her with reproving murmurs of "Really! At this time?" Unable to relate to the grief of strangers, she had gone away happy,

261

with a fluff of blue net carefully packed in tissue paper.

"Phew!" Gwen groaned, as she tottered through the twilight. The sky was still an unnaturally bright pink, but she was too tired to care. She thought only of her clean bed, with David, solid and reliable, snoring on his side of it.

"Where's your dad?" she asked Mari, as she took off her Sunday hat, black velveteen with a bunch of feathers held by a *diamanté* brooch, and laid it carefully in its box.

The girl lifted a wan face from gloomy contemplation of her arithmetic book and wiped her pen nib with a piece of blotting paper. "I don't know, Mum. I'm scared. It's late for him."

"Ach, he's probably doin' overtime. What did you do with his bit of fish pie?"

"I kept it hot for a while. Then it got so dried out in the oven, I put it back in the pantry."

"Good girl."

Good girl? Mari chewed the end of her plait nervously, and sighed, and tried to forget the extraordinary sensations within her.

About midnight, David staggered in and thankfully plunked down his heavy tool-box.

"Worked late and then I had to walk home," he told them as, regardless of the guns roaring outside, they scuttled round to get him his supper. "There's a proper raid on down town. The sound of the planes diving, as I come along, give me the willies, they did. Hope our Em's all right."

Gwen had forgotten entirely about Emmie and now she paused, tea caddy in hand, a twinge of conscience striking her.

"Anyway, we can't do anything about her," he went on practically, as he sat down to his fish pie. "We should go to bed. They're not bombing round here — too busy with the town to bother us." He turned to Mari and said with a grin, "Your room's a deal safer with the window being boarded up. Maybe young Patrick did you a good turn."

Mari stared at him for a second, her smile frozen on her face. Then she said diffidently, "I suppose he did."

Gwen climbed nervously into her bed and pulled the clothes over her head, to shut out the sound of chugging aeroplane engines. Two hours of sitting on the basement steps had made her back ache and to lie down was a blessed relief. David put his head

262

on his pillow and began to snore immediately. Mari lay quietly in the stuffy darkness of her room and wondered what had really happened to her. Could you have a baby if a boy touched you?

None of them heard Emmie's flagging footsteps, when she came in. Groaning sleepily, they got up again at six o'clock in the morning and were astonished to find her sound asleep in David's chair, a cold cup of tea beside her on the bookshelf.

SATURDAY, 3 MAY 1941

I

Gwen stared unbelievingly at the shattered windows of Blackler's store. She seethed with indignation. An attack on Blackler's was, she felt, an attack on her personally. It was her store.

She glanced along its usually immaculate frontage. Little piles of swept-up glass stood waiting to be shovelled away. The gaping holes, which had once been windows filled with merchandise labelled with large, cheerful notices of special bargains, had been cleared; only one or two, where the glass, by some fluke, remained intact, still bravely displayed for the benefit of the weekend invasion of shoppers from Wales a collection of special offers.

And the Welsh were coming in in force. Dressed in their best, they came by train and bus not only to buy but to make holiday, joining shoppers from the Liverpool suburbs in touring the damage wreaked on the city and viewing the roaring fires. People from slum and suburb alike walked into cafés and grocery shops whose fronts had been blown out, and stood around feasting on food not yet salvaged. Rowdy groups, dodging the already harassed police, calmly looted anything they fancied, laughing and joking and getting drunk on wines and spirits they found in the grocery stores. Not a few owners defended their little broken shops with cricket bats, battered symbols of integrity.

As, later on, she snipped lengths of material for a customer who spoke, with disgust, of the behaviour of a group of hooligans she had seen, Gwen said bitterly, "You'd think we was a circus, the way they gape — and a free-for-all. Rob their own mothers, they would."

"Aye," the customer agreed heavily. "Who'd have believed it?"

267

II

David usually finished work at twelve noon on Saturdays, and Gwen had left a dish of stew in the oven for his midday meal. It grew dryer and dryer and finally shrivelled up on the plate, because David had not, that morning, been pursuing the incredible intricacies of the plumbing of the Royal Infirmary. He had, instead, been pounced on by his supervisor, immediately upon his arrival, and had been sent by taxi out to Bootle, together with his mate, Arthur, a grizzled ancient, back in the work force after four years of retirement.

"Bloody chaos out there," the supervisor had told them. "No water. Gas lines flaring up in the streets. Electric's out. Report to the town hall. They'll tell you where to go."

They were joined by two electricians, who had also been impounded, and as they sat in the taxi, tool-boxes rattling in the luggage compartment by the driver, they looked out in astonishment and no little trepidation at increasing turmoil, the further north they proceeded.

The driver had to pick his way through miles of littered streets made muddy by burst water lines and, in places, lacings of fire-hoses temporarily abandoned for lack of water pressure. Timber yards crackled and smoked on both sides of the road, the draught of the flames making it hard for the driver to keep the taxi stable, for a scarifying few minutes. Occasionally, they would be redirected by police or special constables to detour a mass of masonry spread across a street.

When they finally found the streets they were to work in, after being redirected by a series of city officials, they stood for a moment bewildered, their tools at their feet, wondering where on earth to start. Civil defence workers of every kind toiled amid the havoc, while the homeless scrambled over the debris in an effort to pick out some belongings which might still be usable. In desperate efforts to help families still entombed, some of them got into the way of rescue workers cautiously digging through piles of bricks, mortar and shattered wood, to get at victims for whom there was little hope. Others stood in forlorn groups, an occasional sob indicating some poor soul for whom it was all too much; still others were unnaturally cheerful, thankful to have survived;

the true hardship of their situation would hit them later.

A hundred yards up the street, a cracked gas line gave way. A white sheet of flame roared upwards, its deadly heat threatening further damage. Rescuers and inhabitants scrambled over debris to a safer distance.

"Good God!" exclaimed Arthur, and turned to run.

David caught his arm. His breath came in frightened gasps, but he said, "It could blow the whole street up. Better find the valve. See if we can turn it off." He grabbed a tool from his box and followed by a protesting Arthur ran towards the explosion. While wardens shouted to them to come back, they searched likely spots for the valve they needed, and, within a minute or two, found it. A quick twist and the flame subsided. David stood very still for a moment, holding on to Arthur, while the pain in his chest subsided, a shivering unsung hero, like many others that day.

Soon, watched anxiously by housewives, black-shawled against the morning coolness, David and Arthur were set to work by a city hall official to reconnect a major break in a water line. The women were desperate for water to clean their damaged homes and wash the dirt off their children and themselves. The Women's Voluntary Service brought food both to workers and watchers, and they stood around in the street, their children about them, while they thankfully sipped mugs of tea. Their voices were shrill with nervous tension and they wound their shawls tightly round themselves for comfort. To David, it seemed particularly wicked that people so painfully poverty-stricken should have their tiny, crowded homes broken open like eggs. "And the men at sea — or struggling to keep the docks working," David muttered angrily to Arthur.

There was no question of going home that night; the need of them in Bootle was too grave.

As twilight approached, he and Arthur paused to stretch themselves and eat the sandwiches brought to them by the indefatigable WVS canteen staff. They both became aware of a general movement in the neighbourhood. Women, pushing perambulators or pushchairs loaded with children and bedding, were so numerous as to form a long procession in the now partially tidied up street.

"Where do you think they're goin'?" he asked Arthur.

"Walkin' out to Huyton, to sleep in t' fields, I expect. It's a deal safer'n staying here overnight."

David nodded. Except for an occasional shout to a child to mind himself, the procession was strangely quiet. There was a dull acceptance in the passing faces, framed in dusty, tousled hair. Dragging boots made a slow shuffling sound on the gritty street.

"They'll be back in t' mornin', bright and early no doubt," remarked Arthur, "to check on their homes — and send t' kids to school — if the school's still there."

III

Mari and her friend, Dorothy, went to the Saturday children's programme at the cinema that afternoon and then went home to Dorothy's house for tea.

While his mother sat on the front step, nursing Michael and enjoying the sunshine, and Ruby and Nora played skipping on the pavement, Patrick sloped around the alleyways, hoping to find Mari. Unsuccessful, he irritably teased his father's fighting cocks and for his pains got a long scratch on the back of his right hand.

Conor Donnelly's area had been mercifully free from incidents on the previous night, so while he had a comparatively quiet day, he wandered down to the Hercy Dock to see if he could find an American sailor off a tanker, with nylons or lipsticks for sale. Both fetched good prices on the black market.

IV

As Gwen bustled into her home about eight o'clock that evening, she felt more energetic than she had done for some days. A few hours of good sleep, despite the noise of the raid, had restored her, and she had enjoyed at Blackler's the close feeling of unity amongst her companions, engendered by their joint dislike of the large influx of sightseers and ill-intentioned riff-raff into the town.

Mari was sitting alone, by the fire, slowly turning the heel of a sock, one of a pair she was knitting as a contribution to a parcel being made up for the men of the King's Regiment. Two of the girls in the class had fathers serving in it, stationed at Hull. Mari was a good knitter, having been taught by her mother as soon as she could hold a pair of butcher's skewers and a ball of wool.

"Yer dad not in?" Gwen inquired, as she once more returned

270

her best hat to its box.

"No." Mari paused, needle in stitch.

Mari was feeling a little less panic-stricken about Patrick. She had stuck close to Dorothy all day, and after tea they had rearranged Dorothy's doll's house and put up new curtains in it. Mr Hale, Dorothy's father, who had to go to a chapel meeting, had kindly walked her home, since it was on his way. They walked slowly because he limped; Dorothy said he had been wounded in the First World War at a terrible place called Passchendaele, and, as had sometimes happened in her grandfather's house, Mari was reminded that the results of war stayed on and on, long after the battles were finished. Did it mean, she wondered fearfully, that her life would be different after the war? Would she, all her life, drag a foot or, much worse, be jeered at because she had been disfigured? She nearly choked, when she remembered that her grandfather had once told her that he had a friend kept permanently in hospital because he had almost no face.

She had thought about this, as she sat quietly knitting; it was all mixed up with a hodge-podge of ideas about Patrick. To her relief, her figure had not swelled up as she knew a pregnant woman's did, so she had begun to think that being caressed all over by a boy's exploring fingers did not produce a baby, and that was a relief; she had heard of girls who had committed suicide because they were pregnant and did not have a proper husband.

The explosive feelings that Patrick had aroused in her must mean something, though. She longed to ask her mother about it, but dared not. Could such an exciting feeling really be wicked? She wondered if she could ask Aunt Emmie; after all, she was engaged and must know something about it.

As Gwen put the kettle on for tea, she was not particularly worried about David; he had done a lot of overtime recently. Both mother and daughter jumped apprehensively, however, when someone thumped on the front door.

"Your dad? Hurt?" Gwen exclaimed.

As they ran along the passage, getting in each other's way in their sudden sense of urgency, they heard Conor Donnelly outside, shouting, "Mrs Thomas! Mrs Thomas!" Gwen reckoned that if the warden brought the news, it must be bad. She flung the door open, letting out a little light from the candle on the hall table.

271

"Get in, get in," Conor ordered testily. "Enough light to guide them from Berlin."

He hastened over the doorstep and shut the door behind him.

"What's to do?" Gwen asked anxiously, while Mari's blank little face went whiter than usual.

"Och, it's all right," he answered, seeing their frightened faces. "Yer husband rang the post, from Bootle, to say he mayn't be back till tomorrer night."

"What? Bootle? What's he doin' there?"

"It's terrible out there, missus. They need every man they can get."

"How'll he get his dinner?"

"Same as the firemen and everyone else workin' out there. From the WVS canteen, I 'spect."

"He's too old to be gallivanting round out there. He needs his sleep." Gwen's voice was angry.

Conor's deep blue eyes registered such scorn that Gwen quailed slightly. "So do we all. We're none of us youngsters, Mrs Thomas."

She was disconcerted at the snub, and her irritation at this man and his slovenly family increased. She said tightly, "Well, thank you for bringing the message. I don't know why he didn't phone earlier."

"Phones out of order, like everything else," he replied, fully aware of her distaste of him.

Gwen went slowly back to the living room and sat down on a footstool close to the fire. It was wasteful to have a fire in May, but she justified it by cooking on it, and now, suddenly, she was grateful for its comforting warmth. For the first time in her life, the idea that she might be widowed occurred to her; Conor's description of the dire straits of Bootle had struck home; accidents happened in such awful situations.

While Mari made tea and toast for their supper, the virtues of her patient lumbering husband surfaced in her mind. She remembered, with a pang, the sturdy Welsh youth who had proposed to her, as they walked soberly in Princes Park after chapel. They had had to wait seven years before they could afford to be married, and, sipping tea beside the fire, she wished they had not wasted their youth. Why, she wondered bitterly, had she been so coldly virtuous? And now it could all end in a holocaust in Bootle.

She and Mari had lain in bed a scant hour, when the air raid warning dragged them out again. "We'll get dressed in the living room," Gwen said resignedly. "It'll be safer down there."

"Poor Aunt Emmie," Mari exclaimed. "Stuck down town again."

V

Ellen Donnelly blasted furiously all them Jerries and their ilk, as she, too, that Saturday night shepherded her family down the cellar steps.

During the day, she had hauled a mattress down into the dank basement and on this she persuaded Ruby, Nora and Brendy to lie down to sleep. It was not quite so safe as sitting on the stairs, but as she remarked, "Beggars can't be choosers."

Patrick sat moodily on the top step, watching his mother nurse Michael to sleep again. The candlelight caught the white hairs amongst her brown mop and deepened the lines on her shiny red face. He felt a sudden twinge of pain that his mother was growing older. Though she was always demanding to know where he had been and what he had been doing, he loved her with a passion that frightened him sometimes. He was inordinately jealous of his father, and, when his father struck her, he boiled with inward anger that he was too small and cowardly to defend her. When I'm bigger, I will, he always told himself. He resented the succession of babies that occupied her lap, and only Ruby, eleven months younger than him, escaped being bullied by him whenever he was in a bad temper.

The noise of the anti-aircraft guns began to shake the old house.

VI

Unaware of the frantic clean-up done by candlelight after the previous night's raid, a dozen men were lounging round the tables of the sailors' canteen, gossiping amid the usual cloud of tobacco smoke.

Mrs Robinson arrived at the same time as Emmie. She was carrying two parcels and Emmie took them from her. "These are heavy," she exclaimed.

"Crockery oddments, my dear. After last night, we're dreadfully short. These are a donation from Lewis's — I went in to see them

273

this morning."

In the kitchen, Peggie Evans, another paid member of the staff, was tidying up the last of the muddle from the lunchtime rush. "'T' fish is finished," she told Emmie and Mrs Robinson, "t' butcher brought plenty of sausage, though, for tonight. And there's still a lot o' dried egg."

As she put on her overall, Emmie told her how the fish had been covered with dust the previous night. "At first we was goin' to throw it out. Then Mrs Robinson said what waste. So we washed it very carefully and put it in the larder. Did you have any complaints?"

"Never a word. Deep fried, there'd be nought the matter with it." She took her coat off a hook and her handbag out of a drawer. "Was I ever glad I wasn't here last night. It must've been awful."

"I were scared out of me wits," admitted Emmie. "I got a proper laugh, though, out of the note you've pinned on the sandbags round the door. 'Open for business — very open.'"

"Aye. I thought t' lads 'd believe we'd given up on 'em, with the shutters closed, like."

"You know we had the till cleaned out, during the raid?"

"No?"

"Somebody took the whole night's takings. Must've done it while we was in the shelter. We didn't stop to lock the front door."

"Stinking buggers," said Peggie forcefully, as she clapped a blue beret on her head. "Tara-well."

Doris did not arrive. She lay dead in the arms of the seaman who had taught her to smoke, under the wreckage of a shop doorway which had suddenly collapsed on them, taking both their lives while they made love.

A white-haired grocer's wife, Mrs Atkins, and the silent, elegant Lady Mentmore were redeployed to cover the work. "Perhaps she'll phone later," suggested Emmie.

"Is the phone working?" Mrs Robinson looked harried. She was bone-tired, her plump, middle-aged body refusing to run at its usual pace.

Emmie went to the table by the window and cautiously lifted the receiver and put it to her ear. "It's still dead," she announced.

"Oh, dear! What a nuisance! The crater down the street must

274

be responsible for that. I saw the Post Office Telephones van there, as I came in."

Mrs Atkins looked up from her carrot scraping. "It really was an awful night. And it could have been worse. I heard this morning that they were worried about a munition ship called the *Malakand* in Huskisson Dock. It's being loaded for the Middle East. And with the fires and that being so bad up the north end — poor Bootle — they were mortally afraid it would explode."

Emmie froze, the fork with which she was pricking sausages poised to stab. "The *Malakand*?" she exclaimed in horror. "My Robbie's on that." She turned a stricken face towards the carrot scraper. "He never told me it had munitions in it."

Mrs Atkins soothed, "Well, nothing's happened to it yet. Perhaps it will sail today."

Emmie nodded assent and slowly and heavily she pricked the neat pink rows of sausages. She tried not to weep. To sail the Med with ammunition in the hold! Even if he got out of port safely, it could be a death-warrant! She wanted to scream 'No' to God. Was He really almighty? She wanted to faint, to escape the fear which pierced her. But she could not, must not. In a war, she must not give way. Quietly, she went on with her work and missed the pitying glances of Mrs Atkins and the countess. The countess said practically, to Emmie's back, "I think we all need a cup of tea."

As she filled the four cups from the samovar, she herself was not feeling very well. The previous night, an incendiary, apparently a dud, had fallen through the thatched roof of her house, and it had taken the combined efforts of her two elderly maids and herself to lift it out of the water tank into which it had fallen. They had thrown it out of the attic window on to the lawn, where it had unexpectedly exploded. A small incident, not worth mentioning, but it had tired her. She yawned behind a heavily beringed hand, as she added lots of sugar to Emmie's tea; she understood that the lower classes enjoyed plenty of sugar.

VII

Saturday night, when you should be down at the local, sitting by the fire and telling funny stories over a pint of bitter; instead you were stuck in a sandbagged shop labelled A.R.P., listening to the pandemonium in the skies and hoping that nothing fell on you. The strain was telling on Conor Donnelly. He told himself irritably that he had had it up to here. And to add to it all, he had quarrelled with Ellen over a drop of whiskey — and she was still as sour as yesterday's milk. He went to the door and glanced up at the sky.

The brilliance of the flares had put the stars out, and the air smelled as if a million rubber tyres were burning. The shriek of bombs descending on the flaming city centre, about a mile down the hill, could hardly be heard above the concerted roar of their impact, the drone of heavy engines and the scream of night fighters as they dived. Nearer, in the park, the anti-aircraft guns kept up a steady barrage at the bellies of the bombers, which glistened like slugs, in the light of darting flames.

Inside the post, three women wardens were placidly waiting for a tin kettle of water to boil on a primus stove, their imperturbability belied by their ghostly faces. A grey-haired voluntary warden, Montague Smith, who came in each night there was a raid, was snatching a nap on a camp-bed. In the daytime, he was the manager of the bank round the corner.

Conor had always thought that anyone who had a bank account, never mind worked in a bank, must be hopelessly stuck up. But this pot-bellied man had won his admiration the previous November. He had crawled into the shifting debris of a house, to hold the hand of a dreadfully injured old man until a doctor crawled in, too, to give the victim an injection to ease the pain while they got him out. Then they had worked the remainder of the night together, under enemy machine-gun fire.

The half-washed Irish labourer and the well-shaven polite banker supported each other. Conor never gave himself credit for the friendliness he exuded, the enthusiasm with which he would do a good turn. Montague — our Mont, to all the wardens — had a quick, orderly mind, able to size up the immediate needs in some of the horrid situations which they faced together.

"G' us a cuppa tea, Glynis, luv," Conor asked one of the women. He was hungry. In a day or two, Ellen would get over her sulks and boil up a good stew. Meanwhile, he could whistle for it. A short burst of machine-gun fire directly overhead made everyone

276

duck instinctively. He wished suddenly he had made it up with Ellen. What was a drop of whiskey anyway, in a world where one bullet could finish him? He chewed his thumb uneasily while Glynis made the tea.

Glynis Hughes eased her tin hat further back on her head and grinned up at him. She was a small, brown-skinned woman, suggesting descent from the little people who roamed Britain before the Celts arrived. Her husband was serving in the South Lancashires and she was temporarily living nearby with her mother. She worked in a factory which made aircraft parts and she made many a lewd joke about her production of joysticks. She was used to coping with the appetite of a labourer in a steelworks and she still shamelessly bought any food she could find on the black market. Now she asked, "Like a Spam sandwich?"

"Ah would, if you can spare it."

She took out from a shopping bag a white, confectioner's paper bag and from this she carefully drew out a sandwich two inches thick with a thin slice of Spam in it. "I brought some bikkies for you girls," she told her companions, "Chocky ones."

The other two women's faces lit up. "Mm. Where did you get them from?" They, too, were housewives permanently scrounging through the shops for extra food. To earn the money for it, they worked as labourers, cleaning oil drums at a petrol installation.

Glynis giggled. "Ask no questions, you'll be told no lies."

Conor wolfed the proffered sandwich and a chocolate biscuit. He felt much better and walked outside to take another look at what was happening.

The sky was a brilliant pink, with rolling billows of smoke making rosy cushions above him. There was no one, not even a cat, in the street. He went back into the tiny shop and leaned against the wall by the telephone girl, to gossip.

He was jolted upright by a fast puffing sound, closer than the general roar, then a pause, while everyone held their breath. A heavy crump and everyone breathed out.

"Land-mine," Conor said. "Unexploded."

"Must have fallen in the park," Glynis commented, relief exuding from her.

"Here comes another," squeaked the telephonist, as she laid

her head on her table and clasped her arms over her tin hat. The trainlike sound came again and Conor tensed.

An enormous explosion shook the old shop, reverberating round them in swelling waves. The telephone girl was nearly lifted off her chair, and cracks ran up the grubby walls. Mont was on his feet in a split second, clapping his helmet to his head. "My God!" he exclaimed.

A colossal growl, like that of some huge animal, indicated the fall of heavy masonry; it was followed by a rapid tattoo of smaller pieces on to the roof and into the street.

"The tenement?" breathed Glynis through chattering teeth. "The Dwellings?"

"Could be," Mont replied, as he loosened his torch from his belt. All of them dreaded a direct hit on the huge five-storey tenement nearby. It was built in a circle, round a communal yard, and was packed with young families.

Conor had already gone. He ran madly down the pink-lit street and turned left. He was brought up short by an impenetrable cloud of dust. Other than the heavy grumble from the skies, there was a weird silence.

Then, from beyond the dust cloud, came scream after scream of pain and panic. "Oh, Jesus, help us," shrieked a woman's voice.

Doors of the row houses close to the warden banged open, as shaken tenants came rushing out. Mont panted up to Conor, and said, "I'll tell Josie to phone R. and P. We're going to need a lot of help."

Conor cleared his throat and spat. "Better have a closer look first. Could be only the houses facin', not the tenement itself."

They both took out handkerchiefs to cover their noses from the cloying dust; it was so thick that the beams of their torches were reflected back, as if they faced a wall. They turned the lights down to their feet and picked their way round huge slabs of concrete and piles of bricks, interspersed with threatening electric wires. The dust, now mixed with a strong smell of gas, made Mont cough. He tripped over a broken beam and fell, barking his shins and hands painfully, and got up again. Behind him, Conor could hear other people scrambling over the wreckage; they were shouting to each other, as they converged, and above and beyond the sound of their voices came the screams of the half-crushed.

278

" 'Allo, la," Conor called. "I'm the warden. All men come to me. Dear God, send me some wi' a bit o' savvy, he added to himself. Judging by the curses behind him, he was not going to have to *ask* people to help tonight, which was a welcome change. He hoped Tom Massey was on duty — biggest bloody rozzer in the whole police force. He knew he could use a dozen heavyweights for this job.

A shrieking woman blundered into him. She clutched his arms and shook him. "Me lads — me lads!" she yelled into his face. She was naked, her clothing blown off her, and long, black hair flicked across his mouth, as she half turned to look back at the carnage slowly emerging from the fog.

"Hold on there, luv. Did it hit clean on The Dwellings?"

"Aye, into t' middle yard." She clawed at him. "For Jesus' sake, get me boys out."

Throughout the raid, Conor and Mont, with the Rescue Squad, sweated and cursed their way into the ruins, sickened frequently, occasionally triumphant when they brought out the living, until in the early morning, a filthy, bloodstained Conor went back to the post to write out his report. New orphans, new widows, new cripples and a band of homeless. And what for? What was it in truth all about? God's curse on them all. He rubbed his torn and dirty hands on his overalls and reached for his pencil.

VIII

Arms round each other, Gwen and Mari cowered on the cellar steps, certain that each strident screech above their heads would be the last thing they would ever hear.

The petrifying crash which destroyed The Dwellings made both of them scream. Tinkling glass and a rushing draught told them that the windows had blown in.

"Me sitting room! Me aspidistra!" Gwen wailed. Her Holy of Holies would be exposed to the weather — and thieves!

Mari began to cry.

The roar of the attack on the city centre was undiminished, but locally it was as if everything held its breath, as if the explosion of the land-mine had taken everything with it. Gwen and Mari loosed their grip on each other and raised their heads.

279

The quiet was broken by a frantic banging on the back door. "Missus, missus! Come quick," a boy's voice cried.

Patrick! Mari scrambled to her feet.

Her mother caught her by her bare ankle. "You stay here, miss. I'll go."

In the pink light coming from between the flapping remains of the blackout curtains, it was easy to see the familiar terrain of the brick-tiled kitchen. She flung open the back door. Five shadows tumbled in together, wailing like forgotten babies.

Gwen surveyed five shocked faces, in the uncertain light. "For Heaven's sake, what's to do?"

"It's Mam. She's hurt real bad," Patrick gulped. "Coom and help her."

Gwen swallowed. "Where is she?"

"She's lyin' by t' front step. Ah can't move her. Coom quick." The usually bumptious Patrick was beside himself, his face ashen.

Crowded close to him, the other children broke into loud howls. Ruby led the hullabaloo. Her mother, her only defence against the terror of the raids, was lying inert at the door of her home; and Ruby was convinced that all the houses would collapse any minute and she would again be buried.

Despite Gwen's own nervousness and confusion, the sickly smell of the children's unwashed bodies penetrated to her. Repulsed by it, she snapped at them, "Now you be quiet. I'll get a candle and go and have a look at your mam."

As the candle was lit, the howls tailed off into small sobs. The flame showed the small, barefoot crew in more detail. They all had white rivulets down their dirty faces.

For safety's sake, Gwen decided that the children could not return to their home with her; the gunfire was too heavy. She lit another candle and handed it to Patrick. "Sit on the cellar steps with Mari — all of you. Get a move on, now. It's not safe up here. And mind your feet on the floor — there's glass all over. I'll be back in a minute."

Ruby, dragging a protesting Michael, led the way timidly. Patrick wiped the tears from his face, put on a defiant air and stood on the top step, leaning one shoulder against the wall to stop himself shaking.

Mari half smiled at him as she looked up the steps, but he did

280

not even glance at her. She felt unexpectedly hurt. She turned her attention to Ruby. Gosh, how she smelled.

The clangour of fire-engine bells came clearly through the roar of the blitz, as Gwen, candle in hand, hesitated in her front doorway. What would she find next door?

A string of incendiaries slithered down a short distance away. Vicious pencils of flak suddenly peppered the road in front of her. She bobbed back into the hall. The candle blew out. With it still in her hand, she crept down the two carefully whitened steps of her own front entrance, as if by making no sound she could outwit the German pilots. Then she turned into the immediately adjacent front doorway of the Donnellys and stared into their hall. In dismay, she dropped the dead candle and it rattled away on the pavement.

Just inside, Ellen half lay, half sat, against the weathered door. One hand was flung across her breast. Her eyes, wide with shock, stared at the wall opposite her.

"Oh, my goodness!" Gwen took the two steps in one stride and knelt down by the woman. "Mrs Donnelly? Are you hurt?"

There was no reply. Gwen put out a careful hand and touched her face. She did not move. The body was surrounded by the effluvium of human excrement, and a primeval fear of death clutched at Gwen's throat. In an agony of indecision, she glanced up at the small piece of sky she could see above the roofs opposite; in the flushed torment there, the battle raged on. Her breath came in short pants and she wanted to run away, out of Liverpool, away from the dirty horde on her cellar steps, away from this scarifying hulk of a woman. But there was nowhere to run to; even the street across the doorstep was a death-trap.

She took a big breath and pulled herself together. How did one make absolutely certain that a person was dead? She might still be alive — in shock — wounded only.

A resonant bang nearby, followed immediately by a shower of bricks and mortar on the doorstep, galvanised Gwen into action. Still kneeling, she leaned forward and tried to heave Ellen further into the hall. Ellen's arms flopped and her whole body reeled towards Gwen's tiny frame. In horror, Gwen let go and scrambled to her feet. Ellen slumped to the floor.

Doing her best not to vomit, and risking the descent of further missiles, she ran a few steps to the nearest street shelter and called hopefully through the doorway, "Anybody there?" But only a faint echo came from its stinking darkness.

She ran back to her own house and scuttled through the length of it. On the cellar steps, the children were sitting as rigidly as images; one little boy was crying heartily. At the sound of her footfall they turned to look up at her, the whites of their eyes gleaming in the candlelight.

"I'm going through the alleyway to Mr Baker's next door but one," she told them quickly. "To get some help for your mum. You all stay close, now. Everything's going to be all right."

She ran through the brick-walled back yard, out of the tall, plank gate and down the alley, which, with its narrowness and high walls, seemed to offer more protection than the front street. She reckoned the Baker family, also, would be in the basement and they would hear her knock more easily if she tried the back door.

"Mr Baker," she shrieked, above the rat-tat-tat of machine-guns. Fearfully she glanced upwards and then renewed her bangs with her fists.

"Wasser marrer?" inquired a richly Liverpool voice, as the door was opened a narrow crack.

"It's Mrs Thomas. Mrs Donnelly's hurt bad and I can't lift her into the house meself. And Mr Donnelly's on duty and me husband's in Bootle." The words poured out, as she wrung her hands helplessly.

The door swung open immediately to reveal, in the light of a kerosene lamp, an elderly man who looked, thought Gwen, a bit like a tortoise wrapped in a dressing-gown.

The wide mouth in the crumpled face opened. "Step in, step in. Let me get me slippers and tell Mother." He padded away, towards the cellar door.

Gwen thankfully entered the kitchen and shut the door behind her. By some fluke of the blast, Mr Baker's kitchen window was still intact. As fear gave way to resentment, she wondered crossly why her windows should always be those to be broken. Why should she get landed with someone wounded? And have to let in five disgusting kids?

Mr Baker came panting up the cellar steps again, his dressing-gown now tightly belted, his misshapen feet encased in carpet slippers.

"Where is she?" he inquired.

"By her front door. It's open."

"Coom through then."

Seething with suppressed vexation at the unfairness of fate, she followed him through his front door, round the tiny bay windows of his home and that of the Donnellys, and up the latter's front steps. From behind the closed door of the kitchen, Sarge began to bark.

Mr Baker put the lamp down on the floor. Very gently he lifted Ellen's arm. A piece of shrapnel was deeply embedded in her side. He held her wrist for a moment, but there was no sign of a pulse.

He got laboriously to his feet. "Let's get her in and shut the door."

As a postman, he was used to lifting awkward weights and he soon pulled her along the bare wooden floor, by putting his hands under her arms from the back. Then he quietly shut the front door; it cut off a lot of the noise from outside.

He looked carefully at the wound. It had bled little and he toyed with the idea of pulling out the piece of shrapnel. Better to leave her as she was, he decided. With womanly care, he turned her on one side to look at her back. Another sliver protruded for about an inch from under one shoulder-blade.

"I reckon she were hit first in her chest and she half turned into the house, and the second piece hit her in the back," he said to a shocked Gwen. "She's dead for sure." He laid the body flat on its back and gently closed the staring eyes. Then he glanced round him, puzzled. "Where's all the kids?"

Gwen licked her white lips. "All in my house, with our Mari."

"That's proper kind of you, Mrs Thomas." He took a crumpled handkerchief out of his dressing-gown pocket and, with a grimace of distaste, wiped Ellen's life-blood from his hands. Gwen stood uncertainly before him, her hands clasped tightly together. Her irritation had faded and she felt numb, unable to make herself think.

"It's more'n anybody's life's worth to go up to the post in this," Baker went on heavily. "As soon as the All Clear sounds, I'll get up there and tell him — and get some help to move her." He rubbed his almost non-existent chin, grey with a day's beard, and then smelled the dried blood still on his hands. Sickened, he dropped them to his sides. "The kids'll do fine with you." He looked down kindly at the small wraith in front of him. "Five of them, isn't there? Poor little buggers — excuse the language."

At the remembrance of the repellent collection sitting on her well-scrubbed steps, Gwen felt nauseated again. But she could not, in all conscience, send them back home, while their dead mother lay where she did. "Donnelly'll have to get a relation to come in and look after them," she said.

"Aye," he agreed. "I'll leave it to you how you tell them."

Gwen stared up at him, aghast. How could *she* tell them? Surely it was not her responsibility? But Mr Baker's mind had gone on to other things, and he said, "I'll let the dog out in the morning, if Donnelly isn't back."

In her own house, she faced the children, as they rose expectantly from their uncomfortable seats on the steps. Ruby held a sleeping Michael; she looked as if she might faint.

Mari was in the kitchen, calmly making cups of cocoa for their guests, while the early morning breeze fluttered her long white nightgown and made the gas jet dance.

The sounds from outside indicated that the attack had shifted slightly to another part of the town, though the rhythmic beat of engines overhead continued.

Gwen looked resentfully at the little crew and cleared her throat uneasily, while the children waited like marble statues in a cemetery. She said carefully, "Your ma's hurt rather bad. Mr Baker next door but one is looking after her. He'll send her to the hospital." She cleared her throat again, some pity for them seeping into her. "You're not to worry. Everything's goin' to be all right."

Relief dawned on Ruby's face. She said to Nora and Brendy, aged 7 and 6 respectively, "See, I told yer so. We're all goin' to have a nice cup o' cocoa, and when the raid's over, we'll go home to bed." She turned to Gwen. "I could go to Mam now — the kids'll be all right with you and Mari."

"No. No," Gwen responded hastily. "Your mam wants you to stay to comfort them."

When she turned to fuss round the cocoa maker, Patrick followed her and stood squarely in front of her. His face was grim and the fine, blue eyes looked at her fearlessly. "I *know*," he said scornfully.

"Well, don't you say nothin' for the minute," Gwen murmured out of the side of her mouth, like a convict. Then, feeling ashamed, she added, "I'm real sorry, lad." She felt like adding, I'm sorry for me, too.

Mari glanced up from her stirring, surprise and fear mingled in her expression. Patrick's face crumbled, tears welled up again.

He's only about 13, Gwen thought, for all he's so big. Instinctively she moved towards him and put her hand on his shoulder. She tried to reassure him. "It'll be all right when your dad comes," she said.

Mari bit her lips to restrain her own desire to cry. She put four cups on a brightly printed tray, filled them and took them to the children on the steps. She said with forced cheerfulness, "Here you are, ducks."

When she turned back to pour out cocoa for her mother and Patrick, she saw with a pang of jealousy that her cold, fastidious parent was holding Patrick's head against her skimpy chest and crooning, "Never mind, luv, never mind." And Patrick, tough cruel Patrick, was actually crying as if his heart would break. Her own lips quivered, as she took down some more cups from their hooks.

Gwen herself was in torment. The children must stay with her until their mother's body was removed. That meant they would probably have to sleep the rest of the night in her house; and they probably had nits in their hair — she would have to burn the pillows afterwards, which would make David thoroughly angry because of the cost of new ones. But what else could she do?

She was personally revolted by their dirtiness; even this beautiful boy smelled as if he had never had a bath since he was born. With a sigh, she urged, "Have a cup o' cocoa, luv. Make you feel better." She took a cup from Mari and handed it to him. "What was your mam doin' at the door on a night like this?"

He took a small gulp of the scalding liquid. "There were a terrible bang — and then it were dead quiet, like. So she run up to see if it were the houses opposite what were hit — 'cos they'd need our help, if they were." He faltered, and then went on, "I heard her cry out and I run up meself — and there she was on the floor — and she never said nothin' — and I knew." His cup rattled against his teeth, as he took another sip.

"God rest her." Gwen put her empty cup down on the drainboard. "We'd better get down the steps. You, too, Mari. We'll wash up tomorrow."

SUNDAY, 4 MAY 1941

I

Ruby's arms were stiff from holding the dead weight of young Michael. Every so often in his sleep, he would nuzzle into her non-existent breasts, looking for the comfort of his mother's milk. Then, frustrated, he would whimper and sleep again.

Patrick sat with eyes closed and fists clenched. He was tortured by the idea of his mother lying alone in the house next door. He wanted to go to her, look at her, try to wake her from her long sleep. But he was afraid of the demons in the sky, afraid of facing alone the fact of her death. After a while, his head fell forward, his mouth opened and he, too, slept.

Just before five o'clock, they all awoke with a jerk to a profound silence, except for Gwen who continued to snore.

Mari shook her mother's arm. "Ma, it's stopped. They've gone."

"Who? What?" Gwen jerked her head from against the cellar wall and blinked. She had been having a nightmare, a nightmare in which the whole house crawled away as a result of the infestation brought in by the Donnelly children. Through her fogged brain, she heard the long, thin cry of the All Clear.

"Phew!" she exclaimed. Then she gazed blearily down at the appalling weight of responsibility sitting on the inhospitable stone steps below her.

Brendy, aged 5, struggled awake and stood up on wobbling legs. He stared round the alien staircase and then roared tearfully, "Where's me mam?" He started to struggle past the knees of the other children, to get to the top of the steps, howling like a miserable dog. Nora, a year older, turned to follow him. She began to whimper. As she threatened to teeter backwards down the steps, Ruby grabbed her wrist.

"Leave me go," the child yelled savagely. She began to beat her big sister in the face with a small clenched fist.

Patrick got up slowly. With frightened, bloodshot eyes, he glanced down at his hostess and then at the other children. A curling spiral of unvented rage ran through him. "Brendy! You shut up or I'll clobber yez. Mam's been hurt and can't come to yez."

Brendy's howls came down a full octave, and Nora stopped trying to get a hold on Ruby's hair to tear it out; when Patrick decided to hit someone, he often distributed the favour throughout the family. Nora's white-lashed eyes narrowed and she made an obscene gesture at Ruby.

Patrick addressed his snivelling siblings again, his voice suddenly placating. "Mrs Thomas is going to let us stay here, aren't you, Mrs Thomas?" His eyes were on Gwen now, pleading, defeated.

Gwen was dizzy with lack of sleep and could not bring her mind into focus. She rubbed her face and then ran her fingers through her frizzy hair. She nodded. Even if Ellen Donnelly's body had been removed, the children would feel the absence of their mother more keenly in their own home and would ask more questions — and she did not want to have to break the news to them that they would never see her again. Better by far to keep them in her own home and let Donnelly do the job in the morning.

She stood up. Her whole body ached. And where was David in all this? He should be at home taking charge of everything. It was unfair that she should carry the whole burden. She began to simmer with resentment. And Emmie hadn't turned up either, to give her a hand.

"I want to pee," wailed Brendy, clutching at himself.

"For heaven's sake, take him down the yard," she ordered Patrick, as she yawned mightily. "Tut, he hasn't got any shoes on — lift him over the glass in the kitchen — and no socks neither — 'is poor little feet is purple."

It was as if Brendy's sad straits forced her awake. She turned to her drooping, equally sleepy daughter. "Mari, get the dustpan and

brush, and get the glass off the kitchen floor, so the little boy —
and the little girl — you ain't got no shoes neither, luv? — don't
cut their feet."

Nora was not to be wooed by a kindly tone. She stuck her finger in her mouth and looked sulky. Gwen turned to Ruby. "And
you, what's your name?"

"Ruby, missus." From beneath her shaggy fringe two sad eyes
gleamed dully.

"Well, you got shoes on. You bring the baby upstairs with me,
and we'll put him on a potty and then into bed. The little girl can
wait in the living room a minute, till Patrick comes back with the
little lad." She lifted a stiff, unyielding Nora up the stairs and deposited her on the living room hearthrug, which seemed to be
clear of broken glass. The child ignored her and stared around the
strange room.

Thankful that someone seemed to know what to do, Ruby trailed
upstairs, a fretful, complaining Michael in her arms. She looked
with awe at Emmie's bedroom into which she was ushered. Though
its pretty, rose-covered curtains, which normally masked the blackout curtains, had been torn by glass, to Ruby it looked like a film
star's bedroom. A matching curtain hung from a corner shelf, to
make a wardrobe, and Ruby eyed its cascade of printed flowers
wonderingly. The window glass had fallen in a rough heap beneath the sill, and Gwen leaned over it to slip the ripped blackout
curtains across the casement.

Ruby shivered in the draught. She felt as if she had expended
every scrap of energy she had, and she was sick with apprehension about her mother; she was silently counting the minutes until
morning, when she could ask her father how she was and whether
she could go to the hospital to see her.

Gwen pulled out a rose-wreathed chamber pot from under the
bed. Michael objected violently to being held over it, and kicked
and screamed. Gwen persisted until he made water — she was
not going to have her beds soaked. A puddle was left on the heavily patterned linoleum. With the enraged child under one arm, she
pulled back the bedclothes, to expose the whitest sheets Ruby had
ever seen, and then shoved the little boy into bed.

"Now you be quiet," she ordered sharply. "Your Ruby's going
to come and lie by you and make you warm, aren't you Ruby?"

Ruby assented and started to climb into bed, shoes, dress and all, but Gwen looked at her in such a scandalised fashion that she hastily reversed herself and pulled off her faded cotton dress and hooked it on to the bed knob. Then she kicked her worn lace-up shoes under the bed.

"That's better," Gwen approved.

Emboldened by the approbation, Ruby inquired, "Me mam? Which hospital did they take her to?"

Gwen looked at the whey-faced, skinny child nearly as tall as herself, the bony chest half-covered by a grubby vest. She knew nothing of the silent terror with which Ruby had faced the night; she saw only that the girl was swaying on her feet. She replied carefully, "Mr Baker was going to see about her being taken to hospital. I don't know which one, though. But you don't have to worry. Mr Baker is proper kind, and Mrs Baker will have gone in to comfort her, until the ambulance arrived." The latter statement made her realise what an accomplished liar she could be, but she cringed at telling the brutal truth. "Now you get into bed, and in no time your Dad'll be here and tell you all about it. Mr Baker was going to send a message up to the post as soon as the All Clear went."

Ruby smiled weakly and climbed into the wonderful bed. Two pillows and real white sheets — and blankets. Gwen tucked her and the complaining child into the bed and left them, taking the candle with her. As soon as she had left the room, Ruby got out again and felt around for the chamber pot.

"Our Emmie is going to have to make do on the sitting room sofa, when she comes in," Gwen told Patrick, who was waiting by the cold fireplace in the living room. He was still holding Brendy. Brendy's head had sunk on to his brother's shoulder and he was sound asleep. Patrick had managed to light the gaslight which hung from the middle of the ceiling, and a bright shaft lit up the back yard. Gwen tushed, and ran to the window to close the dusty blackout curtains over the flushed dawn sky. The breeze blew them up into the room, so she hastily picked up her work-basket and balanced it on the sill, to hold them down. A clatter of glass dropped into the kitchen rubbish-bin told her that Mari had done what she had been ordered to do. Gwen sighed, and turned to survey her remaining unwanted guests. "Now, what to do with you?"

"Dunno," responded Patrick mechanically. Round and round inside his head went the picture of his mother as he had last seen her; nothing else touched him.

"I know. I'll put the girl here ..." She paused, and then asked, "What's your name?"

A malevolent, pinched face was turned up towards her. "I'm Nora," the tight lips spat out.

Gwen recoiled slightly. What a horrid, wizened-faced brat. "I'll put you and the little lad here — Brendy, isn't it? — in our Mari's bed. Mari can sleep with me." Not for all the wealth in China could she bring herself to put any of the children in her own huge double bed; she would never sleep comfortable in it again, she told herself. "And you, Patrick, can kip down on the sofa here. I'll get a blanket out for you. But first bring the kids upstairs."

She preceded him, the candle flame streaming a thin line of smoke behind her. "The whole place smells of smoke," she remarked over her shoulder, "but it's all from outside. Nothin' to worry about."

Patrick did not care what the place smelled of, as long as he could lie down, curl up and try to obliterate the fact that his maddening, bossy, beloved mam was dead.

Nora's stony expression relaxed and she followed Gwen up the carpeted staircase, sidling along like a stray dog in search of something to eat, sniffing, touching everything. She went straight to the dressing table and, standing on tiptoe, reached over to pick up Mari's most prized possession, a china lady in a crinoline.

"You put that down!" Gwen's face was dark with immediate anger. "You don't touch nothin' in this house, young lady."

Nora glanced up at her with pale, expressionless eyes. Slowly she opened her hand and let the china figure drop. It broke into three pieces.

"You naughty little vixen," Gwen shrieked at her. She caught the child by the shoulder and gave her a sound slap on her bottom. "Our Mari'll be broken-hearted, she will, you little devil. Get your frock off and get into bed afore I mairder you."

With a look of complete satisfaction on her face, Nora removed her dress, to show only a pair of tattered knickers.

Gwen pulled a chamber pot from under the bed, this one with a pattern of violets to match the mauve curtains. "You pull them

293

panties down and pay a call," she ordered a bridling Nora. Nora did not seem to hear, so Gwen took her by the shoulder and shoved her down on to it.

Patrick had stood with Brendy in his arms, waiting for Gwen to finish with Nora. He was used to loud voices and slaps and to Nora being a trial to his mother; it was nothing out of the ordinary.

Boiling with rage, Gwen whipped back the bedclothes and he thankfully put Brendy, fully-clothed, into the bed. "And you get in, miss, and let's have no more trouble," she ordered Nora. Nora, knowing the precise breaking point of most adults, felt it was wise to comply.

Outside the bedroom, Gwen and Patrick came face to face with a bewildered, sulky Mari; she did not like her room being taken over by two dirty kids. "You get into our bed, Mari — on your father's side. I don't know what we do when he comes home. And I don't know what he's going to say."

She opened a drawer of a fine oak chest on the landing, one of the pieces of furniture appropriated from Emmie's home, and took out two thin, but clean, blankets. "You go make yourself comfy on the sofa in the living room," she told Patrick.

She had to repeat her command before Patrick took any notice. As Mari passed, she had caught his hand and squeezed it. "I'm sorry," she had whispered, and he realised with a gleam of comfort that she understood how he felt. He wanted to cry on her shoulder. To Gwen he said, "Yes, missus."

While Gwen lay, rigid and awake, beside Mari, Mari suddenly remarked, "You know, mam, it's over half an hour since the All Clear went, and Auntie Emmie isn't in yet."

"Your aunt's big enough to take care of herself. She'll be in just now — probably gossiping somewhere." Gwen could not take any more; she had been tried beyond endurance, and the very thought of Emmie and her Robert added to her grumpiness. The sly bitch and her greediness about the furniture.

Though Emmie went through the motions of being a good sister-in-law, her bitter resentment against Gwen's refusal to help with her sick parents was all too apparent. Mari's reminder that Emmie had not yet returned made Gwen feel that she did not care if the woman never came back; yet, underneath it all, her

Methodist conscience smote her hard — Emmie had carried a terrible load which Gwen could have eased. Angrily, she turned over in her bed. If Emmie were dead, she would be free of the remainder of her own sins of omission. Savagely, she *wished* her dead, as she lay seething with frustration at her current predicaments.

Suddenly, as a new horror occurred to her, she sat up in bed beside the sleeping Mari. She had never looked to see what had happened to her precious sitting room — the aspidistra in its big, green pottery bowl, set on a table in the bay window, the settee and two easy chairs which she had recently recovered herself in bright orange-flowered cretonne, and the piano, still not quite paid for, which Mari was learning to play, taught at a shilling a lesson by Mrs Cooper down the road. Was it all ruined by the blast?

She could not bear it, if it were all spoiled. She started to turn back the bedclothes, to go down and look, and then flung them back over herself. She could not endure to know now, and she turned her face into her pillow and quietly wept herself to sleep.

Patrick, too, cried — into the patchwork cushion on the sagging horsehair sofa. The pain was so great that it was as if the shrapnel in his mother's body had pierced him.

A light tread descending the staircase made him lift his head abruptly. Was Mari coming down?

"Pat, where are you?"

"Here, Rube." He let his head fall back on to the cushion.

"I were so scared, Pat." She crept towards him through the darkened room and knelt down by the sofa. He sat up and her seeking arms went round him.

"It were the worst raid." Patrick's voice was more gentle.

"I'm worried about our mam. Mrs Thomas don't say much."

Patrick ran his tongue round his lips. Then he said very softly, "She's dead, Rube. Didn't you realise it?"

"Oh," she gasped, putting her hand against her mouth to control an involuntary shriek. "No, Pat. I thought she'd fainted."

She put her head down on his blanketed lap and he could feel her shivering. Then she began to sob. He sat stiffly under her weight. "Don't, Rube," he muttered. "Don't."

"I can't help it. What are we goin' to do without Mam?"

"Dunno," he replied thickly. But he did know. It happened all

295

the time when mothers died. Ruby would take her mother's place. Like many another motherless girl, she would learn to wash and cook for the family and tend little Michael. He was glad he wasn't a girl. He lived for the day when he would be big enough, hefty enough, to go down to the docks and stand in the pen, to be picked again and again for work, because he was the biggest and best. And he would bring home real wages and take a pretty girl, like Mari, to the pictures. Ruby would slave most of her life for nothing, because her mother was dead.

No wonder Ruby wept.

II

During this terrifying Saturday night and Sunday morning, while Gwen coped with her unwelcome visitors, five hundred German bombers converged on the already stricken city, with orders to wipe it out, make it unusable by the convoys of ships from the United States.

They were met by Defiant fighter planes darting bravely in and out of the searchlight beams, in an effort to confuse and harass them. But the Defiants were too slow and their guns were wrongly placed, and not all the gallantry and skill of their crews could compensate for the planes' deficiencies.

There were not many seamen in the canteen that night, nor had the firewatchers come in for their accustomed snacks. Deckie Dick was seated in his usual place at the centre table, from which vantage point he could look out of the window to watch the passing scene and also observe all that was going on in the canteen itself. He idly shuffled the deck of cards, from which he derived his nickname, from one hand to the other, as he regaled a bored younger merchant seaman with the story of the rescue work he had participated in the night before.

When the first bombs whistled down, neither staff nor customers sought the shelter of the basement, but when suddenly the attack seemed particularly near and intense, everybody dropped what they were doing and fled for the stairs. As they tumbled down the curving flight, the window shutters flew open with an angry rattle; the front door was blown off its hinges and shot across the canteen, followed by a torrent of sand from burst sand-

296

bags. As the blast receded, the door flew out again, to crash against the lamp post on the pavement.

Miss Piggot, one of the volunteers, had tripped on the bottom step and fallen, taking a swearing, flailing Scot down with her. Now, they both picked themselves up off the stone floor and ruefully rubbed their knees. "My poor stockings," wailed Miss Piggot, lifting her skirts to look at the tears. Mrs Robinson pushed her to one side and quickly closed the stout door which guarded the foot of the staircase. She sat down on one of the benches and smiled at a thin, pimpled Royal Naval rating already perched there. He was rolling himself a cigarette, with trembling fingers. "Soon be over," she told him comfortingly. He replied wryly, "I'd rather be at sea." And her plump face creased with laughter.

"Phew!" exclaimed Emmie, as she sat down by Deckie Dick. "That were close." She shivered and rubbed her bare forearms, as if she were cold.

"Aye. Looks as if we're in for a bad night." He looked tired beneath the grey stubble of two days' beard. As a night watchman, he was not used to heavy physical labour and he had spent the previous night heaving beams and chunks of stone out of the way of rescue squads. As he glanced down at Emmie's anxious face, he was thinking he would be thankful to be back at work on Monday night, when he could, between his rounds, kip down in a warm corner of the warehouse which he watched. He leaned his bald head, with its fringe of white hair, against the whitewashed wall and closed his eyes against the glare of the single electric light bulb hanging from the ceiling. Pity the lodging house in which he lived was so noisy; otherwise he could have slept in a bit longer that morning.

As the raid progressed, the electric light began to flicker, so Mrs Robinson opened her capacious handbag and took out a candle and some matches. She lit it and then glued it down on to the corner table, by drips of its own wax. Then she blew it out.

The uproar outside became intense. "Good thing they're bringing in mining engineers, to help out," remarked Dick, his eyes still closed. "They can advise the heavy-rescue men."

Emmie nodded and leaned forward to rest her face on her hands, to stop herself shaking.

Mrs Robinson turned to the taciturn countess, who was seated stiffly opposite her, her ankles crossed neatly, her skirts precisely arranged around her. "I wish I had shut the canteen at ten o'clock," she remarked. "I had an uneasy feeling this morning that there would be another raid tonight."

The countess looked down her Norman nose and sniffed delicately. "On no account should you have closed. It would show that we are intimidated." Her wonderful diamond rings flashed, as she dismssed the Luftwaffe with an impatient gesture.

The naval rating drew on his cigarette and stared at her. Proper rum old dame, she was. If he were as rich as she looked, he would be thirty miles away from any place like Liverpool.

A gaunt and hunched ship's stoker, sitting cross-legged on the floor playing cards with three others, suddenly looked up. "Can yer smell smoke ?" he inquired nervously of the company.

"Be funny if we couldn't, after last night's effort," grunted one of his fellow players. He shuffled his cards secretly, close to his face.

"I mean in here," the stoker responded irritably. Holding his cards to his chest, he got up, went to the door and opened it. Conversation ceased. He crept up a couple of steps and peered around, then bolted down again, as a huge swish followed by a roar and the sound of tumbling masonry indicated a hit nearby.

"Shut the door, you bloody fool," shouted a highly alarmed voice.

"Had to take a look-see," grumbled the equally shaken stoker. "T' canteen might've bin bairnin' over our heads."

Emmie fidgeted unhappily beside Deckie Dick. Why planners never put lavatories in air raid shelters was beyond her. It was certain that they must live far away from air raids; otherwise they would have known that the banshee wail of the warning was like a switch turning on your waterworks. She wondered if some of the fellows felt as she did, and she giggled shakily.

Deckie Dick opened his eyes. "What's ticklin' yer, luv?"

She blushed and whispered into his ear. He laughed, and replied, "I'm in the same boat."

The card players had been murmuring together. Now the owner of the pack knocked them together and put them in his back pocket. They got up and stretched. "Got to get back to the ship," they informed Mrs Robinson, "raid or no raid."

Mrs Robinson, alarmed, half rose from her bench. "You can't

go out in this, Mr Petersen. No one would expect you to." But she read the panic in their eyes, and she sank down again. A ship out in the river might seem a safer place than the bedlam surrounding them.

Their opening of the door let in a dull roar, punctuated by occasional shouts and the sound of lorries from the docks being driven in low gear, as drivers tried to get themselves and their loads to safety. They scurried up the steps, only to throw themselves flat on the littered floor at the top, as another deafening detonation made the old building shudder and sent bits of plaster flying from the ceiling. The subsequent rumble of falling masonry confirmed their opinion that, if they *could* get away, they preferred to be aboard ship. Who wanted to be buried under eight floors of eighteenth-century stone blocks?

As they scrambled over the remains of the sandbag wall, they were shaken to see that the street was as light as day.

"Get under cover," shouted an irate auxiliary policeman, running towards them half sideways, like a crab, to gain the greatest protection from the office walls.

The men took no notice of him and sped past him, bent on reaching the overhead railway which might well still be running and would take them south, away from what appeared to be the raid's main targets. In so doing, they saved their lives.

With her face buried in her lap and her arms clasped over her head for maximum protection, Emmie prayed that Robert was safely out of the port. She jabbed Deckie Dick with her elbow, and shouted above the noise, "Do you think Robbie will've sailed yet?"

Dick paused before answering. He knew that the *Malakand* had not yet left dock and he knew what she was being loaded with. But why add to the girl's worries? He answered her quite cheerfully, "She may have got away this mornin'."

Relieved, Emmie returned to worrying about the need to go to the lavatory.

In No. 2 Huskisson, Robbie heaved the last of a series of spitting incendiaries off the foredeck and into the water.

"Watch it!" shrieked one of his mates, and pointed upwards.

Robbie whipped round.

A barrage balloon, half deflated, loosed from its moorings, was settling into the rigging.

Someone shrieked to Robbie, "Get away. It'll explode."

Robbie scrambled aft and with the rest of the crew watched helplessly as the grey monster was pulled and pushed by the breeze. A particularly strong gust loosened it and it flopped on to the for'ard deck.

Several men started towards it, but they were grabbed and held back by more cautious seamen.

A second later, the grey, silky mass burst into flames, a huge, scarifying ball of fire.

Regardless of the deadly cargo beneath their feet, the officers ordered hoses out and for fifteen agonised minutes the crew deluged the roaring fire with water, while more incendiaries were scattered down on to the hapless freighter.

A Nazi bomber swooped along the nearby dock sheds dropping a further load of incendiaries. Orange flowers of flame burst from the roofs, and in minutes a mighty conflagration stretched from Huskisson to Seaforth, like a brilliant multicoloured curtain. The wind generated by the fire sent huge fingers of flame out to the boat, and the crew found themselves surrounded by fire licking along the ship from stem to stern. Robbie could see the raw terror which struck him reflected in the eyes of the others; yet they and the auxiliary firemen sent to help them held on to their hoses until, through the noise of the blaze, came the firm voice of the shore relief master, "Abandon ship."

Black, singed and panting, they regrouped on the dockside and were immediately put to work jetting water into the holds, while a special tender was sent for, to bring oxy-acetylene apparatus to the boat.

"Goin' to try scuttlin' her - cut a hole in her side," a fireman said to Robbie, as they sought to hold a wriggling hose towards the ship.

"Aye, they'd better be quick," Robbie gasped, "or we're all for Kingdom Come, and half of Liverpool as well."

III

There was a fumbling at the door of the canteen shelter. Mrs Robinson hastened to open it, and an air raid warden entered in a puff of smoke. His tin hat was askew and he was swaying with fatigue. "Just checkin' who's here," he assured them, and, pointing to each person, he counted the number present.

"What's happening up there?" asked Mrs Robinson. Her face was wan and her lipstick smudged, giving her a clownlike appearance.

The warden flopped down on the end of a bench and the weary shelterers turned towards him. He took off his tin hat to rub his bald head. Emmie noticed that his trousers were thick with dust and there were holes in the knees.

"Lewis's store is a raging inferno," he said to Mrs Robinson, in answer to her query. "Must've lost most of their firewatchers. T' firemen is stuck for water." His dispirited voice lifted a little, and he grinned, "T' fire brigade has pumped all the water out of the Adelphi's swimming bath into Lewis's. That'll larn that snobs' paradise."

A ripple of laughter at the expense of the city's finest hotel went through the company.

Too bad about the firewatchers, thought Emmie, but if you didn't laugh at what was funny you'd soon go mad.

"Our telephone at the post is out," he went on more soberly. "Bloody havoc without it. Seen a couple of post office engineers just now, slinging lines every which way, to get us connected up again. And there's another two of them sittin' in a crater right in the street here, splicin' telephone lines as calm as if they was havin' afternoon tea at Lyons'." He stood up and stretched. "It's a bloody miracle they're not dead."

"Should we try to move out of here?" asked Mrs Robinson.

"Nay. You're safer here than anywhere. South Castle Street, at the back here, is a shambles, what with fire and direct hits. I'll come back and tell you, if the firemen think you should move."

"Do they need men up there?" inquired a lanky individual in battered beige denim trousers, as he got up clumsily from the floor.

"Not now, they don't. They will when the All Clear goes, though."

"Not tonight, Josephine. Sit down again," cracked a wit.

The warden clapped his helmet back on to his head, grinned in a friendly way and clumped back up the steps.

A collective sigh went through the company and they settled back to wait again.

The light went out. Mrs Robinson quietly lit the candle. Its flame

301

seemed to emphasize the lined faces of the men and women, picking out a drooping eyelid, a blackened tooth, the sole of a shoe with a hole in it, the glitter of a cheap ring on a chapped hand.

From the gloom, a forlorn young voice informed its neighbour, "Me leave's up at eight o'clock tomorrer mornin'. Got to be back in camp by then. I were on me way to the station when this lot started. Ah coom in 'ere, thinkin' it'd all blow over in an hour."

"You got a bleedin' hope, mate. You live around here?" Deckie Dick inquired.

"Aye, wi' me gran. Lives in Pitt Street. She were scared enough last night, without this on top."

Emmie remembered that a heavily built youth in battledress had scuttled into the canteen when the first bomb fell. Poor lad. No more'n eighteen, he must be.

The young voice continued, a little muffled from the owner's face being buried in his lap, his tin hat perched atop the back of his head. "Dunno whether to go back home or go t' station and show up late at camp anyways."

"Report back to camp," rumbled several voices, and Deckie Dick added, "Aye, you'll be in real trouble if you don't — absent without leave, they'll jump you for. There's people as'll look after your gran." He raised his head from his lap, to look at the crouching boy. "I'll go meself, if you like. You give me your address and her address. I'll go and see her tomorrer — and I'll write to you straight away. You'll get it the next day."

The boy glanced up quickly at Dick's ruddy, good-natured visage, faintly lit by the candle. "She'd be proper pleased. She's real lonely," he said somewhat more cheerfully.

With Mrs Robinson's fountain pen, he clumsily printed the addresses on the back of a café receipt and passed the paper to Dick.

Dick folded it up carefully, put it into a shabby wallet and returned the wallet to his back pocket. Above the wallet he pushed in a grubby comb; he always said that a comb was the best defence against pickpockets or even plain losing your wallet. Now he thought that it would not hurt him to go and sit with some old Irish biddy for an hour, to help a youngster. It would be something to do. He had been lonely ever since his wife's death a year earlier.

The noise outside gradually lessened, as if the main target of

302

the raid had been shifted. Ears pricked and heads were cautiously raised.

Emmie thought for a second that she heard women s voices outside. Women's Voluntary Service van, she guessed, feeding the firemen and the wardens. My, she could use a cup of tea herself.

"I'm goin' upstairs," announced Deckie Dick heavily. He winked down at Emmie.

Emmie promptly jumped up. "I'll come, too."

It was evident from a lewd gesture on the part of Deckie Dick where he was going, and Mrs Robinson said apprehensively, "Emmie, you should not go upstairs yet; it's too dangerous."

Emmie was immediately defensive. Nobody was going to tell her any more what she should or should not do; she'd had a bowlful of that from her parents. Besides, if she didn't go soon, she'd wet her knickers.

Emmie smoothed her skirts and tossed her head. "I'll be all right, Mrs Robinson. Dickie'll look atter me." She glanced teasingly at Dick, as if single-handedly he could force the Luftwaffe into retreat.

Left to himself, Dickie would have run up the stairs and urinated just outside the front door, and then returned as fast as his tired legs would have carried him. But Emmie would be counting on his going through to the backyard privies.

The man sitting next to Dick yawned and glanced at Emmie. "You lucky bastard," he muttered to Dick.

Dick laughed. He felt that at his age it was a compliment.

In the middle of the wrecked canteen, they paused to look through the gaping hole where the window had been, at the dancing shadows on the wall of the building opposite.

"Good Heavens!" Emmie exclaimed fearfully. "There must be an awful fire behind our building."

"T' warden said as we were OK. Come on now, quick." His words were nearly drowned in the rumble of a series of bomb explosions, as the Luftwaffe took a run at the centre of the fire they had started alongside No.2 Huskisson.

Except for glassless windows, all the buildings round the light well seemed undamaged, though the sky glowed red above them. They ran across the cobbled yard, glass crunching under their feet, and with sighs of relief paid the long-delayed calls.

Close to hand, the tumbling roar of a wall collapsing brought them both out at a run, Emmie still pulling up her knickers. It buried the warden beneath its shattered stone, as he ran along the street. Another bomb exploded in the fire at the back of them, sending a shower of sparks into the air. Emmie screamed.

A further swish and crash made Dick hurl her to the ground, his plump body on top of her.

"Jesus, save us!" she shrieked, as she hit the unfriendly cobble-stones. She clung to him

"Keep yer head down. God, that was ..."

With a deafening crash, the whole of the canteen was blown out.

An agonised blow on the forehead made her yell again, as she and Dick were lifted by the blast. Then, clinging to Dick, she was rolling and falling. She saw the ground beneath them crack and open in a tremendous yawn, as if in some unearthly dream. Dick seemed to slip from her, as she hit sliding rubble and then half fell, half slid, down and down on to a shuddering floorspace, mercilessly bumped and bruised as she went. She was aware, in a split second, of the earth closing over her as if a great door had been slammed, of a dreadful weight on the lower part of her body and of an ear-rending storm of noise. Then silence, except, from nearby, thin horrifying screams like souls crying out in Dante's *Inferno,* as she sank into oblivion.

IV

In smothering dust, Emmie fought for breath. As she coughed and choked and spat, the pain in her head was all-encompassing. She endeavoured to raise a hand to clear her face of rubble, but both hands were pinned against her stomach by a huge, warm solid mass; she shuddered as she realised what it might be.

She tried shaking her head and then moaned when the movement not only added to the pain in her head, but pulled her hair as well; its longer strands appeared to be caught under some unyielding weight.

Suddenly she sneezed enormously, her nose ran and she could breathe a little more easily. Small anonymous pieces of rubble, dislodged by the sneeze, slipped down the sides of her face.

As greater consciousness seeped back into her and she laboured for air amid the cloying dust, the dawning knowledge that she was buried made her tremble violently.

She became aware of stinging pain all over her face, in addition to the throbbing in her head. Cautiously, fearfully, she opened her eyes a slit. She could see nothing.

She was blind! She was sure of it. The trickles she could feel from her eyes must be blood, not tears. She screamed in horror, a howl of pure terror. Dust again entered her throat and the screams became strangled coughs. Then the pain in her head overwhelmed her and she faded into unconsciousness again.

She came round slowly, aware now of being surrounded by reverberating, booming noise. The ground under her, if it were ground and not a floor of some kind, vibrated continuously, adding to her own shuddering. The sagging weight on her body also moved slightly. At first her fogged mind believed the movement was also caused by the noise; then a large breath was exhaled, followed by a series of coughs.

In sudden joy, she croaked, "Is that you, Dick?"

Though she got no reply because of the paroxysm of coughing, she felt a hand run down the side of her and heard a faint rattle of what sounded like pebbles falling as the same hand apparently explored a little further. Then, with a satisfied grunt as the coughs eased, the body carefully rolled over until it was positioned tightly beside her. A series of muffled curses in a man's voice came from close to her ear. Thankfully she took a larger breath, to ease her constricted lungs, only to set off a further desperate coughing which threatened to cause her to vomit, as powdered plaster cloyed her throat again.

Above her, there was a series of ominous creaks, and in the distance the sound of water trickling. The surrounding uproar seemed to have decreased.

"Hold it, luv. Hold it," came a frantic whisper. "Yer noise'll bring the whole issue down on us. Breath shallow, if you can."

She did her best to control the coughing, lifting a hand, tingling with pins and needles, to cover her mouth. Between efforts to clear her throat, she giggled hysterically, "Oh, Dickie, I'm so glad you're here."

"*I'm* not," came the dry response. The body packed tightly beside her fidgeted slightly. "God spare us!"

She began to laugh wildly at this, only to choke again and to have her hair pulled painfully as she moved.

"Hold your hush, luv," he cajoled softly and caught one of her hands as if to comfort her.

She sobered as best she could. "Are you hurt, Dick?" she inquired hoarsely.

"Not much, I don't think. Wind kicked out o' me." His breath came laboriously. "Feel like I did after a fight once, in a bar in New York. Got beat up." He squeezed her hand. "How about you ?"

He could feel her trembling increase. Carefully, he lifted an arm round her, as she whimpered, "Dickie, I think I'm blinded. I can't see anything. Me hair is caught under something — and me face is all wet and sticky. I'm afraid to touch it."

He did not reply for a moment and then he assured her, "Well nobody could see in this dark. Are you sure? Open and close yer eyelids. Do they work? You're lying on your back, aren't you?"

"I can move me lids. They're awful sore."

"Humph. Well, try touching round them, very lightly, to see if the eyes is still in their sockets."

Sickened by the implication, she nevertheless moved her fingers cautiously round her cheeks and over her closed lids. She moved her eyes from right to left and then blinked. "They seem all right," she announced with marked relief. "They're running like mad."

"Aye, you probably got dust in them; but it's my bet you'll be all right, when there's light to see by. I were lucky — I had me face against you when we fell. Can you move your legs?"

Diverted, her trembling lessened, and she obediently bent her legs slightly and wiggled her feet. He felt the movement, when she arched her back. "All of me seems to work," she announced with a tremulous laugh. "I can't turn me head, though, 'cos me hair's caught under summat.

They lay quiet for a minute, while the dust thinned. Then she asked pitifully, "How long will it take 'em to get us out, Dickie ?"

He sighed — carefully, so that he did not commence to cough again. He had been thinking about this and was privately convinced that it would be a miracle if they were ever found. While Emmie had been unconscious, he had lain over her, dazed by the

306

fall, his mind trying to grapple with the mystery of where they were.

They had been in the light well, lying on the ground, against the wall of the canteen under the little kitchen window. They must, he argued, have fallen straight through a fissure opened up by the bomb explosion. Yet, could they fall through a solid yard? He had definitely fallen through open space — he would remember the sensation until the end of his days.

The answer seemed to be that they lay in some old cellar under the cobbled yard. And who would dream of looking for them there? Only the people in the shelter knew that he and Emmie had gone into the yard, and judging by the fearful groans and shrieks with which his ears had been tortured for a moment or two after the bomb fell, those in the shelter were either dead or dying.

If all the buildings had come down, there could be sixty feet or more of debris above them. This had to be the end. And yet in him, bruised and scared as he was, lay a tremendous passion to live.

"How long, Dickie?"

"Dunno." The dust was settling now and it was much easier to breathe, but delayed shock caught up with him and he fainted. Emmie felt the body stuffed in beside her relax and she thought he had died. She poked him with her elbow. He did not respond. "Dick! Oh, Dickie!"

Total fear engulfed her again and she began to scream helplessly, rendered almost insane with fright. She gibbered at him, as she tried to reach his face and finally succeeded in running one hand over it. Then she felt his chest heave slightly. She quietened and it seemed as if he were sleeping, and indeed he did pass into a light slumber.

She lay sobbing softly and between the sobs prayers tumbled from her lips. Promises to lead an immaculate life if only God would get her out of the tomb in which she lay came almost incoherently forth, as she tried to make a pact with the Almighty.

"I'll never hate Gwen no more. I'll help her all I can. She can have the bloody furniture. Oh, Jesus, hear me. What will Robbie do if I die? He's been so lonely for lack of a wife, oh, God. Have pity on him, if not on me. I know I'm as wicked a piece as ever was made, but I'll never miss chapel again, I won't. God have pity on me."

Deckie Dick became gradually aware of this litany, as he awoke and his mind began to clear. He was himself afraid of death, particularly a painful death. How would the Grim Reaper strike? Would the debris shift, to slide down and crush them? Would they die of thirst? Or starve like rats? Or worse still, be eaten by rats before they had a chance to starve?

There was an increasing smell of escaping gas, faint but distinct. Deckie Dick also addressed his prayers to whatever Gods might be to let the gas thicken and engulf them. It would be a comparatively quick death; he had thought of sticking his head in the gas oven after his wife had died. With one son, Georgie, killed at Dunkirk and the other one, Billie, long since emigrated to the States, there was no one left to care about him. Now he wished, prayed, that this quick death might be granted to him and to the sweet woman lying next to him. Selflessly, he begged that there be at least sufficient concentration of gas to render her unconscious, so that she never knew what hit her, even if it was not sufficient to snuff out a tough old devil like himself.

V

Conor staggered into his crowded post, and Glynis Hughes looked up from tending a stout woman with a knifelike pain in her chest. The woman was nearly purple in the face and Glynis had been trying to keep her from going into hysterics, until one of the First Aid men, who had been called from the Dwellings, arrived with some more nitro-glycerine. The man followed Conor in, pushed him aside and plunged through the crowded room. Glynis snatched a spoon from a used teacup and handed it to him. She held the struggling woman, while he forced the life-saving liquid down her throat. In seconds, the pain abated, and Glynis thankfully left her to the care of the new arrival, while she pushed her way over to Conor, who stood like a zombie amid the crowd, his eyes half closed with fatigue. He was covered with grey-white dust, except across his knees and stomach, where his uniform and the dust were stained dark red. Around him, the room hummed with voices, through which cut the sound of the telephonist relaying details of casualties and damage as they were brought to her. The line had been broken during the night and, despite a quick repair, the telephonist was having difficulty, as she laboured in a high-pitched voice to overcome the crackling of the line.

"Got a cup o' tea, Glynis?" his voice grated, as she reached him.

She eased her little buttocks past the back of the telephonist's chair and laid a hand on his arm. "Sure. I'll get you one. But — but first I got to tell you somethin'. Come out in the street a mo'; it's quieter."

How am I going to do it? she worried. He always teased about his old woman, but he was fond of her for certain. And she was a kind woman, me mam always said. Dumbly, Conor allowed himself to be ushered into the street and a little away from the gossips by the door. Glynis turned and looked up at him compassionately. "Conor," she whispered.

"Is it one of the kids?" he asked, suddenly alert.

"No, Conor. It's Ellen." She grasped one of his hands hanging limply by his side. "She's gone, Conor. Mr Baker came earlier. Said she got a piece of shrapnel straight to her heart. 'Twas instant. She didn't suffer. I'm so sorry, Conor." She was trying not to cry, as he stared unbelievingly down at her. "The kids are all right. Your next-door neighbour — Mrs Thomas, isn't it — she's got them all and is taking care of them. The house is OK, too."

Conor licked his dry lips. "Where's Ellen?"

"She's laid out in the church hall — along with the others from The Dwellings. Monty got her picked up from the house real quick, in case your kids went in there. He's still here, if you want to pop over and see her."

His hand clenched hers tightly and the weary eyes closed. "I'm accursed," he said bitterly. "Accursed."

Glynis shivered. "Don't say that."

"First we lose everything we got, and nearly little Rube as well. And now Ellen."

"Go and see her," urged Glynis, a little desperately. "Father O'Dwyer'll be there, no doubt, to talk to."

"And what good will that do, to me or to him? And what good can I do for Ellen — Ellen!" He almost shouted and then his voice broke.

309

"You have to arrange her funeral — I'm sorry to say it."

He looked round him, like an animal trying to escape when cornered, then back at the tearful woman still holding his hand. "Glynis, down behind the filing cabinet in the post there's some whiskey — there's half a dozen bottles and more in the cellar. But don't say nothin'. Just get one out for me."

She smiled through her tears. So he did indeed smuggle whiskey. "To be sure," she said. "Trust me. We'll have a hot cup of tea with a good swig in it. You come back in, lad, and sit down a minute."

When she returned to him with a steaming cup of tea smelling strongly of whiskey, he was seated on a wooden chair, his face in his hands, and was weeping. Opposite him a middle-aged man, wrapped in a blanket, his bare feet sticking out from under it, sniffed and caught the odour of the spirit. Out of the corner of her eyes, Glynis saw the tired eyes light up. "I'll bring you a cup — exactly the same," she promised. "In a minute."

She put the cup and saucer into Conor's hand and then put an arm over his shoulder. He turned to her and hid his face against her breast. The tea slopped into the saucer. "I'm damned, Glynis," he mumbled. "Why Ellen? She never done anything wicked in her life!"

"I don't know," she replied sadly, and patted and stroked him, as if she were comforting one of her children.

VI

When Gwen heard the knock on the front door, she thought it was David returning and that he had mislaid his key. She flew down the stairs clad only in her long, white nightgown and thankfully swung open the door.

She did not recognise for a moment the anguished man on the door step. Then a familiar Irish voice, with an unaccustomed wheeze in it, greeted her politely. "Mornin', Mrs Thomas. I'm told you kindly took me kids in?"

In the interests of modesty, she wrapped the cotton folds of her nightgown more tightly round her. Then she said, "Yes, indeed, Mr Donnelly. They're here. I think they're still asleep."

Without being invited, he stepped into the highly polished hall.

310

Gwen's lips tightened, when he failed to wipe his feet on the door-mat, a new one with the word *Welcome* knotted into it.

He brought with him a strong smell of whiskey — and raw meat, was it? She shivered as she shut the door quickly behind him.

He looked uneasily round the hall and then sighed. "Do they know?" he asked her bluntly.

"No. Come in here for a minute." She ushered him into the small sitting room, and nearly cried out at the sight of her biggest aspidistra lying smashed in a pile of earth on her new red, imita-tion Belgian carpet, a carpet which had only two more payments to be made on it before it was entirely hers. Despite the breeze coming through the glassless windows, the room smelled cold and dank from disuse. Both the cretonne curtains and the black-out were in shreds. Gwen felt, in sudden rage, that she could hap-pily strangle a German with her bare hands.

"What happened?" Conor almost snapped at her, as he turned to her.

A little frightened of the tight, frozen look of the filthy, tear-stained face in front of her, she stuttered an explanation. "Patrick knows," she finished up. "He's asleep on the sofa in the other room."

"I'll have to tell 'em, Mrs Thomas." He looked at her implor-ingly, hoping she would do it. But she was on the defensive now. There was a limit, she told herself. Enough that she had had these dreadful children thrust upon her. She couldn't.

"What if I get Patrick in here, and you talk to him?" she sug-gested.

He nodded, and turned to look out of the devastated window, while she gathered her nightgown even more tightly round her and went to get the boy.

"No!" she exclaimed in genuine horror, as she looked down at Ruby and Patrick tightly intertwined under the blankets on the sofa. She bent down and tapped Ruby on the shoulder. The girl woke with a jump. "Your father's here," she announced frigidly. "He wants to see Patrick in the sitting room. You stay here, miss." She would deal with their shocking indecency afterwards. Brother and sister sleeping together! She was scandalized.

Hardly comprehending what she had said, the two children

looked up at their outraged hostess. Patrick yawned and then, without a word, he swung himself off the sofa and lurched unsteadily out of the room. Mrs Thomas pursed her lips and stared down at Ruby. Ruby slowly laid her head back down on the cushion she had shared with Patrick. She began to cry helplessly.

Gwen turned towards the fireplace and rolled back the hearthrug, preparatory to making the fire. "I should think so, too," she muttered angrily. "Such behaviour I never did see."

Yesterday, Patrick would have sworn that he hated his father. But now the object of his jealousy was dead and his father suddenly seemed a pillar of strength. He stumbled towards him and Conor held him, while they both wept heartily. Finally, Patrick snuffled, "Rube knows."

In the living room, Gwen put down her poker. She was suddenly cold. Without a word to the weeping girl, she ran quickly upstairs to get her dressing-gown.

Immediately she vanished, Ruby sat up, untangled herself from the blankets and ran, barefoot, into the sitting room and flung herself into her father's arms.

With an arm round each of his children and tears smudging his dusty face, Conor asked them not to tell the little ones that their mother was dead. "Tell 'em she's in hospital being mended," he suggested. "Better they know when your gran comes down from Walton. I tried to phone the post there, so as to get hold of her quick — it were dead — so I wrote to her, but with it being Sunday today, she won't get it till tomorrer." Gran was his own mother. Ellen's mother lived in Dublin — and he realised suddenly that he must write to her as well.

"You all stay with Mrs Thomas, till I can get home. And you help her, Rube."

Ruby agreed sulkily that she would help her. "Pat, you feed me cocks — and beg a few scraps from Mrs Thomas for Sarge." The boy sniffed lachrymosely and nodded agreement. He could hear Gwen in the next room raking out the fireplace. Even the sound of the poker seemed angry.

Gwen was just putting a match to the paper of the newly laid fire, when Conor entered, Ruby hanging on to his arm. Patrick followed, his face stony.

Conor loosed himself from his daughter and bent down to seize

312

one of Gwen's coal-blackened hands and shake it hard. His breath stank of whiskey; still kneeling, she recoiled from him.

"It's proper kind of you to take in me kids, Mrs Thomas. I'll not forget it. Mr Baker said you would keep them for a while. By the looks of things, I won't be home until tomorrer — at least. It's terrible up at The Dwellings. You never saw anything like it. Keep the kids away - it's no sight for them. I've written to their gran, but with everything being upset in the town she probably won't get the letter till tomorrer afternoon at earliest." He paused for breath and looked at her anxiously.

"I — but — I ..." she began, a fearful sinking feeling in her stomach.

He burst into speech again. "I tried to get the wardens' post up there on the phone. Can't get through to anybody." He seemed to take it for granted that she would keep the children with her, and went on, "We won't tell the little ones their mam is gone, till their granny comes to comfort 'em." He took a turn about the room, while Gwen watched him, speechless for once. "You can say she's in hospital, doing fine, soon be home, like."

She opened her mouth, to make an excuse for not keeping the children, but he deflected her by asking, "Where's your hubby?"

"Still workin' out at Bootle. And our Emma isn't in yet."

Overwhelmed by his own troubles, Conor failed to realise that Emmie must have been in the thick of the air raid. He said mechanically, as he hugged Ruby again and turned towards the door, "She'll probably be in just now."

While the children saw their father out, Gwen leaned forward and mechanically struck another match to light the fire, which had failed to kindle. She sat on her heels, watching the flames creep through the newspaper and wondered what to do. There was not enough food in the house to feed everybody and little money in her purse to buy more. David would be furious if she exceeded her housekeeping money. Mechanically she gave the fireplace a quick whisk with a brass-handled hearth brush, and then continued to sit listening to the wood crackle, feeling exhausted, defeated.

Ruby watching her, hesitated in the doorway and then advanced diffidently. She put her arm shyly round Gwen and said, "Don't cry, Mrs Thomas. I'll help yez."

313

Startled, she turned in the curve of the child's arm. A little stiffly, she put her own arm round Ruby. "Well, thank you, Ruby." The girl smelled to high heaven. Hadn't her mother taught her to wash herself? Perhaps she hadn't been taught not to sleep with her brother, either, she meditated grimly. She scrambled to her feet. She *must* do something.

While Mari still slept, Ruby and Patrick were set to work, she to sweep up the remaining glass in the living room and he to tack some pieces of old lino culled from the cellar, over the gaping windows. The table was laid and a small helping of cornflakes put out for each child.

"And after breakfast, if you're going to be here overnight, everybody had better have a bath."

Both Ruby and Patrick were taken aback. They had never had a bath; only an occasional wash all over in the kitchen bowl; they were saved from having to reply by Nora and Brendy rushing down the stairs in a panic, having forgotten where they were. They surveyed the living room with popping eyes, broke into roars of tears and demanded to go home to Mam. Ruby mothered them both and soon they were shovelling cornflakes into their mouths, while they watched very suspiciously the preparation of the tin bath set in front of the fire.

Michael shrieked from upstairs and Ruby ran up to him. He had soaked the bed and was standing on it, holding the brass head rail. In the half darkness of the room, Ruby held him to her and told him Mam would be coming soon to fetch him. No amount of soft talk, however, would persuade him to eat cornflakes or even drink milk from a glass. He wanted his mother's breast.

Gwen surveyed him in harassed silence for a moment, as he sat on Ruby's knee kicking out in a furious paddywack. Finally she said wearily, "He'll eat when he's real hungry. Let him be for now. We might as well bath him first." She moved the dish of cornflakes away from Michael's flailing arms. "Do you have any clean nappies or pants for him at home? And any clean clothes for the other kids?"

"There's some," Ruby answered her doubtfully. "Me mam washed Thursday." She dreaded that Gwen might command her to go to fetch them. Her stomach churned at the idea of finding her mother lying so still in the hall.

Patrick came in from the kitchen, carrying a steaming bucket of water to tip into the tin bath. "I'll go and get 'em," he said heavily. "I got to feed the birds — and Sarge. They'll have taken Mam to hospital by now — won't they, Mrs Thomas?"

Gwen had forgotten about Ellen. She hesitated, and then said, "I think so, lad."

Mr Baker had remembered to let the dog out into the tiny back yard, and Sarge greeted Patrick ecstatically. He padded into the house behind the boy.

Patrick went straight to the front hall, almost hoping that his mother would be lying there, made comfortable by nurses, and that she would open her eyes and say she was fine, just waiting for the ambulance. But there was only the quilt from Ruby and Nora's bed piled against the wall. Slowly an all-consuming rage spread through him, that strangers had taken away his mother without his seeing her again. He kicked angrily at the quilt, and Sarge, who had been nosing round it, slunk back, tail between legs. He stamped his feet and then banged his fists against the wall, bent his head and hit that too against the hollow plaster. "Yer pack of sewer rats," he screamed at the anonymous ghosts who had come in the night to carry away his mother. He forgot about the clothing he was supposed to collect and ran through the house, up the stairs and down again, kicking open doors, screaming obscenities which echoed through the house, yelling what he would do to a German if he ever met one. He picked up some used cups from the kitchen table and slammed them on to the floor and crunched the broken pieces under his boots, until the fury of frustration waned and he stood sobbing helplessly in the deserted kitchen.

There an anxious Ruby found him. She put down on the floor an extraordinarily clean Michael, clad only in his jersey. The child was sucking his thumb, tears still wet on his face. He glanced round the kitchen, looking for his mother. Small sobs shook him from time to time and he stared in a dazed fashion at his big brother.

Ruby put her arms round Patrick. "It's no good, Pat. She's gone."

The boy pushed her away and turned his back on her. He mopped his eyes with the end of the woolly tie of his jersey.

"We have to find some clothes for Mrs Thomas."

"Damn her."

"Don't knock her, Pat. She's trying to help. We'd be in a right

315

muddle without her — and no Dad either."

He turned a dark, passionate face on his sister. "I can't stand her. I'm not having no bath. I'm going to see what Dad's doin'."

With a huge sniff, he swung past her, opened the front door and slammed it after him.

Ruby stared after him, her whole body trembling with fear of the responsibility left to her, fear of offending Gwen, fear of not being able to cope with Michael, Nora and Brendy, fear of being terribly alone to face everything — perhaps yet another air raid that night.

VII

"It's quietened," Emmie pointed out. "It must be Sunday morning by now. We've been here ages, Dickie, and I'm so parched. Are you thirsty?" The voice was thin and quivery.

"Aye, I am. 'Could use a pint." He cleared his throat. "Yer know, there's a bit o' water here, somewhere. I can hear it trickling — faint, like."

"I know. It's not very far, but I can't move 'cos of me hair." Emmie's voice quavered and threatened hysterics again.

"There's a straight wall on t' other side of you, isn't there?"

"Yeah." She raised her arm up as far as she could reach, and winced with pain from bruises acquired in her fall. "There's enough space above me — I think — for me to sit up." She ran her fingers along the obstruction above her. "It feels as if there's a very big rough stone over us. It slopes down towards you, till it must touch you. If I could turn on me side, I could give you more room."

"Sardines in a bloody tin," he snorted. "Can you reach over your head to your hair where it's caught?"

"Mm. I've bin tryin' to pull some of it loose."

"I've got a penknife in me pocket. I doubt I can get it out, though. I've hurt me wrists, and me hands is as sore as hell."

"Oh, Dick! You never said you was hurt?"

"It's nought terrible. Could you reach in me right-hand keck pocket?" She felt him wriggle himself slightly upward, so that he was more level with her.

With her long, bony Lancashire fingers, she hunted feverishly down his side, stretching as far as she could. She touched his belt.

316

"Lower," he instructed her. "Look, I'm goin' to ease meself a bit across you. "She felt his head move across her shoulder till it lay against hers. He tried to ease the dead weight of his body over her arm. He grunted." That's it. See if you can reach now."

The long fingers ran down his thigh, paused and then scrabbled at the pocket opening. "If you truly can't get it, I'll put me own hand in — but it's that tender, I don't want to."

"Hold still," she advised him. "I'll winch the pocket lining out." She giggled nervously. "You've got all sorts in here. I got your hanky out."

"Well, don't lose it. Put it where you can find it. We'll wipe our faces with it."

She obediently hauled it out and stuffed it down her chest.

Again the long, exploring fingers. He gritted his teeth; not with pain, but to control the sudden arousal which her warm nearness and her gentle fingers was exciting. The tendrils of hair against his cheek were having their effect, too. Many times, when he had seen Robert and Emmie walk out of the canteen with arms around each other, he had been pierced with envy and wondered what she would be like to bed. Now, however, crammed in a hell-hole which was likely to be their coffin, his desire for her was so strong that he longed passionately to roll back on top of her and have her.

She was his best friend's girl, he reminded himself forcefully, and with eyes screwed tight he kept himself rigidly still, until she almost shouted, "I got it. I got it."

"Good," he muttered, and took a large sighing breath and promptly sneezed.

She was panting with the effort she had made and began to cough again. When the paroxysm had passed, she cleared her throat, and said, "Afore I start sawing at me hair, I'm going to wipe your face with the hanky." She paused, and then added with a tremor in her voice, "Me own old dial is too sore. I'm bleeding a bit, I think."

"Ta." Poor kid, he thought. If her face is ruined, how'll she endure life, even if we are rescued?

She could feel his breath on her cheek. "Is *your* face hurtin' at all, afore I touch you?"

"No, Em. I think I were pressed against you when we fell."

His face was carefully wiped. She spat on a corner of the hanky and ran it clumsily around his eyelids. God, how he wanted her. She was surprised, yet pleased, when a kiss was planted on her cheek. She pushed the hanky back down the front of her blouse. "Now," she said almost cheerfully. "I'm goin' to start chopping. Proper sight I'll be when I'm finished." It was comforting to feel the man's warmth against her, especially when a particularly loud crash made the whole structure above them vibrate, and small rushes of debris slithered down on them.

The smell of gas had gone, Dick realised. The firemen must have managed to turn off the main. So much for that. He did not know whether to feel relief or disappointment. Willy-nilly, as shock had receded and been replaced by more mundane yearnings, a faint hope crept into him, that maybe the bomb that hit the canteen was not engraved with his and Emmie's names, that they might, by some miracle, be found.

Whimpers came from the girl next to him, as she tugged and cut hair by hair. She sighed and stopped work, to rest herself for a moment. Then she said without preamble, "We must have fallen into somebody's cellar — right under the yard, 'cos we was still outside — and I fell and slid quite a ways." Her voice was mournful. "I ache all over from it. Who'd build a cellar under a yard?"

"Plenty o' people, not too many years ago — about a coupla hundred, maybe. For keeping smuggled goods in - or privateers hiding their loot."

"They would? How'd they bring the stuff in?"

"A hidden door from the cellar under the building — where the shelter was, like."

"There weren't no back door out of that shelter."

"Could've been bricked up when they built the present building."

She sighed, and recommenced the cutting of her hair. If she could get her head free, perhaps she could move enough to find the water that trickled so maddeningly close to her. As they lay at present, Dick could not move much either.

VIII

Though the raid was over, and to Emmie, deep in her prison, the din seemed less, the noise outside from the roaring fires was sufficient to make everyone converse in shouts.

318

With shoulders hunched and bodies bent close to their jetting hoses, firemen had managed to advance a little into the raging inferno of South Castle Street, at the back of Paradise Street. Then the water pressure fell to a trickle and they had to beat a hasty retreat. Petrol in a pump caught fire and it blew apart. Dispirited men watched helplessly as, fanned by a light breeze, the flames began to eat their way towards Paradise Street. Wandering wisps of smoke worked their way through the wreckage. Neither Emmie nor Dick said anything, as they lay rigid with fear in the face of this new menace.

The building in which the canteen had been housed had blown outwards across the street. It effectively blocked the movement of traffic, already in difficulties because of the bomb hole further down, in which Post Office engineers struggled to restore some kind of telephone service for the authorities.

A gang of Army Pioneers, aided by volunteers, both civilians and servicemen, inched their way down the centre of Paradise Street, shovelling smaller rubble into wicker skips; larger pieces were hauled to one side. "For Christ's sake, why don't they bring in some cranes?" groaned a man in blue mechanic's overalls, as he heaved and shoved in company with a German Jewish pioneer. They turned to move a huge metal desk which had lain upside down under the girder they had just shifted. "Jesus!" the mechanic exclaimed, as he stooped to get a grip on it. With all his strength he heaved and rolled it on to its side — and looked down in horror at what had once been little Dolly, the firewatcher.

Her uniform had been blown off her. Terribly crushed, her entrails spread out, only the long gleaming hair indicated that there lay someone who had been soft and pretty.

The Pioneer looked down at her in silent pity, while the less hardened civilian shouted, "Curse them, curse them!" beside himself with horror. He bent down and gathered the frail, sticky remains up as best he could and took them to the pavement. There was nothing to cover her with. Soon, he knew, somebody would come along with a bag to put her in. Weeping, savage with rage, he went back to work.

Help *was* coming. Through moonlit lanes and narrow streets snaked a stream of fire engines and ambulances, water tankers, kitchen lorries, mobile canteens and vans of food. Rescue parties,

319

including miners and demolition experts, spent an uncomfortable night crammed into trains as they converged on Liverpool. Through broken roads, spanking clean American soldiers manoeuvred bulldozers and dump trucks, and great shovels, also mounted on caterpillar tractors, bigger than anything most Britons had seen before. They would eat into the choked thoroughfares and make a path for other vehicles.

The looters came gaily from the suburbs and the countryside, to rob those who had already lost so much.

IX

An unexploded land-mine, sitting quietly at the back of a deserted insurance office, suddenly blew up and the ear-splitting bang shook Emmie's and Dick's tiny refuge. It shook not only the debris above them, but the ground on which they lay, like some huge earthquake. In terror, they clutched each other, their heads buried into each other's shoulders, to avoid the dust which rose once more around them. Bits and pieces rattled and fell above them. The great stone over their heads held, however, though the beam which was holding down Emmie's hair shifted slightly and the remaining strands of her hair were freed.

"My God!" Dickie's teeth were chattering helplessly, as the bang was followed by a series of rumbles, gradually dying away into quiet.

Ears pricked, they waited for the next onslaught, but there was only the creaking and shifting of the ruins and the occasional splash of water. Very dimly, they also could hear what might have been slow traffic and, at times, felt the faint vibration of it.

As the dust settled again, Dickie muttered to a whimpering Emmie, "It *has* to be morning — that bang were too big for a bomb — it were something special. Come on, luv. Now's the time to feel around for a stone and bang on that wall by you, so a rescuer knows where to look."

Emmie stirred and half sat up. Dickie exclaimed at her sudden movement.

"Me hair came free in the last shake-up." She laughed tremulously and felt round for a likely stone.

For nearly half an hour, they banged steadily, to no purpose.

During that time they had both, shamefacedly, to urinate and now lay in wet clothes.

As they rested, feeling surprisingly weak, Emmie said, "David — me brother — 'll be out lookin' for me. What about your folks?"

Dickie explained that he had nobody and that this was his weekend off from his duties as night-watchman at a seed warehouse. "They'll wonder where I am come Monday, though, when I don't turn up for work."

"Gwen — that's Dave's wife — she won't bother. She hates my guts. Be glad to see me dead, I truly think. All she cares about is her house. If you breathe out, she'll dust all round you."

Dick laughed. "She can't be that bad."

"She is," insisted Emmie. "Dave's proper patient with her. It'll be him as comes to find us."

"The wardens and the Rescue Squads is good at finding buried victims," Dick replied, to reinforce her hope of help.

David was, however, sound asleep on a bunk made of chicken wire in a street shelter in Bootle. He had worked until the siren went, on repairing water pipes in narrow, badly damaged streets, while housewives and children hung round him, waiting for the taps, or at least the fire hydrants, to start gushing again. They also had no gas with which to cook, and often torn chimneys made it impossible to build a fire in a grate. Once water was restored, a good many kettles got boiled in the back yard on a fire made from splintered beams. In most cases their tiny stores of food were ruined, tins laced by slivers of glass, the contents of cupboards blown into pieces and lost in the general mess of broken plaster.

On Sunday morning, fed by a grateful housewife, David and his mate, Arthur, continued to work, laying new water pipes. Two streets away, another gas main sent a scarifying sheet of flame into the sky, threatening to engulf the slums around them in fire.

A little soothed by the thought that David would be seeking her, Emmie said to Dick, "You'd better have your knife back afore I lose it in the dark."

He fumbled round until he found her hand and the knife. As he slipped it into his shirt pocket, he felt her begin to sit up again.

"My God! Me poor back," she groaned, as the stiffened muscles were stretched.

"Now watch it," Dick warned. His voice sounded muffled, the

words coming reluctantly from a parched throat. "Move carefully. If you touch something solid, don't push it or we'll have an avalanche down on us."

"OK." If she could stop shivering, she thought, she would be less clumsy. The shivering would not stop, however. As she sat up, it became a wild shaking, her teeth chattering uncontrollably.

Dick heard her wincing, and the shuffle of her skirts against the loosened earth, as she finally got herself seated upright. Instinctively, she turned towards him, to bend forward and touch him. "Ow!" she squeaked, as she hit her head on the sloping stonework over him. When she rubbed her scraped forehead, it hurt much more than she had expected; there was a trickle, which might have been blood, down over one eyelid, and she whimpered slightly as she carefully wiped it away with a shaky finger.

"Steady on, girl."

"Suppose I move too far away and I can't find you again?" she croaked.

"Na," he assured her. "We're like a pair o' mackerels in a tin — waitin' for the tin-opener."

Her shaky laugh was close to being a sob.

She heard Dickie sigh with relief as the pressure of her body on him was eased when she moved. Very carefully she tucked her feet under herself and then kneeled up. She promptly hit her head again and sat back dizzily until the throbbing stopped. In a wild hope that there might be an aperture through which they might creep to greater safety, she rapidly ran her hands up and down and along the wall beside her. Her spirits fell, when she found that the huge rough-hewn stones of the wall met tightly with the sloping slab which roofed them over. There was enough height on the wall side for them to sit up, if they kept their heads bent, and she reported this to Dick.

"That'll be a relief," he replied. "I'll stay put till you've felt right round."

She crawled with difficulty a foot or two along the wall, until, where her feet had rested, her exploring fingers found what felt like a metal girder sloping the opposite way to the stone above her. She tried to reach over it, but the way was blocked with rubble; she managed, however, to slip her hand under it and work her fingers through a pile of cobblestones and plaster. As she eased

322

her hand carefully in, there was a loud creak and dust began to rise.

"For God's sake!" Dick's voice held panic.

She snatched her hand back under their sheltering slab. "I'm doing my best," she said crossly, and then sneezed. The sound was answered by another small rattle of debris from the same direction. She stayed frozen until the last small piece seemed to have dropped. Then she voiced the need of both of them. "I wonder where the water's running?"

"Let's listen hard."

The sound indubitably came from somewhere beyond the iron girder.

She burst into tears.

"I'm comin' up beside you, Em. Just sit still. Steady as you go, there's a girl."

He wriggled out of his narrow niche, his shoulders aching sharply, the rest of his bruised body complaining bitterly. Guided by her whimpering, he hauled himself alongside her. He sat, panting and dizzy, half leaning against her, and then he straightened up. "Phew, that's better." He listened again, and then said, "There's water there all right. May be from the pipes leading to the canteen taps."

Emmie sniffed. "Doesn't matter where it's from. It's on the other side of a bloody great girder, and the girder's too big to either climb under or over. Even if you could, there's a lot o' smallish bits very loose there." She tried to still her chattering teeth, and then quavered, "I don't know what we did to deserve this. We're not wicked."

Dick gave a rattling laugh. In the pitch-darkness, he tried to visualise the tiny space in which they found themselves. Then he said ruefully, "War's like the weather; it falls on the good and the bad alike. Only them what starts it takes care to be well away from it." Then, with determined cheerfulness, he went on, "Never mind that. First, I'm going to move forward a bit, so you can lie along this big wall. You lie on your stummick, and very, very slowly slip your hand under the girder again and work your fingers into whatever's there. See if you can feel wet. It'll be easier for you to do than me — 'cos o' me weight, like. I'm plain fat."

"Right." Her voice was a little firmer. After a tight squeezing

323

past each other, she managed to do as he had suggested, and she worked her arm further and further under the girder until part of her shoulder lay under the unyielding metal. It was all bone dry.

With her arm still stretched into the rubble, she lay and listened carefully. "It's no more 'n a foot beyond, I'm sure," she wailed in despair.

"Not to worry," Dick wheezed. "It might make a puddle in time and we'll be able to reach it. Have you still got me hanky?"

"Yes. Down me chest."

"Good. If it makes a puddle we can reach, we'll get at it by soaking the hanky in it."

She remained prone for a moment, while she mentally savoured the joy of cold water. Then she cautiously withdrew her arm and heaved herself round until she could sit up.

"Eh, I'm that sore, and you must be, too," her tremulous voice came out of the darkness. "Why don't they come? It's been pretty quiet for a while now. It has to be morning. Surely they'll be lookin' for us?"

"As soon as you hear anything that sounds like them coming, we'll shout as hard as we can, so they know we're here. And we'll bang with the stones again."

"'T' warden what come to the canteen counted us all. He'll tell the rescue men how many people to look for."

"Aye, he will."

Outside in the street, the Pioneers carefully consigned the warden to the mortuary and, with him, the remains of the police constable, who would at least have known there were people sheltering in the canteen basement.

Further down the street, in a bomb crater, a newly bathed and clean-overalled Post Office Telephones engineer relieved his exhausted colleague. Elsewhere, linesmen continued to string wires from anything they could hang them on, in an effort to re-establish communications within the city.

As less fatigued aid arrived from other towns, a mood of ebullience spread amongst the toilers. This was the end of this run of raids, they told each other. Everybody would be able to go to bed tonight and sleep it off, ready for work on Monday.

Emmie found Dick's hand and held it, as she dozed. Sometimes a very distant rumble shook their tiny lair; it sounded like big lorries moving, a promise of rescue, and they were comforted.

Without warning, there was an enormous roar, a detonation greater than any previous one, and the whole ruin in which they lay shivered and groaned. Loud cracks overhead made Emmie scream. She flung herself against Dick; in equal terror, he turned and clung to her. Again, a tremendous dust enveloped them. Instinctively, they ducked their faces into each other's shoulder, cowering together as they nearly choked.

The pandemonium died away to a rumble, only to be followed immediately by a whole series of explosions which shook their precarious shelter. Almost directly overhead they could hear the fall of masonry followed by the lesser sound of smaller debris slithering like a hundred snakes down through the wreckage. The great piece of stonework above them shuddered.

A terrified rat scuttled across Emmie's lap, sending her into hysterics.

Despite the desperate efforts of its crew and the fire brigade, fire had finally reached the main hold of the *Marakand*. Surrounded by flames, dive bombed all night, firemen and crew had been unable to scuttle her, and now, under whatever cover they could find, they crouched defeated. A four-ton anchor, blasted into the air, fell into the engine-room of a hopper and sank it as well. Acres of dock and warehouse were mowed down by the tremendous blasts and the ever-encroaching fire. Only after seventy-four hours of almost continuous racket did a weird silence descend on the embers of a whole district.

"I never want to see anything like it again," Robbie muttered fervently to his deckhand friend, as their captain checked his sooty, worn-out crew. "I'll be thankful to go to sea again."

Fogged by fear, unable to produce even one more scream, Dick and Emmie lay tightly together, both breathing shallowly. Each time the torn building over them lurched, a fresh poof of dust would surround them and they would cough and splutter.

Outside, the late spring morning was made horrible by a blizzard of burned paper which blew about the city, getting into people's eyes, clinging to clothes and faces like black snowflakes. The burned records of innumerable enterprises flattened during the night had been caught by the wind and whirled out of every broken building. Up and up they went into the smoke haze, to descend again in a supernatural storm. Through the smoke, flames still licked greedily.

By noon the road outside the canteen was passable to a single line of traffic driving very carefully, and further efforts were being made to find the remainder of the firewatchers assumed to have been on duty with Dolly. The air raid warden on day shift and new police, all looking wondrously spruce, had come on duty, and a heated altercation broke out between a demolition squad foreman puttering along the edge of the debris, and the new warden.

"How was I supposed to know there was a canteen there? There weren't no warden around, nor a cop for that matter, on this street. Thought it was all offices — and as for firewatchers, I've only got one unaccounted for now."

"Well, there *was* a canteen here and it'd be open," replied the warden irritably, "and we'd better get weaving on it." By his accent the demolition foreman must be from Manchester, presumably one of the over three thousand men which the warden had heard were being sent to Liverpool. No wonder the man didn't know where anything was.

"How many people, do you reckon?" inquired the foreman resignedly.

"Could be as many as forty."

"Good God! Somebody should've told me." He scratched his crew-cut hair and put his helmet more comfortably on his head. "They didn't say nothin' in the command post."

The warden raised a gloomy face from contemplation of the anonymous piles of wreckage round him. "The command post lost nearly the whole shift."

As he strode towards them, the police constable in charge of the area looked bleary-eyed, despite a clean and tidy uniform. He had just arrived, to commence his shift, only to find a new command post being assembled and nobody very sure of what the situation was. "Looks as if Constable Wilson got it last night. We can't find him," he was told. Heavy-hearted, he had taken the first telephone call on the re-established line. Now he shouted towards the warden, "There's a phone inquiry about a Miss Piggott — serving in the Sailors' Canteen — do you know if that's bin tackled yet?"

"I only just coom on duty," replied the warden defensively. "And

326

t' command post's only just bin replaced — pack of strangers. There weren't nobody in a fit state to tell nobody nothin'. Joe, here, he just coom from Manchester." He cocked a thumb towards the lugubrious foreman, who looked even more glum.

The constable's face went red with suppressed rage. Bloody fool, why didn't he use his common sense and show the new foreman? Poor Wilson and the command post couldn't help being dead.

"Get a bearing on where the entrance was," he ordered the warden through gritted teeth, "and explain to the foreman how it were laid out. I'll get you more help, and alert ambulance people. The entrance to the shelter underneath the canteen was to the left of the entrance from the street." He ran back to the newly reconstituted command post.

While the warden, like a questing terrier, trotted up and down the partially cleared street, the foreman assembled his squad and checked that they were equipped with shovels and crowbars — and skips to hold the rubbish they would have to remove.

The warmth of the fires, further over, was borne towards them, making them sweat. The hiss of water hitting flame and the drum of pumps bewildered the warden. If it were only quiet enough to climb the rubble and listen; then they would stand a chance of hearing survivors tapping. There were other noises to add to the confusion: explosions from No. 2 Huskisson dock; detonations, as Lancashire mining engineers showed another demolition squad how to break a way through mountains of wreckage, without bringing an avalanche down on themselves; the lives of men with demolition experience were to be preserved at all costs — their peculiar skills were all too rare. In a nearby street, a huge bulldozer manned by American soldiers was slowly crunching its way through a blockage, and that also added to the racket.

"I've got it," shouted the warden triumphantly, as he rubbed one eye watering with a mote in it. "Opposite the stump of this lamp-post."

Huge and ponderous as the foreman was, he immediately began to climb the fall opposite the broken lamp standard, walking with surprising lightness, probing gently with his crowbar, before committing his team to the search. When he was satisfied that he understood the lay of the pile, he set his men to work. "Come on, lads. Quick — but careful — mind." His melancholy expression

327

fell still further. "Doubt anybody's alive under that."

A portly gentleman in a business suit and bowler hat accosted the watching warden, "Excuse me. Can you tell me where the Sailors' Canteen is? My wife was on duty there last night, and she has not come home this morning. When I tried to telephone, I could not get through."

The warden looked up sharply and then bit his lip with tobacco-stained teeth. "Aye," he said slowly, with a sigh. "It were here. They're workin' on it now, as you can see."

The gentleman's ruddy complexion went glistening white. His grey, military moustache quivered; words would not come. Finally, he breathed, "I was afraid of that."

The warden caught his arm, concerned that he might collapse. "Sir! They could be safe in the shelter — it were a good stout cellar." The warden had not an iota of hope. But then, he told himself, you never knew what quirk of fate could save the life of someone. "What was — is — her name, sir?"

"Clara Robinson, Mrs Clara Robinson." The man was already out of his black jacket and folding it neatly. He laid it down by the lamp-post stump and placed his bowler hat on top of it. "Thank you," he said fairly steadily, as he got a grip on himself. Then he turned and picked his way over to a labourer clearing a path from the edge of the fall inwards. "Give me a shovel. I'll help you," he said between tight lips.

"Best stay back, sor," a middle-aged Irish navvy, working ahead of the other labourer, advised him. "It's dangerous." He lifted his pick again and swung it down on the obstruction before him.

"I *have* to do something," Alec Robinson said firmly. He undid his gold cufflinks and rolled up his shirt sleeves.

The foreman came carefully down the slope of the pile, placing each foot precisely so that he did not fall into the debris. The warden shouted up to him, "T' cellar had a pavement light what led right into it."

"That'll save a lot." The foreman's face lifted slightly, as he redirected his men, to facilitate the unearthing of this narrow window of heavy glass framed in iron and set directly into the pavement to give some light to the cellar. If it had not been pounded into the ground, it could give the rescuers immediate access. Then he turned and sized up the blenched business man who was working his way towards him.

"You could clear some space at the edge of the pavement," he told him kindly. "Make a way through to where the road has been cleared. We'll need a bit of space to lay 'em down, maybe, when we bring 'em out." He saw Alec Robinson's eyes widen with horror, and added hastily, "They could be hurt." He turned to the labourer. "Find 'im a shovel."

Alec Robinson thankfully took the proffered shovel and bent to the task, his heart heavy. An ambulance was already nosing its way cautiously along the street, followed closely by a fire pump. A wobbly stream of water was directed at the ruins further back, to damp them down and possibly contain the fire raging behind them, until the rescuers had finished their work. The stream was weak because of fractured mains, and the turbulence in the air caused by the fires themselves blew much of the water back on to the firemen and the rescuers. Still, they persisted.

While the workmen picked their way in with meticulous care, para-medical personnel, black bags in hand, came at a shambling run along the littered pavement opposite.

They were too early, so, with tin hats pushed to the back of their heads, they lit cigarettes and stood gossiping about a new film one of them had seen.

In what seemed to have become their own private bomb crater, the clay-bespattered telephone engineers continued their patient splicing of lines.

When Alec Robinson paused to mop his forehead, he was approached by a tall cadaverous man dressed in the grey uniform of a chauffeur. The man took off his peaked cap, revealing a bald head across which a few wisps of white hair had been carefully plastered. "Sir, I'm looking for the Sailors' Canteen. I'm Higgins, sir. The mistress has not come home, and we — that is, Mrs. Fleming, the housekeeper, and me — thought I should come down on the bus, to see if she's all right — the car being mothballed for the duration, sir." He turned and surveyed the appalling wreckage. "I trust I'm not looking at the canteen?"

Alec Robinson replied gruffly, "You are. Who is your mistress?"

"The Dowager Countess Mentmore. She's a volunteer."

A minute later, a chauffeur's cap and jacket were carefully laid by Mr Robinson's bowler hat and black jacket, and the demolition foreman had to find work for another volunteer.

The rescuers worked like moles, shifting obstructing masonry, splintered woodwork, pieces of filing cabinets and desks, a slippery cascade of law books, a huge Victorian lavatory, all interlaced with electric wires which might still be live, and miles of water pipes and gas pipes. A lot of this was passed back and piled on the pavement. Stout pieces of timber, desk drawers, finely panelled oak doors, all were used by the labouring men as props in the twisting passageway they were making. Every time there was a further explosion from No. 2 Huskisson this perilous little entry was shaken by the blast, but still the men persevered.

X

That dreadful Sunday, as Emmie lay in Dick's arms, her mind wandered. Both of them were drained by fear, thirsty beyond words and very hungry. It seemed to her that she was lying in Robbie's arms on the sandhills, behind the great sea wall at Meols, and they were talking of building a small cottage not too far from there, with a good slate roof and a parlour for best occasions.

She woke suddenly, not sure what had alerted her. Instead of the sunlight on the waving, coarse grasses of the sand hills, she faced a midnight blackness. She touched Dick's face with her hand, and he stirred and muttered hoarsely, "OK, luv?"

"Mm," she replied. She shivered; the wall felt cold against her back.

It felt wet! Her cotton blouse and petticoat were sticking to her back. She must have sweated heavily or wet herself again. But there it was once more — a cold drop, a trickle down a strand of her torn hair and across her neck.

"Dickie," she gasped. "Wake up. There's water running down the wall behind me back. I can feel it."

Water? He swallowed and tried to answer her, but his dried lips would barely move. He felt clammily cold and he shivered.

"Sit up, Dick. I'm goin' to turn meself over."

"Can't sit up, 'cos of the slope over me," he managed to reply thickly. She was right, though. He could smell the odour of water on dust — and he could also smell an increased amount of smoke. His heart leapt with fresh apprehension. He eased himself away

330

from Emmie, to help her turn.

Emmie was as excited as if they had already been rescued. Her mind cleared as, wild with hope, she knelt up and ran her hand along the wall. There *was* a steady dribble down it at one point. She put her sore cheek against it and then turned to lick it. Her tongue was promptly covered with grit, but it was moistened, none the less. She tried again and spat out the grit. "There's only a bit," she announced in a fractionally clearer voice. "I'm going to try and soak your hanky, though."

The water flowed faster, forming a small pool round her knees. The handkerchief was soon quite wet and she passed it to Dick to suck. He thankfully wiped his lips and put a corner in his mouth. He too had to spit out grit, but the relief was tremendous. He managed to move a little out of his niche and curve himself round Emmie as she knelt, to dip the hanky again into the wondrous little pool.

Emmie undid her skirt button and awkwardly hauled off her blouse, cursing roundly when she caught her elbow on the rough wall. She pressed the garment into the tiny stream. As it became wetter, she struggled to get out of her cotton petticoat in order to soak that also. "It'll make a little store of water," she puffed.

"I'm sorry I can't see you."

She blushed, and managed a small giggle. In the dark, she had not considered her nakedness. Thankfully, she pressed the sopping blouse to her throbbing face. She tried to wipe it gently but it hurt too much.

All around the great slab that protected them water began to drip, to a point where, no matter how they lay, they became wet, and they again huddled in each other's arms, to keep warmer, while they speculated on the source.

"Could be a leak from a pool which built up somewhere above us," offered Dick. "And now it's sifting down to us."

Their little lair shuddered, as a quick series of explosions from the *Marakand* shook it; a heavier splatter of droplets fell round them. Dick felt Emmie begin to tremble and he held her closer. Again he was tempted to take her, now that the air felt cleaner and he could breathe properly. She wriggled more tightly to him and he knew that she wanted him. She turned on her back and he moved on top of her, so that there was space above them.

331

Despite the limited space, it was a wild lovemaking, as if both of them were young and filled with the frantic desire of youth. Every terrifying shift of the broken buildings above them; every great blast that numbed their ears as the deadly cargo of the *Marakand* wreaked havoc, though adding to their fear, also intensified their passion, until finally they lay exhausted and almost unbelievably at peace. They continued to caress each other, Emmie with a strange wonder that some one other than Robbie could make her feel so good. As she stroked him, she murmured incoherent endearments and he chuckled. "Not bad for an old man, eh?" he joked, and fell asleep.

He was awakened by her hoarse voice saying, "Dickie, I thought I heard something scrabbling about then."

"Eh, what?"

"Listen? Is that a voice?"

They held their breath; then without a further word felt round for the stones they had used to bang the wall with.

Frantic with hope, they both banged, and shrieked, "Help! Help! Help!"

Emmie's voice was much weaker than she realised, her throat swollen from her earlier screams, and Dick's was not much better; he realised ruefully that he had exhausted himself with Emmie; it was hard to get breath enough into his lungs to yell.

They paused to listen again. They could hear only the groans of the pile above them, as it slowly settled. Emmie began to cry.

XI

Gwen felt, that Sunday, that her life had been broken into, just like burglars broke into houses, that her house was as good as doorless and anybody could plunge in and out of it without so much as a by-your-leave. Never before had she had to extend a hand to anybody; she prided herself on minding her own business, on having the whitest doorstep in the street, the best-dressed daughter and the cleanest-looking husband — and, of course, getting her washing out on the line before any of her neighbours, on a Monday morning. Sunday was a day to meet one's friends at chapel and show off the hat one had retrimmed, and to anticipate with pleasure eating one's meat ration, slowly braised in the oven while one was at service.

And instead, she was surrounded by the most awful bunch of little horrors anybody could have wished on her. She surveyed them grimly, as they sat round the table at midday, eating like starving dogs. It was a pure miracle, she thought, that she had managed to provide a dinner at all; just like the story of the loaves and fishes. The Thomases' meat ration had been extended into a stew with the aid of a bag of potatoes, culled from Mrs Donnelly's kitchen, and three pennyworth of fades — discarded, shrivelled vegetables — from the corner shop. Nora, who had been entrusted with the message to the corner shop, had also brought two loaves of yesterday's bread and some milk — on credit. "The first time in me life I ever arst for anythin' on tick," moaned Gwen.

Patrick had been soundly clouted over the head by his father, for coming to view the ravaged Dwellings, and he now sat sulkily shovelling stew into his mouth, while Gwen slapped a couple of spoonfuls of it on to her own plate. She picked up her knife and fork and began to cut the tiny cube of meat, when suddenly she remembered.

"Emma!" she exclaimed, and put down her fork.

Ruby looked up from her task of feeding an unwilling Michael with bits of bread sopped in a saucer of gravy. Mari, who had got up only in time for the meal, asked with a small yawn, "Isn't she in bed?" She smiled across at Patrick, but he dropped his eyes and did not smile back.

"It were such a hectic morning, I clean forgot her. She never come home."

Mari stared at her incredulously, while Ruby stuttered, "Do you think she caught it last night?"

Mari licked her lips. "What about Daddy?"

"He'll be all right." Gwen's reply was automatic. Her husband was always all right, as dependable as the Liverpool one o'clock gun, which, before the war, had marked the time for the city. No one had told her of the carnage in Bootle — or, indeed, in the city itself; the wireless had merely reported a raid on a north-west town.

She sighed, as she looked round the table. Only Ruby and Mari were interested in Emma; the others continued to eat, Brendy happily pushing bits of vegetable into his mouth with his hand. "Really, Brendy," Gwen expostulated. "Use your spoon, you naughty boy." He took no notice and she leaned across the table and gave his hand a small slap; then she stuffed a spoon into it. He tried shovelling.

She turned to Patrick, as being the only older male present, and said agitatedly, "I'll save her some dinner, anyway. And you, when you've finished, run over and tell your dad she's missing. He'll know what to do. He'll ask about her for us."

Patrick nodded agreement. If he had a real message to deliver, surely he would be able to stay to watch the men at work on The Dwellings. He quickly ate the last mouthful on his plate and half rose from the table.

"Have your pudding first," Gwen ordered. "A few more minutes ain't goin' to make no difference."

Pudding as well. For the first time that day, Patrick's spirits rose a little, and he ate eagerly the large helping of bread-and-butter pudding she put in front of him.

"Where did Miss Emmie go?" he inquired.

Gwen explained about her job in the Sailors' Canteen in Paradise Street and that she was on the evening shift. She ran her fingers through her greying red curls. She had been too busy to comb it and had not even washed her face.

"I'll take me dad's bike and tell 'im first; then I'll ride down to Paradise Street and see what's to do there." He looked excited at the prospect and gave Gwen the same beguiling, conspiratorial grin that had mesmerised Mari in the air raid shelter. Mari, seeing it, felt again the extraordinary sensation which his exploring fingers had introduced her to. She flushed and went slowly on with her dinner.

"I hope she's all right," Gwen said mechanically. "She might've gone over to see Robert Owen's mother." In her heart she felt that Emmie was a deliberate nuisance in not turning up for either breakfast or dinner. Serve her right if she'd got killed. Decent girls came straight home. And then there were all those merchant seamen hanging around the canteen — a lot of no-goods with only two ideas in their heads, drink and women.

Patrick could not find his father at The Dwellings because he had taken half an hour off to go to see the local undertaker about his wife's funeral. He reluctantly approached the constable in charge of the incident, who promised to put an inquiry about Emmie in motion immediately, and to let Mrs Thomas know as soon as he had news. The constable refused to allow him to go close to the ruins, so Patrick again mounted his father's rusty bike and sped away to join the sightseers in the town. At the top of Duke Street, he was stopped by a soldier with a rifle on his back, who wanted to know his business and promptly turned him back.

Patrick knew the town like a rabbit knows its warren. He gravely cycled round the corner out of sight, then dived down an alley and proceeded along back ways. He did not return for tea.

XII

Gwen gave the children a tea of bread and margarine and home-made gooseberry jam and sent them out to play in the street. It was the first day in her married life that she had given barely a thought to the condition of her little house, except nearly to weep over the bed which Michael had wetted; it was now being dried out with the aid of three hot-water bottles. She sat with eyes closed, wishing passionately that David would return. He would know what to do about the Donnelly children — and Emma and the windows — and the fact that she was going to be over her house-keeping money.

She was sound asleep in the chair, mouth open, gently snoring, when Conor Donnelly, followed by Ruby, walked in through the open front door.

She awoke, startled to see an awful apparition standing before her on her rag rug. It was white with dust from head to foot, the face caked. Two red eyes glared out at her from under a battered tin hat; ominous brown stains marked the front of him. There was a faint smell about him as if of a butcher's shop, mixed with old sweat. A gap in the face was mouthing something about Emma.

Frightened, she jumped to her feet so quickly that she nearly knocked him down.

"It's me dad," explained Ruby simply.

Gwen forced herself into wakefulness. "Did you say Emma?" she asked. Then, without thinking of the effect on her fireside chair, immaculate in faded cretonne, she said, "My, Mr Donnelly, you look dreadful! Sit down. Would you like a cuppa tea? Have you had your tea ?"

Conor flopped thankfully into the little chair and tried to smile. "Ta, I could use a drop."

"No trouble." To offer a cup of tea was a strict convention, but she surveyed him with dismay. Never in her life had she seen anyone look so dreadful. Even the chimney sweep at the end of a day's work — or the coalman — never looked as bad as that. For once her Methodist training surfaced, and she asked impetuously, "I got a bit o' dinner left. Why don't you wash your hands and face under the kitchen tap, while I make it hot for you?"

He had eaten nothing hot for forty-eight hours and he accepted eagerly.

It was amazing what a bit of hot food would do for a person, thought Gwen in gratified surprise, as she watched Conor polish off the dinner intended for Emma. Scuttling round to make the food ready, she had forgotten again about Emma, but now as he slurped at a cup of tea, she remembered and inquired if he had news.

He sighed. "Aye, I have, Mrs Thomas. The canteen's flat. They're digging into the shelter under it now."

"And Emma's in it?" Her heart bounced uncomfortably. It was one thing to wish a person dead or gone; quite another to probably have the wish granted so promptly.

"I suppose she's there. They're trying to finish the job afore it's dark — same as we bin doin' at The Dwellings."

"Do you know how things are in Bootle?"

Anxious not to scare her unnecessarily, since her husband was out there, he played down the shocking fate of Bootle.

"Me hubby didn't even come home for his dinner," Gwen remarked quite crossly. "Don't they know men have families to look after?"

Conor ignored the remark and pursued the question of Emmie. "Miss Thomas were engaged, weren't she?"

"Yes." Gwen was surprised that he knew. She had forgotten that the engagement of a woman of mature years would have been an interesting piece of gossip to be mulled over by the fire in the local public house.

"Is he at sea?"

"I doubt it — yet. They were loading at No. 2 Huskisson, according to Emma."

"What?"

Gwen jumped. "At Huskisson. Why?"

Conor told her the news, received over the post telephone, of the fearsome destruction wreaked by the exploding *Marakand*. "Most of the bangs you've been hearing today is from her," he finished up.

"Well, I can't say as I think much of him, to be truthful — but I wouldn't wish that on him." She had a sudden picture in her mind of the tall, well-built man, ruddy-faced and blue-eyed, and knew in her heart that she was deeply jealous of Emmie. Emmie was so content, so satisfied, as if part of the time she was moving in a dream. David had never made her glow like that. She felt a surge of longing go through her thin frame and she examined her nails carefully so that Conor would not read her feelings in her face.

Conor said heavily, as he got up from his chair, "I'll see if we can trace him. Robert Owen, deckhand, on the *Marakand*, wasn't it?"

She nodded absently.

MONDAY, 5 MAY 1941

I

Neither Emmie nor Dick admitted to each other an increasing hunger; hunger was something which had been with them, on and off, all their lives. At her brother's house, Emmie had for the first time enjoyed adequate meals, though Gwen was by no means generous in the portions she gave her. Now, however, she endured a clemming misery.

As they became wetter, the water which had been such a Godsend became a trial. Dick shivered constantly, teeth chattering, from the cold as well as from nervous strain.

Not only did they lie in puddles of water, but in their own urine and ordure, and the odour vied with the smell of smoke and wet plaster; the wisps of smoke saved them, however, from attacks by rats, the contemplation of which made both of them heave at times; the vermin with which Liverpool was infested retreated as the fires advanced.

At one point they thought they heard the scrape of metal on stone and then a distant shout. In response, they banged the wall with a stone and cried out again and again. The wall was as thick as a castle keep and if there was anyone there, the frantic cries went unheard.

In a sudden burst of fury, Emmie had said venomously, "if I ever get out of this fix, I'll go into munitions. I'll send them something to make *them* smart, I will."

"You can make good money at it," Dickie replied practically. "A lot more'n you could servin' in a cafe."

This idea had set her off on a laboured, barely audible description of what she would like to do after the war, if she had some savings. "I'd buy a nice little sweet and tobacconist's," she confided to Dick. "It'd give me some real independence — and summat to do while Robbie's at sea."

"He might like to swallow the anchor and help you."

"Nay," she insisted, with unexpected woodenness. "He can have 'is own job. This is for me. I never ever thought o' planning for meself afore this." She contemplated a hopeful future for a little while. Then she said, her voice cracked and broken, "You know, a lot of women get tired of being bossed all the time, but unless you got money you got to put up with it. I'm tired of it. I want to be free — and Robbie will benefit. We'll have more money for both of us. Go on holidays and suchlike."

Sporadically, they planned holidays and dreamed of sunny beaches, until an ache in Dickie's back became a piercing pain; his temperature started to rise and finally his speech to wander, until he was talking to Emmie as if she were one of his sons.

Emmie, too, began to feel light-headed, and the unbroken darkness robbed her of any knowledge of the passage of time. Unaware of the frantic battle being waged in No. 2 Huskisson, in which her beloved Robbie fought as hard as anyone, she concluded from the intermittent booms which shook the ground beneath her that it was night and a raid was taking place at a little distance from the town centre.

Just before midnight, and continuing well into Monday morning, enemy aircraft swept over the east coast, like a cloud of disturbed hornets, curved round over Liverpool Bay and followed the shining Mersey to their target.

The anti-aircraft guns had been reorganised during the day, to good effect, and a heavy barrage greeted the raiders, making it difficult to bomb accurately. Nevertheless, incendiary bombs deluged the city, and the haphazard scattering of high explosives brought out of bed at a run all those citizens brave enough to retire in the first place. People sleeping on the platforms of the underground railway forgot the hardness of their sleeping place and turned over thankfully, and those in air raid shelters or out in the fields beyond the city congratulated themselves on their forethought, miserable as they might be. The stunned victims of the earlier raids, now herded into schools and church halls, faced this further threat to their safety, and more than one such shelter became a bloody grave before morning.

Though night fighting was a new art, the pilots in their slow Defiants used all their ingenuity to defend the port. "Learnin' on t' job, like us," one auxiliary fireman remarked cynically, as he gazed upwards for a moment at the fireworks in the sky. A thin cheer went up from his battered brigade, when a Nazi airman was spotted bailing out and floating downwards, his parachute spread above him. "Hope he gets lynched," cried several savagely tired Liverpudlians; but he was picked up from the river the next morning, drowned, like so many of Liverpool's own men.

Ignoring the pandemonium and the danger, Rescue Squads still picked their way delicately through great heaps of what had once been a city. With the aid of shaded lamps or, infrequently, a floodlight, they peered and called and probed, with occasional success, while searchlights flicked like mad pendulums back and forth across the sky and malevolent pieces of flak flashed like javelins amid the rescuers.

Panting, trying to keep calm, Emmie held the head of a babbling Dick to her naked breast, clasping her arms tightly over him as she sought to protect him. As the hubbub continued, furious sexual desire engulfed her again. It boiled in her, an urgent, primitive need, and she murmured incoherently to him. Dick himself was aware only of a warm, comforting presence in a world of nightmare, as pneumonia took hold of him. His breath came in harsh rasps.

"Don't let him die, oh, God. Don't let him die," she implored, as she realised there would be no response from him. While the ear-splitting din round her increased, she began to believe that he was indeed dying; her self-control deserted her, her mind gave way and she shrieked like a rabbit in a snare.

II

As she saw Conor out of the front door, on Sunday evening, Gwen managed to insert into his monologue the suggestion that the children might now return to their own home, since it was fairly certain, from experience in other raids, that the Germans had finished this onslaught. Shocked, Conor had turned back and vehemently begged her to keep them with her for one more night.

"Their nan should be here by tomorrer night," he assured her. "She'll stay a few days, though she's still got me dad to care for at home. Then Rube will have to manage for us — we'll hope the raids'll be finished by then."

When Gwen still demurred, he insisted, "I *can't* stay home with them tonight. They need every man they can get at The Dwellings. What would people say if I stayed home, I ask you?"

Because of what people might also say about her, Gwen reluctantly agreed to keep the youngsters.

She went slowly back indoors. In the yard, Conor's dog started to bark and then to whine. "Blast him," she muttered viciously. The kitchen door to the yard opened, and Patrick entered, the dog sidling after him. He looked white and strained and glanced at her uncertainly before dropping his eyes to the importuning dog and patting it.

He's scared, Gwen sensed. Frightened to death of something.

"What's up, lad?"

"I don't think anybody's alive down there," he burst out, his breath coming quickly, as if he had been running.

"Where?"

"Down Paradise — where your Emma was."

Gwen felt herself go cold. So the worst had happened. She had wished it and she was responsible. She wanted to be sick.

"It's somethin' terrible down there, missus. You should see the fires." His lips trembled. He had seen what he feared even grownups could not cope with and he was frightened, humbled. Dreadful Mrs Thomas looked suddenly like a pillar of strength; her basement steps a safe stronghold.

The gates of hell yawned before Gwen. If you wished a person dead — and it happened as you wished — it was as good as murder. She gaped at the beaten child whose grubby hands clutched for support at the back of the chair. Then she said very slowly, "What you and I need is a cuppa tea." She tried to pull herself together, and added, "And I'll make you gooseberry jam butties to go with it." She walked unsteadily past him to the kitchen and he and the dog followed her forlornly.

Faintly from the street floated the voices of Ruby and some

neighbouring little girls singing a skipping song. The thud of the rope stopped and a quarrel broke out, in which Nora's strident shrieks predominated. A few moment later, a flustered Ruby dragging a recalcitrant small sister interrupted the tea making, and from the staircase another voice chimed in, as Brendy, clad only in his vest, howled, "I want me mam. Where's Mam?" He came pattering into the kitchen, pushing his way past his sisters.

Gwen gulped and half closed her eyes. "Be quiet!" she cried exasperatedly. "Shut up, Nora." She bent down to catch Brendy, who threatened to exit through the back door in search of his mam. "Hey, you're supposed to be in bed, now."

Nora stopped her battle with Ruby and joined in with Brendy. She looked up resentfully at Ruby and cried, "Aye, where's me mam?" She pouted, and rubbed her arm where Ruby had slapped her.

Gwen snatched up Brendy and tried to soothe him. "Your mam'll be back soon," she told him, patting his back gently. "You know she's gone to hospital to be mended."

Though she heard both Patrick and Ruby catch their breath behind her, this was sufficient to reduce Brendy's howl to a sob. "Where's she broken?" he asked with a trace of interest.

Gwen sighed. "She's got a cut — just there." She touched Brendy's protruding ribs. "The doctor'll sew it up — and then she'll get better and come home, I hope."

"Get away," Nora exclaimed in disbelief, her pout wiped off her face. "With a bloody needle?"

"Don't you use language like that round this house, miss," Gwen scolded. "Or I'll wash yer mouth out with soap." Nora bridled, her sly eyes peeping defiantly between the almost white lashes. Gwen went on, "For sure, they stitch cuts up with a needle — and white cotton."

"Well, I'll be buggered!" Nora's eyes opened wide with amazement. "They couldn't?"

Gwen put down Brendy, picked up Nora's hand and smacked it on the back. "I told you to mind your language, you little vixen."

Nora scowled and was silent.

Brendy pulled at Gwen's apron. "When'll she come?" he asked piteously.

"Soon, luvvie, soon. Now you come up to bed. You'll get cold

345

down here."

After Gwen, Ruby and Patrick had shared a pot of tea and he had told them some of the details of the shambles in the town, including the information that the rescue squads were still digging for survivors, Gwen sat white and silent for a moment. Then she said heavily, "You'd better go and feed your dad's cockerels."

He went grudgingly into his own back yard and stood watching the birds in their separate cages pecking at the black market corn, as he sprinkled it in front of them. When he unthinkingly put his fingers on to the chicken wire which held them in, one bird pecked him. He swore at it. The burst of anger brought him out of the lethargy into which he had sunk, and as he sucked his finger, he watched with interest a plane high in the sky. It climbed in the pearly atmosphere until he could hardly hear its engine, and slowly a great ambition rose in him, to fly himself, to be a bomber pilot and give the Germans what for. He looked at the closed back door, where his mother had been fond of leaning, her latest baby in her arms, to catch the sun and wait for him to come back from school. Tears welled up and with them a murderous desire for revenge, a boiling tide of feeling which stayed with him for years. "I'll teach 'em!" he cried, as tears of grief ran down his face.

III

Gwen crawled into bed beside Mari. In the next bedroom Michael whimpered fretfully.

"I wish Ruby could shut that kid up," she fumed uselessly.

Mari stirred uneasily. "He's hungry, Ruby says. He wants his mam. She used to feed him from her breast. I seen her."

"Good Heavens! That's not decent. He's far too old for that."

"Ruby says that's why he wants his mam so bad."

Gwen cleared her throat, a little embarrassed. "Well, a little girl like you shouldn't be talkin' about such things." She turned over, and buried her head in her big feather pillow. Mari thought she had gone to sleep, but she said abruptly, "I'd better get him a titty-bottle from the chemist tomorrow." She sighed, and then went on, "Till I can teach him how to drink from a cup."

A resounding crash, an hour later, took the corner grocery shop, and the sunken-cheeked woman who kept, it straight into oblivion.

346

Mother and daughter flew out of bed. Nora, Brendy and Michael were howling in unhappy unison with the air raid siren.

Ruby met them on the landing, with a bawling Michael in her arms. She was panting with terror, her big grey eyes nearly popping out of her head. Nora and Brendy crowded behind her.

"Downstairs, quick," ordered Gwen, as she struggled into her dressing-gown. "And you, Mari, take the candle — and don't drop grease on the stair carpet."

Patrick had opened the front door and was watching the Defiants darting in and out amid the searchlight beams. "For goodness' sake, come in," yelped Gwen in nervous concern. "That's how your mother caught it."

He shut the door reluctantly as the other children scampered through the living room to the kitchen and the cellar steps. Inspired, Gwen snatched her sweet ration out of the sideboard drawer as she went past, and what had threatened to be a weary, noisy gathering became suddenly happily quiet when she distributed toffees all round.

At half-past four on Monday morning, they went gratefully back to their beds.

At five o'clock, David was dropped at his door by a car intended to carry the walking wounded.

He staggered into his home and sank thankfully into the familiar depths of his easy chair. He leaned his head back and the pain in his chest surged again. To hunt for the matches and light the gas jet was out of the question; he concentrated instead on trying to breathe. Finally, the spasm passed and he sat absolutely still, beads of perspiration coating his forehead, until he heard Gwen running down the stairs. She hurried in, tying her plaid dressing-gown round her, as she pattered across the linoleum. Patrick stirred but did not wake.

"Dave!" she exclaimed. "Am I ever glad to see you." She peered at him in the half light. "Golly, you look dirty. Have you had any tea?"

David felt as if he were floating along in a mist, everything distorted, nothing close to him. He breathed with effort, afraid to move much, lest the pain recommence. The staircase up to bed loomed as an impassable barrier. "I'd like a cuppa tea," he managed to reply. He closed his eyes, and the faintest smile broke the exhaustion of his face, as he envisaged the whole of Liverpool afloat on pots of tea.

Gwen quickly folded back the little hearthrug. "Aye, David, what a time I've had. I've got all the kids from next door here. Patrick's there." She gestured towards the sofa, half hidden in the gloom. "Poor Mrs Donnelly — struck down in her prime."

"Dead ?"

Gwen was kneeling in front of the fireplace, quickly raking out the ashes and then stuffing balls of newspaper and pieces of firewood into the grate. She paused and turned a pinched, weary face towards him. "Saturday night."

As best he could, David tried to pay attention to the story of the children, the windows, the broken aspidistra bowl, the dog in the back yard and Emmie's absence. Finally, she said, "And last night the gas went off. I put a whole shillin' in the meter and nothin' happened."

David sat with his eyes closed. Emma! "What did you do about Emmie ?"

"Told Mr Donnelly and he's inquiring."

He knew he could not go out himself to look for her, so he simply nodded and said, "You can draw a couple of quid from the Post Office Savings. Aye, I hope she's all right." After these garbled instructions, he allowed himself to rest.

He was hazily aware of her feeding a horde of children, correcting them sharply and dispatching them to school. He woke sufficiently to return a hearty kiss and a hug from his daughter, doing his best to appear merely tired. Gwen had handed him a cup of tea, but he sat with it on a little table beside him until it went cold.

When Ruby left him, Michael yelled and had to be held back from following her. As the front door slammed, he threw himself on to the floor and kicked and screamed, arms flailing.

David was thankful when the piercing howls became sobs and then the sobs were separated by silences, as the little boy discovered David staring at him. The blazing blue eyes closed and, thumb in mouth, he went to sleep on the hearthrug at David's feet.

Gwen had run upstairs to put on her clothes, and now she came down and said, "Thank goodness, that's over. He won't eat, 'cos his mother used to feed him herself. I'll get him a titty-bottle from the chemist when I go down the road." She turned to survey David.

"Would you like some cornflakes for your brekkie? Or do you want to get washed first?"

"Nay," he replied slowly. "See if you can get the doctor to come. I keep getting a pain in me chest."

"Pain? Why didn't you tell me? You don't look well, that's for sure."

The detail of the cramp in his chest was laboriously explained to her, as she flung her coat over her flowered overall and crammed her beret over her errant curls. She half ran the quarter-mile to the doctor's house.

According to his troubled wife, the doctor had been out all night. She would send him over as soon as he returned.

Breathless, Gwen returned more slowly. She was sick with fear. Was it a heart attack? Or warning of a stroke? She must keep him quiet — and that meant keeping Michael quiet, as well. She'd pick up a bottle and teat from the chemist when she passed his shop, if he were open.

As she went to turn into the chemist's doorway — she could see him inside, though the "Closed" sign still hung on his door — she bumped into Mrs Hanlon, a big, florid woman, the wife of a docker who lived a few doors away. Mrs Hanlon was bubbling with the exciting news of the demise of the corner shop and its owner, which lay in the opposite direction to the doctor's house and had consequently not been seen by Gwen.

"And what you goin' to do, now Blackler's is burned down?" the woman asked, wrapping her black shawl more tightly round her and leaning forward to breathe into Gwen's harassed face.

The news was a real shock to Gwen, and Mrs Hanlon seemed to expand and contract, like a balloon in process of being blown up. Blackler's gone — and with it, presumably, her wages. Gwen's heart sank.

"And Lewis's," went on Mrs Hanlon ruthlessly. "T' firewatchers must've been roasted alive."

Gwen felt as if the whole universe was crushing down on her. "I got to go to the chemist," she intervened desperately. "Mr Thomas is sick."

Mrs Hanlon ignored the interjection and prattled on happily about The Dwellings and the pile of bodies there.

Suddenly, with overwhelming passion, Gwen hated her. Was it

349

really a Roman holiday to her? Didn't she realise that every bomb that fell was like a huge stone in a pool; the effect grew and grew, like ripples in a pool. Not only did it destroy homes; it upset completely the lives of everybody near. And for what? For what?

As the remorseless voice went on and she tried unsuccessfully to ease herself behind Mrs Hanlon in order to rattle on the chemist's door latch, she thought of Michael screaming for his lost mam, and she wanted to run home and take him in her arms and tell him everything would be all right — in a while, when the ripples ceased — and to put a hot poultice on David's chest and tell him the same.

The chemist opened his door and at his polite "Excuse me" Mrs Hanlon moved out of the entranceway. Gwen whirled behind her and left the woman standing open-mouthed.

IV

A frantic Monday for every city official, with one hospital out of commission and several others badly damaged; in Webster Road mortuary over half the bodies nameless; water in short supply; wavering sheets of flame still flaring upwards from burst gas mains; dangerous electric cables snaking over many a road and in and out of wrecked buildings; hordes of hungry and homeless people; and the centre of the city a mighty funeral pyre.

To those Liverpool housewives who still had a home, however, the main problem was that they could not do their washing. Monday was national washing day and on Tuesdays one did the ironing.

As Gwen hurried through her back yard, on her return from the chemist, she realised that even if the trickling kitchen tap provided enough water, she could not hang the washing out in the yard to dry. The air was filled with tiny bits of grit and burned paper — she had a piece in one eye and it was watering miserably. A sandlike film had formed on all her brightly polished window sills, and when she ran her finger along the clothes line as she passed, she found it thick with dust.

She paused for a second, her hand on the doorknob, to get her breath before entering the house, and looked down at the neat sealing-waxed parcel the chemist had made of a feeding-bottle and comforter. Then with shoulders bowed like an old woman, she opened the back door and went slowly in.

David lay on the sofa, asleep. His usually ruddy face was ashen and Gwen noticed with a pang that his two days' growth of beard was grey, not black. He was still in his overalls.

Michael snuffled gently on the hearthrug. He was awake, sucking his thumb as usual. He held the little, brass-handled hearth brush in his arms as if it were a teddy bear.

She ran upstairs to get a woollen shawl with which to cover David and was immediately thrown into a towering rage when she discovered, in passing, that the drawers of the chest in Nora's and Brendy's room had been opened and the contents were scattered all over the floor, amid feathers from a burst pillow. "Blast them!" she cursed, nearly crying.

She had just tucked the shawl over David, who did not stir, when there was a polite knock at the front door. Expecting the doctor, she hastily took off her overall and smoothed down her skirt, before answering. She was still shaking with suppressed anger.

On the unwashed doorstep stood a nun. Gwen glared at the tiny elderly figure in a spotless white wimple and a shabby, but perfectly pressed, black dress. Little highly polished black boots peeped out from under the heavy skirt and a large rosary hung from her waist. Her hands were tucked into her big sleeves. The face in the stiffly starched frame was paper-white and lined like crumpled tissue. Two gentle grey eyes surveyed Gwen and showed faint amusement, as Gwen stepped hastily backwards as if to avoid contamination.

Assuming that the nun was begging, she asked rudely, "What do you want? We're Methodists. We don't give to Catholics." She started to close the door.

"I have come with regard to the Donnelly children. I am from their school." The voice was soft but authoritative and Gwen opened the door slightly again. "I wanted to inquire if you need help with them."

With a long sigh Gwen said, "Well, I'm managing." She bit her lower lip and, remembering her manners, asked, "Will you step in for a minute? The parlour is wrecked, but come in anyways."

The nun floated in after Gwen and surveyed the dying aspidis-

351

tra lying amid its earth and the broken shards of its pot in the middle of the red Belgian carpet, the linoleum nailed roughly across the windows, and the soot in the hearth.

Gwen hastily brushed broken plaster off a straight chair brought from her mother-in-law's house. "Sit down," she invited cautiously.

"Are *all* the children with you?" asked the visitor, seating herself.

"Yes." The word came in a little gasp, and suddenly Gwen was pouring out to another woman, a woman, not a nun, all her worries about Michael, her fears that she could not keep Patrick under control, about Ruby's little shoulders having to carry such a terrible load in the future, and about foul-mouthed Nora and Brendy. "Their gran's supposed to come today," she finished, pushing back her wild hair from the eye that was still watering. "And me husband come back this morning with a pain in his chest. He's asleep back there. We're waiting for the doctor now."

"I understand. I can quite understand your concern." Gwen had been standing in front of her, and now the sister caught her hand and patted it. "I'll have some additional clothing sent over to you — and a box of groceries — you could pass them on to their grandmother — if she arrives safely."

Afterwards, Gwen warmed some milk and put it into the new feeding-bottle. How strange it was. Under all that black cloth lay the kindest of human beings. She said to Michael, who was sitting on the rug, rubbing his eyes and whimpering, "I won't be a minute, luv. Auntie's coming with a nice bottle — and an old lady's goin' to send you some little pants — specially for you." She picked the child up and held him in the crook of her arm, his drooping head against her flat chest, and put the teat into his mouth. After a moment's experimentation, he began to suck eagerly.

V

The shops which had survived were closed. The black-clad assistants were hurrying home, after a frantic Monday of dusting and sweeping and the resorting of stock blown off the shelves. The foreman of the rescue squad wriggled out of the zigzag tunnel he and his gang had moled into the ruins of the air raid shelter under the canteen. He took off his breathing apparatus.

"We're into it," he announced to the anxious little crowd hanging about outside. "But there don't seem to be nobody alive."

Mr Robinson's mouth tightened and Higgins threw away his cigarette end angrily. They climbed as close to the tunnel entrance as the foreman would allow them. There, they leaned on their shovels and waited. Both were covered with dust, their blackened shirts clinging to their backs with perspiration. Not by so much as a quiver did either show their agony of mind; yet Alec Robinson thought that if it were not for the support of the shovel, he would collapse. The tall, thin chauffeur took a cigarette packet out of his shirt pocket and offered a smoke to his companion. Without taking his eyes off the tunnel entry, Alec Robinson nodded refusal.

He was able to identify his wife of thirty years by the modest engagement ring on her crushed hand. The chauffeur, faced with the naked, torn body of his beloved mistress, peered in the gathering gloom at her contorted face and then at the three magnificent rings on her hands, and muttered, "Yes, it's Her Ladyship," before quietly fainting. He had to be carried across to the other side of the street by two exhausted labourers and revived by the First Aid contingent. When the body of Her Ladyship was turned over to her family's undertaker, the rings were missing.

The police reported to the constable in Toxteth that no one answering to Emmie's description had been found.

VI

It was as if the whole population was swaying on its feet.

One more blow and it would, if from nothing else, collapse from fatigue. By Monday evening Gwen had decided that the Sunday night raid must be the last one; the Germans had never before raided four nights in succession; she reckoned they would not come a fifth time. If it wasn't the last of the series, she felt she would drop dead; she could not take any more.

Conor Donnelly had not helped this feeling of despair. He had slapped the children's and his ration cards on the kitchen table, as if they had come to stay another week at least. Then the doctor had arrived, taken one look at David and hurried home to his telephone, to order an ambulance; Gwen had hardly had time to wash her husband's face and hands and help him out of his dirty overalls, before the vehicle arrived and whisked him off to Walton Hospital.

"They would choose the hospital furthest away," she grumbled to Mari, Patrick and Ruby, at lunch-time. "How'm I goin' to get out there to visit him, I'd like to know. This mornin' I'd no one to leave Michael with, so as I could go with him, to see him settled in, like."

Mari ignored her mother's whining complaints. "He's not going to die, is he, Mam ?"

"Of course not, snapped Gwen peevishly. "If they can't cure a heart attack we're in a proper bad way." Her panic regarding Dave must not be conveyed to Mari.

In the afternoon, she announced to Michael, who was having a great game on the heathrug with a collection of saucepans and lids, "Now we got to go and do the ration books — yours as well — 'cos Annie's corner shop's gone with the wind. Got to find a new grocer. And all that beastly red tape, to register again."

As she trudged back home up her own familiar street, carrying a very tired and fretful Michael, she passed the pile of rubble which had been Annie's shop and she stopped to sigh sadly in front of it. The pillar box still stood amid the rubble, and Mr Marsh, the neatly uniformed postman, was just unlocking it to collect the letters from it. "Nice day," he said mechanically, and she laughed almost hysterically, "Aye, I suppose it is."

A few yards further on, she met Bridget Mahoney, her neighbour from across the road. Bridget was looking red-faced and sullen, but she listened as Gwen told her about the Donnelly invasion of her home, something she knew about already. "And to crown all," Gwen finished up, "our Emma is missing down town somewhere, and I'm worried to death about her."

Bridget regarded her dully, as she nursed her bandaged arm, when she had removed the incendiary bomb from the gutter of her house. Her body trembled and she could not answer Gwen at first. Then she muttered, "So's me husband — in Greece. Got a telegram just now."

Gwen was aghast, stuck for words, knowing that she should say something optimistic and comforting.

Bridget swallowed. "I don't know how to tell me boys."

VII

Conor received with some anxiety the information that Emma had not been found in the canteen's air raid shelter. The constable on duty, who had given him the news, added heavily, "Either she were struck down on her way home — or she took shelter somewhere else and got buried there."

"We could try checking amongst the unidentified." Conor sighed. "Could start with the living. I'm off duty now — I'll see what I can do on the phone."

Four unidentified women between the ages of 25 and 35 lay in three different hospitals, their names unknown, though only one had been found in a street Emmie was likely to have traversed on her way home. The voice at the other end of the telephone added laconically, "Of course, there's several hundred unidentified bodies, a goodly number unidentifiable, at Webster Road mortuary."

Patiently, Conor hitched lifts to the various hospitals; looking at the women was the only way to be certain.

One woman had recovered consciousness and had identified herself. Another had been claimed by a frantic husband. The third one had just died and Conor was allowed to view the body before it was wheeled away to the mortuary.

To see the fourth one, he followed hopefully a young probationer through a packed women's ward, filled with lively chatter. Behind a screen, a person lay on her back, arms neatly arranged at her sides under tightly tucked-in bedding. Her breath fluttered uneasily from blanched lips. Her eyes and head were sheathed in bandages, as if a white turban had slipped half-way over her face. Her head was supported on either side by what Conor supposed were sandbags. An angular, elderly nurse raised an eyebrow as Conor intruded softly.

He whispered, "I've come to see if she's Emma Thomas." The nurse nodded and stepped back, while Conor peered down at the end of a nose, prettily curved white lips and a rounded chin with an unexpected dimple in it, totally unlike Emmie's long narrow face.

The nurse's face softened, as he nodded negatively. "Poor little lass," she murmured. "It's her eyes, you know."

With a dreary ache in his heart for Ellen, mixed with sorrow for

355

the pretty young woman he had just seen, he decided that he would try the dead.

A delivery van driver gave him a lift to within a couple of streets of his destination. He had to wait, while a calm, slender woman in a white coat dealt with a sailor in a tight-fitting Royal Navy uniform, who could not have been more than nineteen. The sailor stood timidly at the counter, his round white cap clutched in both hands in front of his chest. The acne spots stood out on his face and neck against an unnaturally pale skin. Together, he and the woman went through a series of large brown envelopes holding the effects found on or near the bodies in the mortuary. Time and again he nodded affirmatively, as he recognised the pitiful possessions. Sometimes he hesitated uncertainly and the woman put those envelopes on one side.

Conor nor felt himself reeling at the strong smell of disinfectant mixed with the ghastly odour of disintegrating bodies. He lit a cigarette and drew on it heavily, as he watched the pile of envelopes in front of the hapless sailor grow and grow. Finally, the woman drew the shaking boy further into the building. Conor began to whistle softly to keep his courage up; he had seen enough at the shambles of The Dwellings to understand what the youngster was going through. Thanks be to the Holy Mother that his Ellen was decently wrapped in a winding sheet in a proper coffin, and tomorrow, when his mother had arrived, they would see her respectfully committed to her own grave.

The sailor suddenly bolted past him and out of the front door. When the woman turned inquiringly to Conor, tears were streaming down her face. "He's from Seaforth," she burst out, as if she must share her agony of mind with someone. "He had fourteen bodies to identify, and some of them were a mess."

She had no trace of anyone who could be Emmie; the only likely corpse, picked up in Whitechapel, which was the continuation of Paradise Street, had been identified.

She rubbed her damp eyes with the back of her hand. "I'm sorry, Mr Donnelly. Try the temporary mortuary near the scene." She paused and tapped the table with the end of her pencil. "If I were you, I would talk to the men on the spot."

Between the mortuary and Paradise Street lay Emmie's home. He thought he should drop in *en route* and assure Gwen that the fact that he had no news of Emmie was probably good news.

He was surprised to find the front door open and, after a per-
functory knock, he walked in.

He was immediately engulfed by his children, their faces smeared
with jam, as they rushed from the tea table. They were followed
by Gwen holding a feeding-bottle. Behind her, a man half rose
from his chair by the fire. Robert Owen had duly received the
information through the police that his fiancée was missing, and,
since not much more could be done regarding the still exploding
cargo of the *Marakand,* he had been given a few hours' leave. He
had come just as he was, blackened and reeking of fire, his eyebrows and hair singed. When, at last, he had found a tram blun-
dering along in the right direction, he had endured with suppressed
fury the stares, and occasional giggles, of the other passengers, at
his outlandish appearance.

Gwen looked inquiringly at Conor above the children's heads.
He nodded negatively and she sucked in her lips as her sense of
guilt returned to her. She shouted suddenly, irritably, at the children, "Now, Patrick — you kids — get back to the table and finish your tea. Now, Mike, you come to Auntie and I'll put you on
the sofa, and you can show your dad how you can hold your bottle."

When the child had been propped up on the sofa cushions, he
put the teat in his mouth and looked triumphantly at his father
out of the corner of his eye. His father had, however, other things
on his mind.

"You must be Emmie Thomas's intended," he said to Robert.
"I been lookin' for her just now."

VIII

The air raid siren interrupted Conor's and Robert's conversation
with the police constable they found on duty at the corner of
Paradise Street.

"Oh, blast 'em," rumbled the constable exasperatedly.

Robert's heart sank, as he looked out over the enormous, smoking pyre facing him. He thought he'd seen the worst in Seaforth,
but here was just such another scene of devastation — and possibly his Emmie was under it. He wanted to run across the road and

start tearing it aside single-handed, to find her, but instead he had to listen to the doubts expressed by the constable that there were any more bodies there; certainly nobody alive.

High in the sky anti-aircraft fire flashed white. There were few clouds. Despite the smoke haze, it was much too clear for comfort.

From the south, where Toxteth lay, the guns spat forth. Conor, so tired that he was becoming a little incoherent, prayed in the back of his mind that his children would be spared. With a quivering match he lit a cigarette handed to him by Robert; one more flash of light was not going to help the Germans; the fires still burning would guide them beautifully.

The constable glanced uneasily at the firemen, rescue teams and a demolition squad still at work amid the destruction, and the women of the WVS mobile canteen nearby. The blue flash of the men's lanterns made them look like ghosts. Nobody ran for cover as the gunfire increased. He began to herd the chattering crowd of sightseers into a nearby underground shelter. It beat him where all the onlookers came from. He'd have thought that every man and woman in the city had enough to do at present; and if they didn't, that they would be thankful to sleep. But here they were, come to gloat. Ruddy vultures, the whole bloody lot of 'em. He blew his whistle impatiently, to summon one or two stragglers, and to draw the attention of the solitary telephone engineer, still toiling in the nearby crater.

The engineer took no notice. The whole job was almost completed and he continued to check the lines which he and his colleague had been sedulously splicing together all day. In co-operation with the exchange operators, the reconnected phones were rung in nearby offices. Sometimes the line was still dead, the telephone shattered under the debris. Occasionally, a late-working clerk or a firewatcher or cleaning lady would lift the receiver and assure him that *everyone* had gone home, which never failed to make him smile. Now, with the increasing noise overhead, he was frightened and was glad of these nasal Liverpool voices responding to him. George, he told himself wearily, you're getting a bit old for this game. When a piece of flak whizzed down and buried itself in the clay side of the hole, he clapped his tin hat on to his bald head, clenched his teeth over his cold pipe and went on working.

The constable returned to Robert and Conor and they all stared skyward. Beneath the hissing of water from the firehoses and the rhythm of the pumps, they could hear the steady chug of engines from the east, and they moved to the shelter of the sandbags surrounding the entrance while they discussed what could have happened to Emmie. The sandbags had been pierced by flak and were slowly bleeding their contents on to the pavement. Conor absently poked a bigger hole with his finger, while the constable assured him, "They cleared the shelter, the rescue squad did — they were proper tired — and then they went home to get some sleep." He turned, to rebuke someone trying to leave the shelter, and then, in answer to an impatient query from Robert, he said, "Well, you could talk to the new incident officer — the other one was killed last night."

A series of thuds not very far away announced the arrival of the Luftwaffe, and George nervously collected his tools into his tool box and said to himself, "Me lad, this is where you beat it."

He hastily had the line he had been working on rung by the operator. It failed to ring, and he cursed his wasted effort. The exchange operator said sharply, "Mind your language, if you please," and transferred her plug to another call. He made a face and was just about to remove his instrument from his ear, when distantly down the line came a hoarse female voice singing falteringly *Men of Harlech*. He grinned. The receiver must be off the hook and some cleaning woman probably dusting round it. He listened for a second; the sky directly overhead was quiet, though more distant sounds of combat warned him not to linger. The song became a series of harsh sobs. It seemed to him that very faintly he heard also the rumble of a male voice, and then, a little more strongly, the tune again sung in Welsh. He gave a small laugh. Welsh miners sang it a lot better, probably because they were always singing; he had been told that they sang even when they were entombed in a mine accident.

Entombed! My God!

"Can you hear me?" he shouted, in incredulous apprehension. There was no reply, only the weak, cracked voice carrying the tune.

He called the telephone operator. Could she hear it? But the voice had stopped and the operator told him loftily not to be so daft. Lips pursed, he put a clamp to mark the line and scrambled out of the hole. Like a lumbering bear with a tin hat on its head, he ran down the newly cleared pavement, looking madly for the constable.

The WVS volunteer, a mug of tea in each hand, directed him to the entrance to the shelter.

"Get away," exclaimed the constable, when he poured out his suspicions to him.

"I'm not joking," spluttered George furiously. "I tell you I heard it. It's possible, I tell you. And buried miners always sing — and this woman was singing in Welsh. Me grandmother was Welsh — I know Welsh when I hear it. Damn it."

"It's her," Robert interjected with conviction. He caught at the constable's arm. "Come on. Who do we have to see to start 'em digging?"

The constable swallowed, while Conor said simply, "Emmie Thomas is Welsh."

George looked a little bewildered at this exchange and they hastened to explain to him about the missing woman. "And you think this is technically possible, that the telephone fell somewhere near her and still managed to remain connected?" the constable asked the engineer.

"You've just said the canteen was on the ground floor. It wouldn't have far to fall, if it wasn't blasted out; if it were protected by a wall that didn't give, like. Anyways, I heard her."

"Let's try the line again," Conor suggested impetuously. He started to move out of the sheltered doorway, but the constable held him back and pointed to the bit of sky they could see above the sandbag wall. It was filled with flashing light, and a series of reverberating booms came from the direction of the docks. "You're chancing your own lives," warned the constable. "What number was it?"

"I've forgotten. I can find out. I marked the line."

"For God's sake, let's try it," Conor urged. "Come on," he called to George and Robert. He started to run across the road, George skittering unhappily behind him, followed closely by Robert. A shrill shriek overhead sent the three of them into the gutter, hands clasped over heads, noses in the dirt.

The missile passed over them, to fall into a fire slightly closer to the river. Its explosion sent a mass of burning debris flying into the air, to start fires in buildings hitherto untouched. Firemen dropped their hoses and ducked for cover wherever they could find it, only to regroup a few minutes later and continue their tasks. Conor, George and Robert stayed firmly in the gutter until the remainder of the stick of bombs had been deposited in a neat line across the city, and had sent to Kingdom Come one ambulance driver and her assistant, twenty-two homeless people in a rest centre, two pedestrians never identified, one firewatcher and one special constable; the thin red line was becoming frighteningly thinner.

A series of bombers sweeping the length of the fan-shaped city now dived one after the other to loose their deadly loads, and sent up fountains of rubble as their bombs scored hits. The three men cowered in the gutter, hearts racing, as all kinds of lethal odds and ends pinged and plonked on the road and pavement round them. A group of soldiers and rescue men, their hooded lanterns bobbing, chanced running for the air raid shelter. Robert heard a muffled cry, as one was hit. He crammed himself further into the littered gutter.

During a moment of lessened hubbub, Robert cautiously turned his face to peep upward. The gun flashes were like an enormous storm of sheet lightning. Tracer bullets and flares added to the scarifying display. A further beat of heavy engines made him push his face tightly against the pavement's friendly curb. George, his head near Conor's feet, stretched out a careful hand to touch the warden's boots for comfort. He could feel panic rising in him, but he was haunted by the sound of the quavering voice and he tried to concentrate on the technical arguments why he should be right. He'd *prove* he was right, he would, even if he had to dig for her himself.

In Paradise Street, a big Victorian chimney, balanced by a piece of side wall from the building in which the canteen had been, shivered and fell, its stonework rattling over the wreckage at its foot. The usual cloud of dust spumed upwards. Through chattering teeth, Conor prayed for his life to his patron saint, who had not heard from him for some years. Conor had said bitterly that he was accursed; yet even so, life seemed unexpectedly precious when it looked like coming to an end.

361

The Defiants succeeded in disorganising the raiders and the bombing moved further north. Robert was so stunned with noise and fright that it was a moment or two before he could make himself scramble to his feet, to find the constable bending over George, as he got to his feet, and shouting through the noise, "Come on, get back in t' shelter."

Though terrified out of his wits, George was determined. "I'm goin' to try that line again. Won't take a mo'."

"You're clean out of your mind," the constable bellowed. But he ran with them to the cavity in the street.

They crouched together in the clay hollow. George found the wire with a clamp on it. He clipped on his headphones.

"No." He found also that he could no longer contact the telephone operator.

"It could've been one of the WVS women at the corner singing," suggested the constable.

George boiled with frustration. He checked his splicing again.

Conor leaned closer to him and shouted into his ear, "I believe you."

Robert thought he would lose his reason if one of them didn't do something constructive soon. "It must've been the chimney what fell just now — broke whatever connection there was." He turned to the constable and asked, "Who do we go to — to ask for rescue men?"

"The incident officer, like I said." The constable was feeling most unhappy and cursed his indecision. He was, in principle, the ultimate authority, but he did not want to pressure the incident officer into a wild-goose chase; yet the engineer presumably knew his business. As they crawled over the gummy clay and out of the hole, he said finally, "Let's talk to the incident officer."

A curious chug-chug-chug, like a train coming rapidly into a station, made them all slide back into their refuge and hug the side of it. Not too far away, something crashed into the wasteland. Tensely they waited for the explosion.

Nothing happened.

Cautiously they lifted their heads. Again the sound of a train. Again they pressed themselves into the clay. A tremendous detonation in the direction of Exchange Station drew a string of vivid swear-words from the constable. "Now I know what we got — a bloody land-mine — unexploded. Now isn't that nice?" His sarcasm was bitter. "Blow us all into next week, it could, while we're lookin' for this woman."

TUESDAY, 6 MAY 1941

I

"I've never heard of such a thing before." The hard-pressed incident officer sounded kind, but he was used to survivors clutching at all sorts of straws to assure themselves that a loved one was still alive. "I think you *must* have misheard," he added to George. "It's easy enough."

"We can trace the number," George informed him coldly. "Look in your telephone book and see what the canteen's number was, and I'll trace if the line is the same."

It took a little while and the close co-operation of the telephone exchange supervisor to establish fairly certainly that it was indeed the canteen telephone line. Then, with his nose in the air, George climbed into his van and went home to bed. Let the high-and-mighty incident officer work out *where* she was.

The incident officer wasted no time. He sent for a heavy-rescue foreman, recently off a train from London, and to his surprise the man said calmly, his Cockney accent sounding strange to the men around him, "There was a case like this in London."

The plans of the buildings in the Paradise Street area, carefully prepared at the beginning of the war, had been burned with the command post the previous night, but an off-duty warden, who might know the canteen, was traced with commendable speed, through the warden of his home district; and he tumbled out of the Anderson shelter in his garden and came down on his bicycle while the raid still raged.

He could not suggest where Emmie could be, but, when asked

to draw a plan of the canteen, he included the cobbled back-yard.

"Where was the phone?" asked Robert.

"It were in the kitchen at the back."

"Exactly where?"

"On a little table by the window, as I remember — though I can't be sure." He stubbed out his cigarette. "T' window faced the yard."

"She must be in the yard, or in the wreckage of the kitchen," interjected Conor between a series of yawns. His legs felt like lead and he told himself that once they started to dig, he would go home and kip down for a while.

To Robert Owen, the dark small hours were a nightmare, while with infinite care the heavy-rescue foreman from London and a group of miners from nearby St Helen's, with other experienced people, plotted Emmie's possible position. They decided to explore whatever might remain of the light well.

Robert was sick with fatigue from the battle in No. 2 Huskisson; burns on his hands were a throbbing misery. Conor tried to persuade him to go home for a few hours, but he refused. Someone thrust a mug of coffee into his hand and he drank it gratefully. Then he insisted on going down to Paradise Street to help the rescue squad. Shoulder to shoulder with the miners, he helped to pass debris back to the road, as painstakingly slowly a new tunnel was made, to pass over the huge stone wall which had formed the back of the canteen shelter. Pieces of office equipment, beams, furniture and some precious pit-props were carefully eased into place, to hold the tunnel open. He worked like an automaton, the fear he had felt when he went to the Mercantile Marine office to obtain another ship long since forgotten, lost under greater and more immediate terrors. Nothing seemed to matter now, except that Emmie be found alive.

When the All Clear howled across slateless rooftops, to be followed shortly by the first rays of the rising sun, the pace of work increased. A rotund WVS woman, a flowered wrapover pinafore covering her uniform, brought mugs of tea and a basket of fresh scones with a scraping of margarine on them. "Made them myself before I set out," she told them proudly. "We've still got gas on our side of the water."

Her face showed the same weariness as that of the rescue team, but she was so fresh and clean that Robert felt as if his mother had come all the way from Hoylake to help. "Have you heard her yet?" the woman asked.

"Nay. T' foreman's goin' to go in a bit further, now he's got a block and tackle rigged. Then he's goin' to ask the fire engines and everything to be quiet, while he listens — afore the streets get busy, like. Couldn't do it while the raid was on — no point in it, with guns and all."

She touched his arm and said comfortingly, as the weary group munched and slurped thankfully. "Och, you'll find her if she's there. You're all great lads."

Robert lifted his mug to her, his eyes twinkling suddenly. "You're great ladies," he said.

It was only when the new police constable on duty managed to organise a short period of quiet that Robert realised what a shambles of noise they had been working in. In the stillness, he was surprised to hear a seagull squawk, as it came to rest on top of the broken roof of the building behind him. Not very far away, burning wood crackled, and from the direction of the river a ferry boat hooted cheerily.

The squad waited, tense as Olympic runners, while a miner as small as a jockey eased his way along the tunnel they had made. Apart from his torch, he carried a piece of piping to use as a listening device.

To Robert, it seemed a lifetime before a soft rustle and a tumbling pebble heralded the man's careful emergence. Once clear, he stood up and removed his mask; he coughed helplessly to rid his lungs of dust. His watering eyes made little rivulets through the dust on his cheeks. He nodded negatively.

Robert's teeth began to chatter. He clutched the foreman's arm. "Let me go down," he pleaded.

"No, son. You're too big."

II

During Tuesday morning, Gwen, with Michael on one arm, squeezed into the stuffy privacy of the nearest public telephone box. It was still functioning, so she telephoned Walton Hospital.

A tired, uninterested voice assured her that Mr Thomas was

369

resting comfortably.

Gwen determined that on Wednesday morning she would keep Ruby home from school to care for Michael while she attempted the journey across the town to visit the hospital. She fully expected, however, that keeping Ruby home would not be necessary. Grandma Donnelly would surely arrive in time for her daughter-in-law's funeral that very afternoon, and would remain to care for her grandchildren. After lunch she must see that Ruby and Patrick were clean and tidy, ready to accompany their father to the funeral.

She had had a sharp spat with Patrick that morning about the necessity of going to school. The broken nights had taken their toll and he wanted to remain in bed. It had ended with her slapping him hard across the head and threatening to complain to the headmaster, if he did not go. At first she had thought he would slap her back, but he had got up and gone sulkily to school with the other children.

At lunch-time, as she handed him a bowl of soup and a cob of bread, she said to him, "You're a bright lad, Patrick. If you learn to read and write as good as Mari, you'll never be hungry or out of work. And I would like that for you, scamp that you are."

He had nodded agreement and lost some of his sulky look. He dreaded the afternoon. He was afraid he would cry at the funeral.

Ruby sat silent, steadily drinking her soup. She knew *her* reading and writing days were over. She looked down at the soup bowl, spoon poised, and wondered what happened at funerals. Her thin lips quivered.

A box of groceries, some children's clothing and a parcel of nappies were delivered immediately after lunch by a cheeky youth on an errand boy's bicycle. Gwen smiled. The nun had not forgotten.

A worried Conor, looking incredibly neat in a clean blue overall, washed and ironed for him by Glynis Hughes, collected Patrick and Ruby. "Their gran and me brothers' wives haven't come from Walton yet," he told a very sober-looking Gwen. "Here's a slip of paper telling 'em which church. Will you give it to them, if they come late?"

"Where you goin'?" asked Nora, held back firmly by Gwen, while Brendy sucked his thumb and stared at the funeral-goers.

370

"Never you mind," Patrick told her savagely. "You and Brendy go to school." Ruby began to cry.

"You stay with me, and after school we'll go down the street and buy a sweetie ration." Gwen shepherded the youngsters back into the house, where Michael was trying to feed Mari's long-discarded wooden bricks to a patient Sarge.

Grandma did not arrive that day, nor did any other relation, and an extremely hurt Conor went straight back to his post after returning Patrick and Ruby to Gwen's house. "I'll try to get through on t' telephone to the warden up there and ask him to send a message. They may've got t' lines restored by now."

Once more a resigned Gwen saw her charges scrubbed from head to foot and put into bed, Michael soothed with a bottle of milk and Brendy happily sucking his brother's dummy.

"What about me mam?" asked Nora, sitting up suddenly in her white bed. "A girl at school says she's dead. What's dead? Is it like when the cat was run over?"

Gwen gulped, while Ruby shivered by her in one of Gwen's own nightgowns. Ruby's eyes were huge and imploring. Gwen said coolly, "They're still mending your mam. You don't have to worry about her. And soon your gran'll come to take care of you."

"Well, what is dead?" Nora insisted, as she unhurriedly pulled the blanket over herself, and Gwen tucked the sheet round her chin.

"It's when you go to Heaven," replied Gwen, and added almost wistfully, "It's proper peaceful, like, and you're with God."

"Oh, aye," replied the child, just as if they were talking about lollipops, "Sister Theresa talks about it sometimes. Do you get lots to eat there?"

Gwen laughed, for the first time for a week. "To be sure," she replied promptly. "No shortages at all."

She waited for Ruby to climb into her bed beside Michael. The girl looked drained and as hagridden as Bridget Mahoney from across the road had looked that afternoon. Impulsively Gwen bent and kissed her on the cheek. "Now you cuddle down and sleep and don't worry about nothin'. You'll feel better in the morning."

When she went into her own bedroom to see Mari, the girl was sitting on the edge of her bed, pulling off her socks. She, too, looked older than her age, her eyes black-rimmed. "I wish we had

371

news of Auntie Emmie," she greeted her mother.

Gwen sighed. "They'll find her. Don't worry. Now hurry up and get into bed and get some sleep."

She went slowly down the darkened staircase, automatically holding a corner of her apron under the candlestick, to catch any wax before it fell on to the stair carpet.

In the living room Patrick was sitting on the black, horsehair sofa. He had his head in his hands and was crying.

She put the candlestick down on the table and held him against her apron. "Now, don't take on so, luv. She's at peace now."

She took her handkerchief from her pocket and bent and wiped his tears. He took it from her and blew his nose hard.

Gwen felt as if she herself had hardly got into bed before the air raid siren went, followed almost immediately by a tremendous run of explosions. Once more, she gathered her frightened brood and hastened to the cellar steps, where, for four hours, she tried to cope with tears and quarrels, while outside a thundering tumult raged.

WEDNESDAY, 7 MAY 1941

I

As clerks and typists struggled over the debris to report for work in non-existent buildings, the incident officer offered to send a relief crew, to replace the men hunting for Emmie. The men refused to be relieved.

The incident officer did not argue with them. Amongst the motley gangs of workmen there was a stiff pride that they did not stop work until they had themselves carried the victims out.

An intact corner of the light well had been reached. The searchers tried listening there, but heard nothing. They did, however, find a woman's shoe and this gave them new incentive to continue.

Robert could hardly stand, but he continued mechanically to pile rubbish into skips and to lend a hand where he could. He could not identify the shoe as Emmie's.

Gathered as close as the police would allow was a large crowd of sightseers, clerks in well-pressed business suits, their female counterparts in neat black dresses with white collars and white summer hats, housewives in spring suits, with pretty baskets on their arms, and the male flotsam and jetsam of a port, who, despite two years of war, seemed to have nothing particular to do.

An untidy little office girl came out of a building still standing behind the crowd and pushed her way into the middle of the partially cleared street. She held a saucer of milk. "Kitty, kitty, kitty," she called, and, as a thin black cat sidled up to her, she put the saucer down, and explained to a young woman standing watching, "It's the offices' pussies. They got no home now." Another

375

cat approached tentatively, and she renewed her call.

Young typists and clerks were searching the edges of the ruins for filing cabinets, account books, any records which would help to re-establish their companies, when it was agreed that a miner particularly experienced in mine rescues should go down the tunnel and decide how they should proceed further. In a moment he was gone, flicking himself along the tortuous zigzags and ups and downs, like an eel through rock-patterned water. Though the smell of this disaster was different from that of a mining accident, the dust was the same, and when he felt cobblestones under him, he paused to readjust his mask. It was surprisingly quiet, as he flashed his torch along the lines of what cracks he could see. It was clear from their angle that, further on, the yard had collapsed. This puzzled him. He turned the torch upward, to examine the fearsome mass above him. To move further in, he decided, could be dicey.

" 'Allo," he called tentatively, not too loudly — it wouldn't take much to start a fall, he reckoned. " 'Allo, there."

Dead silence, except for an uneasy movement overhead. Blast it. He drew his piece of piping from inside the front of his singlet and this time put it to the cobbles — afterwards he could give no real reason why he did so. He bent his ear to it and listened intently.

It seemed to him that he did hear something, a movement, other than the rustles in the wreckage bearing down round him. But it was from underneath him.

He laid his head, ear down, against the unfriendly cobblestones and held his breath. Very carefully he tapped on the stones with the end of his torch.

The girl couldn't be under him? Or could she? He tapped and listened again. There was a small, strangled cry. And it was from underneath, but a good distance further to his right, he guessed. Taking a chance, he cupped his hands round his mouth and put his face to the stones. At the top of his voice, he shouted, "We're coming. Hold on there."

She heard him, a muffled echo. With overwhelming joy, she tried to shout back, but she had screamed so much, was so exhausted by fright, hunger and thirst that the noise was not enough for him to hear. Beside her, Dick muttered incoherently in a high

376

fever, as if he had pneumonia.

Perplexed, the miner ran his torch again along any cracks he could find, to see their direction. He tapped the surface in several directions as far as space would allow, but there was no echo, and no further cry. He backed down the tunnel as fast as he dared, trying to imagine, as he retreated, how parts of the light well might have fallen, and into what kind of space. It had to be a cellar, he decided.

As he emerged, panting, scratched and mystified, Robert ran lightly up the debris to meet him, followed by a protesting foreman. "You shouldn't run over it like that, you fool," he bellowed. "Bring the whole mess down!" He forgot his complaints, however, when the miner said there was indeed someone there. "Under you?" he exclaimed in disbelief. "But it's a yard — a light well. Cobbled. Seen it meself when I went down a bit back."

"Well, get down there and get her out." Robert was nearly beside himself.

"Hold on, lad." The foreman was aggrieved. "These buildings've bin blasted several times from different directions. It's not that simple." He turned to the miner again. "You're sure you heard her?"

The man smiled, his teeth flashing white in his filthy face. "I heard somebody, all right."

"Thank God!" exclaimed Robert in relief. But anguished dread then filled him. What horrifying hurt might Emmie have suffered? He fought down a wave of nausea.

The returned miner was talking again. "She must be lying in a hole under that yard. But most of the yard must be supported by solid earth — otherwise the cobbles would have caved in years ago. They'd be a dead weight."

"Some kind of arches might be supporting 'em," another man suggested. "Arches can hold up cathedrals."

"Aye, but we *could* be digging down through solid rock, if we go down through the cobbles."

"How far into the yard, measuring, like, from where you was lyin', do you think she was?" The foreman rubbed his heavy-muscled arms which ached intolerably. He was bent on pinpointing as accurately as possible where they must penetrate.

"A way," the miner said immediately. "I went over the stone

377

foundation wall what you told me about — back o' where the canteen shelter must've been — and all me body was on cobbles. She must've been at least twenty feet from me, bearing half right; and I tell you, the voice came from below — not level with me."

Robert caught the foreman's arm. "I know!" he broke in eagerly. "Me grandad told me often enough. Privateers — and smugglers — used to have hiding-places for contraband — and you said the cellar of the canteen was much older than the building above it. Could be there's some merchant's old cellar under that light well."

The foreman sighed and pursed his lips, and then said rather condescendingly, "It's an idea. But God knows how she fell into it."

"This fella here said it would be hard to go down through the light well itself. Could you still get into the shelter?" asked Robert, fatigue forgotten, and the plan of the building he had seen the warden draw clear in his mind.

"Oh, yes. It was all well nigh cleared out by the time we'd finished. Have to go down carefully, because of the big chimney collapsing over there, last night."

"Did you see any doors in the walls?"

"No, lad. We'd 've gone through 'em if we had — to make sure nobody was there." The tone was scornful now.

"Look again," Robert persisted. "If they had a secret cellar under the light well, then they had a place to get into it. Maybe it were bricked up when they built the offices. Round here they've bin building and rebuilding for centuries — even the offices were real old. There must be all kinds of little places built over — even small rivers have been."

The men stood round arguing amongst themselves, while the foreman thought this over. The ultimate responsibility was his and he was not going to put his men at risk unnecessarily.

Finally, when Robert had begun to think he could not bear another moment of suspense, he said, "OK. I'll go down meself and look." He turned to a young miner who was particularly small-made. "You, Evans, you can come with me."

They had been squeezing slowly round the shelter's walls for nearly five minutes, before Evans said triumphantly, "I've got it. See, this is brick, not stone."

The foreman flashed his torch along the wall. Once pointed out, it was possible to see a line under the whitewash where the texture of the wall changed. He crawled closer to the younger man and then carefully tapped on the brick and listened. No response.

II

Some of the rescue crew, who could do nothing for the moment, went down to the WVS van to get some lunch, while, amid the smell of wet plaster mixed with that of a charnel house, the foreman dug out the first bricks with the care of a surgeon. The wall would be weaker at this point and the old brickwork could crumble suddenly under the weight of the wreckage above.

The wall proved to be four bricks thick, and when the fourth one suddenly gave and fell out on the other side, a poof of surprisingly cold, damp air blew out at them.

Evans broke into excited Welsh; then remembered his English. "The lad up there was right. There's space here." He put his face close to the hole they had made, and shouted, "Anybody there?"

In the light of the foreman's torch, his face fell. "Try again," the foreman urged.

"Anybody there?"

Very faintly came a croaking sound that could have been a human voice.

The wall was broken as fast as human hands could do it without causing a fall. As soon as the hole was big enough, young Evans wriggled through feet first. He felt around with the toes of his boots, to make sure he was not dangling over a hole. Cautiously, he stood upright.

"Lend us the torch." The foreman passed it to him and he flashed it round. "It's like a blinking castle dungeon," he reported. And then he called, " 'Allo! 'Allo!"

From beyond a massive blockage facing him came a faint response, a distant sob.

"We're coming. Hold on. Are you by yourself?"

The reply was unintelligible.

Evans tried again. "Are you badly hurt?"

There was a pause and then Evans clearly heard an effort at a

379

throat being cleared. "No," came the answer.

Meanwhile, in preparation, other men worked feverishly, pushing pit-props and tools down the tunnel and through the hole in the wall. They whistled when they saw, by the light of a powerful lantern, parts of hefty stone arches. There was room to stand against the wall through which Evans had clambered; but the rest seemed to be an almost solid mass of wreckage.

"She's on the other side of that," said Evans, his young face gloomy in the light of the lantern, as he gestured to his right.

The foreman, who had followed Evans through the hole in the wall, glanced quickly round. He said, with more optimism than he felt, "We'll find her. God, it must be five hundred years old, this place. They knew how to build in those days — and that's what's saved her, though there's more'n one fall here." He rubbed the end of his nose and then went on, "Reckon she's tucked up not far from the wall we've come through, but it's goin' to take a while afore we get through that lot."

The floor of the cellar was earthen, which at times was a help to them, in that they could loosen large pieces of debris by digging for a little way under them. Miners can almost sink into the earth when they dig, but a bucket brigade had to be formed, to move earth and debris out of the way as it was dug, and these men had difficulty in keeping up with the moling miners.

"At this rate, we'll be home in time for tea," one of them joked.

The moles themselves, though fast, moved with the greatest care, with the minimum of noise, with the least disturbance of the dense mass poised above them. A faint smell of burning made Evans shiver; occasionally small runnels of water would cascade down on them. "From the fire-hoses," the foreman told them firmly. "Water and gas is turned off. You're not goin' to drown."

Every so often the gasped curses would cease and the leading man would call to Emmie, partly to reassure her, but partly to keep them on course.

She would answer them with a faint croak. Every tired nerve alert, she had listened through an eternity of time to the muffled sounds indicating that help was coming. Sometimes the men had paused, to consider how to deal with an obstruction facing them; there was no sound, and at such times her spirits would sink. They had given up, deserted Dick and her. Dreadful, agonised fear went

380

through her parched, starved body. She tried to shout but little noise came. She felt around the sick man beside her, to find her petticoat with which she had earlier wiped Dick's burning face. It was half under her, and she laboriously hauled it out, to suck it and dampen her mouth. Though they were lying on wet ground, it seemed impossible to do more than moisten their lips and tongues.

She found the stone with which she had tapped earlier and hit the wall unsteadily with it.

"That's good," said a voice surprisingly close to her. "Every time I call, you tap, eh?"

She tapped once in acknowledgment and prayed she would not pass out.

Outside, Robert Owen stood hunched in his Red Cross, brown jacket, nearly out of his mind with the frustration of the long wait. As he mechanically emptied buckets or handed in pieces of wood, his mind would hardly function, and suddenly he heeled over and fell face down on to a pile of debris. The watching crowd murmured and shuffled.

A First Aid man who had been checking his canisters of milk and water, and the tube which he could poke through a small hole in the obstruction between himself and a victim, and thus feed the sufferer until he was freed, dropped his satchel and ran to Robert. He went down on one knee and gently turned the exhausted man over. The doctor and driver from the ambulance also hastened across the street and together they lifted the limp figure and laid him down on the pavement, which had earlier been so sedulously cleared by Alec Robinson and Lady Mentmore's chauffeur. The lady doctor knelt to wipe gravel from his bruised face and half turned him on his side, so that he was less likely to choke if he vomited. She checked that he had no false teeth in his mouth and then lifted one of his eyelids. She smiled and took his pulse. Still amused, she got up slowly, dusted down her slacks and said laconically, "Gone to sleep on his feet."

She turned to the warden, who had come from helping the constable keep back the crowd. "Better find out who he is," she suggested, "and send him home."

"He'll be right mad if I do. It's his girl what's bein' dug out." He ran his tongue round broken teeth. "I'll get a couple of blankets

381

and we'll lay 'im in the hallway of the office opposite."

The First Aid man returned to digging through his satchel. For the third time, he checked its contents: hypodermic syringe, pain-killers, sterilised pads, sticking plaster. A stretcher had already been carried as close to the tunnel entrance as possible. There was nothing he could do but wait. He envied Robert, sound asleep in the hallway. It was thirty-six hours since he had been to bed himself.

Far below the horrifying ruins, the miners burrowed like ferrets, thin sinewy arms flashing in the lantern light, flat-stomached bodies swinging in rhythm, as they passed buckets of earth back to a space near the broken entry to the old cellar.

Jimmy, the foreman, moved his helpers around as if he were playing a complicated game of chess, his seamed face a picture of intense concentration, as he improvised the steps of the rescue. No two rescues were ever the same; no two buildings ever fell in exactly the same way — their stresses and strains had each to be weighed up anew, and their constant tiny shifts watched with feline intensity. Not only had he to rescue those buried; he must at all costs ensure the safety of his team, and as he sometimes remarked, "Me old woman would be proper put out if I buried meself and she was done out of a good funeral."

They came up within two feet of her, to a tight tangle of splintered wooden beams and what might have been part of an iron girder, the same obstruction Emmie had felt in her first search for the dripping water. Now she squeaked with shock when her foot was grasped by a warm hand slipped under it.

They were stalled.

"Sufferin' Christ!" The foreman's disappointment was as bitter as if his own daughter lay beyond the girder. "Get First Aid to bring some water and a shot for her, while we decide what to do."

The nervous young man crawled down the tunnel and fed both Emmie and Dick with water and then a little milk through the tube he thrust over the girder. She refused any sedation. Without a hint of his inward horror of the tight confinement of the suffocating tunnel, he whispered encouragement and told her that her fiancé' was waiting outside.

"He's there?" Her voice was suddenly comparatively clear. "Thank God, thank God." She began to weep, soft, helpless crying in which was mingled a tremendous joy. He was there, he was safe.

When the miners were ready to start again, he backed down and told the surprised foreman that he had two living victims to get out.

Like dogs getting at a bone buried under a tree root, Evans hollowed out a space in the earthen floor under the girder. He then grasped her ankles firmly and told her he would help her wriggle down and under, on her back. When her knees were through, he grasped her bent legs and heaved her upwards. She cried out at the scratches she received, but she was through, her eyes dazzled excruciatingly by the blaze of the torch held by a second man behind Evans.

After calling Dick and getting no response, Evans turned himself on his back and squeezed himself into the space Emmie had occupied. He flashed his torch quickly round the tiny refuge, sickened by the stench. Near Dick's head, neatly wedged between a piece of stone and what looked like the remains of a table, was a telephone. So the engineer had been right. With a grin, he turned to the job of easing the barely conscious Dick out.

With difficulty, the warden managed to wake Robert. "They're bringin' her out," he said, a smug satisfaction in his expression, "and she's not badly hurt."

Without a word, Robert stumbled to his feet. Across the road he saw her being carefully carried down the slope of the debris. She was wrapped in a white sheet and strapped to a stretcher.

He pushed his way through the crowd of excited onlookers and ran across the road. Emmie was alive — and absolutely nothing else in the world mattered.

III

On its way to Walton Hospital, the ambulance carrying Emmie, Dick and Robert passed the bus in which a very subdued Gwen was travelling back home from her visit to David in the selfsame hospital.

Regardless of the thirty-odd other men in the ward, she had put her head down on the white coverlet of David's bed and cried. Too ill to do more than hold her hand, he had been staggered when she had laid her cheek on his work-scarred palm and told him he must get better, because she could not face life without him. She had paused to give a weepy sigh, and added, "Half the time I dunno what to do for the best."

"I'll be all right," he had whispered with an effort, and closed his eyes. It was nice to be wanted and not to be regarded as merely a walking pay-packet.

When she got home, Nora and Brendy were rolling round on the kitchen floor like a pair of angry young wolves. Patrick was kicking them none too gently in an effort to separate them, while Mari watched him from the living room, where she was seated at the table, trying to do her arithmetic homework. Ruby sat near her with Michael in her arms, feeding him from his new bottle. She was shouting, "Leave them be, Pat. They'll stop of themselves in a minute."

Gwen took one look at the fighting youngsters and total exasperation seized her. She strode through the crowded living room and squeezed quickly behind Mari's chair and into the kitchen. "Stop kicking 'em," she ordered Patrick, and he slunk back, muttering, "I were only tryin' to stop em."

Nora rolled triumphantly on top of a beleaguered Brendy, and Gwen bent down and administered the heaviest slap she could on the girl's small cotton-covered bottom. As quick as a cat, the child loosed Brendy and jumped to her feet. A stream of invective poured from her, as she rubbed her stinging bottom.

"Any more of that and you get no jam for tea," threatened Gwen, as she picked up the kettle to fill it from the kitchen tap. Nora made a face at her, and Ruby hastily called the little girl to her. "You coom 'ere afore you get into more trouble, our Nora."

Brendy lay on his back and laughed, as he watched her go.

Patrick had a tin bowl of grain in his hand, some of which had spilled on to the kitchen floor in the mêlée. He squatted down and began to scoop the precious seeds together. "I were goin' to feed the micks," he told Gwen defensively.

"Aye, feed the pigeons — and you'd better do your dad's cocks, too."

After he had fed the cockerels, Patrick stood, empty bowl in hand, and looked round the familiar muddle of the Donnelly backyard. He burst into tears. Where *was* his mother? Where had

384

she gone after death? Her body had been in the coffin the day before, but that wasn't her — not really her. Would he never again come through the back yard, to see her leaning against the door-post, waiting for them all to come home from school? He did not know how to bear the pain within him.

An hour later, Gwen surveyed her troublesome brood across the littered tea table and prayed that their grandmother would turn up soon.

Patrick looked as if he had been crying. Deep compassion for him and for Ruby welled up in her; they must both be feeling terrible despair. Yet they were being very brave. Impulsively she leaned forward and pressed Patrick's grubby fist lying on the tablecloth. He looked up at her, startled, and saw the pity mirrored in her faded blue eyes. Quickly, he withdrew his hand and picked up his piece of bread and margarine. "Everything's going to turn out all right," she assured him, feeling a little shy herself.

He nodded.

She turned to Ruby. The girl looked crushed. She was staring vacantly at her empty plate. "Would you like another butties, luv? I can soon cut you one."

"No. I'm all right."

"Coom 'ere."

The girl rose and went to stand by Gwen's chair, like a school-girl called before the headmistress. Gwen put an arm round the thin body and gave her a hug and a smile. "Come on, now. Cheer up. Your gran's goin' to come soon — and I'm goin' to be next door all the time, and you can ask me." The girl smiled faintly, and unexpectedly put her arms round Gwen's neck, as she had so often done with her mother. She did not cry.

Mari watched in jealous shock. Her mother never hugged her. All she ever got was a peck on the cheek and an admonition to be a good girl. She had endured the invasion from next door, because of the strange magic of Patrick's presence. Now she wished crossly that they would all go back to their own house and that her father was home to give her a smacking kiss and call her his pretty young lady.

At midnight, she was sitting on the cellar steps, reading *Gone With the Wind* aloud to Patrick and Ruby, while one of the worst raids Liverpool had ever experienced raged outside.

On a mattress dragged down to the bottom of the steps lay Nora, Brendy and Michael, mercifully sleeping the sleep of the totally exhausted.

Gwen nodded over a cold cup of tea, while her mind went round and round in weary confusion. What if Emmie is injured — not killed? Do I have to nurse her as well as Dave? It would, she felt be a fit judgment on her, for not helping Emmie with her parents; the pain-filled face of her acid-tongued mother-in-law haunted her for the duration of the raid.

THURSDAY, 8 MAY 1941

I

Constable Doyle consulted his notebook and then knocked on Gwen's front door. At least for this family he had good news — as far as it went.

He made himself smile as the door opened, to reveal Gwen in her dressing-gown, followed by five children in differing states of readiness for school.

"Me husband?" Gwen faltered, at the sight of the uniform.

"No, missus. Miss Emma Thomas live here?"

Relieved, Gwen replied that she did normally, but she was missing.

"Well, missus, you'll be pleased to know she's resting comfortable in Walton Hospital. Be out in a few days."

"Thank you kindly for stopping by to tell me," she began to close the door.

The constable cleared his throat. "I should tell you, missus, that we've heard as the hospital was bombed last night. We don't know the extent of the damage yet. I'll know in an hour or ..."

Through white lips, Gwen murmured, "Dave!" and fainted on her neglected doorstep.

Though the constable was resigned to carrying news that had this kind of result, Gwen's collapse was unexpected. He helped to carry her in and lay her on the living room sofa. She came round within a minute or two and, through chattering teeth, asked if he or Mr Donnelly would let her know when they had more news of the hospital. "Me husband's in there, as well as Emma. I'll go over

389

meself as soon as I've got the children away to school."

"The north end's a shambles," Constable Doyle warned. "I doubt you'd get through. I'll come as soon as I've any news." He turned to Ruby and Mari — never had he seen two sisters so totally unalike — and told them to make a strong cup of tea for their mam. "Lots of sugar in it — and see she rests a while."

II

On the previous Wednesday, the day before the raids began, Mrs Owen, Robert's mother, had said a thankful farewell to the evacuated mother and children who had occupied her spare room for some months. "I can't stand the quiet out here a day longer," the mother had told her. "I'm goin' home to Great Homer Street."

Now, on this perfect spring morning, she asked Mr Burnett, the chemist in Hoylake village, for something she might sprinkle round the newly scoured bedroom, to kill off any vermin that her unwelcome guests might have left there. "Me daughter-in-law elect is coming out to live with me. She's in Walton Hospital at present, recovering from being buried under the canteen she worked in. Poor girl. She's real nice. I'll be happy to have her."

Mr Burnett looked over his gold spectacles. He swallowed. "Do you know Walton was bombed last night?"

Mrs Owen's hand flew to her throat. "Oh, no! Poor lass, poor lass — and poor Robbie."

She had trouble waking Robert from the sleep of the absolutely worn out. He would have to go into Liverpool, anyway, she told herself, to be signed off from the *Marakand* and then find himself another berth. She sighed at the thought.

When he heard the news, he was wide awake in a moment and jumped out of bed. He seized his trousers and struggled into them.

"The phone to the hospital's dead. I tried it — or rather, Mr Burnett did."

"I can go over."

"Well, you have some tea first. The kettle's boiling." Dear Lord, what a mess he was in, too. A black eye, hardly any eyebrows or eyelashes — all singed off — likewise his front hair. And both hands bandaged by the hospital, because of the burns on them.

390

III

Conor had not been home since before his wife's funeral on Tuesday. Now, on Thursday morning, after what Glynis Hughes described as a lively night but not in the usual sense, he hesitantly opened his front door. He had snatched an occasional nap at the post, but now he knew he must really sleep; otherwise, he would collapse.

On the floor of the passage inside, lay his letter to his mother, returned through the dead-letter office. A wobbly hand had scrawled in pencil on it, "Address Unknown. Return to sender". Then in brackets the writer had added, "Whole street bombed. Tried to trace in Rest Centre without success."

He stood in the narrow hall, paralysed. He could not believe it. He had been so harassed himself that he had not thought about his parents' danger.

If they were hurt or killed, why hadn't his married sister, who lived in the same street, let him know?

A slow coldness crept through him. From bitter experience, he could visualise the scene so well. A dozen houses down, a whole series of families related to each other carried out dead or dying; no one surviving long enough to give names to the authorities. Those same authorities, hopelessly overloaded by the sheer magnitude of the raids, would in time name most of the victims — but not yet.

He leaned his head against his paintless front door, and cried aloud, "Holy Mother have pity on me!" He beat his fist against the unresponsive wood. "I'm damned! Accursed!"

Nearly demented, he fled back to his post — and the telephone.

With some difficulty, he got through, on the newly restored line, to the wardens' post nearest to his parents' house. Then he came slowly back to his own street. Instinctively, he sought the only people left to him, his children; he turned the rapidly tarnishing brass knob of Gwen's front door and walked in.

Michael was asleep on the sofa, an empty feeding-bottle lolling by his cheek. From the kitchen came the splash of dishes being washed.

"Are you there, Mrs Thomas?"

The splashing stopped immediately and Ruby came running in,

wiping her hands on a dish towel. "Dad," she cried eagerly.

He held out his arms to her. She ran into them and with his head bowed over her he began to sob helplessly. She drew back. "Dad, what's up?" she whispered, frightened by such a lament.

While she sat on his knee in the muddled room, he told her. He wept unrestrainedly, unable to hold in his despair and grief any more.

Half girl, half woman, she listened quietly, arm around his neck. Then she started to comfort. "Don't cry, Dadda. We'll manage," she said hoarsely. "Mrs Thomas'll help me — while I get started, like." She clung to him while he tried to control himself.

"I'm sorry, luv," he said, and wept on.

She was frightened to see her hot-tempered father cry, but it also put him on a level with Patrick, and she said, "Aye, everybody cries sometimes, Dadda," and gritted her teeth and hugged him closer.

When her father's weeping ceased, she said quite eagerly, "Let's go and buy a bit o' food, Dad, so as we can move back home."

That afternoon, Gwen and Mari sat and looked at each other over their teatime toast and dripping. The house was extraordinarily quiet and seemed to exude the misery of its damage and neglect. Gwen thought her heart had never been so heavy. By dint of taking three trams in a circular route and walking quite a distance, she had managed to reach Walton Hospital. The fright engendered by the bombs on the hospital had given David another heart attack. He had, however, survived, though he would need much nursing and would probably never be able to return to work. She had also briefly visited Emmie, who was heavily sedated and an alarming bundle of bandages and sticking plaster. There she had met Robert, sitting by her bed. He had told her that when Emmie was discharged from hospital, his mother would take care of her at his home in Hoylake, until they were married. It was the only good news of the day. Confound her — and her furniture — she could have the lot of it.

Mari broke into her gloomy contemplation by saying brightly, between sips of cocoa, "Tomorrow's your day for Blackler's."

Gwen nodded. "It's burned down. I'm out o' work — like plenty of others."

"They might start up again," Mari replied. "You could go and see. There's probably a notice set up in the ruins, to tell the staff what to do."

"Aye. I'd be glad of a full-time job, now your dad's so poorly." Her face brightened. "I'll go this evening. People's got to buy clothes and bedding from *somewhere*."

"I'll walk down with you, if you like."

"Would you, dear? I'd enjoy your company."

IV

One of the loneliest people in Liverpool lay unvisited, except by Robert Owen, in a huge, overcrowded men's ward at Walton Hospital. Identified by the pay slip in his wallet, still in his back pocket, Deckie Dick opened his eyes on Thursday evening, to the long glinting rays of a setting sun reflected on a shiny, white ceiling. He was in a bed and shivering; yet at the same time feeling dreadfully hot. He had been vaguely aware of being bundled about, of being sponged and feeling chilled.

A face loomed over him. It was topped by a little white cap above a wrinkled brow. A pair of sharp blue eyes, red-rimmed, peered at him. His wrist was clasped by cold, bony fingers.

A misty mouth said, "He'll be all right now."

Another blanket was tucked over him. He fell asleep, only to be awakened by more fumbling hands. The air raid warning was wailing its devil's notes, and two giggling young women were lifting him out of bed. They stuffed him underneath it. "Safest place," they assured him, and wrapped his blankets round him.

"Where am I?" he asked.

"Walton Hospital," they told him, and he breathed, "Thanks be," and slept contentedly on the floor through the rest of the night.

The entire population of Liverpool had been waiting tensely for the warning to go. Some of those who still had a bed had climbed into it, feeling that they *must* sleep, no matter what happened to them. Now they raised their heads to listen. But the raid was small, short and scattered; many of the townsfolk slept through it. London became the main target, though German squadrons were beginning to regroup in preparation for an attack on Russia. In the days following, mass funerals were held, and people who

393

thought they could not cry another tear wept some more.

One morning, a curiously shrunken and shaky Deckie Dick, dressed in clothing supplied by a charitable organisation, tottered out of Walton Hospital and went back to the room he rented in Pitt Street. The landlady had relet it. "Ah thought you must be dead," she told him. She had, however, stored his few belongings, in case he had a relative to claim them.

Weak and bewildered, he went into a tiny cafe, sat down at a greasy table and ordered a cup of coffee. From his wallet he took out a small piece of paper with an address written on it and he smoothed it between thumb and finger. The granny of the young conscript he had met in the shelter also lived in Pitt Street. Robert Owen had told him that everyone in the shelter had been killed. She must be feeling bad, he ruminated, as he slowly stirred his tasteless coffee. It wouldn't hurt him to go up and see her; the old biddy might even know of a room to let.

Ten minutes later, he was climbing the bare, littered stairs of a lodging house similar to the one he had lived in, though this one seemed to smell even worse.

He did not have to knock at the door of the first-floor front room. The occupant had heard his footsteps and had opened it a crack.

"Mrs Pickles?" he inquired of the one grey eye peeping at him.

The crack widened. In the dim light he could make out only a female form draped in a black shawl. "What d'yer want?" The voice was full of suspicion.

"Ah come about your nephew, Wilf."

A sharp intake of breath. "Well, what about 'im?"

"Mrs Pickles, can I come in and sit down? I bin ill or I'd have come before. I met your lad in an air raid shelter and promised to look you up."

A pause. "Come in."

Inside the bare, clean room, he turned to the woman. She was very small, with a pinched, thin face out of which large steel-grey eyes regarded him with sudden compassion. Her skin looked pale from poor nourishment and lack of sunshine, and was a mass of fine lines. She had no teeth. About 55 years old, he reckoned.

She said, "Aye, you are ill, I can see that. Sit down on the sofa bed. I was just goin' to make a pot o' tea and a bite of toast." She picked up a kettle from off the small fire and poured boiling water into a teapot, much blackened from being kept hot too near the fire.

Dickie sank thankfully on to the edge of the sofa; the springs complained bitterly.

"What about Wilf?" she asked. "You know he were killed? He were all I got — a real nice lad."

As gently as he knew how, he told her about the scene in the air raid shelter and of his promise.

White cup and saucer in one hand, she looked down at him, her mouth quivering. He thought she was going to cry, but she did not. She simply sighed and sat down abruptly. She took the lid off the aluminium teapot and stirred the tea vigorously.

As she handed a cup to him, she asked, "What was you ill with?"

He told her about being buried with Emmie and his subsequent pneumonia, and as he talked some of the stress went out of him.

She listened patiently, and at the end she said, "I don't think any of us will ever be the same again after all this. It's as if all our lives was overturned in the course of a week, isn't it?"

"Aye." He smiled wryly, and stirred his tea. He wondered if he still had a job. Then he burst out suddenly, "Being buried like that — it taught me life was worth having. Funny, isn't it?"

She smiled and her eyes crinkled up with a promise of laughter, when she felt better. "Have another piece of toast," she invited.

Through two pots of tea and a pile of toast, they sat knee to knee, two lonely people tossed together by a war they did not understand.

He stayed with her for the rest of his life.

SUNDAY, 29 JUNE 1941

"It feels proper queer — to be married at last," remarked Emmie. "I thought we'd never make it."

"You mean when you was buried?"

They were wandering along Hoylake Promenade, idly pausing from time to time to watch children digging in the sand, while their elders snoozed beneath copies of the Sunday newspapers, and dogs ran yapping after balls tossed by strolling owners. It was hard to believe that, not too far from them, out to sea, men stalked each other mercilessly and that, in Europe, the art of murder was reaching new heights, while in England itself cities burned.

"Not so much being buried," Emmie replied uneasily, "Though that were bad enough. But you havin' to go back to sea afore I were out of hospital — and bein' so long in the hospital, with me nerves, and lookin' like a piece of red raddle when they took the bandages off me face; I were fit to die when I saw meself in the mirror. I thought you wouldn't want me no more."

"Tush, luv. I'd always want you. There's more to a woman than a face. Anyways, there's nothin' that time and a spot o' warpaint won't cover." He bent and kissed the top of her newly permed hair. No need to tell her that he had been nearly shocked out of his kecks when he had first seen her. But the doctors had been right. She was healing and they'd done some neat stitching on her, which they swore would fade, and the bruises on her poor body were going, too. The doctors had said it was a pure miracle that she had no broken bones and she wasn't blinded.

He tightened his arm around her waist and he saw her wince and immediately loosened it again. Bugger the Nazis. Just wait till

399

he got a chance at one, he promised himself bitterly. He'd never felt such boiling hatred in his life before. It bubbled in him, awaiting only the opportunity to explode.

She turned her face towards him. "I love you so," she said unexpectedly, and he was diverted immediately by a fresh surge of longing.

"Look, duck. Let's nip 'ome. Me mam and dad allus goes over to see me brother on Sunday afternoon. Let's go 'ome and have a little matinee. What say?"

She bit her lip and then grinned quite cheerfully. Why say that so much of you still ached that you could hardly bear to be touched. He'd be gone on the eight o'clock train, back to his boat and the god-damned Atlantic. She'd have weeks of nothing before he returned — always supposing he got back safe. Time enough to get herself well again — and try for a job in munitions, so she could send a bit back to the Jerries with her best compliments.